Philip Caveney, born in ~~North~~ a two-year spell at Manchester's Piccadilly Radio, writing and presenting a weekly film review programme. He is a professional and freelance journalist, and his previous novels include *Speak No Evil*, *Black Wolf*, *Strip Jack Naked* and *Slayground*, all published by Headline. He lives with his wife and young daughter in Heaton Moor.

Praise for his previous novels:

SPEAK NO EVIL
'An exciting story . . . writer of genuine promise'
– *Solicitors Journal*

BLACK WOLF
'A sharp, fluid novel that packs the necessary dramatic punches without sacrificing wit' – *The Times*

'More than the average ration of thrills and chills'
– *Northern Echo*

'The sense of menace Caveney creates is excellent'
– *Eastern Daily Press*

'A book which horror fans should enjoy as much as suspense fans' – Ramsey Campbell

STRIP JACK NAKED
'A powerful and at times violent story . . . It's a triumphant thriller' – *South Wales Evening Post*

'The violence is chilling and graphic . . . keeps you guessing at every twist and turn' – *Metro News*

'Pacy, well-written . . . Caveney's confident, punchy style makes for a compelling read'
– *City Life* (Manchester)

# Skin Flicks

## Philip Caveney

*Philip Caveney* (signature)

HEADLINE
FEATURE

First published in Great Britain in 1995
by HEADLINE BOOK PUBLISHING

First published in paperback in 1995
by HEADLINE BOOK PUBLISHING

A HEADLINE FEATURE paperback

10 9 8 7 6 5 4 3 2 1

ISBN 0 7472 4419 7

Typeset by
Letterpart Limited, Reigate, Surrey

Printed and bound in Great Britain by
Mackays of Chatham PLC, Chatham, Kent

HEADLINE BOOK PUBLISHING
A division of Hodder Headline PLC
338 Euston Road
London NW1 3BH

For the NCT support group –
we soldiered together . . .
and with thanks to Darren
for the timely introduction
to Big Abel.

# Prologue

Did you ever think about your skin? I mean, *really* think about it, consider how it works, what it does for you, what kind of a mess you'd be in without it? It's something we take for granted, like every other part of our anatomy; eyes, limbs, ears . . . we carry them around with us every day of our lives, and yet, the complexity of them, the incredible tasks they perform for us!

Skin holds our internal organs together, helps us to respirate, regulates our temperature and gives us much of the appearance that we designate as human; yet how fragile it is, how easy to tear.

Just lately I've been thinking about skin a lot. After what happened I wonder if I'll ever be able to *stop* thinking about it. And it's not just in my conscious thoughts. No, I have these awful recurring nightmares that people are removing my skin, working away at me with these tiny, sharp knives, hands moving with methodical practised ease. I cannot see the faces of the men that perform the task, I only know that they are tall, warrior-like figures, dressed in hides and feathers.

First they make a long incision, from the top of my head, down my spine and into the cleft of my buttocks. The knife blade is as sharp as a razor and I feel no real pain, only a

1

brief, stinging sensation. They make similar cuts along the backs of my arms and legs. Then they start working with their flat-bladed flaying knives, working them in under my skin, teasing it away from the flesh, muscle and sinew beneath, taking their time so that they don't tear or damage it.

I'm frightened, naturally, but also kind of fascinated, particularly when they get to my hands and start prising the skin off the fingers like a pair of tight-fitting gloves. I lie there watching them work on me and I marvel at their patience and precision. When everything is off my back they gently lift me and turn me over and there's this weird moment when they peel the skin off my face and, for a second, my sight is obscured. It's like they're lifting a bedsheet off me.

Finally, they do this really fancy move; I don't know how else to describe it. You must have seen at one time or another that classic trick where a magician takes hold of a table-cloth and whips it off a table without knocking over the place settings? It kind of reminds me of that. The warriors take a firm grip on the extremities of my hide – for this is what it has now become – and with a single, fluid motion, they tear it right off my body. It makes a noise like sticky tape being ripped off a cardboard package.

And I'm left lying there, an exposed mass of quivering red flesh. I'm still in no pain, but what's somehow infinitely worse, I'm starting to get really, really cold . . .

That's when I wake up and find that it's *actually* happened to me. I'm lying in my bed and the sheets have turned a sodden scarlet and I can't move so much as a muscle, because the merest touch of cotton against my flayed flesh is enough to send a jolt of flickering agony through me. I can only lie there and scream at the top of my lungs . . .

And that's when I *really* wake up, to find that I've thrown off the bed covers and I'm lying there naked with my arms wrapped around myself, my teeth chattering, but my skin, *thank God*, still very much where it's supposed to be.

From time to time I've mentioned this dream to friends (once I was at a dinner party and several portions of lasagna were promptly consigned to the dustbin) and they usually give me some line about how it's only understandable after what happened to me, anybody would be the same. Then after a suitable pause they'll add, in a helpful tone, that there are people you can talk to about things like that, you know, *professional* people and maybe it wouldn't be a bad idea just to book myself a couple of sessions. Nobody ever comes right out and says the word 'shrink' but I get the general idea. I always tell them that I don't believe in all that bullshit and that the nightmares will ease off in time. After all, it's only been a couple of months.

Then another friend – a more sensible one – suggested that it might help to write it all down. 'Only by confronting our fears can we ever really hope to overcome them,' she said. I don't know if this was an original theory or something she'd memorised from the back of a matchbox, but on reflection, I decided that she might have a point.

Anyway, what the hell? Here I am, sitting at her word-processor and, scrolling back up the screen, I see that I've already made a start, of sorts.

And looking back I can see that it was pure chance that sent me down Sobriety Street that rainy morning in October: or rather, a whole network of little coincidences that conspired to ensure that I, Danny Weston, would be there on that particular day to witness something that will stay with me to the grave.

Sure, you can laugh, that's a cliché. People say it every

day, usually in jest, but I really mean it. At the age of thirty-two, I'd already seen some bad things in my life but this . . . this was something else entirely. It affected me profoundly and seemed to me to be the end of everything I knew and believed. I didn't realise it at the time, but it was really only the beginning . . .

# PART ONE

Skin for skin, yea, all that a man hath will he give for his life.

*Job* 2:4

Clear the air! clean the sky! wash the wind! take the stone from stone, take the skin from the arm, take the flesh from bone, and wash them.

T.S. Eliot
*Murder in the Cathedral*

# Chapter One

The first time I was ever on Sobriety Street I was kind of lost: which I suppose, neatly sums up my life.

What happened was, I was taking a portfolio of my photographs up to a catalogue company in Ardwick, Manchester, in the feeble hope of scaring up some freelance work. My car was temporarily out of action, so I took the train to Piccadilly Station. Having already passed the company's offices back up the line, I decided to make the most of an agreeable autumn day and walk, telling myself that if I simply followed the tracks back in the right direction, I would eventually arrive at my destination.

Shortly afterwards, I found myself strolling along this decrepit stretch of road, flanked on one side by the high, crumbling brick wall of the railway viaduct and on the other by a series of mouldering warehouse buildings. I got the feeling then that there was something timeless about this little chunk of the city, the distinct impression that it probably didn't look a great deal different to the way it had looked a hundred years ago. I passed under a rusting metal bridge, the ground beneath it plastered with layer upon layer of pigeon droppings, dried to a spongy crust beneath my feet. On my left, beyond a low parapet, a stretch of stinking canal passed into a culvert beneath the level of the street, the stagnant black water choked with the detritus of the throw-away generation: brightly coloured carrier bags, cans and bottles, even the inevitable half-submerged supermarket trolley.

I found myself wishing I'd brought a camera with me. You see, I've always been drawn to places like that. My photographer's eye has never been interested in capturing the conventionally beautiful – I would rather dwell on the angular, the grotesque, the misshapen. Little wonder I'd never made it as a fashion photographer.

I moved on, beneath the dark overhang of the bridge, past a series of railway arches set into the viaduct, ancient wooden doorways opening on to dark, uninhabited interiors. And then, as I approached the last of them, out from the open doorway came this huge rat, sauntering along as though he hadn't got a care in the world. He registered me standing there and I made a shooing noise to hurry him on his way, but he took not a blind bit of notice of me. He strolled on along the street as though he owned it and turned around a corner out of my sight.

I paused by the open doors of the railway arch and peered into the gloom. I couldn't see more than a few yards, but out of the interior gusted a musty smell of neglect and decay. I caught a tantalising glimpse of rotting roof beams and rusting machinery piled up near the doorway and was sorry that I didn't have a torch with me.

At any rate, I shrugged my shoulders and walked on to the interview for a job I'd never get; but I mentally filed the railway arch away in my head, telling myself that I'd come back there one day with the right equipment and shoot some black and whites. And with that, Sobriety Street slipped clear out of my mind for something like eighteen months.

Then one day my manager, Vincent Spinetti, phoned me

up and asked would I like to do an exhibition at The Wedge. Would I? *Christ, Vincent, do bears shit in the woods?* The Wedge was currently the city's hippest arts centre, with three cinema screens specialising in obscure sub-titled films, a café, a bar and two floors of dedicated gallery space.

I paused dramatically and made the obligatory humming and haahing about having to look in my diary: whereupon Vincent told me to *cut the crap*, because the fact was that a major photographer had pulled out of there at short notice and there was a prime slot available in two weeks time. *Did I want it, yes or no?*

Naturally I said *yes*. It was only after I'd rung off that I started wondering if I'd be able to pull something together at such short notice. Tell you the truth, I wasn't totally unprepared, I'd got some great material in an old people's home a few month's back, lots of grainy black and white close-ups of all those lined, gummy faces; and I'd been toying with a vague notion of juxtaposing them with images of urban decay, that kind of thing. That's when Sobriety Street jumped back into my mind.

So there I was, Danny Weston, thirty-two years old, freelance photographer of this parish, ready to make his bid to be the new Robert Doisneau, driving my little green Citroën 2CV in the direction of the city centre in search of material for what I thought of as my first *real* exhibition.

I should point out here and now that this was an unusual situation for me – not the kind of photography I usually made my living from. For the last couple of years, my main employer had been the *Manchester Evening Post* – if they had somebody or something they wanted immortalising on celluloid, I was amongst the half dozen regular contributors on whose services they called. It could be anything. Visiting celebrity, old age pensioners' outing, new extension to municipal car park, cat stuck up tree . . . I've photographed them all in my time. And don't think I'm being sniffy, either. After years of struggling on the breadline, I was grateful for the regular employment.

But deep down inside, there was a part of me that longed to do something more demanding – something that would make the city's culture vultures sit up and take notice. I was about to achieve that, but not the way I had anticipated.

I parked up on Sobriety Street and hauled my equipment out of the boot. I'd brought my trusty Pentax SLR (currently held together with sticky tape after being dropped down a flight of stairs but still doing nicely, thank you), a powerful Olympus flashgun, a selection of lenses and filters, which slotted into the leather harness I wore strapped around my waist and – great foresight this, I thought – a torch to light my way. The camera was loaded with HP5, my preferred mono-chrome film and there was a tripod in the boot should I have need of it later. I put on a baseball cap, a recent promotional give-away from the *Manchester Evening Post*, complete with a lurid MEP logo and, remembering the huge rat I'd seen last time I was here, I took the added precaution of securing the legs of my jeans with a pair of bicycle clips. I don't have a particular problem with rats, you understand, but like most people, I'm wary of them. Feeling that I'd prepared myself for just about every eventuality, I turned towards the doors of the railway arch.

And then something spooked me.

I didn't know what it was and I certainly wasn't the kind of person to jump at shadows – not *then*, I wasn't – but as I stood looking into the black, chilly maw of the archway, I was taken by what I can only describe as some kind of premonition. My blood temperature seemed to drop a couple of degrees and my scalp began to prickle alarmingly.

For a moment there, I was on the verge of turning around and going straight home.

No such luck. I told myself I was being ridiculous: actually said it aloud, which on reflection isn't too convincing. I switched on the torch, took a deep breath and stepped into the arch.

Christ, it was cold in there! I was aware of my breath clouding in the glow of the torch, as I directed the beam around the damp interior. Actually, damp is an understatement. The walls were running with moisture, years of rain seeping through the porous red brick. Above my head, a series of ancient wooden beams ran horizontally from side to side and above them, the black, mould-encrusted curve of the brick roof was occasionally visible, festooned with thick grey cobwebs, made by spiders, that it seemed to my overheated imagination, must have been the size of dinner plates. In places, steady drips of water hurtled down to smash into fragments on the puddled stone floor.

To my left, stacked along one wall, were heaps of rusting machinery; cog wheels, girders, brackets and things I couldn't identify but which seemed to suggest to me that they had once been part of a train. Above them, pinned to the wall, there was a mottled, fly-blown calendar, only a couple of years out of date, with a photograph of a Page Three girl, a buxom blonde smiling cheesily at the camera. But dark patches of mould had blossomed like tumours on her bare flesh and an incongruous patch of grey fungus had sprouted from the top of her head.

'One for the family album,' I muttered; and moved in closer to take a shot. Not as easy as I had anticipated. I had to wedge the torch into my belt to provide suitable illumination, while I lifted the camera to my face and focused on the woman's rotting grin. I'm blighted with poor eyesight, an absolute curse for somebody in my line of work, and have to wear spectacles, so I require a decent level of light to get my focus spot on. When I was happy that I was as close as I was going to get I took the shot. The flash momentarily illuminated the whole of the interior with a lurid, high-contrast light. I turned away from the calendar, retrieved the torch and turned to walk deeper into the arch.

Something scuttled away from the torch beam and ran into a pile of discarded black rags off to my right, something sleek and grey and very fast. The beam momentarily picked out the glow of its eyes and I couldn't suppress a shudder of revulsion. My flesh crawled and once again, I thought wistfully about abandoning the expedition – but I gritted my teeth and told myself not to be so pathetic. I moved on and my fleet splashed through a pool of viscous, oily liquid. Then I registered a smell, different to the musty, wet-paper smell I'd detected before. This was a gamey, raw stench that inexplicably brought back a memory from years before, a time when I'd come back from a two week holiday in Greece and had opened the fridge to discover a pork chop I'd forgotten to throw out before I left.

*Probably a dead rat around here some place*, I told myself.

I raised the torch to examine the stout overhead beams and liked something about the rigid pattern they made, marred only by lumps of yellow fungus sprouting out of the black wood. The fungus resembled ancient skin, whorled and lined as if by the passing of years. I had a mental picture of this image hanging alongside a portrait I'd got from the OAP shoot, a ninety-four-year-old lady with some weird polyps growing on her cheek. The juxtaposition of the two images would be disturbing, even shocking – and the pundits at The Wedge would probably cream their 501's over it.

Once again, I was obliged to hook the torch into my belt as

I raised the camera to my eye. By wriggling my hips in a kind of bizarre John Travolta routine, I was able to illuminate the section I wanted to photograph. In this poor light, it was hard to envisage what the end result would look like. But what the hell? It was worth experimenting with a few shots. Besides, some of my most pleasing pictures have been little more than happy accidents.

So I fired off a shot and in the brief glare of the flash, I glimpsed something hanging from one of the beams just ahead of me: something large and pendulous. It was the briefest of glimpses, seen in something like a hundredth of a second but it was enough to fire my curiosity. I let the camera hang around my neck and moved forward again, wrestling the torch out of my belt as I did so.

I had miscalculated the distance. I almost walked right into the thing, but at the last instant, the torch beam caught it and I froze in my tracks. My first reaction was one of puzzlement. It seemed to me that I was looking at a huge joint of meat. The torch beam picked out a red, blotchy carcass hanging from a length of rope.

Then, quite suddenly, I noticed a lot of other things. I noticed them all at once. A grinning upside-down mouth, blank staring eyes that seemed to gaze right through me, outflung limbs culminating not in hooves or trotters but fingers—

*Fingers? What the—?*

Realisation hit me like a clenched fist in the gut, literally driving all the breath out of me. I took an involuntary step backwards. Part of me registered the strange sucking noise made as I lifted a foot from the ground, but I couldn't think about that yet, because . . .

I was looking at the body of a naked man, hanging by his heels from a roof beam. He was naked in the most extreme

13

sense of the word. As far as I could tell, there wasn't a scrap of skin left on his body.

Breath came back to me in a sudden, uncontrollable rush. I panted like a dog as I tried desperately to hold down my mounting panic. My impulse was to turn and run the hell out of there, but something about the nightmarish figure turning slowly at the end of the rope, held me transfixed in a kind of morbid fascination. The man – I thought it was a man, though I couldn't even be sure of that – was little more than a bloody, glistening mannequin made up of exposed nerves, muscle and shocking red flesh. The upside-down mouth seemed to be smiling serenely but when I thought about it logically, much later on, I realised that it was really down-turned in an expression of agony.

I took another step back and again there was that sticky, sucking noise from beneath my feet. Glancing down, I directed the beam of the torch into what had initially appeared to be a puddle of black oil. I registered now that I was standing in a pool of the man's blood.

That was the moment when I came closest to losing it completely. For a couple of seconds there, I was very close to breaking. Somehow I didn't. Instead, I reached for my camera.

At the time, this reaction surprised me, though really I suppose, it shouldn't have. In cases of adversity, my profes-sionalism always rises to the surface, like some lifebelt floating up from the deck of a sinking ship. I started taking photographs.

Looking back, it's hard to know if there was any ulterior motive at work – whether I figured some tabloid newspaper would hand over a small fortune for images like these. I'd like to think that such an idea never occurred to me, that I was merely performing this particular function to prevent myself from running around in the darkness, screaming like some madman. Then again, I *was* a freelancer and times were hard.

At any rate, I lifted the camera to my face and went to work, completing the task quickly and methodically.

I went first for a close-up of the dead man's face, focusing on the eyes. I noticed the dull, flat stare of them in the glare of the flash. Then I stepped back (*splotch, splotch*) for a torso shot, the outflung hands just skimming the foot of the frame and I noticed the thick purpley lines traversing the undersides of the arms like lengths of rubber tubing and I found myself wondering, *Christ, how did somebody remove the skin without damaging the veins*? No, I shouldn't allow myself to think about that. I moved back another two steps (*splotch, splotch*) for a full figure, noticing the way that the ankles had been knotted expertly together with a thick coil of bloody rope, then how the rope had been slung over a roof beam and secured off in the corner to a metal stanchion on the wall.

Circling around for a back shot, I noted the knobbly vertebrae just beneath the sticky flesh, then moved in for a close-up of the hands – *Look Mum, no fingernails. Christ, think about it, no fingerprints either!* The shoulders, the buttocks, the hairless skull – and all the time I was clicking away, the motor-drive turning on to the next frame with a brief whirr. Turning aside I noticed the two words scrawled large on the brick wall to my left in what must have been some of the man's blood. Two big, childish-seeming words that at the time meant nothing to me whatsoever.

## FOR ZIPPY

I photographed that too and was momentarily surprised as the flash seemed to flare briefly back at me from the shadows to the left of the writing; but then suddenly I was at the end of the film, the spool was rewinding itself and I was left standing there in the darkness with the thing I had been photographing. I started to tremble violently. Tears burst from my eyes and acid welled in my throat as I turned and stumbled towards the doorway. I got just a couple of steps out into the fresh air before the vomit exploded from my mouth, but still I had the presence of mind to hold my camera at arm's length out of harm's way. I made it over to the car and leaned one hand on it for support. A part of me noticed as I coughed up more vomit, that my shoes seemed to have been liberally dipped in maroon paint.

A man came wandering along the street, a bearded middle-aged guy dressed in navy blue overalls. He eyed me suspiciously as I divested myself of the last few scraps of my breakfast.

'You all right?' he muttered.

I shook my head, pointed feebly at the doors of the railway arch. 'In there,' I gasped.

'What?' He glared at me.

'Dead body,' I muttered. 'Man, I think.' I spat emphatically and made an effort to compose myself. 'Is there a phone?'

'There's one up at the warehouse,' he said. 'But I dunno if . . .'

'Call the police,' I told him. 'Tell them there's been a murder.'

'What?' He looked at me and then a slow, stupid grin spread across his face. 'This is a put-on, right?'

'Don't be bloody silly,' I snapped. 'Get the police, *now*! I'll wait here for them.' I glared at him. 'Go on, hurry!'

He began to move on along the street, but slowly, hands in pockets. He kept looking around as though he was expecting a camera crew to pop out of hiding and admit that it was all a stunt.

'Will you for fuck's sake get a move on?' I yelled; and that seemed to do the trick. He began to trot, then run. He ducked in through the open doorway of one of the big warehouses across the street.

I leaned back against the car and took a deep breath. The camera had stopped rewinding and on impulse, I opened it up, removed the film and slipped it into an empty compartment on my harness. My fingers searched out a new film and loaded it into the camera.

With hindsight, I can see how if I'd only neglected to perform this simple action, everything would have been different. But I had set the oiled wheels in motion now and they would click and whirr through their pre-programmed sequence till they arrived at their logical conclusion. Pointless now to agonise about what might have been. I was already in deep, right up to my skinny little neck.

Like a sacrificial victim, ripe for the slaughter, I stood there on Sobriety Street and waited for the police to arrive.

# Chapter Two

They were prompt, I had to give them that. The police car came cruising slowly down the street about ten minutes after the workman had gone off to make his phone call.

By this time he had alerted all his mates to the fact that something dodgy was happening and a small bunch of men were standing around the entrance of the warehouse, further up the street. They were smoking cigarettes and watching me with open curiosity, but they were keeping their distance, as though they didn't want to get involved. I felt strangely numb by this time. I'd expected to experience a wave of shock or something but instead, I felt detached from everything, watching it all unfold before me like a series of images on a giant television screen.

The police car stopped for a moment alongside the group of men and the one who had phoned pointed me out. Then the car came on again and pulled to a halt a short distance away from me.

Two uniformed men got out, bored expressions on their faces. One was a small, thin, dour-looking individual. His companion was plump, ruddy-cheeked, with baby-blue eyes. I mentally dubbed them Laurel and Hardy as they came strolling towards me.

'Now then, Sir,' said Hardy. 'We had a call. Something about a dead body?'

I nodded, gestured at the open door of the railway arch.

'It's in there,' I told him. 'Hanging from a beam. You'll probably need this.' I proffered the torch and the two men exchanged amused glances, before Laurel reached out a hand to take it.

'I'm on dead body duty today,' he announced gleefully. 'Hanging, you say? Be a suicide I expect. We get a lot of those.'

'I don't think so,' I told him. 'This one's hanging by his feet.'

'Bloody hell,' said Laurel. 'Odd way of doing it. Hang there till you *starve* to death!' He snickered unpleasantly.

I gave him a sharp look. It was evident he wasn't taking the matter seriously. 'It's not a pretty sight,' I warned him.

Laurel gave me a look in return, an expression that suggested that I was trying to teach my Granny to suck eggs. He turned to look at his companion. 'If I'm not back in ten minutes, send a search party,' he quipped. Then he turned and strolled in through the open doors.

Hardy produced a notebook from the breast pocket of his jacket. For some reason, I noticed an egg stain on his lapel. He flipped open the book and licked the stub of a blunt pencil.

'Now then, *Sir*,' he said; the latter word emphasised to let me know that he didn't really like having to call me this. 'Perhaps you'd be good enough to supply me with your name and address.'

I did as he asked, but all the time my eyes kept straying to the open doors of the railway arch and I realised that I was mentally counting.

'And what time did you find the body?'

'About twenty minutes ago. I got somebody to call you right away.'

'I see. And would you mind telling me what—'

But that was as far as he got. Laurel emerged suddenly from the gloom of the arch, moving with more urgency than he had entered it. His face was chalky white and he was holding himself very erect, one hand on his stomach, as though he doubted whether he'd be able to hold back its contents. I couldn't help feeling a twinge of satisfaction. He was taking the matter much more seriously now. Again the two policemen exchanged glances. Laurel gave a curt nod and Hardy's eyebrows lifted in surprise. He turned to move towards the open doors but Laurel raised a hand to stop him in his tracks.

'Don't,' he said.

Hardy stared at him, then swore under his breath. He walked quickly back to the car and reached in to pick up the intercom. He started to talk rapidly into it. Laurel, meanwhile, had moved a few steps off and was gazing up the street, his back to me.

'Skin,' I heard him mutter. 'What happened to his fuckin' skin?' Then his shoulders heaved, he retched and doubled over like he'd just been punched in the stomach. Vomit spilled from his mouth. I could see that the ancient cobbles of Sobriety Street were going to need a good sluicing down before this day was over.

Things happened rapidly after that. During the next half hour there were a lot of arrivals.

Another police car approached along the street, then a third. A black van pulled up and disgorged half a dozen men in overalls. They began to seal off the area around the railway arch with incident tape. The workers further up the street who were still watching the proceedings were escorted back into the warehouse by uniformed men. Then what looked like a portable generator and a whole series of lights were unloaded from the van and carried into the arch. I took the opportunity to snap off a series of surreptitious photographs, using the autofocus and shooting from chest height. It was a technique I'd perfected over the years. You simply adopted a bored expression and masked the whirr of the motor-drive with a strategically timed cough. I told myself that the *Manchester Evening Post* would pay big bucks for a scoop like this.

After throwing up, Laurel had retired to the sanctuary of his car. He sat in the passenger seat now, his pale face tilted back to stare at the roof. Meanwhile, Hardy, completely oblivious to the fact that I was snapping away with my camera the whole time, saw fit to ask me a series of stupid questions, taking down the answers in slow, laborious handwriting, the tip of his tongue protruding from his mouth as he wrote.

'Did you know the deceased?' he asked; a question he wouldn't have bothered with if he'd actually seen the condition of the corpse. I just shook my head.

'And what were you doing in there anyway?'

I gestured at the camera hanging from my neck.

'Taking pictures,' I said. 'I'm a photographer.'

He gave me a suspicious look and I was sure that he didn't believe me. 'Taking pictures?' he echoed. 'Of what?'

'Well, of the interior of the arch, obviously.'

'The interior of—' He was gazing at the notepad in his plump hands now, as if expecting an explanation to materialise on the sheet of lined paper. On reflection, I had to admit that it did sound kind of unlikely.

'I'm having this exhibition,' I elaborated. 'At The Wedge.

You know, the arts centre? I thought I might get some good pictures in there.'

'Pictures of *what?*' muttered Hardy.

I was prevented from answering the question by the arrival of yet another car. It drew to a halt a short distance away and two plain clothes men got out. Simultaneously, powerful lights flared within the railway arch, illuminating the interior with a harsh, naked glow.

'Wait here,' said Hardy, sternly. He hurried across to the newcomers and made an awkward, stammering report to them, though I was too far away to hear what he was saying. He kept pausing and pointing back at me every so often, as though apportioning the blame for all this commotion. The two men studied me intently and I took the opportunity to photograph them.

They were another ill-matched couple. The man nearest to me was a squat, ugly individual in a shapeless tweed overcoat, the neck pulled up as though it was raining. He had a square, almost featureless face, dominated by a large nose that somewhere back down the years had been spectacularly squashed against his face. His eyes were small and beady, his sandy hair cropped close to his skull.

His companion, however, was as handsome as the first man was ugly. Younger by some ten years, he had the smouldering good looks of a 1940's matinée idol. He wore his straight black hair somewhat longer than regulations usually allowed and his tall, lean frame was enclosed in a beautifully tailored charcoal suit. The silk tie at his neck was a brilliantly coloured Aztec design and I couldn't help thinking that he was unlike any policeman I'd ever seen. As I watched, he issued curt instructions to Hardy, then with a casual flick of his head, he instructed the broken-nosed man to follow him into the railway arch. Surprisingly, despite his comparative youth, he was the senior officer.

Hardy came back, tucking the notebook into his pocket and looking very self-important.

'You've to hang on here,' he informed me. 'Detective Inspector Flynn of Homicide wants to have a word with you, once he's had a look at the scene of the crime.' He gazed thoughtfully towards his car, where Laurel's pale countenance was visible through the window. 'Took it bad,' he murmured, sounding bemused. 'Hard to believe, really. Body all cut up, was it?'

'Well, it was still in one piece,' I told him.

'He's seen all sorts too,' said Hardy. '*Terrible* things. I wouldn't have thought there was anything left could shock him. Dismembered was it? Things missing from the body?'

I nodded towards the arch where a couple of waxy-faced men in overalls were currently emerging into the daylight, both of them looking as though they might toss their cookies at any moment.

'Why don't you go and take a look?' I suggested; but he stayed right where he was.

'Got to keep an eye on you,' he explained. 'In case you decide to wander off. Detective Inspector Flynn wouldn't like that, would he?' He looked suddenly grieved. 'Flynn's new here,' he said, quite unprompted. 'Sent him up from London, didn't they? Show us simple Northern coppers a thing or two. He's a bloody magician by all accounts, got his own way of doing things. This will be his first real case.'

I stared at him, wondering why he had elected to tell me all this. Then I noted the expression of intense dislike he threw towards the railway arch and I realised that his remarks were fired by a resentment so powerful, he was incapable of keeping them to himself. He didn't actually add the words 'bloody Southerner' but they were the subtext behind the disapproving set of his mouth, the furious glare in his eyes.

Then yet another car, a red Cavalier, approached and found a place to park. An elderly man in a tweed suit got out from behind the wheel. He leaned in and withdrew a leather case from the passenger seat, then walked briskly towards the arch.

'There's the pathologist,' announced Hardy, with unmistakable reverence in his voice. 'Dr Giles Laughton. He's one of the best in the country.'

'That right?' I leaned slightly to one side and snapped a picture of the new arrival, coughing to disguise the camera click.

The two Homicide officers met Laughton in the doorway and stood talking with him for a while. After a few minutes of earnest conversation, the ugly detective accompanied the pathologist back into the arch. Flynn stood there looking thoughtful, tapping an index finger against his pursed lips. Then he shrugged, walked purposefully towards me.

'Mr . . . West?' he inquired.

'Weston, Sir,' Hardy corrected him. 'Danny Weston. Claims to be a photographer . . .'

'Yes, thank you, Constable. I shan't be requiring you any longer, you may go.' Flynn's voice was smooth, suave even, shot through with a cultured tone that spoke eloquently of a privileged upbringing. A strange kind of copper indeed.

'I'll make a full report back at the station, Sir,' persisted Hardy. 'In the meantime, if you need to refer to my notes . . .'

'Yes, thank you, that will be all,' said Flynn, more forcefully. Hardy scowled and turned away, trudged resignedly back to his car. Flynn turned his attention to me and favoured me with a dazzling grin. 'A photographer indeed! And you work for the *Evening Post*?'

I was taken aback by this sudden show of clairvoyance.

'Yes, but how did you . . .?'

He smiled, indicated the baseball cap I was wearing.

'I haven't been in Manchester that long, but I've learned to recognise the MEP logo,' he said.

'Of course. Well yes. I work for the *Post* in a freelance capacity . . .'

'But,' said Flynn.

I stared at him. 'But what?' I murmured.

'Oh, there's always a "but" in these situations, Danny. Oh, look, do you mind if I call you Danny? Mr Weston seems so very formal, don't you think?'

The car containing Laurel and Hardy moved slowly away down the street and I caught a glimpse of Hardy's ruddy-cheeked, scowling face. He was saying something to his partner and I supposed he was talking about Flynn. From the ugly shapes his mouth was making, I knew it wasn't complimentary.

'Er . . . Danny is fine,' I muttered.

'The "but" in your case, would be . . . oh, let me see now, one of creative conflict, I suppose. Working for the *Evening Post* keeps the wolf from the door but deep down, you harbour aspirations of a more creative nature. You long to be the new Henri Cartier-Bresson.'

'Robert Doisneau, actually,' I said – but I was floored, not only by his insight but by the very unlikelihood of a policeman who'd even *heard* of Henri Cartier-Bresson.

'Ah yes, I should have guessed. Doisneau's enjoyed quite a revival in recent years, hasn't he?'

I tried not to gape. Tried and failed. 'Yes, he has,' I mumbled. 'But how did you know—'

'About your creative conflict? Oh, simple deduction really.' He waved a neatly manicured hand at the railway arch. 'A commercially motivated photographer would hardly have been seeking subjects in a filthy rat-trap like that – and so many people in your profession do things they *have* to do to provide the time and resources to do what they *want* to do. Show me any commercial photographer who doesn't fancy himself as a gifted artist and I'll show you a rare creature indeed.' He considered this for a moment. 'So, you went into the arch to take photographs.'

'Yes, I've got this exhibition coming up at The Wedge . . . oh, that's—'

'The arts centre on Oxford Street. Yes, one of the first things I did on arrival here was to take in the *Images of War* exhibition. Did you see that? Quite devastating, I thought, particularly the photographs by Don McCullin.'

'Yes, they *were* impressive . . . I'm sorry, I'm a bit thrown by all this. I mean, forgive me, but I'm sure there are not many policemen who go to exhibitions at The Wedge.'

Flynn grinned. 'We're not all Dixon of Dock Green types, you know.'

He slipped his right arm around my shoulders, an overly familiar gesture under the circumstances, but I was still so astonished by him, I never questioned it. He lowered his voice to a confidential murmur.

'Isn't it always the way, Danny, that one is never in a position to discuss these matters properly. Photography is something of a pet subject of mine. Oh, I've no flair for it myself, you understand, but I do enjoy looking at it and under different circumstances, I'd love to pursue the subject in more detail. But, alas . . .' He sighed, threw a resentful glance over his shoulder at the railway arch. 'I'm here to do a job. And you, Danny, are in the luckless position of being the poor devil who chanced upon that . . . that *abomination* in there. Now, obviously you must have been deeply shocked by what you saw; but the more you can tell me about how you came to find it, the sooner we can let you get away from here.'

I nodded. 'He's been skinned, hasn't he?' I asked him. It was about the dumbest question I'd ever asked in my life but it just kind of slipped out. I think my mind wanted confirmation of what my eyes had seen. Flynn however, took it in his stride.

'*Flayed* is, I think, the correct term. And a brilliantly executed piece of work it is, too. I don't think I've ever witnessed such craftsmanship. Did you see the fingers, Danny?' He wriggled the fingers on his own left hand in front of my face. 'Meticulous attention to detail. Can you imagine the kind of skill required to—' He must have noticed how I blanched, because he broke off and made an apologetic gesture. 'Thoughtless of me,' he observed. He took his arm from around my shoulders and turned back to face me. 'One question, Danny,' he said quietly. 'And I absolutely have to ask it. Are you in any way connected with the death of that man in there?'

The question caught me off guard. 'N . . . no, of course not!' I protested. 'Christ, you surely don't think—'

He smiled, put a hand on my shoulder.

'I had to ask,' he replied. 'Forgive me. Now, if you'll humour me a while longer? I want you to tell me everything that happened from the moment you arrived here. Every little detail you can recall, no matter how inconsequential.' He took a dictaphone from his pocket and held it in front of me.

I did as he asked. From time to time he interrupted me to elucidate on some small point but for the most part he listened patiently as I picked my way through the day's events. It didn't take long and when I got to the end of it I could see from the expression on his face that he'd gleaned nothing of any value. He switched off the dictaphone.

'Yes, well . . . we may need to get a written statement from you in due course but for the moment, this should suffice. I dare say we can let you go about your business soon – though I would appreciate it if you'd allow some of my forensic boys to have a quick look at your car, before you go. I take it the green 2CV is yours?'

'Yes, I . . .' For a moment, I bridled, realising that he was cleverly manipulating me. 'Look,' I said, 'this has got nothing to do with me!'

'Delighted to hear it, dear boy. In which case, you'll have absolutely nothing to hide from us, right?'

I sighed, nodded. I pulled my keys from my pocket and handed them to him. He beckoned to a couple of men in overalls standing by the railway arch and as they approached, Flynn threw them the keys. 'Just give the car a quick once over,' he instructed. 'I'm sure there's nothing to find but still . . .' The men went to carry out his instructions and I watched them resentfully. 'Don't worry,' Flynn assured me. 'I'm sure they'll be gentle with her.'

Disarmed again, I gave a bitter little laugh.

'What happens next?' I asked.

'A very good question. In a case as unusual as *this* one, we'll likely have to invent new rules. Obviously identification is going to be the bugger. His own mother wouldn't recognise him looking like that; and unfortunately, the killer appears to have absconded with the main means of identification.'

'What, you mean the *skin*? It's not somewhere in the arch?'

'If it is, it's well hidden. We haven't found hide nor hair of it, if you'll forgive the rather ghastly pun. So we'll just have to wait till somebody is reported missing. Then it's a case of

28

comparing blood groups, dental and medical records. A lot of paperwork as I'm sure you'll appreciate.'

The ugly policeman came out of the arch and trudged across to us, his hands buried deep in the pockets of his overcoat. He stopped a short distance away, his brutish eyes flicking over me like the lenses of two tiny cameras.

'What a fucking mess,' he observed. For an instant, I thought he was referring to me; then I realised that he was commenting on the bloodbath back at the scene of the crime.

'This is Detective Sergeant Potts,' announced Flynn and I couldn't mistake the evident distaste in his voice. Potts had a blunt, Lancashire accent and an unpleasant sneer. It was immediately apparent that the two men disliked each other and I wondered who'd had the bright idea of teaming them up.

'Laughton has had a quick decko,' said Potts. 'Reckons the poor bugger was still alive when that was done to him. Christ, he must have made some noise. Would have happened no more than a few hours ago, Laughton reckons.'

'Hmm.' Flynn turned away and stared along the length of the street. 'Well, nobody would have heard anything from out here, that's for sure. Our killer chose his turf well. If you'd been up an hour or so earlier, you might well have caught him red-handed, Danny.'

'There's a small broken window at the back of the arch,' said Potts. 'Looks like that's where he got in and out. We've found clear prints around the frame, the forensic boys reckon he was wearing surgical gloves. Photographer wants to know if he can take his pictures now.'

'Surely. I've seen as much of that monstrosity as I want to.' He dismissed Potts with a nod and the man walked back towards the arch. Flynn glanced at me. 'Now *there's* a way to keep the wolf from the door, Danny. Ever considered a career snapping scene of crime pictures for the Force?'

I grimaced. 'Don't think I could handle that,' I told him.

'Oh, I think that most photographers manage to overcome their natural aversions very quickly. Something in the voyeuristic nature of them. The most hideous things seem acceptable when viewed through the lens of a camera.' He reached out a hand to tap the Pentax around my neck. 'You might think me a suspicious old cove, Danny, but you wouldn't by any chance have taken any pictures in the arch, would you? Only I see that your film counter is currently set to number twelve . . .'

I laughed nervously. 'Do me a favour,' I said. 'I ran out of there the second I saw the body.'

'Hmm.' He looked far from convinced. 'Well, I'm afraid I'm going to have to ask you for the film in the camera. Just to be on the safe side.'

'Look, I already told you—'

'The film, please. If I wanted to get difficult, I could demand every roll you have with you.'

'OK.' I upturned the camera and grumblingly rewound the spool. 'I don't suppose for one moment I'll be reimbursed for the cost,' I muttered.

'I'll do better than that. I'll have it developed for you. And if I find nice photographs of verdant fields and pouting leggy beauties, I'll bring you round a set of quality prints at absolutely no expense. If on the other hand, I find pictures that I do not deem acceptable, I'll confiscate them and I will personally bring round a fresh spool of . . .' He examined the film casing as I handed it to him. 'HP5,' he concluded. 'Now, I can't say fairer than that, can I?'

'I wouldn't want to put you to any trouble,' I said hastily.

'No trouble at all. Actually, Danny, I have a feeling we'll be seeing a lot more of each other before this is over.'

I didn't like the sound of that, not one little bit. Not that he wasn't an interesting man, but he was a cop and I didn't much like the idea of him hanging around the place, scaring all my friends.

The forensic people were finished with my car. They moved back towards the arch and in passing, one of them gave Flynn a brief shake of the head, then handed him the keys. He in turn, presented them to me.

'Well, it would seem that you're free to go, Danny.' He looked thoughtful for a moment, then once again he gave me that movie-star smile. 'This may sound odd, but for some time now I've been thinking of having my portrait done. You know, a proper studio portrait. You wouldn't have a business card with you, I suppose?'

I frowned, but took out my wallet and found him a card. He examined it carefully, as though looking for clues. 'Danny Weston,' he read aloud. 'Studio Seven Photography. Why Studio *Seven*?'

I shrugged. 'It's my lucky number,' I told him.

'Mine too.' He slipped the card into his breast pocket. 'I'll be in touch,' he said.

I turned and walked back to my car, stowed my equipment in the boot. Flynn just stood there watching me in silence. This was unnerving and it seemed to take ages before I was ready to go. Finally I got in, slammed the door behind me and started up the engine. Flynn lifted a hand in a brief wave as I drove away. I could see him in my rear-view mirror, standing and watching me intently, until my car turned the corner at the end of the street.

# Chapter Three

Fifteen minutes later I was struggling up the staircase to my city centre apartment-cum-studio. I was heavily laden with the camera equipment which I didn't dare leave in the boot of my car. I still felt curiously unmoved by recent events and was beginning to worry about my apparent insensitivity to the violent death of a fellow human being.

The apartment was just off Oldham Street, an area that up until comparatively recently had been a seedy, disreputable part of the city, full of boarded-up premises and down-at-heel pubs, haunted by incoherent drunks who specialised in backing you into corners so they could ask for a few pence for 'the bus home'. But Oldham Street was currently undergoing the process of urban regeneration, lots of alternative cafés and bars opening up, lifestyle boutiques and 'indie' record shops. True, there were still plenty of incoherent drunks hanging around, but these days, at least they tended to have more interesting haircuts.

I'd secured the tenancy on the large upstairs apartment at a propitious time, a good two months before regeneration had begun in earnest and rents had risen accordingly. There were three good sized rooms up there, together with a small kitchen and bathroom. My landlord, a charming Bangladeshi gentleman called Mr Bhopal, had been experiencing difficulties in letting them out, mostly because of the pungent aromas that drifted up from his take-away curry emporium directly below. As somebody who adores Asian food, I didn't think this would cause me any problems, but I hummed and haahed enough to obtain a substantial reduction on the rent, before signing on the dotted line.

Mr Bhopal proved to be the ideal landlord. I received a visit from him on the first day of every month when the rent was due and he always softened the blow by bringing me up a little paper box full of Asian sweets. Aside from that regular visitation, he left me to my own devices and hadn't complained once about the various changes I'd made to his premises.

The first thing I'd done was to convert the largest room into a studio, rigging up lights, a selection of backdrops and a couple of movable reflectors. I partitioned off one corner with plasterboard to create a small darkroom. I'd begged, borrowed, scrounged a lot of the stuff I needed and taken every opportunity to frequent the regular sales of bankrupt stock around the city. The result looked pretty ramshackle but I ended up with a place where I could photograph and process to a professional standard in monochrome. For colour work, I was still obliged to use one of the bigger processing labs in the city, but the cost of rigging up for that kind of work was well beyond my meagre budget.

Still, everything went along swimmingly at first. I was getting regular work from the *Evening Post* and more than enough commissions from other sources to keep me busy. And then it occurred to me that I still had one room that was largely unused and I began to think about the possibility of taking on a photographic assistant. I couldn't afford to pay much but the successful applicant would get free accommodation, plenty of hands-on experience with the equipment and best of all, the benefit of my years of professional expertise.

So I advertised in *Metro Magazine*, interviewed upwards of twenty potential assistants, each one of them positively brimming with enthusiasm and somehow – don't ask me how – I ended up with Roz Birchill.

Looking back, she *did* make a good impression at the interview; a punky, tomboyish twenty-three-year-old with a shock of spiky red hair, a scattering of freckles across the bridge of her snub nose and a no-nonsense attitude that made a refreshing change from some of the goody-two-shoes I'd previously talked to. She was passionate about photography, she said, particularly the confrontational, sexually ambiguous style of Robert Mapplethorpe. She wasn't afraid of tackling the more mundane darkroom chores either, since she believed that it was important to acquire as much technical knowhow as possible. And – this was the clincher for me, I'm afraid – she browsed through my portfolio and declared herself 'genuinely excited' by what she saw in there, she figured there was a lot she could learn from a talented professional like myself.

Sure, she'd sucker-punched me, but by the time I realised it, Roz was already installed in the spare room and proving to be a lot more difficult than I had anticipated.

Unlocking the door, I stepped into the kitchen area, looking vainly around for an empty stretch of work surface on which to dump my camera case. Roz was sitting at the table, dressed in her Batman pyjamas. At the decidedly decadent hour of one-thirty PM, she appeared to be having her breakfast. She looked up from her bowl of Sugar Puffs and gave me a welcoming sneer.

'No, no, don't get up,' I told her, sarcastically.

She grunted something I didn't quite catch and went on

with the serious task of consuming her cereal. I finally managed to locate a bare stretch of floorboards and set down the heavy case and tripod with a sigh of relief. Then I moved to the worktop and switched on the kettle with the intention of making myself a cup of coffee.

'There's no milk,' said Roz, at the same time lifting a spoonful of that very liquid to her mouth. I sighed, turned towards the breadbin, deciding that I'd have toast instead.

'No bread either,' she informed me, matter of factly. 'I finished it last night.'

I looked at her sharply, then mentally counted to ten. It did absolutely no good to lose your rag with her. That would just make her snap right back at you. I'd discovered very early on in our 'working' relationship that Roz could be as stubborn as a mule and any criticism of her tended to result in a show of rage that would put the Incredible Hulk to shame. Actually, I'd discovered a lot of things about Roz since she'd moved in, few of them designed to fill me with joy.

I now knew that she was a dyed-in-the-wool Marxist, a women's libber of the most extreme kind, a smoker (at the interview she'd sworn she never went near cigarettes) a karate expert and most distressingly, a Cure fan with a predilection for playing their records, full volume, in the early hours of the morning. Furthermore, Roz was one of those people who believed that the world owed her a living. She thought that the work I did for the *Evening Post* was a sell-out of Trotsky-like proportions and took every opportunity to ridicule it. Most infuriating of all, she seemed to see no reason whatsoever why she should lower herself to perform the kind of demeaning chores that I had actually engaged her to do.

Yes, I'd learned a lot of things about Roz; and yet,

conversely, I didn't have the least idea of what made her tick. And the problem was that deep down, I really *liked* the girl. When you caught her in the right mood, she could be funny, engaging and great company. Unfortunately, these occasions were few and far between.

I sat down opposite her and for want of more suitable sustenance, I took a sugar lump from the bowl on the table and sucked it contemplatively. A long silence unfolded between us, interspersed only by the clunking of Roz's spoon as she ate her Sugar Puffs. Finally, she felt obliged to acknowledge my presence with a little conversation.

'Where've you been, then? Out on a job for the *News Of The Screws*?'

She always called the *Post* that, though it was hardly the sordid, gutter-tabloid that she made it out to be.

I shook my head. 'Something for the exhibition,' I told her.

'Hmmph!' This was a bit of a sore point, since Roz and one of her feminist cronies were currently collaborating on an exhibition of their own, which had recently been turned down by The Wedge. This wasn't a great surprise to me, since their 'installation' as they preferred to call it, imaginatively entitled *Private Parts*, was to consist of three-hundred-and-sixty-five photographs of the penis. They'd finally managed to get a tentative venue at the Greer Centre. Only now, Roz was discovering how difficult it was to persuade men to pose for such pictures. The ones who *would* generally had dodgy ulterior motives and Roz's training in karate had proved useful on several occasions. She currently had eleven willies 'in the can' and a lot of ground to make up. Meanwhile, she seemed to consider it fair game to criticise my upcoming photofest at every opportunity.

'So what was it this time?' she wanted to know. 'More old age pensioners?'

'No. Actually, it was this old railway arch behind Piccadilly Station. I thought I might get some interesting stuff in there, but . . . well, it didn't exactly go as planned.'

Roz couldn't suppress a smirk of delight.

'You're going to have to pull your finger out,' she informed me. 'There isn't much time left.'

'Yes, well thanks for pointing that out. And how is the willie-count progressing, I wonder? Getting any nearer to that magical three-six-five, are we?'

Roz frowned. 'Actually, I was going to have a word with you about that. I was wondering if you fancied getting on the other side of the camera for a change?'

'No,' I told her bluntly. 'Don't even think of it. I've no wish to have my family jewels put on display for the general public, thank you very much.'

'Oh go on, nobody will know it's you. We won't show your face or anything.'

'Roz, read my lips. No!'

She scowled into her breakfast bowl. 'So you're thinking of doing *buildings* now?'

I nodded. 'I've been toying with the idea of urban decay,' I told her. 'I thought I could contrast the OAP photographs with images of derelict buildings, crumbling walls, rotting beams . . . that kind of thing.'

She made a face. 'Bit derivative,' she said.

'Derivative of what?' I protested.

'Of things I've seen elsewhere.'

'*All* art is derivative,' I argued. 'It's part of the creative process. And frankly, Mr Shankly, I don't think that prick pictures are so startlingly original, either. Didn't Yoko Ono do stuff like that in the early seventies?'

'That was *arses*,' she corrected me. 'This is pricks. There's a big difference.'

'You don't say.' I picked up another sugar cube and crunched it absent-mindedly.

'That's a very annoying habit,' she told me tartly, then took a slurping mouthful of milk and cereal. 'Anyway, you were a long time gone considering you didn't get anything you could use.'

'No, it got kind of complicated. I found a body.'

'Yeah?' She went on chomping her Sugar Puffs and I decided that she couldn't have heard me properly.

'I mean like a *dead* body.'

'Uh huh. Anybody I know?'

I glared at her. I couldn't make up my mind if she was being deliberately cool or was just genuinely indifferent to the news.

'Is that all you've got to say?' I cried. 'I am talking about a dead human being. *Murdered*. I've just spent a couple of hours being interviewed by the old bill.'

'Why, did they think you had something to do with it?'

'No, of course not,' I said; though I didn't feel entirely convinced of this fact myself. I remembered the way Flynn had gazed at me as I drove off, as though watching for an indication of guilt. 'I was just the poor sod who found this guy's body, wasn't I? Jesus, it was *horrible*.'

At last, Roz sat up and took notice.

'How was it done?' she asked me.

'What do you mean?'

'Well, was he stabbed, shot, strangled . . .?'

'Christ, you're a right ghoul, aren't you?' I thought for a moment. 'Well, I don't know exactly what killed him. It was hard to tell. He'd been skinned, you see.'

She pushed the remains of her cereal away and gave me an

accusing look, as though she was holding me personally responsible for the method of killing.

'You *did* ask,' I reminded her.

'I know, but *really*!' She threw me another look and for an instant, I thought I glimpsed the genuine article behind the hip facade. Momentary concern flickered in her brown eyes. 'You seem surprisingly calm about it,' she observed. 'It must have been pretty awful.'

'Yeah, well, it *was* at the time. Now I feel kind of numb. Tell you the truth, I don't think it's hit me yet. Looking back, it's like a film I saw. Like it happened to somebody else, you know?'

'You don't have to say "you know" to me,' she snapped irritably. 'I'm not stupid!'

And suddenly the more familiar Roz was back again, prickly, defensive, totally unsympathetic. I wondered what had happened to her back along the years that had made her so schizoid.

'Look,' I said, 'I didn't mean to—'

'Forget it,' she said. 'It just annoys me, that's all. You say it all the time, you know?' She realised what she'd just said and looked distinctly annoyed with herself. I refrained from rubbing it in. The brief pleasure it would have afforded me would soon have been obliterated by the days of contempt I'd have to endure as a result.

Roz got up from the table.

'Anyway, I'd love to stay and chew the fat, but I've got to go out. It's my assertiveness class this afternoon.'

I tried not to smirk. Roz needed assertiveness classes like Arnold Schwarzenegger needed a Charles Atlas course. Mind you, she was fond of her classes. She also did creative pottery, reflexology and Aikido, so she had a busy schedule.

'I'm meeting Vincent Spinetti at The Wedge bar later,' I told her. 'We're going over some ideas for the exhibition. If you want to meet up with us . . .'

'Wouldn't dream of it,' she assured me. 'I hate playing gooseberry.' She didn't really approve of Spinetti, who she always said was a 'wide boy'. Actually, this was a description that suited him well enough, though in a manager, it was probably an essential requirement.

'Make sure he buys a drink,' she muttered darkly, referring to Spinetti's uncanny ability to avoid putting his hand in his pocket whenever it was his round. 'And don't let him bully you. Remember, it's *your* exhibition . . .'

Then, as if sensing that she was once again edging dangerously close to displaying friendly concern, she turned on her heel and stalked off in the direction of her room.

I took the edge off my hunger with a couple of handfuls of dry Sugar Puffs, then carried my equipment through to the studio. I went straight into the darkroom and set about developing the film I had shot earlier. Once the negatives were dry enough to handle, I switched on the red lamp, laid them in strips on a sheet of photographic paper and popped them under the enlarger to produce a sheet of contact prints.

As the images began to appear in the developing tray, I anticipated that they would rekindle a sense of horror in me, but they didn't. I was able to observe them with a dispassionate, critical eye and to decide that yes, they *were* a powerful set of images, savage, uncompromising, shocking in their explicitness. Too graphic for any magazine or newspaper to use, that was for sure and yet . . .

I slid the paper into the fixer, then pegged the sheet up to dry on the line. I was now able to switch on the main lights to get a proper look at the contacts.

They seemed even more impressive now. The camera had

captured every ridge of wet flesh, every twist of muscle, every exposed vein. If you didn't think too closely about what you were looking at, there was almost a weird, alien beauty to them.

And for the first time, I thought about how they'd look blown up to life-size in stark, high contrast monochrome. How they'd look in an exhibition . . .

I should have obeyed the instinct that followed – a powerful rush of self-disgust. I should have bundled up the negatives with the paper and burned them, then and there. With hindsight, it's so easy to see that I was on the verge of doing a stupid and irresponsible thing.

But part of me – the dark part that has always relished the grotesque – was intrigued by the possibilities. And the other side of my personality was too malleable, too easily led. It wouldn't allow me to rule out the idea entirely, not until I had consulted somebody else.

So I decided to make a half dozen enlargements and take them to show Vincent Spinetti. Maybe he'd help me decide.

# Chapter Four

I got to The Wedge fifteen minutes late and went in through the glass swing doors.

I stood for a moment, portfolio under my arm, gazing around the packed but cheerless interior, but there was no sign of Spinetti. There were a lot of other punters in, most of them grabbing a quick drink before going off to see their respective movies. Everybody – myself included – seemed to be wearing a black leather jacket but as always, I was struck by the sheer diversity of the haircuts on display; there were quiffs and flat tops and suedeheads and spikes and dread-locks, bobbing and swaying like a collection of furry animals beneath a fog of cigarette smoke.

The bar itself was fashionably severe – bare off-white walls, scuffed, beer-stained floorboards and a couple of tall black metal assemblages that looked like modern sculpture but which on closer inspection, turned out to be radiators. There were a few metal tables and uncomfortable wooden chairs off on the periphery of things but most customers here opted to stand around the bar, striking don't-give-a-fuck poses, propping themselves on one elbow while they sipped designer beers straight from the bottle. Off in one corner, a fifties-style jukebox was currently emitting a grungy techno-pop instrumental at an ear splitting volume.

By all accounts, The Wedge bar was still one of the hippest places to be seen in, but it was a mystery to me why anybody should choose to drink there. It was cramped, dirty and decidedly unfriendly and I got enough of that at home.

I pushed my way to the bar and ordered a pint of something cold and gassy. Right on cue, as if by magic, Vincent Spinetti appeared at my shoulder and I was obliged to pay for his drink too, a tall silver container of Japanese beer that was his current favourite tipple.

'All right?' he shouted, above the din of the jukebox. 'Sorry I'm late, I got held up. Been here long?'

I looked at him. Spinetti was about my age, tall and thin with a prominent nose and slightly bulging eyes that seemed to suggest an over-active thyroid. As ever, his short dark hair was meticulously cut and groomed and he was wearing a loose-fitting Armani suit in midnight blue, several sizes too big for him, but still hanging perfectly from his lean frame. An uncharitable side of me couldn't help thinking that he must have been waiting around outside The Wedge till I got there, to ensure that I paid for the first round of drinks. I told myself I was being unfair and handed him his can – apparently it was considered uncool to drink the stuff from a glass – then followed him across the crowded room in search of a vacant table. I was just telling myself that we hadn't a hope of finding one, when Spinetti spotted somebody reaching for a coat. He made a decisive sprint for the table in question and had himself safely installed in the one vacant seat before the current occupants had quite realised they were leaving.

This little incident seemed to me to be the essence of the Spinetti character. The man was a brilliant opportunist.

A Londoner by birth, he'd lived in this city long enough to be considered a permanent fixture. Shortly after his arrival, he'd recognised the need for a decent 'What's On'

publication, along the lines of London's *Time Out* and had
promptly founded *Metro Magazine*. For the first year or so
it had struggled fitfully for survival, lurching from one cash
crisis to the next. Its contributors were kept going on
peanuts and promises, it's many creditors were constantly
hammering on the door. Only Spinetti's undoubted flair
for bullshitting his way out of trouble had kept it from
going under. Somehow it had survived and prospered,
whereupon Spinetti had brought in people to run it for him
and these days restricted his involvement to attending a
weekly editorial meeting.

From that point he had diversified, getting his fingers into
all manner of pies – promoting concerts and raves, exhibitions, stand-up comedy festivals, New Age book fairs . . .
you name it. He acted as manager to a whole stable of
odd-ball entertainers and artists. I was just one of them.

With so many diverse strands to his business dealings it
was little wonder that he had become a hyperactive streak of
nervous energy, constantly glancing over his shoulder to
check for somebody he owed money to, whilst keeping one
eye skinned for the main chance. He sat opposite me now,
his fingers tapping out a furious rhythm on the table top as he
surveyed the room and the faces in it. Every so often, he'd
nod to somebody he knew, an almost imperceptible gesture
but you'd see the recipient beam back at him, lift a hand in
acknowledgement, looking well pleased with themselves
because – and this was, I think, the key to his success –
people genuinely wanted his approval.

He turned his attention to me now, looking at me thoughtfully, as though considering what he might do with me next.

'So, what's happening, *Maestro*?' he asked. 'Tell me some
exciting news.'

'Well . . .' I said; but I had hesitated a fraction too long.

Spinetti was off and running. He loved to gossip.

'See him at the bar? Guy with the spiked hair and shades? He's the bass player with the Serial Messiahs. Heard their demo the other day, reckon they've got potential.' He took a gulp of his beer, ran the fingers of one hand through his hair. 'Anyway, I've been trying to talk him into a management deal, but get this, he wants to stay with this no-hoper who's handling the band because he's an old friend from college. I ask you, what chance have they got with an attitude like that?'

I shook my head. 'Unbelievable,' I said. Actually, it sounded fair enough to me but I didn't want to get involved in a long conversation about some band I'd never even heard of.

'It's like I was telling him, you want to make it in *that* business, you can't afford to be sentimental. And the scene is so *blinkered* now, you know? I mean, you only have to look at what's happening with William K. That guy is such an awesome talent but can I get anybody to give him a fair hearing? Can I fuck!'

William K was one of Spinetti's earliest signings, a bearded young Bohemian whose admittedly original act consisted of him sitting cross-legged on the floor, beating out a rhythm on the back of a stringless acoustic guitar whilst improvising lyrics about whatever took his fancy at the time. Spinetti was convinced that William K was going to be huge some day, that his unique brand of 'anti-pop' would be the next big thing. I couldn't see it myself but then, what did I know?

'Bloody hippie music establishment,' growled Spinetti scathingly. 'They can only think in terms of "who is he like?". I keep telling them, he's not like anybody else, he's a genuine one-off. And you've heard the demo, Danny. If

*Pig-Dog-Trance-Dance* isn't a potential hit single, I'll eat my old jockey shorts.'

I frowned, took a contemplative sip of my lager. My own feelings about the song in question were that it was the kind of thing you'd put on to get rid of guests who'd outstayed their welcome, but if I'd learned one thing over the years, after seeing so many mediocre talents shoot to stardom, so many gifted individuals languishing in obscurity, it was that at the end of the day, everything came down to a little hard work and a lot of luck.

'Anyway,' said Spinetti, 'we didn't come here to talk about the shortcomings of the rock business. What's been happening with you?'

'Well . . .'

'Hey, Danny, see her over there? Chick with the pill-box hat and no tits?'

'Er . . . yes . . .'

'She's a clothes designer, good one too, has a stall up at Afflecks Palace. I keep telling her, she needs to open up a boutique on King Street, whack up her prices by about six hundred per cent and sell to rich hippies. She's worried about supplying the demand, so I told her, easy, what you do, right, is you get yourself a little sweatshop in Cheetham Hill, slap a half dozen Asian girls in there running up the gear to her original designs. Then she starts bleating about exploitation and how is she going to maintain the quality control? I said to her, I bet Vivienne bloody Westwood doesn't lose any sleep over stuff like that!' He took another pull at his Japanese beer and shook his head. 'I hate to see that, Danny. Genuine creativity held back by a *conscience*.'

'Absolutely . . . er, Vincent?'

'What?'

'About the exhibition. You remember, we were going to

go over some ideas?' I tapped the portfolio on the table top meaningfully and he gave it a wary look.

'Yeah, all right,' he said, with visible reluctance. 'Let's see what you've got then.'

I untied the small folder and handed it across to him, remaining silent as he browsed through the fifteen or so images that were in there, glancing perfunctorily at each one in turn.

'Old people,' he muttered at one point. And he glanced at me hopefully, as though expecting me to announce that this was some kind of joke, that these were not the real pictures at all. He went back to his browsing and quickly reached the end of them. 'Pictures of old people,' he concluded. 'And a couple of buildings.' He didn't sound very enthusiastic.

'You've got to use your imagination,' I told him. 'There'd be a lot more pictures of buildings. Well, more *details*, really. Close-ups of crumbling brick facades, rotting wooden beams, rusting strips of metal – classic images of urban decay. And they'd be counter-pointed by these portraits of—'

'Wrinklies,' said Spinetti, flatly. 'Old age pensioners.'

'You don't like them,' I said.

'Not at all,' he corrected me. 'I'm sure they're very nice. Very characterful. But . . .'

'But what?' I asked him and remembered something that Detective Inspector Flynn had told me earlier that day.

*Oh, there's always a 'but', Danny.*

Spinetti took another swig of his beer and considered for a moment, searching for the right way to phrase what he was about to say.

'Look around you, Danny boy. This is The Wedge we're in, not the fucking Darby and Joan club. It's a young, gutsy venue. A place with *attitude*. Pictures of wrinklies and buildings are all very well but they're not for an audience like this one, are they?' He took out a packet of Silk Cut, lit one up with his gold plated Zippo and blew a cloud of smoke into my face. 'I don't have to tell you the importance of this gig, there's a lot of people would give their right arms for the chance of a show in here. We've been very lucky to grab this opportunity, let's make no bones about that, it wasn't because they *asked* for you . . .'

'I know that, Vincent, but I still think this could be quite hard-hitting. If you'll only—'

'Hard-hitting?' He leafed through the pictures again as though searching for something he might have missed first time around. 'No offence, Danny, but these wouldn't look out of place on somebody's bus pass.'

That hurt. I bridled angrily.

'That's unfair,' I protested. 'Those are *good* pictures, you'll need to reserve judgement until you've seen them blown up to full size.'

'Danny, get real.' Spinetti was shaking his head pityingly now. 'This is your chance to make some waves, mate. You're going into the market place and putting your goods out on display, but you've got to offer something that will stop them in their tracks, rock them back on their heels. What we want is something raw, exciting, something *shocking*!'

I glared at him for a moment. 'You want to see something shocking?' I snarled. 'All right, you'll find a large envelope at the back of the prints. Open it and take a look at what's inside.'

Spinetti glanced at me warily.

'Now look, mate, don't get me wrong . . .'

'Just look in the envelope, OK?' I took a big swallow of my lager and watched as Spinetti did as he was told. He pulled the enlargements from the envelope and turned them around to look at the first one. His eyes narrowed for a few moments, as though trying to puzzle out what they were looking at. Then they widened in sudden shock and he flinched visibly in his seat. I couldn't resist a smirk of satisfaction.

'Jesus Christ,' he whispered. He glanced up at me and was unable to mask the expression of horror in his eyes. But he didn't have anything more to say, not just yet. He began to leaf through the other photographs, swearing softly under his breath with each successive image, pausing occasionally to figure out some particular detail that he could not, at first glance, identify. When he had got to the end of them, he sat back, reached for his drink and took a big swallow.

'More the kind of thing you had in mind?' I asked cuttingly.

'Jesus, Danny,' he said. 'Where the fuck did you get these?'

So I was obliged once again to recount the day's misadventure, noticing as I did so, how I added more details this time around, as you do with a favourite joke, drawing it gradually into a fuller, more satisfying narrative; and I also noticed that for the first time that evening, I had Spinetti's undivided attention.

'Incredible,' he said, when I'd finally reached the conclusion. 'And to think you had the presence of mind to take these pictures before calling the Old Bill.' He shook his head in evident admiration. 'Well, Danny, we've got to use them. It's as simple as that.'

'I don't know,' I reasoned. 'I won't pretend the idea hasn't already occurred to me – but Christ, can you imagine how shocked people would be? And I'm not sure of the legal implications.'

'Bollocks to that! You were the first on the scene and you happen to be a photographer. It was your scoop. It's only right you should be the one to benefit from it. And besides, didn't I just say it should be shocking?'

'Yes, but Vincent, there are *limits*. Surely this could offend public decency?'

'With any luck,' he said gleefully. 'These all of 'em?'

'No, there's plenty more. I shot nearly a whole film, thirty plus exposures.'

'Excellent.' He picked up a photograph from the first batch of pictures, a portrait of an old man; then selected a close-up shot of the corpse's upside-down face. 'Look at that,' he murmured. 'Now there's the contrast you've been looking for. Before and after!' He considered for a moment. 'That's the key to it,' he said. '*Skin*. Now you see it, now you don't! What you do, right, is you blow these wrinklies up big and grainy, so you can see all the lines and creases on their skin . . . maybe get some other stuff featuring close-ups of different kinds of skin. Black, white, pierced, tattooed. As you go into the exhibition, those are the images you see. Make it kind of a labyrinth, right? Then, in the very centre of your exhibition space, maybe there's this kind of little partitioned-off area you can go into . . .'

'Chamber of Horrors?' I asked drily.

'Call it what you like. We could even put health warnings up, you know, "people of a nervous disposition", that kind of thing. Maybe do the old William Castle stunt of offering to insure anyone who drops dead with a heart attack . . . no, but seriously, right, they go into this thing and wham! A man with no skin! Think of the impact, Danny. Think of the *outrage!*'

'Think of the publicity,' I added caustically, but couldn't deny that the idea *was* intriguing. If the function of art was to stir people's emotions, then this was sure to be the result. But still, there was a part of me that felt decidedly uncomfortable.

'I could wind up in prison,' I said.

'For what? You only photographed what was there. And you didn't exactly lie to that copper, did you? I mean, he asked for the film in your camera and you gave it to him.'

'Still . . .'

'Oh, come on, Danny, you know full well if you don't do this, you'll kick yourself for the rest of your life. I mean look at the exposure that Hirst geezer got for just sawing a dead cow in half. He's laughing all the way to the bank.'

'With respect, Vincent, I think there's a major difference between a dead cow and a dead human being.'

He waved a hand impatiently at me.

'Sure, sure, I take the point. But we'd be stupid to let this chance go, wouldn't we? Now, let me see, we'll need a snappy title. Something with the word "skin" in it, maybe?' He began to extemporise, gesturing with his hands like he was trying to pull something out of the air in front of him. '*Skin and Bone*? Too obvious. *Skin Job*, *Skin Head*, *Skin of the Teeth*, *Skin Game* . . .'

'How about *Skin Flicks*?' I asked him.

I thought he was going to lunge across the table and kiss me. 'Yes! Danny, that's fucking brilliant! It's an allusion to film but it also has a sleazy, low-life feel to it.' He made a gesture with his right hand, drawing an imaginary title in the air. '*Skin Flicks* by Danny Weston. I can see the posters now.'

The trouble was, so could I. It's like I told you before. I'm too easily led. And sitting there in the civilised interior of The Wedge, Spinetti made it all sound so *reasonable*. Why couldn't a skinless, dead body qualify as a legitimate subject for an exhibition? Was it any more unlikely than the Tate

Gallery's infamous bricks, a dead cow sliced in half or even Roz's three-six-five willies? And if it should earn Danny Weston, mild-mannered photographer, a little notoriety, hey, so much the better!

'OK,' I said. 'What the hell? Let's do it!'

'That's my boy!' He rewarded me with the famous, lopsided Spinetti grin. 'Let's celebrate with another round,' he suggested.

'Don't mind if I do,' I said; and drained the remains of my beer.

But Spinetti was reaching into his pocket for his mobile phone. 'While you're at the bar, I'll ring this young artist I know, he owes me a favour. Reckon he'll do us some brilliant invitations and posters. I am very excited about this, Danny, let me tell you. I'll have the same again.'

He began to dial and I slunk obligingly to the bar to get the drinks in, experiencing as I did so, a mental image of Roz's disapproving expression. I shrugged it off and pushed my way through the three-deep crowd that thronged the counter.

I ordered the drinks and carried them back to the table, where Spinetti was concluding a heated discussion with the artist he'd mentioned.

'Of *course* you'll get paid! Yeah, yeah, sure, I'll call round tomorrow. OK? Yes, *with the money*. Jesus! OK, talk to you later, man. Love to Debbie and the kids. Ciao!'

Spinetti hit the 'off' switch and slipped the phone back into his pocket.

'Gordon Bennet,' he muttered. 'Why does everybody give me such a hard time?' He winked at me, then lifted his can of beer in a toast. 'Anyway, I figure Pete can do us something that will look the business. All you have to do is concentrate on getting a few more images to supplement what we've already got.' He thought for a moment. 'Actually, I can give you a tip there. There's a bloke dances at the Adonis club, most nights. He's got these brilliant tattoos, pictures like you've never seen before. You should have a word with him.'

'What's his name?'

'I'm not sure, but you'll know him if you see him. And a lot of these New Age kids go in for body piercing. Be an idea to find out where they hang out.' He tapped the portfolio on the table top. 'I'm feeling really good about this, Danny. I reckon this could stir up a right old hornet's nest in this town.'

I frowned. 'And that's good?' I asked him doubtfully.

'Danny, that's exactly what we want. By the time we're finished you'll be able to wipe your arse on a piece of paper and flog that to the Tate for a four figure sum. Think you could handle that?'

I considered for a moment before answering in the affirmative – without considering that notoriety can be double edged, that it can swing back and cut to the bone.

Spinetti and I stayed at The Wedge until closing time, drinking one round after another – all of which I somehow wound up paying for. Whenever it was Spinetti's turn to buy he was always in the loo, or off talking to somebody else, or answering a call on his infernal mobile phone. After about five lagers, I was too pissed to care anymore. I bought one last round, drank it, then shook hands with Spinetti before we went our separate ways. I ended up staggering back to my place with a skinful of ale, stumbling and weaving through the crowds of exuberant night-clubbers making their way to Rock World or The Hacienda. When I got back to the flat, Roz had already turned in for the night so I went straight to my room and crashed out.

And dreamed that I was back in the railway arch. For

some reason, I'd taken Flynn up on his offer and had become a police photographer. Flynn was making me photograph a corpse – *the* corpse, a red, wet mannequin of exposed flesh and muscle. He was making me photograph it in great detail, close-ups mostly, urging me to get in nearer and nearer until the awful raw meat smell of the thing was in my mouth and nostrils and a powerful nausea churned in my guts.

I kept having to turn away to snatch a breath of air and every time I did, there on the wall were those two puzzling words, written in the dead man's blood: FOR ZIPPY.

'What do you think it means?' I asked Flynn. He gave me that dazzling smile, tapped the side of his nose meaningfully.

'Oh, you *know*, Danny, you're a creative person. You can figure it out, surely?'

And with that he instructed me to go back to work. I took what seemed like hundreds of pictures, pressing the shutter release until my finger ached and the glare of the flashgun made my eyes swim. But still Flynn wasn't satisfied, and so it seemed to go on, all through the night: point the camera, press the button, hideous details picked out in the flare of the flash. Then I awoke with a start to the sound of a fist hammering urgently on the front door.

I groaned, shook my head, fumbled for my glasses. The world swam gradually into focus. A glance at the clock told me that it was just past ten AM. I'd slept a lot longer than I'd meant to. I threw a bathrobe on and stumbled bleary-eyed into the hallway. Roz's door was open but there was no sign of her.

The fist kept up its relentless hammering. 'Yes, yes,' I muttered and went to open the door.

'Morning, Danny,' said Detective Inspector Flynn, smiling sweetly. 'Mind if I come in?'

# Chapter Five

Flynn looked almost indecently fresh and alert. He breezed past me into the kitchen and I caught a whiff of expensive cologne.

'Looks like I got you out of bed,' he observed.

'I had a bad night.'

'Hardly surprising under the circumstances.' He turned back and smiled disarmingly. 'Look, if it's inconvenient, I dare say I could come back later.'

'No, it's all right.' I gestured vaguely at the kettle. 'Coffee?' I suggested.

'Don't mind if I do . . . no, tell you what, you sit down, Danny, *I'll* make the coffee.' He moved across to the washbasin and selected a couple of mugs from the jumble of unwashed crockery piled in the sink. 'Not much of a house-keeper, are you?' he observed reproachfully and rinsed out the mugs under the hot tap.

'I er . . . don't think there's any milk,' I warned him.

'Good. I never touch the stuff.' He busied himself filling the kettle, while I took a seat at the table. His easy-going, affable mood was making me feel decidedly wary.

'So . . . why the visit?' I inquired.

He switched on the kettle, then spooned instant coffee into two mugs. 'There've been some interesting developments in our murder case and I rather wanted to sound you out on them.'

'Oh?' I didn't know what to say to that, so I just sat there and waited for further information; but Flynn's attention had been momentarily distracted by a framed photograph hanging on the wall, a large black and white self-portrait that I'd taken some months earlier, one night when I was bored. I'd shot it in the studio, using a high-contrast lighting rig and self-timer. In the picture I was staring into the lens with a manic, bug-eyed leer. I was holding this big two-handed axe, which was raised above my head as though ready to strike. I was stripped to the waist and my face and chest were liberally splattered with stage blood. At the time it had all seemed like a great joke – now it wasn't quite so funny.

Flynn glanced back at me and raised one eyebrow in a quizzical expression.

'Portrait of the artist as a young psychopath?' he murmured.

'It was just a bit of a laugh,' I told him; but he didn't look particularly amused and I didn't feel like laughing. There was a long silence then while we waited for the kettle to boil. It seemed to take forever. Finally, steam poured from the spout, making a shrill whistling sound. Flynn filled the two mugs with boiling water and brought them over to the table. He set one down in front of me and watched as I dropped a couple of sugar lumps into mine.

'Not good for you,' he observed.

'Sorry?'

'Sugar. Useless calories. It beats me how you keep that sylph-like figure, Danny.'

'It's the worry,' I told him. 'So you were saying there'd been . . . developments?'

'Yes, we've made big strides since yesterday. We already

know who the deceased was. Didn't take us long to place him, either. He'd already been reported missing and he was quite well known.'

I frowned. 'Would I have heard of him?' I asked.

'Better than that, Danny. You *photographed* him.'

'What?' I stared at Flynn. For a moment, I thought he was referring to the shots I'd taken of the corpse and I must have looked as guilty as hell. But then I saw that he was taking a photocopied press clipping from his jacket pocket.

'About three months ago. You did a shot of him outside the Royal Theatre. Sebastian Kennedy.' He handed me the photocopy, an article from the *Evening Post*. Of course I remembered it. Kennedy had been one of the leading lights in local theatre. He'd still been only in his twenties when he landed the plum job of directing an all-gay cast in a production of *A Midsummer Night's Dream*. I remembered that certain wags at the newspaper offices had made cheap wisecracks about this being the first production of the play to use genuine fairies. That was what passed for wit in those quarters.

'Christ,' I said. 'Sebastian Kennedy.' It seemed unbelievable that the slim, dark, good-looking man in the photograph could have been transmuted into the vile, bloody carcass that I had found hanging in the railway arch. 'You're sure?' I asked Flynn.

He nodded solemnly. 'We had to check with dental records to confirm it,' he said. 'Obviously, quite aside from the loss to those who loved him, it's also a terrible blow for the artistic community. Mr Kennedy was currently rehearsing a cast in a revival of *Hedda Gabler*. When he didn't turn up to rehearsals yesterday morning, a member of the cast got worried and contacted the police.' Flynn took a sip of his coffee, then turned his blue eyes full on me for a moment.

'So how well did you know him, Danny?'

'Me? I didn't know him from Adam. I knew *of* him, of course . . .'

'But you did take his photograph.'

'Jesus, I took Madonna's photograph once, but I don't know her either!' I tapped the article on the table. 'This was just an assignment. I do hundreds of them.'

'And you never met him socially?'

'Never. Why do you ask?'

Flynn frowned. He made a steeple from his hands and rested his chin on the point of it. 'I talked to members of the *Hedda Gabler* cast. Several of them had been with Mr Kennedy at a club in town, the night before he died. A place called Adonis. You know it?'

'Yeah, it's on Princess Street. Gay club. It's currently the hot place to go. It also has a certain reputation.'

'What reputation?'

'Well, that it's the kind of place where men go to pick up other men. There's quite a few clubs like that in The Village.'

'The Village?'

'That's just an area in town that the gay community have kind of claimed as their own.'

'And this Adonis place is part of that?'

'It's in the general area. Tell you the truth, I'm a bit vague about the actual geography of it – where it starts and finishes, you know?'

'And you weren't at Adonis the night before last?'

'Me? No, of course not!'

Flynn's eyes narrowed suspiciously.

'Why "of course not"? Do you have something against places like that?'

'Nothing at all. I mean, I go there quite often and so do my friends. I'm not gay myself, you understand.'

'You're not?' He seemed surprised to hear this. 'Forgive me, Danny, I'd assumed that you were.'

'Why do you say that?'

'Well, for one thing, I couldn't help but notice that you wear a small gold sleeper through your *right* ear. I'd always understood that this implied . . .'

'Yes, I've heard that too. And it does sometimes cause misunderstandings. But see, what happened, me and a friend got pissed one night when I was about eighteen and we decided to pierce our ears. We simply didn't know there was any difference between left and right.'

Flynn grimaced. 'You did it *yourselves*? Didn't it hurt?'

'It did when I'd sobered up a bit.'

'So . . . if you're not gay, why go to those kind of clubs?'

'Well, they're less of a meat-market, I suppose . . .' I reflected that under the circumstances, this description was somewhat unfortunate. 'There's . . . there's no pressure on you to be rampantly male. You don't feel you have to chase skirt, sing football songs, indulge in fist fights. And they're mad about Abba. I've always had this irrational liking for them, even when it wasn't hip to admit it, so . . .' I realised that I was beginning to jabber and decided that I might serve my cause better by piping down a bit. 'Look,' I said. 'What's all this about? I suddenly feel very defensive and there's absolutely no reason why I should. I found the body. That's not a crime, is it?'

'Of course not.' For a moment Flynn looked almost sympathetic. 'But you see, Danny, the thing is . . . I talked to the cast members who were with Mr Kennedy at the club. They said that he met somebody there, a slim, *bearded* man. They left the club together, earlier than had been planned. That was the last any of them saw of him.'

I stroked my own beard nervously.

'Oh, now, come on, a slim, bearded man? That description could fit hundreds of people!'

'Yes, it could. So I had one of them in to talk to an Identikit artist.' He pulled a sheet of paper from his breast pocket, unfolded it and laid it out gently on the table. 'Remind you of anybody?' he asked.

I gazed at it and I swear that my heart stopped beating for several seconds. Identikits are usually odd-looking creations, you see them on *Crimewatch* and they're so cartoon-like, you think, 'Christ, *nobody* could look like that!' But typically, this one had been put together by a veritable Leonardo da Vinci of the Identikit world. This one looked like a real, living, breathing person. This one, even I had to admit, looked like me without my glasses.

I didn't say anything for quite a while after that. I *couldn't* say anything. I was dumbstruck. I think I tried to speak several times and all that came out was a series of gasps. Flynn sat there, regarding me in silence, taking occasional sips at his coffee, while he waited patiently for me to compose myself. Eventually, I managed to find some words.

'It's a horrible coincidence!'

'Is it?'

'Well of course it is! Look, if I'd had anything to do with that murder, would I have called you out to it?'

Flynn shrugged. 'Wouldn't be the first time somebody had tried that stunt, somebody trying to set themselves up with the perfect alibi. But usually they make one stupid mistake.'

'That may be so, but I can assure you that I am totally innocent!'

He smiled at that. 'I'm sure you're going to tell me that you spent the early hours of the morning in question with somebody who can provide you with an alibi.'

I thought for a moment, then felt my spirits sink. I shook

my head. 'I was asleep in bed,' I said.

'Alone?'

'Well, there was Roz, my assistant . . .'

'She was in the same bed?'

'No, it's not that kind of arrangement. But her room is right next door, she'd have heard me if I'd gone out. Believe me, she doesn't miss much.'

'I'm sure. Did this Roz see you *go* to bed?'

'No, she was out somewhere. But I heard her come in around midnight.'

'And did you call out to her, give some indication that you were in your room?'

I shook my head.

'Oh dear,' said Flynn, flatly. 'It doesn't look good, does it?' He plucked at a loose thread hanging from the sleeve of his jacket. 'I wonder what would happen if I were to bring you down to the station and put you in a police line-up? Get those cast members to look for the man they saw in the nightclub.'

'Don't, for God's sake,' I muttered. 'The way my luck's going, the bastards would pick me out like a shot.'

Flynn laughed at this and I felt slightly cheered by his reaction.

'Well, Danny, let me assure you of something,' he said. 'If I thought for one moment that there was the slightest chance you were our man, we'd be having this conversation down the nick. God knows it couldn't look much worse, but all the evidence we have is purely circumstantial. This bearded man was only glimpsed in a room full of flashing lights by people who cheerfully admit to being out of their heads on booze and poppers.' He picked up the Identikit and gazed at it thoughtfully for a moment. 'This does have an unfortunate resemblance to you, but the witnesses were all adamant that the man they saw wasn't wearing glasses. It's quite obvious to me that you'd be as blind as a bat without your spectacles and furthermore, you're not the kind of person who would wear contact lenses.'

Once again, I was knocked out by an observation that was uncannily accurate.

'How can you possibly know that?' I asked him.

'Because people who wear contact lenses do so for reasons of vanity. And somebody who dresses as you did yesterday, couldn't possibly possess an ounce of the stuff.'

I scowled. I wasn't sure but I thought that I might just have been insulted.

'And what about people who dress like you?' I snapped back at him.

'Me? Oh, I'm as vain as a blessed peacock. Always have been.' He thought for a moment, then continued with his theorising. 'The other factor that must be considered is the skill of the murderer. The artful butchery that was practised upon that body. It would have to have been perpetrated by somebody with specialist knowledge of flaying – a slaughter-man, perhaps, an ex-hunter? Hard to say, but not the kind of pastime that I'd expect a photographer to be adept at. And you, Danny Weston, have been pretty much employed in that capacity since leaving art college. I know that because I've done some checking up on you.'

'You've been busy since I last saw you,' I observed drily.

'Quite so. And I'm happy to admit that I don't see you as a potential murder suspect. I'd have been a bit happier if you'd had that cast-iron alibi but . . . well, let's just say you've got an honest face and leave it at that. But, Danny . . .' He leaned forward across the table and fixed me with a penetrating glare. 'Other people are less convinced of your innocence. Detective Sergeant Potts for example, thought that your story was suspicious from the start. If it was down to him you'd be banged up in an interview room by now. He's a different kind of copper. He's from the old school, the sort that grabs at coincidences and doesn't look too closely at the elements that don't add up. So my advice to you is to keep your nose very clean until all this has blown over.'

'I intend to,' I assured him. 'But it hardly seems fair. All I did was go out with the intention of taking some photographs.'

'That reminds me, I got your film processed. Some charming shots of my men going about their work and rather a nice one of myself and D S Potts; but I'm afraid I can't let you have them back. So here.' He dropped a spool of HP5 on the table.

'Thanks,' I said. I was surprised that he'd remembered and felt slightly touched by the gesture. I thought about the other pictures I had taken and part of me wanted to own up about them – but I could imagine Vincent Spinetti's face when I told him that the exhibition was back to the original concept. He wouldn't be best pleased.

'And Danny, this is really important, so I'm going to ask you one more time. Are you gay?'

'No, I promise you. Why does it matter?'

'Because I know that lots of gays are afraid to admit the truth. And until we come up with a better theory, we have to consider the possibility that this may have been a homophobic killing. Being gay could prove to be the best alibi of all.'

'Well, I'm afraid I'll have to disappoint you on that score.' I told him.

He shrugged. 'The ritual side of it is what particularly disturbs me. The flaying. It must have taken the murderer hours to carry out that task. Now, obviously it's very important that the details of the killing are kept secret. Have you mentioned it to anyone?'

'Well, only Roz, my assistant.'

'Nothing much we can do about that. But I certainly don't want the gentlemen of the press to get hold of the information, so please tell your friend to keep it to herself. I want a tight lid on this. The other puzzling thing is the message on the wall. FOR ZIPPY. I take it you noticed that?'

I nodded. 'What do you think it means?' I asked: and was abruptly reminded of my dream.

'I'm blessed if I know. The only Zippy I can think of was a puppet character from a children's television series. He had a zip for a mouth, so you could shut him up when he got on your nerves.'

'Oh, sure, *Rainbow*. I remember that.'

'But what it could possibly have to do with something like this escapes me, I'm afraid. Does it mean anything to you?'

'Nothing at all, I'm afraid.'

Flynn frowned. 'Oh well, we'll just have to hope that something turns up.' He got up from the table. 'And now if you'll excuse me, I have a press conference to prepare for. We'll have to let our resident newshounds have *something* to write about.'

I smiled weakly, followed him to the door.

'Look,' I said. 'I appreciate this. Thanks for giving me the benefit of the doubt.'

'Oh, don't thank me yet, Danny,' he warned. 'Early days. And I *will* be keeping an eye on you . . . because even *I* am capable of making mistakes.' He opened the door, stepped out on to the landing. Then he paused, turned back with an inscrutable smile. 'Don't leave town, Danny,' he said. Then added: 'I've *always* wanted to say that!'

He went down the stairs, whistling a cheerful refrain. I stood there in the doorway, feeling far from cheerful myself. I waited until I heard the outer door swing shut behind him.

Then I went back into the flat to get ready for my first assignment of the day.

# Chapter Six

Philip Cassiday was a Manchester-based horror writer with a new novel to promote. The *Evening Post*'s weekly colour magazine was planning to do a feature on him and my editor, Barry Summerby, had assigned me to do the photographs. Since it was to be in colour, my own humble studio had been snubbed and a more professional studio in Ancoats had been booked for the occasion.

I was to meet Cassiday at eleven-thirty, so it turned out to be a bit of a scramble. En route to the studio, I pulled up outside an ironmongers shop, ran inside and grabbed a small tin of red gloss paint, with which I intended to create a suitably sinister backdrop. The car was on double yellows, so I slapped a couple of quid on the counter and dashed straight out again.

The cross town traffic was irritatingly slow and I arrived at Focus Studios a good ten minutes late to find Cassiday waiting for me on the doorstep. I'd never met the man before so I had to do the whole bit of jumping out of the car, shaking hands, apologising for my tardiness.

He was a thin, bearded man, around the same age as me, dressed in a trendy black suit, a black shirt and a black leather tie. He had a black leather duffle bag over one shoulder. I wasn't sure if this was his usual mode of dress or whether he'd adopted the look purely for the photo-shoot. He had a dour demeanour and struck me immediately as a man who didn't have much of a sense of humour.

'I hope you're not going to make me look *too* sinister,' he muttered. 'Photographers always seem to feel obliged to do that.' I couldn't help thinking that he needed no help from me on that score. He had a hook nose, prominent, crowded teeth and a pair of piercing grey eyes that had an unnerving intensity to them. The novel he'd written, *Bad Blood*, was, by all accounts, pretty unnerving too. It had recently been reviewed in the *Evening Post* with a 'don't read this in the dark' kind of warning attached to it.

I unloaded my gear from the car and pressed the buzzer on the studio door.

'Yes?' A bored-sounding, electronically compressed voice buzzed from the tiny speaker and I recognised it as the studio's owner, Don Lynch.

'Don, it's Danny Weston.'

'Oh, yeah, Danny, come on up.'

There was another buzz and I was able to push open the door and lead Cassiday into the bare, dingy hallway within.

'Abandon hope all ye who enter here,' muttered Cassiday. I knew what he meant. Lynch wasn't big on house-keeping and the place had the fusty, unpleasant odour of dust and decay. We climbed up the flight of wooden stairs to the small office and peered in through a fog of cigarette smoke at the room's sole occupant. Don Lynch was sitting in a rickety wooden chair with his big feet up on the rickety wooden desk.

If Lynch hadn't actually existed, somebody would have had to invent him. He was the very epitome of the sleazy, hard-drinking, chain-smoking photo-journalist. He was somewhere in his late-forties but looked a good ten years older. His lank, greasy hair was prematurely grey, his pale, saggy face ravished by the lines and wrinkles that spoke eloquently of a life devoted to excess. He had watery blue eyes and large, horse-like teeth that were stained brown with nicotine.

Lynch was also one of the most unsanitary men I had ever met. His clothes were, as ever, filthy and rumpled-looking, as though he had slept in them – a not unlikely occurrence. Today he sported a grubby print shirt with two yellow circles of sweat around the armpits and a pair of khaki trousers with a collection of squalid-looking stains at the crutch. Through the holes in the soles of his shoes, I had a delightful view of a pair of equally ragged green socks. In a token nod to the laws of etiquette, Lynch wore a blue tie around his scrawny neck, but the shirt collar was too small and frayed to be buttoned up, so the tie hung at half mast on his chest. What's more, the tie seemed to be composed of equal parts polyester and careless dinners. There was a thick film of dried grease plastered into the fabric and if immersed in boiling water, it would probably have made a reasonably nourishing soup.

Lynch removed the butt of a cigarette from his lips and gave us a welcoming grin.

'Candles out, girls! Welcome to the shag factory!'

Cassiday glanced at me uncertainly, but this was Lynch's usual greeting to anyone who called at Focus Studios – he was, in addition to his short-comings in the hygiene department, an extraordinarily profane individual. Most people hated him on sight and I could see that Cassiday would be no exception. But over the years, against all my better judgement, I'd developed a bit of a soft spot for the old rascal.

'On your own today?' I asked him.

''Fraid so. Gloria had a dental appointment and Reg is doing a topless session for *The Sport* – lucky bugger! So I'm chief cook and sheep-shagger today. I'll even be your photographic assistant, if you like.' He got up from the desk and walked around to introduce himself to Cassiday. 'So you're the writer, are you?' he said, shaking the man's hand. 'Lots of shagging in your books, is there?'

Cassiday seemed bemused. He looked down at his hands as though wondering where the nearest wash basin might be located.

'Sex er . . . really isn't my thing,' he said quietly.

'Sorry to hear that, mate!' Lynch slapped him heartily on the shoulder, making him wince visibly. 'You should try eating more fish. I swear by mussels, myself. If you really want to set yourself on, try eating a dozen of them before going at it. Of course, the wind can be a bit of a problem, but you'll have a knob like *iron*.'

I could see that Cassiday didn't appreciate this advice one little bit, so I intervened before any more damage was done.

'We'd best get started,' I said. 'I've another appointment later on.'

'Busy bugger,' said Lynch. 'It's all right for some, isn't it? Come on then, let's get this show on the road.'

He led us out of the office and down the short stretch of corridor to the studio, talking over his shoulder as he walked. 'Right you are, mate, what do you need?'

'Just a plain white backdrop, please. Preferably one you don't mind me messing up.' I took the tin of red paint from my holdall and looked around for some way of opening it. Lynch moved away to unroll a fresh sheet of paper and I turned to Cassiday, who was slumped in a chair with a bored expression on his face. I showed him the paint and explained what I planned to do. 'Bit of an obvious idea, I'm afraid, but we may as well make the most of the colour. I thought I'd just splatter this all over the backdrop and pose you in front of it looking suitably psychotic.'

Cassiday sighed, rolled his eyes towards the ceiling.

'Ingenious,' he said, 'I'd never have thought of that.'

'Well, look, if you'd rather I just did straight close-ups . . .'

'No, no, that's quite all right.' Cassiday waved a hand in dismissal. 'Do whatever you think fit. Provided you don't ask me to hold up a copy of my book and pretend to be *reading* it.'

I found a screwdriver on the bench and started levering the lid off the tin.

'I'll just need a few minutes to—'

I stared at the contents in dismay. Instead of the red, runny liquid I had anticipated, I found myself looking at a firm, smooth, jelly-like surface. In my haste to get out of the ironmongers, I'd picked up a tin of *non-drip* gloss. 'This may take a little longer than I thought,' I muttered.

Actually, it took the best part of an hour. With no thinners on hand, I was reduced to picking out blobs of the stuff with an old spoon and hurling them with all my strength at the paper backdrop. Instead of splattering bloodily, they tended to hang there for a while in thick glops, until gravity caused them to move down the vertical surface in a series of crab-like lurches. The effect was colourful enough but more Jackson Pollock than Charles Manson.

I rooted out an old paintbrush and used that to disperse the blobs over a wider area. After a good deal of experimentation, I finally had something that I thought I could get away with and I was able to position Cassiday on a stool in front of the backdrop. Under the glare of the overhead lamps, the stench of paint fumes was enough to make you feel dizzy. I fixed the Pentax on to a tripod, screwed in a cable release and started getting the lighting rigged, keeping the principal source low down to imbue Cassiday's face with a glowering, ghoulish look.

'I had no idea it was going to take this long,' he grumbled.

'Nearly ready,' I assured him. I had the lighting rigged as I wanted it and just needed to take a couple of general readings, then set the exposure and aperture accordingly.

'Halle-bloody-lujah,' said Cassiday, rather ungraciously.

For ten minutes or so, it didn't go too well. Cassiday was not at ease and it showed. I snapped the odd frame but knew that the results wouldn't be usable. Things picked up dramatically when I got him talking about his latest book.

'Well, it's called *Bad Blood*. And it's about a man who believes he's not a man. That he's something else.'

'Such as?'

'Some kind of animal. A *predatory* animal, he's never really sure which one, at least, not until the end of the book. He's only aware that he's *changing*.'

I shot off a frame as he spoke this last word, because he said it with such obvious relish, his gaunt face ghoulish in the harsh light.

'Changing into what exactly?' I prompted him.

'Something ancient, powerful. Something that has an all-consuming hunger. Increasingly he finds himself drawn to attacking his fellow man, tearing his flesh apart, feasting on blood.'

I shot a couple more frames as he talked about this, thinking to myself that the subject matter was much more relevant to me than it would have been a couple of days ago. An image flashed briefly into my mind – a bloody carcass turning slowly at the end of a length of rope. I blinked, shrugged it away.

'Sounds scary,' I said feebly.

'Well, hopefully. That's my market.' He spread his hands

in a 'so what' gesture and I snapped a shot of that too.

'And it doesn't bother you?' I asked him.

He narrowed his eyes. *Click!*

'What?'

'Well, that people might read the book and be influenced.'

Cassiday sneered. *Click!*

'Oh, not that old chestnut! Honestly, I'm getting a little bit tired of hearing that argument. Why is it that whenever there's anything bad in the news, people start looking for a convenient scapegoat. If it's not horror writers, it's films and videos, if it's not them it's bloody computer games.' He smashed his clenched fist against the palm of his left hand *Click!* 'When will people accept responsibility for the *real* causes of aberrations like that?'

I frowned, adjusted the focus slightly. 'What's that then?'

'Take your choice!' he growled. 'A government whose policies create an atmosphere of complete hopelessness. A welfare system that fosters a climate of despair and offers young people no hope for the future. An under-funded education system. Immature parents numbed by unemployment and lacking the skills to correctly discipline their children. Those are the real enemies, but what's being done about *them*?'

He was getting really angry now and more photogenic by the second, his eyes bulging, his cheeks darkening with anger. I decided to push him that little bit further.

'Yes, but this horror stuff . . . it's not quality fiction, is it? I mean, you don't see novels like yours winning the Booker Prize, do you?'

Cassiday reacted like I'd jabbed him in the eye with an index finger.

'The tradition in which I write can be traced back through the work of literary giants such as Edgar Allen Poe, HP

Lovecraft and Mary Shelley. Nobody dares to marginalise their works. But writing in this genre today seems to be an open invitation to be heaped with ridicule. "Oh, he writes terrible things, he must be bloody cracked or something—" ' I fired off a whole string of shots at this point and he broke off suddenly, glared at me. The penny had just dropped and he'd realised what I was up to. 'You sly bugger,' he said. 'You were winding me up!'

I dutifully shot the rest of the spool but I knew that I already had the best pictures in the can. By the time Don Lynch shuffled back in with two mugs of coffee, it was really all over, bar the shouting. I took a last few frames, then we packed up and both of us risked potential poisoning by drinking from Lynch's ancient, chipped mugs.

After that, Cassiday announced that he had to be elsewhere, but before he left, he pulled a hardback copy of his new novel out of his bag and signed it with a flourish.

'Here,' he said, handing it to me. 'You can judge for yourself how depraved I am.'

'Thanks,' I said. 'Tell you what, why don't I return the favour? Give me a note of your address and I'll send you an invitation to my exhibition. I've got a feeling it could be right up your street.'

'I'll look forward to it,' he assured me; and after handing me a business card, he went out of the door, towards the exit.

I examined the novel Cassiday had left. The grainy cover showed a shadowy, man-like figure skulking in front of a window. In the foreground, a pair of manacled hands clamped to a metal rail, gestured helplessly. 'Well, that's my bedtime reading taken care of for the next few weeks,' I said. Opening the book I saw that before his signature, Cassiday had written, *To Danny Weston. I'll get you back, one day!* I slipped the book into my shoulder bag and went to collect my camera.

'What was that about an exhibition?' asked Lynch, lighting yet another cigarette from the previous stub. 'Couldn't help overhearing. Don't suppose there'd be another ticket going spare?'

'Well, I don't know if it would be your kind of thing, Don. Won't be a tit or a bum in sight, I'm afraid.'

He shrugged. 'You never know, I might learn something. Besides, it'll be a free drink and buffet, if nothing else.'

I smiled. 'Things can't be as bad as all that, surely?'

He frowned. 'Ain't that shaggin' good, neither. You know I told you Gloria and Reg were otherwise occupied? That was just for Cassiday's benefit. The truth is, I had to lay them off.'

'Don, I'm sorry, I had no idea. When did all this happen?'

He sighed, shrugged. 'Been coming a long time, mate. I'm not getting the volume of work I used to, it's as simple as that. I blame all this new technology, myself. Victim of the computer age, that's me. I'm pulling in just about enough to keep the old place ticking over. And I've had to diversify, to make ends meet. I'm getting into the video business, making movies for a *specialist* audience. Trouble is, it ain't strictly legal, you know what I mean?' Lynch inhaled on his cigarette and blew out a cloud of pale blue smoke. 'I've often sailed pretty close to the wind before this, but I've never ventured on to the crooked side of the fence. Don't get me wrong, I've got nothing against *stag* movies. But these I'm doin' at the moment, they're a different kettle of KY Jelly.'

'How do you mean?'

'Ah, you don't want to get into all that, mate.' He seemed to make a deliberate effort to change the subject. 'Anyway, enough of my troubles. You just send me that invite, eh? It'll be nice to see somebody who's doing well for themselves.'

'Yes, I think it'll make a splash, Don. Get me a bit of publicity. *Bad* publicity, maybe, but . . .'

'There's no such thing as bad publicity, mate.'

I had all my gear packed now and I was ready to go. I pointed to the paint-splattered backdrop. 'Want me to clear that away?' I asked him.

'No leave it,' he said. 'Makes the place look like it's being used.' There was a terrible sadness and a sense of resignation in his voice and I realised that beneath the jovial, couldn't-give-a-fuck exterior, he was really cut up about his plight. He'd probably have benefited from a long talk about the situation, but frankly, I wasn't in the right frame of mind to handle it. So in the very best journalistic tradition, I slapped him on the back, made my excuses and left.

# Chapter Seven

I drove up to Ardwick to drop off the Cassiday film at Photolab, the place where I usually got my colour transparencies processed. They were a good company, quick, reliable and unlike some other firms I could mention, they charged a fair rate for their services. Unfortunately, as far as I was concerned, their days were numbered.

The *Post* was soon to upgrade its own processing facilities and plans were afoot to install state of the art equipment at the newspaper's offices, in the New Year. When it was in place, every conceivable problem could be taken care of in-house: and like Don Lynch, Photolab would be just another victim of the computer age.

When I went in, Trevor Bird was at the counter and as ever, he had something to show me. Trevor was an enthusiastic amateur photographer who fancied himself as a professional. He only worked at Photolab in order to make full use of the equipment and all his spare time was spent taking photographs, which he would then send to magazines such as *Amateur Photographer* in the hope that they would publish them; but they never did. The plain truth was that he wasn't really any good. He didn't have 'the eye', that indefinable instinct for composition that is the single most important quality a photographer can possess.

Bird was a chubby, bespectacled fellow in his early twenties. I always thought of him as a kind of Billy Bunterish figure – hapless and oafish, but oddly likeable; and it was *because* I liked him that I found it impossible to be truthful about his work, whenever I was asked for an opinion. I'm afraid to say that I probably encouraged him to pursue his burning ambition, when it might actually have been kinder to tell him to his face, that he didn't have what it took to make the grade.

He was beckoning to me now, as I approached the counter, and was reaching under it to pull out a plain brown envelope, a sure sign that he was about to seek my opinion on his latest effort.

'Just take a look at these, Danny, tell me what you honestly think!' He was beaming at me, hardly able to contain his enthusiasm.

I tried not to look wary as I slid the monochrome enlargements out of the envelope. I've always had a problem keeping my expression blank. I'd make a lousy poker player.

The photographs were all of the same subject – nude studies of a young woman, lying on a couch. Nothing unusual about that in these liberated times but what did give me cause to raise my eyebrows was the fact that this particular woman was somewhat larger than one might usually expect. To describe her figure as 'ample' would have been something of an understatement – she must have weighed in excess of twenty stone. There she lay in a series of uninhibited, would-be sexy poses, each one more revealing than the last.

'Who er . . . who's the model?' I asked warily.

'That's Mo. My girlfriend. Why?'

'Oh, I was actually wondering if she was a professional. She's . . . she's quite something, isn't she?'

'I'll say! Look at the next shot!'

77

I did as he suggested and nearly flinched, as I was presented with an open-legged pose of quite staggering immodesty. I doubted whether her gynaecologist had seen so much of her and I felt my cheeks colouring up. I simply didn't feel right looking at pictures of his girlfriend, I felt as though the two of us were colluding in some voyeuristic act.

I pushed them back into their envelope and handed the package back to Bird. I forced a smile.

'Well?' he asked me brightly.

'Unbelievable,' I told him. 'They're really very . . . original, Trevor.'

'Think so?' He seemed happy enough with this appraisal. 'Well, we'll see what the magazine thinks of them, anyway.'

'They might be a bit explicit for *Amateur Photographer*,' I warned him.

'That's what I thought. That's why I sent them to *Cosmo*.'

I stared at him in disbelief.

'You've sent these pictures to *Cosmopolitan*?' I murmured.

'Sure.' He spread his hands in a 'why not' gesture. 'Well, they're always going on about fat being a feminist issue, aren't they? How they really want to get away from anorexic birds with no tits. So I thought they could do a feature on a *real* woman for a change. You know, somebody with something you can get hold of.'

I looked at him sadly and tried to picture the magazine's editor, opening her mail one morning. Frankly, Bird would be lucky if they didn't set the cops on to him.

'Well, good luck with it,' I concluded lamely.

'So, what can I do for you?' asked Bird, coming over all business-like.

I handed him the roll of film.

'Something for the *Evening Post*. The colour mag.'

'No problemo, *hombre*. You'll want transparencies then?'

He pulled out a printed pad and started filling it out with well-practised ease. 'Anything interesting?' he asked me. He was always very nosy about my assignments.

'Horror writer, name of Philip Cassiday. We're doing a feature on him.'

'Oh yeah, I know *him*. Read his last one. Bit weird. Bloke's got a screw loose if you ask me. It was all blood and guts, people having their eyes pulled out, people sticking pins into their privates . . . sick it was. Couldn't put the bloody thing down, could I?'

He tore off the receipt and handed it to me.

'Thanks,' I said, turning away. 'I'll pick them up some time tomorrow . . .'

'Hang on a minute!' Bird virtually lunged across the counter to restrain me. 'You thought over my proposition, yet?'

'Proposition?' I looked at him blankly, though I knew perfectly well what he was referring to. Bird had been pestering me for weeks to let him have some time at my studio. I don't think that there was anything in particular he couldn't shoot at home, he just had this idea that working in a 'real' environment would help him to achieve better results. I'm not sure why, but I was curiously resistant to the idea. Perhaps I thought that I'd get roped in to assist him.

'I don't know, Trevor, I'm very busy at the moment.'

'I know that, Danny, but . . . oh, go on, just a few hours. You've got all the proper lights and everything, I'd just love to be able to say I've worked once in a professional studio. Look, I don't mind paying, if that's the problem.'

'No, don't be daft. I wouldn't dream of taking any money off you.'

'Well, then, I'd be really careful with all the equipment.' He stood there looking for all the world like a particularly helpless twelve-year-old and my resolution began to crumble.

'I tell you what, Trevor. I'm working on stuff for my exhibition right now. Once that's out of the way, I'll sort something out for you, how would that be?'

'That would be *brill*,' he said, grinning hugely. 'Get me in there and I'll be a regular star.' He lifted his plump hands to frame an imaginary subject. 'Give me more expression, baby!' he said, in an unconvincing American accent. 'Yeah, give me more hair! Take me all the way!'

I tried not to laugh. Bird's idea of a professional photographer seemed to have been based on repeated viewings of David Hemmings in *Blow Up*. The boy was in for a rude awakening, one of these days. He looked suddenly wistful. 'An exhibition,' he said, drawing the word out slowly as though he liked the feel of it in his mouth. 'God, Danny, you're really on your way now, aren't you? The Wedge, no less! I hope you're going to throw an invitation in *my* direction.'

I smiled. 'Naturally,' I said. 'I'd value your opinion. After all, I'm always giving you mine.'

He looked as pleased as punch. 'Oh, well, that's very kind of you to say, Danny. Gosh, if you think it would *count* for anything . . .'

'Every opinion is as valid as the next,' I assured him. 'But when somebody's in the same line of work . . .'

He flushed. 'Oh, I'm just learning,' he said dismissively. 'But who knows, one day I could be up there with you.'

This was getting embarrassing. Oh, it was great being 'up there'. Why, only the other day I'd photographed the guest speaker at a Women's Institute meeting, but I was trying not to let it go to my head.

'I'll have to get moving,' I told him. 'Another assignment later on.'

'Yeah, busy man, eh? Busy, busy, busy! Hey, this exhibition. You got a title for it yet?'

I opened my mouth to tell him: but the words seemed to stick in my throat. What had sounded so sharp and innovative in the crowded bar of The Wedge, seemed merely cheap and tawdry in the cold light of day. I shook my head.

'We're still thinking about it,' I said.

'I've got a suggestion.' Bird paused dramatically then made a gesture as though drawing a line of type in the air in front of him. '*Danny Weston – a man and his camera.*' He leaned his head slightly to one side, as though considering what he'd just said. 'What do you reckon?' he asked me.

'Not bad,' I said and started to move in the direction of the exit. 'I'll er . . . consider it.'

'Or even, "*Danny Weston – a life in pictures*".'

'Yes. Bye, Trevor, see you tomorrow.'

I stepped quickly out into the street and closed the door before he could shout out his next suggestion. I turned and walked briskly back to where I'd parked the car. I had an afternoon assignment in the city and it occurred to me that apart from a handful of Sugar Puffs, I hadn't eaten anything that day. So I climbed in the car, started up the engine and drove off in search of a 'square' meal.

# Chapter Eight

Actually, it wasn't so much a 'square' meal as an *oval* one – a huge nan bread stuffed with chicken tikka masala and fresh salad. I found it at the Green Room, an alternative theatrical venue on Whitworth Street that, eerily enough, was located in a converted railway arch. I settled down at a vacant window seat, to consume my food and watch the world go by.

As it happened, one of the first people to pass by was Roz, trudging along the street with one of her buddies in tow. Wanda was one of those big, shambling women of indeterminate age, with hair shaved to a stubble and enough studs and rings banged into her ears and nostrils to run the risk of picking up satellite television. She wore shapeless black clothes and big Doc Martens boots and it wouldn't have taken Sherlock Holmes to work out that we were talking lesbian feminist here with a capital LF.

I wasn't really sure about Roz's sexual politics. She had friends of both sexes but so far as I knew, she wasn't going to bed with any of them. But as I said, she was secretive about things like that. Who knew what she got up to in the privacy of her own room? There'd been a time after she first moved in with me when such thoughts had occupied me a great deal. I'd lie in bed at night and imagine her, lying in bed in the next room and I'd wonder what would happen if I just got up, went next door and asked her if she wanted a little company. Probably what would have happened would be Roz performing a flying drop-kick to my skull. At any rate, after several months of total disinterest on her part, I'd given up and gone back to fantasising about Michelle Pfeiffer, who unfortunately wasn't quite as handy for dropping in on.

Still, I was always happy to see Roz, whatever the situation, so I leaned forward, tapped on the window and waved at her. She saw me, I know she did – but she pretended not to, which really pissed me off. Maybe it was because she considered it uncool to wave to somebody who currently had a mouthful of chicken tikka masala, or maybe she just didn't want to let on to Wanda that she was on speaking terms with a *man*.

Anyway, I was determined not to lose sleep over it. I went on with my meal, taking leisurely sips at the beer, enjoying the feeling of not doing very much at all. Basically, I was just killing time till my next appointment, at the Midland Hotel.

I didn't really know much about it. Barry Summerby had left a garbled message on my answerphone the previous evening, telling me to be there for two-thirty. Something to do with Mexico, he'd said.

At any rate, I finished my beer in good time, went out to the car and drove down Oxford Street to the Midland. I found a parking spot outside the G-Mex exhibition centre, retrieved my camera equipment from the boot and walked back around the corner to the hotel.

Up in the function room, the party was already in full swing – not that it was exactly what passed for a party in my book. In other words, it wasn't a bunch of pissed-up maniacs dancing to very loud rock music. This was one of those stilted, official affairs, lots of awkward-looking people in suits, standing around and making polite conversation, whilst sipping glasses of wine and picking at bowls of Twiglets. In the background, Latin American music played at an almost subliminal volume. As I entered, some flunky handed me a presentation pack with the words *Viva Mexico!* printed in bright red letters. I stood for a moment, feeling decidedly under-dressed in leather jacket and jeans, as I scanned the room for familiar faces.

There were quite a few of those in evidence – prominent members of the city council, the Mayor and Mayoress, naturally, representatives of the city's theatres and art centres, even a few local TV celebrities. Over by the buffet table, I spotted the morose hamster-like visage of *Evening Post* journo, Geoff Greenhalge, who was currently demolishing a plateful of tiny triangular sandwiches. I made my way over to him and set down the camera case.

'You're a bit late,' muttered Greenhalge. 'It started at two o'clock.'

'Sorry, mate. Barry told me half-past.'

'You might at least have put a jacket and tie on.'

Greenhalge was a short, thick-set individual with thinning hair and a mousy beard. A native of Birmingham, he had a flat, adenoidal voice and always sounded as though he was suffering from the effects of a bad cold. He'd been at the paper a good few years longer than I had and the two of us had covered a lot of stories together. He was OK, I suppose, but I'd never really warmed to him. He was, frankly, a bit of a misery.

'Barry didn't tell me it was going to be a posh do,' I explained. 'Otherwise I'd have broken out my best bib and tucker. Anyway, what's it all in aid of?'

Greenhalge gave me an annoyed look and tapped the folder which was clutched under my left arm.

'All the info's in there,' he said. 'Since somebody's taken

the trouble to print it all out for you, you could at least browse through it.'

'Bugger that, I haven't got time to wade through all this. You fill me in on the details, while I get set up.' I crouched beside the camera case and unlatched it.

'This is the official start of *Viva Mexico!* A two week festival of Mexican culture.' He pushed the last of his sandwiches into his mouth and appeared to swallow it without chewing.

'Uh huh.' I threaded a new spool of film into the Pentax. 'And what does that involve, exactly?'

Greenhalge looked exasperated. 'Well, there's going to be *loads* of events, isn't there? They've brought over dance and theatre groups, poets, novelists, artists . . . there's a full run-down in the festival programme. It all culminates on Halloween night with a masked ball at the Town Hall.'

'Oh yeah, I seem to remember Roz blathering on about that. Fancy dress, isn't it?'

'That's right.'

'I think she's blagged a couple of tickets through a mutual friend who works there. So the Mexican's celebrate Halloween, then?'

'Not exactly.' Greenhalge put down his empty plate and picked at a shred of food stuck in his teeth. '*El Dia de Muerte*,' he said, through his stubby fingers.

'Beg pardon?'

He removed the hand and said it again. 'Means *The Day of the Dead*,' he explained. 'It's celebrated in every town and village in Mexico. Actually, it's really November the first and second, but I suppose they decided to tie it in with our celebrations on the thirty-first. They start with All Soul's Night. People spend it in the graveyard with their dear departed; then next day, they have a fiesta. Everybody buys a candy skull with their own name written on it in icing. And they sell little dolls in coffins, stuff like that.'

'Yeah, I think I've seen that on TV. Why here though?'

'It's some kind of exchange deal the city council's cooked up. Some time next year, a large contingent from Manchester will be heading over to Mexico City to attend a festival of traditional British culture.'

I smirked. 'Christ, what would that consist of? Pissed-up Mancunians running round, waving meat and potato pies and singing football chants?'

Greenhalge smiled thinly. 'I think it would be more of a "hey nonny no, let's all dance round the maypole" kind of affair.'

'Oh yeah, we do lots of that, don't we?' I clipped the electronic flash into position on the camera, stood up and took a quick light reading. 'OK,' I said. 'Ready.'

'Hold your horses a minute.' Greenhalge was looking at me intently. 'A little bird told me that you're involved in this murder case. The body they found yesterday morning. Sebastian Kennedy? I understand it was you who discovered him.'

I frowned. 'Which particular little bird was this, Geoff? He'll have a bent beak if I catch up with him.'

'Oh, a good reporter never reveals his sources, Danny. But this new DI, who's heading up the inquiry . . . what's his name, Quinn?'

'Flynn,' I corrected him.

'That's the one. Bit of a smarmy bugger, I thought. Anyway, he was at the official press conference at lunchtime. Played it all very close to his chest. Wouldn't give us any details of how Kennedy was killed or how he came to be found so quickly in such a lonely spot. Luckily, I was able to grab an unofficial chat with a friend of mine on the Force.'

I was immediately convinced that the blabbermouth was Potts. I don't know what made me think that, though I could just see him and Greenhalge getting on like a house on fire. A couple of miserable buggers together.

'Anyway, my man wouldn't be pressed on the method of killing, but he did let slip that the person who found the body was a freelance photographer who did a lot of work for the *Evening Post*. Process of elimination, wasn't it? I've tried all the others and they swear they know nothing. Which just leaves you.'

I frowned, then shrugged.

'Yeah, well, what can I tell you? It's true.'

Greenhalge perked up considerably at this news.

'That's great. So you can give me a bit more information?'

'Er . . . I don't know if I should. Flynn told me to keep it under my hat.'

'Keep *what* under your hat? There must have been something bloody unusual about this killing. And how come it took so long to make a positive ID? Kennedy was a well known face on the Manchester scene. Even *you* would have recognised him.'

'Er . . . well . . .'

'Shouldn't have taken them ten minutes, but we were kept waiting more than twenty-four hours. So something's funny.'

I laughed nervously. 'He *was* hard to recognise.'

'How come?'

I sighed. 'Look, I really don't think I should say any more. If I tell you, it'll be all over the front page and Flynn will know it was me that told you.'

Greenhalge looked vaguely insulted by this remark.

'As a card carrying member of the NUJ, I wouldn't dream of reporting anything without your express permission. This would be purely for my own edification.'

I looked at him doubtfully.

'You promise? If I tell you, you'll keep it to yourself?'

'Of course! If I've learned one thing in twenty years as a reporter, it's that you have to be a man of integrity. Trust me, Danny, I won't breathe a word. Scout's honour.'

'All right.' I lowered my voice and leaned in close to him. 'Sebastian Kennedy was skinned,' I whispered.

'SKINNED?' he shrieked, at a volume that seemed to turn every head in the room. The hubbub of conversation died abruptly to be replaced by a silence so deep, you could hear people swallowing their wine. Greenhalge flushed and glanced apologetically around the room, a sheepish smile on his face. Gradually, the conversations resumed and we were able to continue.

'What do you mean, *skinned?*' whispered Greenhalge.

'Exactly what I say. He was just this mass of flesh, blood and muscle. He was hanging by his feet from a roof beam.'

'Blimey O'Reilly,' said Greenhalge softly. He considered this for a moment. 'Crikey,' he added, more forcefully. 'Danny, you've got to give me a story. An exclusive! *How I found Death Skin Horror Victim by Danny Weston.*'

'Death-skin-horror-victim?' I said incredulously.

He waved a hand in dismissal. 'We'll sort out the wording later.'

'No, Geoff, I don't think so.'

'Oh, come on! It'd make a great piece. We'd be able to scoop the nationals with it. Barry would be over the bleeding moon.'

'I don't doubt it, but just take no for an answer, OK? Flynn will skin *me* alive if I go blabbing to the papers.' I gestured at the crowded room. 'Now let's get on with it, shall we?'

Greenhalge stared at me pleadingly.

'Just tell me you'll think about it,' he persisted.

'Will you please tell me who I'm supposed to be photographing here?'

He sighed. 'Just get a snap of anybody who looks vaguely foreign, preferably chatting to somebody from *Coronation Street*. I'll write down the details and we'll let Barry pick his favourite shot.'

'Let's make it snappy.' I winced at the unintentional pun. 'I've arranged to meet a friend this evening.'

We moved around the room, me photographing whoever came into range, Greenhalge taking down their names and occupations. The Mexicans were very easy to spot. For one thing, they were the only people in the room with decent sun-tans. The men were small and dapper, with jet black hair and dazzling teeth. The women were sultry Latin beauties who seemed naturally photogenic. Few of them could speak English, which necessitated me miming my intentions to them. They soon got the general idea and one by one, I photographed them, as they shook hands with town councillors, arts administrators and minor television celebrities.

And then, all of a sudden, as I was peering through the lens of my camera, I noticed this particular woman standing off in the corner of the room – not the most beautiful woman at the party, at least not in the conventional sense, though she was still some looker, tall, slim, vaguely androgynous and oozing sexuality from every pore. Her glossy black hair was pulled back into a long pony-tail, her skin was the colour of milky coffee and she had these big, dark brown eyes that seemed to me to be lit with an inner glow. Her mouth was wide and expressive with thick, pouting lips. It was lust at first sight.

She was wearing a simple black dress over which she wore a kind of ethnic shawl, secured at her throat with a brooch in the form of some kind of tribal mask. She was talking to a man, another Mexican I thought, a handsome young fellow with a neatly trimmed black beard. He made a remark and the woman tilted back her head and laughed, revealing her perfect white teeth. I envied the smooth-talking bastard. I had never perfected the knack of talking to women and only ever made them laugh when I didn't want them to. I was about to turn away when the woman muttered something to the bearded man. For some reason, she started to walk across the room straight towards me. It seemed to my addled senses that she had the natural grace of some wild animal. I saw her long, brown legs, unsullied by tights or stockings and something suspiciously like desire lurched in the pit of my stomach.

I was vaguely aware of Geoff Greenhalge jabbering something in my ear but sensing an opportunity, I ignored him and stepping towards the woman, I raised the Pentax to take her photograph.

Her reaction was extraordinary. An expression came to her face, a look of extreme panic, and she flung out a hand to block the lens, just as I pressed the shutter. As the flash went off, the camera was pushed back into my face and the corner of it jabbed me in the eye, making me yelp with pain. I let the Pentax drop back around my neck and stood there dismayed, lifting a hand to cover the injured eye.

'I'm sorry,' I mumbled. 'I didn't mean to . . .'

'Oh no, *I* am sorry!' she said. 'That was unbelievably clumsy of me.' She had an attractive, husky voice and spoke English with only a trace of Latin intonation.

'It's my fault,' I insisted. 'That was very invasive. I just assumed that I could take a picture.'

'You don't understand. I just didn't want you wasting your film. I'm *nobody*. I don't even belong to this group.' She saw that I had my hand over my eye and stepped closer to me in evident concern. 'You are hurt?' she asked.

'Oh, it's nothing, really.' Close up I could smell her perfume, a musky, sensual fragrance that made me feel quite breathless. I remembered what I'd had for lunch and cursed myself for choosing something so spicy. I probably had breath like Hiroshima.

'No, please, allow me to look.' She reached up to pull my hand away from my face and peered at me closely, so that our faces were inches apart. 'It looks a little red,' she observed.

'I'm fine, honestly. See?' I blinked furiously and tilted my head to show her the eye: but I must confess, I was in no great hurry to step away from her. Part of me wanted to just take her in my arms and kiss her, like they do in those old movies, John Wayne grabbing Maureen O'Hara and snogging her into submission. She would struggle for a moment, then melt into my arms, hungrily returning my kisses . . . except of course, that this wasn't a movie and it *was* the age of political correctness and she'd probably haul off and give me a punch on the nose, which would serve me right for having such sexist thoughts in the first place.

So we stood there looking at each other for what seemed like minutes, but were probably just seconds – and finally the spell was broken and we each took a step backwards, so we could converse at a polite distance. I held out a hand and she shook it gently.

'Danny Weston,' I said.

'Julia Moreno. Pleased to meet you. And I'm sorry about the misunderstanding. As I said, I'm not part of this circus.'

'That doesn't matter,' I assured her. 'My instructions were to photograph everyone in the room. Besides,' I added, with uncharacteristic boldness, 'a beautiful woman is always worthy of a photograph.'

I couldn't believe I'd said that. I felt my cheeks reddening even as the words were leaving my mouth but she seemed pleased by the compliment.

'You are very kind,' she said. She glanced towards the buffet table as though she was thinking of moving on, so I made a clumsy attempt to detain her.

'So you're a . . . a translator?'

'Oh no, I just came here with a friend. I happen to speak the language. It seems to be coming in very handy.'

'And what er . . . what part of Mexico do you come from? I believe it's a very beautiful country.'

She seemed amused by this observation.

'I'm sure it is. Unfortunately, I've never been there. I live in Stockport, myself.'

I gaped. Boy, did I feel stupid.

'Stockport? Uh . . . yes, well, that can be very pleasant too. In parts.'

She laughed. 'Not the part I live,' she assured me.

'So, you were . . . *born* here?'

'No.' She shook her head and her good humour seemed to fade abruptly. 'I am from Chile. I came here as a young girl after the military *coup*. You know, Pinochet?'

'Uh . . . oh yeah, right.' I had some vague knowledge of the events back in the seventies, that had seen the rise to power of one of the cruellest and most despotic military regimes in recent history. I didn't dwell on the subject. 'That explains how you speak Spanish, of course. How did you come to be invited to this bunfight?'

She smiled. 'I'm sorry? Bun—?'

'Bunfight. Like, you know. The *Bunfight at the OK Corral*?' I prompted her. 'It's just an expression. Surprised you haven't heard it, living down there in good old Stockport. How did you come to be at this event?'

She shrugged. 'Oh, I knew somebody who was organising it and she thought my linguistic skills might come in useful. Actually, the official translator isn't much use at all. She has text book Spanish, rather than conversational. Also, I think she has been rather over-enthusiastic in sampling the selection of wines on offer . . .' She noticed that somebody across the room was beckoning to her. The young Mexican she had been speaking to earlier was having trouble making himself understood to a member of the city council. I felt like telling him that we all had that problem and to bugger off, couldn't he see he was cramping my style here? 'I'm sorry,' she said. 'I think I'm needed.'

'That's OK. Oh look, I'm having an exhibition of photographs in a couple of weeks time. At The Wedge. Maybe you'd like to come along?'

She smiled. 'Maybe,' she said. 'Actually I have rather a soft spot for photographers. My brother was a photo-journalist.'

I noticed her use of the past tense but decided against pursuing it any further. From what I'd read about events in Chile the chances were that he would turn out to be one of those numberless people who had gone missing without trace during the administration of the military junta.

'If you give me your address or phone number, I could arrange to send you an invitation.'

She didn't seem to care much for that idea.

'Oh no, I don't think so. I will look out for details in the press, Mr . . .?'

'Weston. Danny Weston. The show's called *Skin Flicks*!'

I winced. Once again, I had the impression that all conversation in the room had ceased abruptly. 'It's meant to be ironic,' I added, defensively.

She smiled.

'Maybe I'll be there,' she said. Then she turned and walked back across the crowded room, to where she was required. I gazed after her adoringly, watching the graceful swing of her buttocks in the tight black dress. I had never in my entire life been so pole-axed by the mere sight of a woman.

'We'll have to keep an eye on you,' said a voice at my shoulder. I returned to reality and the mournful countenance of Geoff Greenhalge, who I realised, must have been standing beside me the whole time. 'Quite a fancy mover when you put your mind to it, aren't you? *A beautiful woman is always worthy of a photograph?* Christ!' He followed the direction of my gaze. 'Mind you, I can't say I blame you. She looks a bit useful.'

I felt an irrational desire to punch him in the mouth, but managed to override it by counting slowly to ten.

'We were just chatting,' I said.

'Yes, well you'd do better to keep your mind on the job, matey. Besides, didn't you say you were meeting a friend later?'

Grudgingly, I went through the motions of completing the shoot but I couldn't stop thinking about Julia Moreno. By the time Greenhalge and I had finished, I'd decided to blow my friend out for the night and ask Julia if she'd like to have drinks with me. If she declined that offer, I'd ask her out tomorrow. Or the next night. After all, my Filofax wasn't exactly bursting with evening appointments. So when Greenhalge left, I hung around, taking my time over stowing my equipment. I gulped down a glass of wine to provide a little Dutch courage and turned to survey the room.

And she wasn't there. She'd just disappeared along with

the young Mexican she'd been talking to. The party was beginning to break up now and I asked around if anyone had seen her leave, but nobody had. Furthermore, I couldn't turn up one person who knew her or the 'friend' who'd brought her along to the event. I was left with the weird impression that she had been some kind of hallucination – a mysterious Latin lady conjured up by my over-heated imagination.

With a sense of mounting frustration, I left the premises and drove slowly home, where as it turned out, my date for the evening was already waiting for me.

# Chapter Nine

When I got back to my apartment, I found Spike sitting in the kitchen, swigging from a can of Special Brew and helping himself to the contents of the refrigerator. Roz was apparently still out, so Spike had let himself in using the spare key I'd lent him months ago and which he'd never got around to returning.

Spike Hughes was probably my best friend. We'd known each other since junior school and had lived in and out of each other's pockets ever since. Spike wasn't his real name, of course, simply a nickname he'd picked up at school when he'd been the first kid in the class to get a punk-rock haircut. The name had stuck and I was one of the few people in Manchester who knew that his real name was Colin. He didn't look much like a Colin. Mind you, these days he didn't look much like a Spike either. He wore his blond hair long, an impressive mane of curls that hung to his narrow shoulders.

By day, Spike was a heating engineer, employed at the Town Hall, where he had the unenviable task of maintaining the ancient heating system. By night, however, he was the vocalist with death-metal band, Sepulchre, a bunch of grungy looking individuals with a predilection for mercifully brief but horrendously loud rants about satanism, necrophilia and nuclear war. They'd been together about a year and now played regularly around the Manchester clubs, and even managed to attract a small, but fiercely loyal following. Spike was convinced that the band was destined for fame and fortune. Maybe they were. All I knew was that to my ears, Sepulchre made the most appalling, godawful racket I'd ever heard in my life – so they were probably in with a chance.

Tonight, Spike was dressed in the kind of style that was considered essential for any self-respecting death-metal vocalist. His tall skinny frame was enclosed in a black leather biker's jacket, replete with a multitude of studs, emblems and badges. Beneath this he wore a 'Kurt Cobain Lives' T-shirt, tastefully embellished with a picture of the late rock star holding a shotgun. Spike also wore a skin-tight pair of Levis that were literally falling apart with age and from which his bony knees protruded like two islands of white chalk. A studded leather belt with a silver death's-head buckle was clamped around his tiny waist; and a rotting pair of trainers, once white but now a malodorous greenish-grey, completed his wardrobe. You had to admit, he did look every inch the rock star.

As I divested myself of my camera equipment, I saw that he was tucking into a foil container of left-over Chinese take-away, that I knew for a fact had been in the fridge for three days. He glanced up and gave me a welcoming grin.

'Hey, man, thought you'd stood me up! I got peckish waiting.' He proffered the container which contained a greasy, unappetising mixture of foo yung, noodles and fried rice. 'Want some?' he asked.

I shook my head. 'I've eaten thanks. Listen, I could heat that up for you in the oven.'

'Nah.' He shook his mane of curls. 'I prefer it cold.' He

took a swig from his can and belched loudly. 'Where you been, man? I been waiting ages.'

'Out on a job.' I glanced at my watch. 'I'm only ten minutes late,' I protested.

'Yeah, but I was half an hour *early*. Here.' He threw me a can of lager and I caught it one-handed. 'What we doin' tonight?'

I shrugged. 'Not sure yet. We'll have to see what Roz wants to do. She said something about going out for a bop.'

Spike scowled. He and Roz had a relationship that could best be described as 'volatile'.

'We could go to Rock World,' he said hopefully.

'Well, maybe.' But I knew Roz wouldn't be keen on that idea. She regarded the regulars there as a bunch of Neanderthal headbangers and on our previous visits, had spent most of the night pointing at some of the more exotic dressers and laughing out loud. Me and Spike had almost ended up in a fight because of this and believe me, it takes a lot to rile the punters at Rock World, who are mostly very laid back. Mind you, when she really worked at it, Roz was capable of coaxing violent tendencies out of a Buddhist monk.

'We could take in a movie,' suggested Spike.

I frowned. Spike's idea of a good night at the pictures wasn't the usual 'Harrison Ford and a car chase' kind of affair. The last time I'd accompanied him to a cinema, I'd cringed all the way through a film that consisted of the cast members being systematically stabbed, crushed, dismembered and disemboweled. As a finale, the lead villain's head had exploded in slow motion. Spike had afterwards proclaimed it to be the best comedy he'd seen in ages. After recent events in my life, I didn't feel up to anything quite so visceral.

'I don't think I'm in the mood,' I told him. I pulled the tab on my beer and the contents spurted out in a gush of foam, obliging me to get my mouth over the opening, pronto. Spike laughed gleefully.

'Must've got a bit shook up,' he observed, which struck me as a patently obvious remark. I moved over to the table and sat opposite him.

'So, what's happening with you?' I asked Spike.

He chewed contemplatively on a mouthful of cold noodles, before answering. 'Big Abel's been giving me some grief. Spent an hour up there today, didn't I?'

Big Abel was not some troublesome relative living in his attic, but the huge bell in the Town Hall's clock-tower. Spike had recently been assigned the extra responsibility of maintaining the thing, which was proving to be more time-consuming than he had anticipated. Apparently, despite the relatively recent addition of an electronic timing system to the clock's ancient mechanism, it was becoming increasingly erratic, striking the wrong number of beats to the hour, striking too quietly, too loud or sometimes not even striking at all. The clock tower was perched one hundred and eighty feet up in the air, so it required a brave soul to go up there every day: but Spike seemed fearless in that respect. To him the whole thing was nothing but a monumental chore.

'Honest,' he muttered. 'You'd think the bastards could find somebody else to do it, wouldn't you? Somebody *qualified*. As if I haven't got enough on my plate. You know the latest thing they've asked me to take care of? On Halloween, they're having this big do in the Grand Ballroom . . .'

'Oh, yeah, I was just talking about that earlier.'

Spike rolled his eyes. 'Some bright spark on the council has come up with the idea of having the bell ring thirteen times at midnight, right? Only you can't set it to ring more than twelve times automatically. So guess who's going to be up there on a ladder with a big wooden mallet in his hand.'

I couldn't help smiling. 'It'll be like J Arthur Rank Presents,' I observed. 'Still, at least they'll have to pay you some overtime.'

He scowled. 'Don't matter. I'm sick of having to do things I ain't trained for. Mind you, I did write a song about it.'

'What, about the Town Hall?'

'No, not exactly. But the bell sort of inspired me, didn't it? Got me thinking about the bubonic plague. You know, the Black Death? They used to go round ringing bells all the time. So I wrote this song called *Bring Out Your Dead*. Could be our first single, I reckon.'

'Right . . .' The workings of Spike's mind never failed to amaze me. I'd heard the Town Hall clock strike the hour many times and had never once thought about the Black Death, nor been prompted to write a song about it.

'Pity I ain't got my axe with me,' said Spike. 'I could have played it for you.'

I was just about to concur that this was indeed a tragedy of epic proportions when Spike's ever mercurial mind flipped neatly on to another track. 'Hey, that reminds me. You know Sepulchre are playing the Mandrake club in a couple of day's time? I was wonderin' if you'd do some photographs for us.'

'What, more? I only just did some.'

'Yeah, but they were *publicity* shots. We could do with some "in concert" stuff. You know, try and capture the excitement of a live gig? We don't mind paying for your expenses and that.'

'Er . . . well, sure, if you think it would help . . .' I wasn't wild about the idea. Having witnessed on several occasions the frenzied, drunken débâcle that was the average Sepulchre gig, I would be extremely reluctant to take my precious camera equipment into the midst of it. But Spike was my best friend, so . . .

'By the way, I think your manager is coming to check us out,' added Spike.

'Vincent? How come?'

'Wrote to him, didn' I? Sent him a copy of our latest demo, told him all about the gig. I reckon we've taken it as far as we can under our own steam. What we need now is proper representation. A seven-gali.'

'I think that's *Svengali*,' I said.

'Yeah, whatever. Someone who can put us on the map.'

I considered this information. Part of me wanted to warn Spike not to count on Spinetti's support for the idea; but then I thought about William K and told myself that Sepulchre weren't any worse than him. At least they could play their instruments. After a fashion.

'What about you, Danny? What you been up to?'

I thought about Flynn's warning not to tell anybody else about my grisly discovery in the railway arch. Thought about it for all of five seconds, then decided, what the hell, this was my best friend I was talking to, of *course* I'd have to tell him about it. So once again I found myself recounting the story of my grim discovery on Sobriety Street and it really was getting better with each successive telling, I was learning how to build the suspense, tease the story out before I got to the 'punchline' – the image of the flayed body hanging from the roof beams. Spike listened agog till I reached the conclusion, then reacted with evident enthusiasm.

'Fuck me,' he said. 'Danny, that's brilliant!'

'Hardly the word I would have used,' I muttered.

'No, 'course, it must have been a bit 'orrible at the *time*. But it's a real stroke of luck on your part. I mean, it's going

101

to put you in the public eye, isn't it? Just when you need all the publicity you can get. Hey, is there any chance of copping a look at these pictures?'

'Oh, you'll be seeing them soon enough. Vincent's persuaded me to include them in the exhibition at The Wedge.' I looked at him warily. 'What do you think of that idea?'

He stared at me for a moment, a look of shock on his face. I thought he might actually be about to slag off the idea. But no, no such luck.

'It's fuckin' brilliant! Shit, I hope I'll be invited!'

I smiled. When I'd first mentioned the exhibition to him, he hadn't been anything like as enthusiastic as this.

'Naturally. Do you think *other* people will want to come?'

''Course they will! That is a brilliant gimmick. And that was Vincent Spinetti's idea?' Spike slammed a fist on the table, making the cans of beer jump. 'Jesus, I have got to persuade that guy to handle our band. He is my kind of manager!'

'You can hardly put it all down to Vincent. I mean, it's not as if he arranged the murder in the first place, is it?'

Spike grinned. 'Not as far as you *know*,' he said.

'I'd already had the idea of using the pictures. I was just worried that it was a really scummy thing to do.'

'Oh, it *is*!' Spike assured me. 'That's what's so great about it. Specially with it being a local celebrity and all that.'

'Hmm.' I stroked my beard thoughtfully. It occurred to me that when Spinetti had first seen the photographs, the identity of the corpse was unknown. I wondered if this would make any difference to his plans. 'Anyway,' I said, 'it goes without saying that I'd like you to keep all this to yourself. If word gets out about what I'm planning to do, the exhibition's liable to be banned before it ever opens. And don't tell anyone about me finding the body either. People could put two and two together.'

'You can rely on me, mate. I won't breathe a word. Who else knows about it?'

'About finding the body? Only Roz . . .' I said; and we exchanged worried glances.

'Christ,' muttered Spike, pulling a face. 'You may as well have broadcast it on *Metrosound* radio. It'll be all over Manchester by now.'

'Oh no, I warned her not to say anything,' I told him doubtfully. But I couldn't help thinking that Spike had a point. Roz wasn't the greatest respecter of privacy the world had ever known. The more I thought about it, the more worried I became. Thank God she didn't yet know about me using the photographs in the exhibition. I imagined her telling one of her radical women's groups about it. These were people who would form a protest group about the incorrect use of an apostrophe, so what they'd make of that, was anybody's guess.

By the time Roz came home, fifteen minutes later, I'd worked myself up into a right old lather, convincing myself that she had informed every tabloid reporter in the phone book about my discovery of the body; and the moment she stepped through the door, I asked her about it.

She looked quite indignant at the idea.

'Of course I didn't tell anybody,' she protested. 'You asked me not to.'

I breathed a sigh of relief.

'Apart from Wanda, of course.'

I glared at her.

'You told Wanda? You told Ms Mouth Almighty? Oh, that's great! Perfect! I've got no worries there, then.'

Roz gave me a cross look.

'That's unfair. How can you call her that? You don't even know her. You've only ever met her occasionally.'

This was true enough and I had good reason to remember one of the occasions. It had happened some twelve months earlier when Roz had brought Wanda along to an amateur exhibition of my photographs at the Central Library. After perusing the rows of pictures for ten minutes, Wanda had stalked over to me, given me an oily smile and informed me that my work was 'reactionary, derivative, penis-driven shit.' With that she'd swept out of the door, leaving me stunned and speechless and wondering how a series of Lancashire landscapes could possibly be thought of as 'penis-driven'. Now that self-same woman was putting together an exhibition of her own that was really worthy of the term, but I supposed the irony of it would have been lost on her. Like most of her ilk, Wanda had absolutely no sense of humour.

'I wish you hadn't told her,' I muttered.

'Oh, come on. Wanda's my best friend, of course I told her.' She nodded at Spike. 'I bet you told *him*, didn't you?'

'That's different. I found the body. It's up to me to make that decision.'

'Yeah,' said Spike. 'And besides, he knows I won't tell anyone, other than the guys in the band.'

I glared at him. This was getting out of control.

Roz slipped into a vacant chair and studied Spike for a moment. 'Still in mourning, I see,' she said, prodding Kurt Cobain's face with her index finger. 'It's been nearly a year now, for God's sake.'

He shrugged. 'So? James Dean's been dead for forty years and I still see people wearing T-shirts with him on.'

'Only desperately sad people,' Roz assured him.

Spike grinned. 'How's the great one-eyed trouser snake hunt proceeding?'

Roz scowled. 'If you're referring to *Private Parts* it's coming along nicely, thank you.'

'Ooh-er, missus!' Spike made Frankie Howard-like gestures. 'Anyway, if you've been left a bit short, my offer still stands.' He waggled his eyebrows suggestively.

'Forget it,' Roz told him bluntly. 'There's no way I'm wasting time on the insubstantial scrap of meat that dangles between *your* legs.'

'Not so insubstantial. You'd need a wide angle lens to get this on film.'

'Dream on,' Roz told him. She glanced at me. 'You had any more thoughts about posing?'

Spike looked affronted by this news.

'You asked *him*, but you keep turning *me* down? How come?'

'Because I suspect your motives. We've already had more than our fair share of sexist males with an Errol Flynn complex, thank you very much. Danny is different. He hasn't got a sexist bone in his body. He's sex*less*.'

'Gee thanks,' I muttered. I glanced at Spike. 'Is it my imagination or did I just get insulted?'

Roz seemed to tire suddenly of the banter. She glanced meaningfully at her wristwatch.

'Are we going out then? Or do we sit here all night talking gibberish?'

'Tough decision,' I observed. 'OK, I'm game. Where we going?'

'How about Rock World?' said Spike, who never gave up on an idea.

'You've got to be kidding,' said Roz. 'What, spend the night surrounded by spotty Keith Richards look-a-likes and busty women who took *Red Sonja* too seriously for their own good?'

'Sounds all right to me,' said Spike.

'I don't doubt it. But here's Roz Birchill's recipe for the perfect night out.' She reached over and took a big gulp of beer from my can. She wiped her mouth on the sleeve of her jacket. 'First, a couple of pints and a few games of snooker down the *Peveril of the Peak*. Next, a couple more pints and some heated discussion down *The Briton's Protection*. Then, once we've had last orders, we head for a brilliant club where we can dance till the early hours . . .' She glanced at Spike cuttingly. '. . . and where they have a very liberal dress code.'

I swigged down the last mouthful of Special Brew.

'What are we waiting for?' I asked her. 'We're relatively young and the night lies before us like a treasure house to be plundered. Last one out of the door gets in the first round!'

The first round cost five pounds and sixteen pence. I know, because I bought it.

# Chapter Ten

'Oh no, Roz, you've got to be kidding!'

We were standing on the pavement outside the entrance to Roz's chosen nightclub, looking up at the pink neon sign above the door. Adonis. The place where Sebastian Kennedy was last seen alive. The place that Flynn had expressly warned me to stay away from.

'What's the problem?' Roz wanted to know. She'd downed more than a few pints before leaving our last port of call and was swaying on her feet, her hands crammed into the pockets of her jacket. Her warm breath clouded on the chill October air.

'Yeah,' said Spike, mystified by my reaction. 'S'OK in here, so long as you keep your arse to the wall!' He sniggered unpleasantly. Roz shot him a look but didn't say anything, realising that he was simply trying to bait her.

'You don't understand,' I told them. 'I can't be seen going in here. I'm supposed to be keeping my nose clean.'

Roz made a face. 'Coming over a bit homophobic in our old age, aren't we?' she muttered. 'I thought you liked this club.'

'I do! And it's nothing to do with homophobia. It's . . . it's kind of complicated . . . look, we'll just have to go somewhere else, all right?'

107

'Like where?' she protested. 'All we'll get now is shite hetero clubs full of beery males with toupees and medallions. They'll all be leering at me over their pints of bitter, while I'm trying to strut my stuff.'

I looked at her. Standing there in her baggy boilersuit and sheepskin flying jacket, she didn't exactly strike me as an object of male fantasy, but I refrained from commenting on the fact. Besides, I was supposed to be sexless, so what would I know about it?

'There's other decent clubs we could go to,' I reasoned.

'Don't be ridiculous!' Roz indicated Spike's torn jeans and rancid trainers. 'Who'll let him in dressed like that?'

'Rock World?' ventured Spike hopefully.

She ignored him and turned to walk towards the nightclub entrance. 'You two do what you want,' she snapped. 'I'm going in. And if I get raped and murdered on my way home, it'll be your fault.' Spike and I looked at each other as we realised that she was resorting to the most powerful weapon in a woman's extensive arsenal – emotional blackmail. I was just about to tell her that such a trick wouldn't sway me, when Roz paused and glanced slyly back over her shoulder. 'I forgot to tell you. Tonight's a special Abba night. A whole hour of Scandinavia's best export from midnight.'

I stared at her. 'You're lying!' I protested.

'No way. Check out the poster, if you don't believe me.'

I looked in the direction she was indicating. Sure enough, there it was out front of the building, those four magical letters spelled out in dayglow orange. I was now in a real quandry. Sixty minutes of Benny, Bjorn, Agnetha and Frida? That was a very tempting proposition. Very tempting indeed.

'But look,' I reasoned. 'I told the police I'd keep my nose clean.'

Roz shrugged. 'What are you, a man or a mouse?'

'Well . . .'

'And you've got two witnesses with you, who will testify that you were a good little boy. Right, Spike?'

'Right!'

'So what's the problem?' Roz walked on towards the open doorway, humming a fair approximation of *Dancing Queen*. Once again, Spike and I exchanged glances. I could feel my willpower crumbling alarmingly. Also, hadn't Spinetti mentioned a photogenic tattooed man who danced in here most nights?

'Let her go,' said Spike. 'We'll hit Rock World, just the two of us. Whaddya say?'

That finally convinced me. Without another word, I trailed dejectedly in Roz's wake and after a brief hesitation, Spike followed. We went in through the shabby doorway and down the steps to the illuminated glass rectangle of the pay-box. Behind the screen, a hefty transvestite in a gold lamé ball gown sat taking the money. She had an elaborately coifed beehive hairdo, make-up that must have been applied with a bucket and spade and, when she handed over the tickets, the longest red-painted fingernails I've ever seen in my life.

We moved on, pushed through a set of swing doors and found ourselves in the club itself, a large, open plan area arranged on three different levels. We were up on top, alongside the bar, which was tricked out with plastic bamboo beams and a grass roof to look like a Hawaiian beach hut. The back wall had a tacky photographic tropical sunset projected on to it.

Down a short flight of steps, plastic patio tables under gharish thatched umbrellas ran off to left and right along a strip of ground that was the colour of golden sand. Beyond that, was the sunken dance floor, painted to resemble an

empty swimming pool, upon which an enthusiastic crowd of
punters were currently cavorting to the sound of Erasure. A
state-of-the-art lighting system bombarded them with different combinations of colour and every so often, clouds of dry
ice rose up from hidden grills, making menacing shapes in
the flicker of the strobe lights.

I stood for a moment, observing the dancers. There were
moustachioed clones in black leather and Brando-hats, TV's
dressed in flamboyant gowns that wouldn't have looked out
of place in a Carmen Miranda movie, severe-looking dykes
with cropped hair and pierced noses. There were sober-
suited business gents, out for a night on the town with a
difference, the occasional New-Ager with dreadlocks and
patchwork loonpants. There were ravers and trancers, old
hippies, young hippies, bikers, bimbos and beefcakes.

Roz and Spike moved down the steps in search of a vacant
table and I turned to walk to the bar, which ran almost the
full width of the room. I saw instantly that somebody was
leaning on the wooden counter, giving me the eye in no
uncertain manner. Presuming that somebody had been mis-
led by the gold sleeper in my right ear, I returned the man's
gaze for a moment, giving him this blank, disinterested
expression that I'd perfected over the years and which
generally did the trick. But the man didn't look away as I had
expected. He continued staring at me intently, a curious
smile on his lips. In that instant, I realised that there was
something disturbingly familiar about him. I stopped walking
and was unable to prevent my jaw from dropping open, as I
recognised Detective Inspector Flynn.

He was dressed a good deal more casually than when I'd
last met him. He was wearing a black Levi jacket over a
maroon silk shirt and a pair of khaki chinos. Now he was
beckoning me over. Reluctantly I moved across and stood

beside him at the bar. He leaned forward to talk in my ear, having to shout over the blare of the sound system.

'Danny! This is an unexpected pleasure!'

'Inspector Flynn, I—'

He thumped me surreptitiously on the arm.

'The name's Lawrence,' he corrected me. 'You can even call me Larry if you must, but I could do without the whole place knowing I'm with the Old Bill, thanks very much.'

'Sorry.' I glanced quickly about but decided a man would need bionic ears to have heard anything over the racket of Erasure doing *Chains Of Love*. 'What are you doing here?' I asked.

'I might ask you the same question. I thought you told me . . .'

'Look, I know what I said. I got dragged along by a couple of friends.' I gestured vaguely down at the tables. 'They chose the venue, honest.'

Flynn frowned. He clearly wasn't happy with the situation.

'Danny, how do you suppose it looks, eh? I'm here on surveillance, waiting to see if our mysterious bearded suspect turns up in search of another victim and bingo! Up you pop like the bloody white rabbit!'

'I can't help that. What was I supposed to do, desert my friends?'

He sighed, shook his head.

'Oh, God forbid that you should have to do something as drastic as that! Well . . . you're here now, so I suppose we'll just have to make the best of it.' He leaned back against the bar, propping himself on his elbows, while he watched the dancers. 'It's OK here, isn't it?'

I shrugged. 'It's all right. Apparently, they're playing an hour of Abba from midnight.'

'Yeah?' He looked enthusiastic. 'That's right, you're a fan

aren't you? What would you say is their best song?'

I thought for a moment. '*Knowing Me, Knowing You*', I replied.

Flynn considered this for a moment, then shook his head.

'Good choice, but I'd vote for *The Name Of The Game*. That walking bass line? And those harmonies against the chords on the twelve string acoustic? Absolute genius.'

Well, he was a man of constant surprises, I had to say that for him. A policemen who knew about photography, who frequented art galleries and who liked Abba? If there was another cop like this one, anywhere on the planet, I'd be very surprised.

I waved a hand at a passing barman and managed to get his attention. I ordered a jug of something called Long Island Tea, a cocktail made with several spirits and a lot of iced cola.

'Can I get you anything?' I asked Flynn. He plumped for a Lucozade Light and I figured he probably never touched alcohol, even when he was off duty; he looked too healthy for that. 'Any progress?' I asked in his ear.

'Not much. We figure it's probably a homophobic attack; we can't seem to find any other motive. To hear his friends talk he's Mahatma Gandhi, Mother Teresa and Saint Francis of Assisi, all rolled into one handy package. But he must have done something to piss *somebody* off. You don't string a guy up by his feet and remove all his skin, just because he looks at you funny.'

'I guess not,' I said.

'It's the ceremonial quality of the killing that keeps bugging me,' he said. 'It's hardly a straightforward murder in any sense of the word. I wondered if he might have been mixed up in black magic rituals or something like that. But nobody seems to be able to tell me anything about his private life, other than the fact that he was an ardent club-goer. Talking to his friends and colleagues is a bit strange. I get the impression that there's something they aren't telling me. It's as though they've drawn themselves into a protective circle and are putting out their horns to keep me from getting inside.'

'Why are you telling me all this?' I asked him.

He looked genuinely puzzled. 'Do you know,' he said, 'now that you ask me, I haven't got the faintest idea.'

I picked up the jug of 'tea' and three cocktail glasses.

'I'd better get back to my friends,' I told him.

'Of course.' He smiled. 'I'll probably see you on the dance floor later on.'

Assuming he was joking, I made my way down the stairs to the next level, holding the jug carefully, to avoid spilling its contents. I found Roz and Spike ensconced at a table overlooking the dance floor. Under the glare of the overhead lights, this area had the ambience of a sunlit beach and Spike had actually put a pair of Ray Bans on.

'About bleeding time,' he said ungraciously. He grabbed a glass and filled it from the jug. 'You could die of thirst in this heat.'

'Who was the hunk at the bar?' Roz wanted to know. Bloody woman never missed a trick.

'Oh, that's er . . . Larry,' I told her. 'Friend of a friend of a friend.' I filled up the other two glasses and sipped at mine experimentally. It tasted like iced coke, which it mostly was. If these jugs had contained anything like the mixture of spirits mentioned on the menu, one jug would probably be enough to drop a bull elephant in its tracks.

At midnight, when we were on our second jug, the lights changed and the DJ cued the intro to *Does Your Mother Know?*

'Come on,' said Roz. 'Time to bop!' She grabbed me by the arm and dragged me in the general direction of the dance floor. She didn't even bother asking Spike, who wouldn't have dreamed of desporting himself to something as frivolous as this. So we left him to it and proceeded to shake some action.

Now, I'd be the first to admit that I was not a great dancer. Stone cold sober, it always struck me as a vaguely surreal way of carrying on, but once suitably fuelled up with copious amounts of alcohol, I would at least give it my best shot. This largely consisted of me moving my left foot over to my right foot and back again, then moving my right foot over to my left. Whilst doing this I would pump my arms vigorously like I was running a marathon. It was rudimentary, sure, but on a crowded dance floor, I could just about get away with it.

Roz, on the other hand, was a spectacularly uninhibited dancer, who relied on no particular technique whatsoever, but preferred to interpret the music instinctively. This particular record was inspiring her to gyrate her hips and buttocks in an alarming fashion, whilst throwing her head back and flailing her arms, threatening serious injury to our immediate neighbours on the dance floor. This track segued into *Voulez Vous*; Roz leapt up and down on the spot and used her arms to perform what looked like semaphore. *Voulez Vous* segued into *Take A Chance On Me*, during which Roz mimed the act of sexual intercourse with an imaginary midget and kept punching the air with a clenched fist, at one point coming perilously close to knocking my teeth down my throat.

All through this *tour de force*, I gamely kept up my plodding routine, but I was beginning to break sweat by now and started to think about sneaking off at the end of the next track. Then I noticed the man who was dancing all by himself, just a few feet away from me.

He was slim but muscular, with close-cropped blond hair and clean-cut features. He was wearing a cap sleeve T-shirt, revealing two powerful looking arms that were literally covered with intricate full colour tattoos. I realised that this was the guy Spinetti had mentioned to me. Actually, the word 'tattoo' failed to do them justice. They were works of art. His skin seemed to teem with a whole menagerie of mythical beasts and exotic characters, all spilling over each other in their mission to cover every inch of available flesh. The guy was also a good dancer – very inventive but *controlled*, not all over the shop like Roz. His hips swayed and his hands made elaborate, mystical gestures as though he was a conjurer pulling invisible cards out of the air.

Spinetti had seemed very keen that I should get some pictures of this man; and emboldened by far more alcohol than was strictly good for me, I determined to ask him if he'd deign to do a sitting at the first opportunity.

When the current record faded out, he left the dance floor. I made a quick gesture to Roz, gulping at an imaginary drink – she seemed oblivious to me anyway – and I followed the tattooed man. I caught up with him halfway up the steps to the next level and tapped him lightly on the shoulder. He turned abruptly, his blue eyes hostile, his right fist raised to strike. I took an involuntary step backwards. He appraised me for a moment, then realising that I posed no threat, he relaxed a little and smiled apologetically.

'Sorry, mate. Thought you were starting something.'

'My fault,' I assured him. I leaned forward to shout into his ear. 'I'm Danny Weston. A photographer. I know this sounds kind of funny, but . . .'

'You'd like to take my photograph!' He grinned, displaying small, white teeth. He had an odd voice, very North

Manchester but also vaguely camp with it. 'Ooh, I get that line all the time. Some people even have *film* in their cameras.'

'Er . . . no, seriously.' I could feel my cheeks reddening and I fumbled in my jacket for my wallet. I found a business card and handed it to him. 'It would be for an exhibition,' I explained. 'At The Wedge.'

This seemed to impress him, as I'd hoped it would. He studied the card intently, as though looking for a catch.

'This be a paid job, would it?'

I frowned. 'I can't afford to pay you,' I admitted. 'But you would get a set of professional quality prints. I could even enlarge a couple of your favourites. It's the tattoos I'm interested in.'

'That's what they're *all* interested in,' he told me. 'Initially.' He seemed to consider for a moment. 'Yeah, well, why not? I could do with some nice snaps. When?'

'If t'were done, t'were best done quickly,' I blurted. It was meant to sound cool but after six pints and two jugs of Long Island Tea, I was probably incoherent. He looked at me, puzzled.

'Come again,' he said.

'Er . . . how about tomorrow?' I suggested. 'Say about ten AM?' The minute I'd said it, I regretted making it so early. The way the alcohol was flowing, the indications were that I'd still be heavily hung over at that time; but the tattooed man was already nodding his agreement.

'You want me to come to this address?' he asked me.

'Er . . . please.'

'Should I wear anything special?'

'Er . . . no, actually, I was . . . more interested in . . .'

'In the tattoos.' He fluttered his eyelashes at me. 'Oh, so it's a tits and bums job, is it?'

116

I felt myself reddening again.

'Good God, no!' I said. 'Umm . . . that is, of course I'll need to see . . . you'll have to . . .'

'Relax,' he said. 'Only kidding.' He slipped the card into the back pocket of his jeans and turned away. 'See you tomorrow,' he mouthed at me, then moved on up the steps towards the bar. Glancing after him, I saw Flynn leaning on the neon-lit rail that edged the top level. He was gazing down at me with interest, an eyebrows-raised, quizzical expression on his face. Feeling resentful about being observed in this way, I went back to our table, where I noted with a vague sense of dismay that Spike had just got in another jug of 'tea'. As I sat down, he filled my glass for me.

'Who's the walking art gallery?' he shouted at me.

It occurred to me then that I'd neglected to get the man's name.

'Just somebody I got talking to,' I said.

'Them tattoos are cool,' said Spike. 'I been thinkin' of getting one. Just a small one on me arm or something. What do you think?'

The DJ segued into *Lay All Your Love On Me*, a dance floor pleaser if ever there was one. Roz was still out there, giving it socks, but somehow managing to not even break sweat. I was going to answer Spike's question but I froze, mouth open, and did a double take. Now another familiar figure was descending the stairs to the dance floor, just a few feet away from Roz.

It was Flynn and he was giving it lots, too: using a fluid, rhythmic style, swinging his hips to emphasise the beat, adding expressive flourishes with his hands. He looked – and I hesitated to admit it – but he *did* look pretty bloody cool. As I watched, I noticed other dancers edging back a little in admiration, to give him room to move. Roz was aware of him

too, she was smiling, moving closer to partner him, the two
of them swaying in time. She hadn't even noticed *me* when I
was on the floor. Now Flynn's hand was coming out to take
her hand . . .

*He's gone too far*, I thought confidently. Roz *hated* stran-
gers touching her up, any second now she'd lose her rag and
Kung Fu him . . .

Except that she didn't. She was responding to him,
giggling all girlie-like. It was unbelievable. She allowed
him to slip an arm around her waist. Suddenly they were
like Fred Astaire and Ginger Rogers.

'Hey, that guy can really dance,' yelled Spike, who never
noticed these things as a rule. I felt like punching him.

I sighed, took a sip of my drink. One more thing to add to
the long list of surprises, I decided. Detective Inspector
Lawrence Flynn liked photography, he frequented art galleries, he adored Abba, he could dance up a storm and Roz was
putty in his hands. Furthermore, he seemed to be very
interested in the movements of a certain, mild-mannered
photographer named Danny Weston. Why was it that this
last point was beginning to fill me with a powerful sense of
trepidation? And why was I beginning to feel guilty when I
had absolutely no reason to?

I would have pondered the question further but the Long
Island Tea was finally taking its toll, exploding at the base of
my skull like sweet fire. What's more the DJ was finally
playing *Knowing Me, Knowing You*. Not for the first time I
abandoned myself to the dubious delights of being joyfully,
decadently, disgustingly drunk.

I was good at this. But then, I'd had lots of practice.

# Chapter Eleven

It's probably Spike's idea, though looking back on it, I'm plastered by this time and I can't honestly be sure that it isn't mine. At any rate, there we are, the three of us, reeling back through the city streets in the small hours of the morning, just about holding each other upright and Spike is singing us the new song he's written – and I *know* I must be pretty far gone, because it actually sounds quite good to me. I'm singing along on the chorus for Christ's sake, which goes something like, '*Bring out your dead, did you hear what I said, the moon is red, so bring out your dead.*' I mean, we are not talking Rodgers and Hart here, you understand, but at two in the morning, with several pints of alcohol sloshing around inside my gut, this sounds like a work of genius, I kid you not.

Roz meanwhile is blathering about what a great dancer my 'friend' Larry is and how come I've never introduced her to him before and do I know if he's married, only she noticed he wasn't wearing a wedding ring, that guy is so sexy, God what a mover! Finally I can't resist it any longer so I tell her, not without a certain degree of relish, that he's a policeman and she laughs hysterically, not believing me at first and when at last I manage to convince her, she seems to quite *like* the idea.

'Imagine,' she keeps saying, 'me dancing with a copper, I can hardly credit it!'

And it's about this point when one of us, I swear I don't know which one, says that they fancy a kebab.

Now, disregarding the fact that I have already eaten a somewhat similar item for lunch, I find myself in full agreement with this idea, even though reason dictates that at such an unearthly hour, there is really only one place that's going to be open and it's Aphrodite's Charcoal Pit, on Oxford Road.

In broad daylight, I wouldn't dream of eating anything that has issued from the filthy, grease-spattered culinary hell-hole that is Aphrodite's. But tonight, when my stomach is only just managing to cling on to its contents, the idea of floating a greasy, half-cooked lump of unidentified meat product on that pool of unstable liquid seems a perfectly logical thing to do.

So we redirect our footsteps towards Aphrodite's, and presently we arrive at its grubby, neon lit exterior to find that a lot of other like-minded individuals have experienced a similar craving and have formed a raucous and disorderly queue at the entrance. Undaunted, we take our places: and in what seems like no time at all, we have progressed to the counter where the sweating, hulking figure of Constantin is doing his level best to supply the demands of his ever eager clientele.

Constantin is from Athens, a dark-skinned, heavy-set gentleman with big stubbly jowls and thick lips. He has an endearing tendency to swear at his customers, as in 'Whadd-adafucka you want?' He is also one of the hairiest men I have ever clapped eyes on, though very little of it is actually on his head. Thick black hairs sprout from his ears and nostrils and through the holes in the grubby string vest he habitually

120

wears. They poke down from his armpits and up from his shoulders and out from his chest. It's as though the hair has got lost *en route* to his head and has taken the shortest distance to the surface. I watch his big hands wrapping up a kebab for the present customer and even his fingers are hairy. Little clumps of the stuff sprout from his knuckles like tiny tufts of grass.

I register all this and still I'm not deterred, my battered old tastebuds are virtually popping in anticipation of the feast to come and assuring me, 'Yep, we're *hungry*!'

And there, turning corpulently on the upright metal spit, in front of what looks rather like a domestic three-bar gas fire is the object of our ill-advised craving. Now, I don't know exactly what a donner kebab is composed of – on reflection, maybe I don't really *want* to know – but whatever it is, it isn't pretty. Furthermore, though we see evidence of the thing dwindling away in front of our eyes as strips of meat are sliced off it, we never seem to be there when it's replaced, do we? Which gives the distinct impression that at night, when the last customers have staggered home, the damned thing simply *grows* back again, like something out of one of those old Quatermass movies.

And the weird thing is, I'm standing there looking at this blob of flesh and the thick, greasy smell of it is in my nostrils and I'm *still* hot for it, and so are my two companions. The three of us order one large donner each. Constantin pauses to mop at his shining features, slaps three pitta breads on to the grill, then turns to get the meat. He picks up a fat encrusted electric carving knife, switches it on and sets to with a will, peeling the brownish pink meat off in long, glistening strips.

And then it finally hits me. The rush of shock I have been anticipating for the best part of two days sweeps unexpectedly over me like a deluge of cold water. And suddenly it is not just a shapeless lump of meat turning slowly on that spit. It is a man's torso, dripping with sweat. It is a strip of soft, pink skin that Constantin's artful knife is cutting away. As the tiny blades glide through the skin, I can see the red, wet flesh beneath. Trickles of fresh blood run down the torso and they hiss as they drip into the hot metal receptacle below.

I close my eyes for a moment, thinking desperately that it's all right, I can simply wish this vision away. I am simultaneously seized by an icy chill that makes my whole body shudder. I open my eyes again and now a second pair of eyes are staring back at me from the spit, the torso has become a huge head, the metal pole punched right through the skull, the blank eyes staring and the open mouth down-turned in a grimace, as the head turns another slow revolution and Constantin's knife slices off a cheek, a lip, the stubby jut of the nose . . .

My stomach lurches violently and I throw up a hand to clap it over my mouth. Spike and Roz glance at me uncertainly.

'You OK?' asks Roz.

But no, I'm not OK, I can feel the sickness rising in me like a flood tide and the smell, that rich greasy aroma that a moment ago seemed so appetising, has become that same raw, gamey stink that I smelled in the railway arch. And the thing still turning slowly on the spit, turning under the blades of the knife . . .

I groan and twist away from the counter, almost knocking Spike over in my haste, knowing that I'm going to chuck my ring up at any second and God help anyone who happens to be in range. I lunge for the door, which is blocked by people queuing to get in and I daren't remove my hand from my mouth in order to ask them to make room. I just have to get outside – quickly . . .

Acid rises in my throat and something warm and viscous spurts from between my fingers. The crowd ahead of me moves miraculously aside, I am like a bilious Moses parting the Red Sea and suddenly I am out in the cold night air. I take my hand away and my jaws open wide, wider, the widest that they've ever opened and I say something that sounds like 'Europe' and the next thing I know, I'm on my knees, throwing up seven kinds of vomit and my head's exploding and the queue out front of Aphrodite's seems to be drifting off in different directions. This is not something you could describe as 'good advertising'; Constantin will probably ban me from the premises. Please God let him do that. Now my stomach is coming up my throat and I swear to God, oh Jesus, never, never again . . .

And finally it seems to be over and I'm left on my hands and knees, my eyes full of tears and I feel totally drained, totally empty. Spike and Roz come sheepishly out of the take-away and they're actually eating their kebabs like nothing's happened. Spike is holding two of the damned things, one still wrapped, intended for me, and he holds the package out to me and I groan and edge away from him, knowing that I mustn't be sick again – all I've got left to throw up are my internal organs.

'Does that mean I can have yours too?' he asks me and I give him a look, which invites him to please feel free to step under the next passing bus. Such charming friends I have. So sensitive. So compassionate. I manage to construct a short sentence.

'I. Want. To. Go. Home.'

'Yeah, well, I'll see you soon,' says Spike. 'Got work in the morning.' He turns and strolls unsteadily in the direction of his own gaff, the paper parcel that is my kebab tucked like a prize under one arm, while he carries on devouring his own.

Roz takes a last bite of her kebab and tosses the remains regretfully into an overflowing waste bin.

'Come on then, dipstick,' she says, with what is for her, an overwhelming display of tenderness. She puts an arm under mine and helps me to my feet. 'I don't know why you bother to drink,' she says, regarding the Technicolour puddle at our feet. 'You never hang on to it for very long.'

We struggle homewards and I'm so far gone, I don't even remember getting there. The next thing I know, the morning light is shining in my eyes, my head is pounding, my sandpaper-like tongue is stuck to the roof of my mouth and my stomach feels like an elephant shat in it. I groan, fumble for my glasses and put them on. The world comes slowly, slowly back into focus. I'm lying fully dressed on my bed and the clock on the bedside cabinet informs me that it's nine-thirty. The tattooed man will be here for his photo-shoot in exactly half an hour.

# Chapter Twelve

Under the circumstances, I got my act together pretty well, I thought. I managed to shave without nicking myself more than half a dozen times: and a hot shower jolted me into some semblance of wakefulness. As I soaped myself, I reflected that throwing up the previous night had probably been the best thing I could have done. God knows how I would have felt with all that poison swilling about in my system. Like one of the undead, probably, instead of just slightly zombified.

I towelled myself dry, threw on some clothes and considered the idea of breakfast for all of ten seconds, but my stomach threatened to rebel at the very idea, so I promptly abandoned it. I made my way through to the studio, noticing in passing that the door to Roz's room was still closed. No doubt she would lie in state till well past noon, sleeping off last night's excesses. Oh, it was a great life for some.

Glancing at my watch, I saw the tattooed man was already fashionably late, but that was OK, it would give me a chance to get ready for the shoot. I spent fifteen minutes or so rigging the lights in front of a plain white backdrop. I'd already decided to shoot in monochrome, go for a graphic linear feel to the pictures, rather than the full colour treatment. I didn't want anything to overshadow the impact of my 'cadaver' shots.

As I worked, I thought back to what I had seen – or rather, *thought* I had seen – in Aphrodite's and I had to mentally shake the image off. I could only put it down to a powerful hallucination, invoked by a mixture of delayed shock and too much alcohol. One thing was for sure, I certainly didn't want to experience anything like that ever again. I resolved to do my level best to lay off the 'sauce' for a while.

At about twenty-past ten, the front door intercom buzzed and the slightly camp voice I remembered from the previous night announced that Kit Marsden was here for his 'session'. I'd neglected to ask the tattooed man his name at the club and reflected that it suited him. I buzzed him up and a few moments later, met him at the kitchen door. He was dressed in a leather biker's jacket and Gap jeans. He had a large canvas bag slung over one shoulder. He glanced uncertainly around, noting the dirty dishes piled in the sink, the remains of Roz's breakfast still on the table where she'd left it. I could see that he wasn't exactly getting an atmosphere of professionalism here, so having ascertained that he didn't want coffee (there was *still* no milk) I led him through to the studio, where he seemed quietly impressed by the sight of all the equipment.

'Ooh, proper lights and *everything*,' he observed. 'Do this for a living, do you?'

'Pretty much. Mostly boring stuff for the *Evening Post*.' I busied myself loading up the Pentax. 'What about you?'

'Me?' He was wandering about the studio, taking everything in. 'Oh, a bit of this and a bit of that. I'm in the entertainment business.'

I smiled, fixed the camera to a tripod.

'What kind of entertainment?'

'I do a drag act. Cabaret turn. Liza Minelli, Shirley Bassey, that sort of thing.' He squinted up into one of the big arc lamps, raising a hand to shield his eyes. 'I'm no stranger to cameras, either. Though usually they're video cameras. I do a bit of acting, on the side.'

'Yeah? Anything I might have seen?'

He looked at me thoughtfully for a moment.

'Could be,' he said. 'Though I think you'd remember if you had.' He seemed to grow tired of the questioning. 'Well, shall we get started?' he suggested.

'Sure.' I took a light reading and adjusted my speed and aperture settings accordingly. 'You can use my room to change, if you like.'

'No need.' He began to take off his clothes, throwing them carelessly on to a nearby sofa. In a few moments, he'd stripped down to a tiny black posing pouch and I was able to appreciate the extent to which he'd taken his interest in tattoos. He had a good body, lean and firm, with hard looking muscles. The head and neck, his hands and feet were free of any decoration, but every other part of him, as far as I could tell, was illustrated. I couldn't discern a square inch of untouched flesh.

As I looked at him, his skin seemed to come alive. He turned slowly beneath the lights to let me have a good, long look. My astonished eyes kept picking out little details, registering a whole proliferation of startling images, but I sensed that it might take months of viewing to take in *everything*. I saw animals: dragons, tigers, eagles, unicorns. I saw faces: demons, film stars, famous cartoon characters. On one shoulder blade, a lunar landscape stretched beneath the glow of an alien moon. On his right breast, a phoenix burst out of a halo of flames. He did a half turn and I glimpsed a *Tyrannosaurus Rex* prowling from the cleft of his buttocks. A huge patterned serpent appeared to be coiled around his left leg, rising up along the length of his spine, threading its way in and out of the other images, before disappearing over one shoulder. At first glimpse there seemed to be no order or logic to the designs, but after a few minute's consideration, it occurred to me that the overall image must have taken careful planning by a skilled artist – and judging by the consistency of the style, by the *same* person.

'How do you want me?' Marsden asked.

I'd thought about this beforehand. I indicated a boom-box in the corner of the room and a pile of cassettes nearby.

'I'd like to get you moving,' I said. 'I seem to remember you're a pretty good dancer. See if there's anything there that turns you on.'

He waggled his eyebrows at me.

'Aren't you the forward one!' he said.

I felt my cheeks reddening again and pretended to be fiddling with my camera.

'I don't want anything too static,' I explained.

'Quite so.' He moved over to the boom-box and crouched down to examine the tapes. 'Bit early in the morning for this kind of thing,' he warned me. 'Mind you, it might warm me up a bit. It's chilly in here.' After a few moment's consideration, he selected an Oasis album and slapped that on. Then he got back to his feet and moved into position in front of the backdrop. He made a few tentative movements to the music, then grimaced. 'I feel a bit of a prat, doing this,' he said.

'It's OK,' I assured him. 'Take your time. Tell me about the tattoos. How did you get into it?'

He smiled. It was clearly a question he'd been asked many times before. He lifted his right hand to indicate a small illustration on his left arm, the place where you'd traditionally expect to find a vaccination scar. The design he'd picked out was a familiar one, a traditional skull and crossbones.

'I just fancied having one, you know. I was only a kid, it was probably a macho thing. Trying to convince myself I was something that I wasn't. Well, I'd heard about this tattoo parlour in Salford. I went along one day and met Scott.'

'Scott?' Marsden was already beginning to relax, moving to the music with more confidence now and I was able to shoot off the odd frame.

'Yes, Scott Banks, the guy who ended up doing all this stuff to me.' Marsden spread his arms out in a revealing gesture. 'Ironic, really. I went up there to try and assert my masculinity and wound up falling for the tattoo artist.' He laughed delightedly. 'Well, it was just an excuse to keep seeing him, wasn't it? I kept going back for more. It must have been dead obvious, but soon enough, he responded. A couple of weeks later I moved in with him and he began to draw up plans for his *masterpiece*. Actually, I found out, much later, that he'd been looking for a willing human canvas for quite some time. I was so green, it never even occurred to me that he might just be leading me along for his own aims. Anyway, I was so happy, I didn't even think about that. Christ, the hours I spent in that chair while he worked on me . . .'

I made a face.

'Doesn't it hurt?' I asked him.

'Of course it hurts! It hurts like hell. But it was a pain I grew to enjoy. And Scott, you see, is a man who likes to inflict pain, both physical and mental.'

I noted the resentment in Marsden's voice and wondered if it was wise to pursue this any further; but frankly, I was hooked.

'So er . . . you're still together, are you?'

He shook his head. He was getting into his stride with the

dancing now and my thumb was punching down on the shutter release with increased regularity.

'Our relationship ended the day he inked his signature into the last free bit of skin on my body. There, see?' He indicated a tattooed scrawl beneath one clean shaven armpit. 'Nothing was actually *said*, you understand. It was simply something I sensed. Quite literally, I'd come to the end of my usefulness; and Scott was already on the lookout for a new subject.'

I snapped another frame. 'So, you're on your own now?'

'Not exactly. I have a rich Sugar Daddy. An older guy. He's not at all like Scott, but he's a useful man to know.'

'And Scott still has this place in Salford?'

'Oh no, he's recently opened a parlour in the Wheat Exchange. Gone up in the world. Tattooing and body piercing have gained respectability, you see. That New Age crowd are into illustration. Pretty mundane stuff, mind you, sun and moon symbols, Yin and Yang, maybe their astrological sign if they're feeling reckless. Still, Scott seems to be doing all right out of it. And it finances his more adventurous projects. I hear he even does *women* these days.'

I couldn't help smiling at the sheer vitriol in his voice.

'What's wrong with that?' I asked innocently.

Marsden scowled.

'It's not just tattoos he's giving them, by all accounts. Scott swings both ways now.' He made a disapproving face. 'I don't agree with that kind of thing. He's getting a bit long in the tooth to go changing the habits of a lifetime. Still, if nothing else, it proves that nobody can ever be sure of their sexuality.'

I must have looked decidedly unconvinced because he fixed me with a sharp look. 'I mean it,' he said. 'You simply never know. Take yourself for example. What are your sexual politics?'

Again I smiled. This seemed a rather pompous way of putting it.

'I'm heterosexual,' I said.

'Are you really? You certainly don't act like it.'

I looked at him inquiringly.

'What's that supposed to mean?'

'Well, let's examine the evidence shall we? You come up to me in Adonis, one of the most openly gay clubs in town. You're wearing a leather jacket, despite the heat in there. You have a ring through your right ear; and you ask me to pose for some semi-naked photographs back at your place. Hardly the actions of a typical heterosexual!'

'I never said I was *typical*,' I told him.

'No, you didn't. But I'll tell you something, you had me fooled. I really didn't expect this photography business to be on the level. Know what I thought? I thought you were planning to seduce me.'

I stared at him, shocked by his candour.

'Then . . . why did you come?' I asked.

'Why do you think? It seemed an interesting prospect. Far more interesting than the actuality of it. Me prancing about like one of Pan's People on a bad night.'

I hardly knew what to say to this.

'Well, I'm sorry,' I mumbled. 'I certainly didn't mean to give you the wrong impression.'

'Didn't you?' He danced a little closer to me and I had to make a conscious effort not to back away from him. 'You must be very naïve, Danny . . . it is Danny, isn't it? Maybe you're on the level. Or maybe you *wanted* me to get the wrong idea.'

I leaned over and adjusted the focus on the camera.

'Why would I want that?'

He shrugged. 'Hard to say. Maybe you're not sure of your own sexuality. Could be you want somebody to take the initiative.'

'That's crazy,' I protested. 'I'm interested in *women*.'

He turned his back to me and gave me the opportunity to photograph the illustrations that stretched across his shoulder blades.

'Oh, so am I, up to a point. Nice to chat to about clothes. Maybe sit with them and watch an old Bette Davis movie, share a box of paper hankies. But when it comes to sexuality, that's a whole new ball game.'

'Not for me it isn't!' I said, perhaps a little too quickly. 'I *love* women. I love them physically.'

'Big ladykiller, are we? When did you last sleep with one?'

'I . . .' For a moment I was flummoxed. It had been a long time, longer than I cared to admit to Marsden. 'It was just the other night, actually. We were at it for hours.'

He laughed at this.

'Methinks he doth protest too much,' he observed, as though there was a third person in the room. 'Well, you'd be surprised how many self-professed fanny-chasers have done a St Paul on the road to Damascus. You'd be amazed how many of them have got all hot under the collar and asked to see the head of the snake.'

'The head of the—?'

Marsden smiled at me over his left shoulder. He reached up his right hand and traced a line with his finger, indicating the thick, patterned body of the serpent that swept over his shoulder. Then he turned and indicated where the snake threaded its way down his chest, winding in and out of the menageries of other creatures that patterned his skin. The snake's body thinned as it reached the curve of Marsden's stomach and then it plunged beneath the line of his black posing pouch. It didn't require much imagination to work out what the snake's head would be.

'Jesus,' I murmured. 'Is *everything* tattooed?'

'Everything,' he assured me. 'And before you ask, yes it did hurt. You really have to trust the tattoo artist. Care to see what it looks like?'

I stared at him. Despite all my protests, I was suddenly aware that I was excited. My mouth was dry, my forehead sticky with perspiration. My heart was hammering along at a mad pace. I barely had the presence of mind to keep pressing the shutter release.

'Look,' I said. 'Maybe we'd better quit now.'

'Before you do something you might regret?' Marsden smiled knowingly, took another step towards me. 'What's the matter, Danny? What are you afraid of?'

'I'm not afraid of anything. I just think we should stop.'

'Well, that's *one* option. There are others. Would it be easier if I was a woman for you? I can be that, if you want. I brought some clothes in my bag there. Stockings, suspenders. I could put them on for you . . .'

'Uh . . . no, that's all right, thanks!'

He gave me a long, searching look.

'Wouldn't you like to see the head of the snake, Danny? Just a quick peek? Hmm? Because it's growing. It's getting bigger.'

I couldn't stop myself. I glanced down and saw that the posing pouch was now bulging as Marsden's penis began to harden. Heat seemed to flood through me. My face burned. Marsden just stood there, his smiling expression simultaneously mocking me and giving a silent invitation to reach out for him. For a long, terrible moment, I didn't know what to do. I just heard Flynn's voice in my head, repeating the same line over and over.

*Are you sure you're not gay, Danny? Are you sure?*

I'd been angry when he'd asked the question, secure in my belief that I was a one hundred per cent red-blooded heterosexual. Suddenly, I wasn't so certain. I wasn't sure at all. I stood there looking at Marsden and he stood there looking at me and I couldn't deny that I was aroused by his advances, that I was perilously close to returning them . . .

And then the phone rang, out in the kitchen, a distant sound that nevertheless seemed to cut through the silence with all the delicacy of a drum kit falling down a flight of stairs.

I remembered to breathe and turning away, I walked quickly out of the studio and into the kitchen, where I'd left my portable phone. I clicked on the receiver and lifted the handset.

'Hello . . . Studio Seven . . . photography. Danny Weston speaking.'

'Danny, you OK? You sound like you've been running.'

'Uh . . . oh, Vincent. I er . . . just ran up the stairs. I er . . . I just got in.'

'You're getting out of condition, mate. I called to tell you to drop by my office this afternoon. I've got the artwork for *Skin Flicks*.'

'Christ, you don't . . . you don't waste any time, do you?'

'Strike while the iron is hot, Danny. Had my man burn the midnight oil to get it done. Wait till you see it, you'll *shit*!'

'Yes, OK, Vincent. I have to drop some film off at Photolab later, so er . . . I'll come by then.'

'Listen, you didn't tell me those photographs were of Sebastian Kennedy.'

'I didn't *know* then. Does it make a difference?'

'I suppose not. If anything, it's going to kick up an even bigger stink. But that's the object of the exercise, isn't it?'

'Uh . . . I guess.'

You all right, Danny? You sound kind of *weird*.'

'I'm fine thanks. I'll see you later.'

I rang off and stood there looking at the phone for a few moments, while I collected my thoughts. Now I was away from Marsden, I could see things more clearly, but he'd really rattled me. I felt very apprehensive about going back into the studio. I was afraid of the consequences.

Eventually though, I plucked up the courage and went back. He was putting his clothes back on. Evidently the session was over. I registered a vague sense of disappointment and wondered at it.

'Saved by the bell,' observed Marsden drily.

I shrugged. 'Maybe.' I waved a hand at the camera. 'I hadn't really finished,' I said.

He laughed. 'I think you got enough to be going on with, don't you? And probably more than you bargained for.'

I smiled sheepishly.

'Well, look, give me your phone number. I'll ring you just as soon as the photographs are ready.'

He searched through the pockets of his jacket, found a biro and a scrap of paper, then scribbled down a number with a Chorlton code and handed it to me.

'You going to deliver them in person?' he asked.

'Sure, why not?' I tried not to sound defensive. I folded the paper and put it into the back pocket of my jeans. 'And I'll bring you an invitation to the exhibition, if they're ready. How does that sound?'

'It sounds like I'm being paid off,' he said flatly. He turned and headed descisively out of the studio. I followed him down the corridor and out to the kitchen. He opened the door, then paused and looked back at me. 'You know, you really missed out on something, Danny. You're going to spend a lot of time wondering what it might have been like.'

Part of me suspected that this was true, but I didn't answer him. I just stood there looking at him blankly and after a few moments' hesitation, he went down the stairs to the outer door. I heard it open and slam shut.

I walked back into the kitchen and tried to make sense out of what had happened. I was feeling vaguely shell-shocked and decided to do a little cleaning up while I thought things over.

Before I was through, I'd washed all the dishes and cleaned the kitchen from top to bottom. I must have been in a worse state than I thought.

# Chapter Thirteen

By the time I got up to Photolab, I'd managed to get the incident into some kind of perspective. I'd decided that it wasn't that I'd suddenly turned gay, or bi, or anything as momentous as that. It had simply been a lust thing.

In the same way that a happily married man might get tempted by a sexy woman coming on to him, Marsden had brought out some instinct in me that normally lay buried deep beneath the surface. He was, undeniably, an attractive individual and the tattoos gave him a distinctly exotic quality. We'd been there in this really loaded, sexually charged situation, him virtually naked in front of me, offering himself for my pleasure. It was only natural that I flipped.

Besides, I asked myself, what was the big deal? I was an unattached male, I'd have been betraying nobody if I'd taken Marsden up on his offer. And it wasn't as if there was anything wrong with being gay . . . was there?

*What are you afraid of, Danny?*

I'd protested to Flynn that I wasn't afraid, but instinctively I knew that this was a lie. Blame it on my upbringing, my parents, my own prejudices, but deep down inside there was a part of me that thought of such behaviour as *wrong*. And that was what worried me the most. Me, Danny Weston, Mr

Liberal, always ready to support gay rights, the man who'd indignantly joined in all those protests against Clause 28, the man who'd bought tickets to see Julian Clary and Eddie Izzard, the man who'd sat through all those interminable Derek Jarman movies because he was a gay director and hey, that was really cool, wasn't it? Could it possibly be that despite everything, I was prejudiced against the very cause I claimed to support?

I was pondering these matters as I stepped in through the hallowed portals of Photolab, to find Trevor Bird in his usual place behind the counter, chatting earnestly with a well-made young lady who unfortunately was all too familiar to me. The last time I'd laid eyes on her, she'd been spread-eagled on a set of monochrome prints. Yet again I found myself blushing to my very roots. Red was beginning to be my colour.

'Danny, what a coincidence! Let me introduce you to my girlfriend and model, Mo. Mo, this is Danny Weston, the photographer I was telling you about.'

I shook Mo's plump hand, telling myself that this was no coincidence at all. Bird had known only too well that I was coming in to collect the trannies of Philip Cassiday today and had almost certainly arranged for Mo to be in attendance. God only knew what he'd been telling her about me.

'Pleased to meet you, Mr Weston. It's always a pleasure to meet somebody in the business.' Mo had a breathy, husky voice which I felt she was putting on for some kind of effect – though the one she achieved was probably not the one she intended. She sounded like a chronic asthmatic.

'Er . . . hello,' I mumbled. I found it difficult to look her in the eyes, so I concentrated instead on her hand which was plump and baby-like, the short fingers glittering with a collection of cheap rings.

'Trevor tells me you were admiring the results of our last photo-session,' said Mo.

'Oh . . . er . . . yes, they . . . they were very . . . distinctive,' I stammered.

'Only I wanted to let you know that I'm not exclusively Trevor's model,' she told me.

I stared at her blankly. 'I'm sorry, I don't . . .'

'I mean I'm *available*. Professionally speaking, that is.'

She was beaming at me, not in the least embarrassed by any of this. I, on the other hand, was virtually crippled with embarrassment, praying fervently for the ground to open up and swallow me, which typically, it didn't. I glanced at Bird and he was beaming at me too, an expectant look on his face.

'This exhibition you're having,' he prompted me. 'I thought, you know, there'd be room for a bit of glamour photography. And what with you expressing such an interest and everything . . .'

'Ah.' The penny dropped with the impact of a large housebrick at the base of my skull; and my brain went into frantic overdrive as I searched for a way to extricate myself without offending anybody. 'Well . . . unfortunately, it's not the er . . . the right vehicle for that kind of approach,' I explained. 'You see, thematically speaking, this show will have a very . . . *negative* vibe.'

'Negative?' Mo looked crestfallen, Trevor Bird merely perplexed.

'Yes. I'm going to be dealing with themes of alienation. I think of it as a 3D concept. Decay, dilapidation and death. Mo hardly fits into any of those categories, does she?'

Bird laughed, hollowly.

'Hardly,' he concurred. 'But, you know, maybe she would lighten things up a bit?'

'I can see where you're coming from, Trevor.' I paused for

a moment, finger and thumb on my chin, as though I was actually giving the idea serious consideration. 'But a photographer has to stay true to his vision. I'm sure you know that better than anyone.'

Bird frowned, nodded.

'I can see that, Danny,' he admitted with visible reluctance. 'Yes, I *can* see that.'

'So, sadly, I'm afraid I'm going to have to pass up on the offer this time.'

Mo's bottom lip began to tremble as though she might be about to burst into tears.

'Which is not to say that she wouldn't be absolutely perfect for future projects,' I added, hastily.

Mo brightened visibly. Bird glanced at her and gave her an encouraging wink.

'See,' he said. 'What did I tell you? Danny thought you were a professional model. Straight up, that's what he asked me. Isn't that right Danny?'

'Absolutely, Trevor.' There was a brief pause, during which I had a brainwave. 'So naturally, Mo, if you'll just supply me with the telephone number of your agency . . .'

'An agency?' Mo looked dismayed. 'I got to be with an *agency*?'

'I'm afraid so. Actually, I'm surprised you're not already with one. I mean, you wouldn't want me to compromise my professional status, would you?'

''Course not,' Bird assured me. 'No, 'course we wouldn't, would we, Mo?'

Mo didn't look so convinced.

'You're saying you can only photograph people who are with an agency?'

'Well, yes, certainly where models are concerned. It's not as if it's a written law or anything, but obviously I have to use the agencies all the time for . . . for specific types. If it came to their attention that I'd been photographing amateurs . . . no matter how good they were . . . they'd probably end up boycotting me. I'm afraid I just couldn't take the risk.'

Bird shook his head, rolled his eyes.

'It's tough at the top,' he observed.

'So how do I go about getting in with an agency?' demanded Mo. I noted that her voice was losing its breathy quality and was getting shriller by the second.

'Easy enough,' I assured her. 'Just take your portfolio around to them. I've got a spare directory of names and addresses at the studio, I'll drop it off with Trevor some time.'

'Nice one,' said Bird. 'And this portfolio . . .?'

'Just a selection of shots in different outfits, different settings. Get one of those clear-leaf binders to put them in. Say, twelve to fifteen of your best efforts?'

'I'll get it sorted,' said Bird, nodding thoughtfully. 'No problemo.' He glanced at Mo. 'We'll get started on it this weekend.' He had a thought. 'Hey, Danny, that's what I could work on when I come to your studio! What do you think?'

'Sure, Trevor. Like I said yesterday, just as soon as this exhibition is finished with. Give me a couple of weeks, OK?' I was feeling magnanimous, now I'd shunted the problem of telling Mo she didn't quite make it into the Cindy Crawford stakes on to some luckless agency director. Not that those people would pull any punches. They'd doubtless give it to her straight; but I couldn't allow myself to worry about that.

I glanced meaningfully at my watch.

'And now, I really must get a move on. The trannies?'

'Oh yeah, got them here for you.' He reached under the counter and withdrew a brown envelope. 'They look pretty good, actually. *Love* what you've done with the lighting. Mind you, that Cassiday character's no oil painting, is he?'

I might have known that Bird would have taken the opportunity to have a good look at the transparencies, but at least he knew enough to keep them in the plastic storage sheets and not get his grubby fingerprints all over them. He obligingly switched on the lightbox set into the counter and handed me an eyeglass. I withdrew the two sheets, placed them on the lightbox and gave them a cursory inspection, just checking that the lighting was OK. Dozens of tiny bearded faces scowled up at me from vivid red backgrounds. They seemed fine but it would be up to Barry Summerby to decide which particular shots would be used.

'I bet *he's* not with an agency,' said Mo, ungraciously.

'That's different,' Bird told her. 'Those are feature shots, aren't they, Danny?'

'Spot on, Trevor.' I slid the transparencies back into their envelope and glancing at the attached invoice, I took out my wallet and paid the bill. I'd include it with my next expenses claim. 'Well, I'd better get up to the *Post*,' I said. 'They'll be waiting for these.'

This wasn't strictly true. The colour mag had a very slow turnaround, an article like this one would be slotted into a chain and probably wouldn't make it to print for weeks yet. But at any rate, it suited me to have them think I was under pressure to meet a deadline. It would at least get me out of range of Mo's basilisk stare and any more awkward questions that she might be cooking up.

'Busy, busy, busy!' observed Bird wistfully. 'Hey, Danny, had any more thoughts on the title of that exhibition. Only I was thinking that—'

'*Skin Flicks*,' I said. 'I'm calling it *Skin Flicks*.'

Bird's reaction was priceless. He just stood there staring at me, his mouth open, one hand raised. I could almost see the counter suggestion frozen on his tongue in mid-utterance.

Mo gave an earthy laugh.

'Sounds like one for the dirty mac brigade!' she said.

I nodded. 'I'll be sure and send you both an invitation,' I retorted; and turning on my heel, I was out of the door before they had time to come up with an appropriate response.

# Chapter Fourteen

It soon became evident that despite all his promises of confidentiality, Geoff Greenhalge had been shooting his big mouth off.

As I pushed through the swing doors into the huge, open-plan office that constitutes the *Evening Post*'s editorial nerve-centre, some wag started humming 'The Funeral March'. I glanced quickly around, trying to identify the culprit but saw only dozens of dishevelled hacks slumped in front of their VDU's, half-heartedly hammering out their respective pieces for the next day's edition.

I walked on along the central aisle in the direction of Barry Summerby's office, a small area separated from the common herd by the strategic placing of acoustic screens. As I stepped into the inner sanctum, I wasn't surprised to see that Geoff Greenhalge was in there with Summerby, the two of them poring over a typescript, which Summerby had liberally marked with red ink. They glanced up at me as I entered, two bearded journos with the sniff of a good story. It was like being appraised by a couple of hungry bloodhounds.

Summerby was a good ten years older than Greenhalge – his hair and beard were iron-grey and his saggy features were a mottled purplish-red colour, the legacy of too many lunches spent slinging back the hard stuff. Both men were in their shirt-sleeves and Summerby had the stub of a cigarette protruding from his lips. Officially, there was a 'no-smoking' policy in the office, but nobody seemed to take a blind bit of notice of it. I think I could count on the fingers of one hand, the journalists I've met who *don't* have the habit and I pitied the luckless non-smoker who got himself employed at the *Post*. Breathing in the muck that passed for air in these quarters was probably equivalent to smoking forty a day.

Summerby appraised me for a moment, his hazel eyes glinting with a spark of mockery. He took the cigarette from his mouth and flicked ash in the general direction of a huge, malodorous ashtray that was absolutely choked with several days' worth of butts.

'Bloody hell,' he said, in his broad Lancashire drawl. 'It's Dr Death.' He paused for a reaction, didn't get one and continued unperturbed. 'We were just talking about you, Danny.'

I stepped warily up to the desk and threw the brown envelope containing the transparencies down in front of him.

'What were you saying about me? Something good I hope.'

'Not exactly. We were wondering when you were going to let us have the full story of your involvement in the Sebastian Kennedy murder.'

I gave Greenhalge a disparaging look.

'So much for your word of honour,' I observed.

'Oh, come on, Danny,' he protested. 'Of course I mentioned it to Barry. He's my *editor*, for God's sake!'

'You don't say.' I indicated the envelope. 'You'd better check those out,' I told Summerby. 'See if they're suitable.'

He frowned, took a last long drag on his cigarette and regretfully ground it into the ashtray. Then he reached into the envelope and pulled out the sheets of trannies. Throwing them on to the lightbox beside his desk, he stared at them blankly.

'Who's this ugly pillock?' he asked ungraciously.

'Philip Cassiday. The horror writer? If you recall, you instructed me to—'

'Yeah, yeah.' He found an eyeglass amidst the debris on his desk and gave them a perfunctory scan. 'What's all that red stuff in the background?' he grumbled. 'Looks like there's been a bloody massacre. And *he* wouldn't give Robert Redford a run for his money, would he? Still, I suppose they'll be all right . . .'

I'd long ago learned that Summerby was incapable of giving anybody a compliment. What he'd just said amounted to a five star review by his standards, so I was quite happy with the verdict.

'We've slotted this in for a couple of weeks time,' he announced. 'I've already got Geoff's copy . . .' He rooted through a pile of dog-eared paper and pulled out a couple of typed sheets, then read the headline aloud. '*Getting Away With Murder.*' He gave Greenhalge a world-weary look.

'I didn't realise how apt the title was till I started reading the book,' said Greenhalge scathingly. 'Load of bloody crap. He gave me a signed copy when we did the interview.'

'Me too.' I felt slightly miffed at this news. I'd thought I was a special case. 'Haven't started mine yet.'

'Don't bother. It's rubbish, I could do better myself.'

This irritated me. People like Greenhalge were always mouthing off about the books they *could* write, if they only had the time. But I'd read enough of Greenhalge's material to know that he was a workmanlike writer at best, lacking the spark of real creativity that sets the best journalists and authors apart from the crowd. Perhaps he was simply bitter. After all, he wasn't getting any younger and he seemed

146

doomed to spend the rest of his working life as an *Evening Post* hack.

'On to other matters,' said Summerby meaningfully.

'What other matters?' I asked – as if I didn't know.

'Geoff tells me you've refused to play ball over this murder business. What's the problem?'

I sighed. 'The problem is a Detective Inspector Flynn, the man leading the investigation. He's told me on more than one occasion that he wants a tight lid kept on the case. He'd be less than pleased to find me shouting my mouth off about the details of the er . . . oh yes, the *Death Skin Horror Victim*.' I gave Greenhalge another contemptuous look.

Summerby scowled. He reached for his cigarettes and lit up a fresh one before continuing.

'Flynn. He's the new face on the squad, isn't he?' He looked at Greenhalge. 'You've met him?'

'Yeah, he was at the press conference yesterday. Bit of a nancy-boy if you ask me.'

'Nobody asked you!' I snapped; and was vaguely surprised by the venom in my voice. The two men gave me puzzled looks.

'Well, we've no worries on that score,' Summerby assured me. 'I'll handle any flak that comes from his direction.'

'It's not just that,' I protested. 'I . . . well, this might surprise you but I actually don't like talking about it, you know?'

This sounded distinctly weedy, but I could hardly tell them the real reason for my reluctance – that in a couple of weeks time, I would be exhibiting photographs of the body and I didn't want anything to upstage that event, or lessen its potential impact. 'I'm . . . I'm still in shock,' I concluded.

'We appreciate that, Danny,' said Summerby. 'It couldn't have been very pleasant for you – but you know, most therapists agree that talking through an event like that is the best way to come to terms with it.'

I stared at him. I could scarcely credit that Barry Summerby, hard-bitten, chain-smoking editor-about-town was attempting to give me his crap, Claire Rayner routine. I treated it with the contempt it so obviously deserved.

'Do me a favour,' I said. 'You'll be offering me counselling next.'

'Geoff here would be handling the story,' continued Summerby, totally unphased by my remark. 'He'd treat the matter with his customary subtlety.'

'Subtlety?' Now I really did feel like laughing out loud. 'He's about as subtle as a car crash! Come on, Barry, all you're interested in is a sordid, slice n' dice horror story and I'm not prepared to give it to you. Unless, of course, you want to offer me an obscenely large payout in return for the goods . . .'

Summerby actually had the cheek to look insulted.

'The *Post* has never been associated with cheque-book journalism,' he assured me. 'And I've no intention of changing that position. Frankly, Danny, I'm surprised at you, making such a suggestion.'

I shrugged.

'Life can be hard for a freelancer,' I explained.

'You want to be careful it doesn't get any bloody harder.'

'What's that supposed to mean?'

'Simply that you're not the only photographer in town. You depend on the *Post* for a living, Danny. It would be bad news if I stopped dialling your number, wouldn't it?'

I studied him for a moment. I didn't think he was entirely serious about the implied threat but I couldn't be one hundred per cent certain. At any rate, he was doing his level best to look like a ruthless news-hound, all gimlet-eyed and lantern-jawed.

'Oh, come on, Barry,' I pleaded. 'You don't mean that. Besides, where would you find another one like me, eh?'

He didn't crack a smile.

'All I know, Danny, is that one of my employees is holding out on me – and I'd like to see a little more loyalty to the hand that feeds him, that's all.'

'Maybe he's already sold the story to another paper,' said Greenhalge suspiciously; and unwittingly, he handed me a possible way out of the situation. I slapped a suitably sheepish expression on my face.

'I didn't want to tell you,' I said. 'Geoff's right. I've already sold the exclusive story to one of the national tabloids. I'm not allowed to speak to anyone else about it.'

Summerby glared at me for a moment in stoney silence. Then a big smile spread itself across his grizzled face.

'Why on earth didn't you say so before? That's a different matter entirely.' This was something he could understand only too well. A better offer. 'Congratulations, lad. How much did you get?'

'Er . . . an undisclosed sum,' I replied. 'Let's just say it'll pay off a few of my debts.'

Greenhalge seemed less easily pacified.

'Which tabloid was this?' he wanted to know.

'I'm er . . . not at liberty to say, I'm afraid.'

'And how did they get on to it so fast? If Flynn's keeping such a tight lid on it, how—'

'Obvious, isn't it?' Summerby interrupted him. 'Danny contacted *them*.' He looked at me. 'Am I right or am I right?'

'It's a fair cop,' I said, going along with the cheery, 'all lad's together' routine. 'Well, a bloke's got to live, hasn't he?'

'Nice one, Danny. Good reporter's instincts. I'm glad to see that some of it is rubbing off.' Summerby was clearly happy enough now he believed that *somebody* would be making use of the story. I'd have to deal with its eventual non-appearance in the tabloids at a later date.

It was at this moment that it occurred to me that here was a stunt I could actually pull off, if I chose to. There were various new agencies in the city that could doubtless drum up large amounts from *The Sun* or *The Mirror* for a story as lurid as this one. But almost instantly I rejected the idea. It wasn't that I was looking for a sainthood or anything like that, but I really wouldn't have felt right making money that way. The exhibition was something I could just about square with my conscience.

That thought led me to make another decision, something I was going to have to explain to Spinetti, later that day. He wasn't going to like it very much but I'd cross that bridge when I came to it.

I could see that Greenhalge still wasn't happy about this latest turn of events. What he'd perceived as a potential scoop, was slipping through his fingers like hot margarine and he didn't like it one little bit.

'Couldn't I still do something with the story?' he asked his boss. 'I had some great ideas.'

'You heard what Danny said. An *exclusive*, he gave them. So forget about that and concentrate on our Mexican friends instead.' He tapped the sheet of paper he'd been so busy editing when I arrived. 'Make the changes and lose two hundred words.'

I perked up at the mention of this.

'What's happening with the Mexicans?' I asked. 'Only there was this one woman I was talking to yesterday . . .'

'Yes, I remember,' said Greenhalge, nodding approvingly. 'Stacked, she was.' He leered gleefully at Summerby. 'Danny started giving her some crap about what a beautiful country

Mexico was. Then she tells him she's from Stockport. I nearly bust a gut laughing at him.'

'I'm glad I amuse you,' I said drily. 'Only I don't suppose you'd know where I could get her address or phone number? I wouldn't mind getting in touch with her again. I asked around at the reception but nobody there seemed to know who she was. Her name's Moreno. Julia Moreno. And before you ask, I've looked in the phone directory.'

Greenhalge frowned, rubbed his chin.

'I don't see why I should help,' he muttered. 'Whisking a shit hot story out from under me like that.'

'Oh, come on, Geoff. Look, I'll buy you a pint sometime, how would that be?'

He sighed, shrugged.

'Well, OK. I've got a sly copy of the electoral register in my desk. She looked old enough to vote. Walk this way, I'll see what I can do.'

We left Barry Summerby to his own devices and moved across the office to the grubby, littered surface of Greenhalge's desk. From between two mountains of crumpled paper and tattered box files, his VDU cowered like a citadel under seige. Pulling open the large bottom drawer, he withdrew a couple of thick computer print-outs and selected the one headed Stockport MBC. He found the M's and traced a stubby forefinger down the list of names – but there were no Moreno's listed.

'Odd,' muttered Greenhalge. 'Maybe she only just moved into the area.'

'No, she told me she'd lived in Stockport since she was a kid. She left Chile when the Pinochet thing was going on. That was in the seventies wasn't it?'

Greenhalge shrugged. 'Well, maybe she gave you a fake name.'

151

'Why would she do that?' I countered indignantly. 'We were getting on like a house on fire.'

'Yeah? She didn't look so keen to me, mate. Anyway, the solution's simple enough, isn't it? She was at the launch of the Mexican festival, right? So . . .' He handed me a copy of the festival programme. 'Get down to as many events as you can manage and you're sure to run into her sooner or later.'

I scowled as I glanced down the list of events. Rock bands, jugglers, musicians, mime-artists . . . who had the time to take in that much culture? I reminded myself that she'd said that she might come to my exhibition. Maybe I was just going to have to be a bit patient about this.

Glancing at my watch, I saw that time was moving on and there were still two more visits to make today. I asked Greenhalge to keep an eye open for my mysterious Latin lady and headed for the exits.

Out on the street, I got to my car seconds before the parking meter clicked into the overdue zone. A portly, female traffic warden who'd been hovering nearby, simply *itching* to slap a ticket on my windscreen, was incapable of keeping the look of disappointment off her face. Cheered by this tiny victory, I climbed into my car, started the engine and drove out on to Deansgate, telling myself that maybe my luck was improving.

Then I headed back into town for my appointment with Vincent Spinetti.

# Chapter Fifteen

Spinetti's office was situated on the upper floor of a scruffy, Victorian red-brick building off Portland Street. A brief glimpse into the gloomy dilapidated lobby gave the impression that it had been long deserted; and only an eagle eye would have noticed the faded plaque beside the open door announcing that 'Spin International Productions' could be found up on the first floor.

I'd long since given up suggesting that a spot of redecoration was in order. Spinetti always told me that the rent here was peanuts, precisely *because* the place was such a shithole. Do it up and the landlord would have no hesitation in doubling or even trebling the monthly tariff. Besides, Spinetti had no interest in attracting passing trade. People knew of his reputation and sought him out regardless of his surroundings.

Tramping up the worn wooden staircase (the ancient elevator seemed to be permanently out of order) I reflected that he could at least engage the services of a cleaner, every now and again. The floors were covered with a thick layer of dust, the windows so grime-encrusted that they barely admitted any light. Spectacular festoons of cobwebs hung from the more inaccessible corners.

Up on the first floor, the windows had at least been

cleaned in the past few months and my nostrils caught the appetising aroma of fresh brewed coffee; but there was also the sound of voices raised in disagreement. I quickly recognised Spinetti's voice, interspersed with the shrill tones of his personal assistant, Juliet Fleming. It didn't take a genius to deduct that she was pissed off about something.

'You bastard!' I heard her say. 'You promised me *today*.'

'Calm down, Jools. Let me explain. It's just a temporary hiccup.' Spinetti was using the calm, placatory tone I'd heard him use so often, only today, it didn't seem to be working.

'You seem to forget, I've got a bloody mortgage to pay. And I like to *eat* occasionally, you know? Now I've waited a whole bloody month, you can't just turn around and—'

'Jools, Jools, a couple of days more, that's all I'm asking. It's a cash-flow thing.'

'No, Vincent, a *rip-off* thing is what it is! I can't believe that I was dumb enough to fall for this. And then to find out what you actually wanted it for . . . my God, Vincent, you've pulled some low tricks in your time, but this . . .'

'Oh, Jools, now you know you don't mean that! Look, supposing I just came up with fifty notes to tide you over? Just till say, Saturday? What do you say?'

'I say fuck off, you scheister! I'm not letting you screw me around like this any longer!'

'Jools . . .'

'No, no, no, no, no!'

I walked through the outer reception, past Juliet's desk and tapped my knuckles on the open door of Spinetti's office. I leaned warily into the room, ready to duck if anything was thrown in my direction. Altercations between Spinetti and Juliet were nothing new, though they didn't normally reach this level of intensity.

'If it's a bad time, I'll call again,' I mumbled sheepishly.

They both turned to look at me. Juliet, a tall rangy blonde in her late twenties, dressed in a houndstooth check Jaeger suit, was standing beside the filing cabinets, her hands on her lean hips. She regarded me with all the apparent pleasure of somebody who had just seen a large cockroach step out of her bowl of corn flakes. Spinetti, who was sitting at his desk, at least seemed pleased to see me, probably because he thought of me as the seventh cavalry riding to his rescue.

'Danny-boy,' he said, beckoning eagerly. 'Come in, come in, have a seat. Juliet and I were just discussing a . . . business matter.'

She rounded on him.

'Correction,' she snarled. 'I was just telling you what a low-down, conniving bastard you are. I was just handing in my fucking *resignation*! You can send on what you owe me, because I'm not working for you ever again. Not ever! Understand?'

I slunk silently to the vacant seat and did my utmost to merge with the decor. Spinetti, meanwhile, tried to defuse the situation with a shrill laugh. It was probably intended to convey to me that he wasn't taking her threat entirely seriously, but under the circumstances, it merely came across as hysteria.

'Jools, I've *explained* how it is. There's this thing called "the recession", right, and—'

'There's also this thing called the "Vice Squad!" You want to consider that before you invest any more of your employee's money in dodgy deals!'

'You've got this all wrong. It's cash-flow, happens all the time. I temporarily over-extended myself and—'

'Over-extend yourself on this,' suggested Juliet, holding up the middle finger of her right hand in a rather rude gesture. 'And *rotate*,' she added, for good measure. Then she

155

turned on her heel and strode out of the door.

'Juliet, if you could just see how ridiculous you look!' Spinetti shouted after her. I could tell it was serious now, because he was no longer calling her 'Jools'. 'You walk out now and I'll be forced to take your resignation *seriously*!'

'Take it any way you like,' she shouted back. 'Take it up your arse, sideways, for all I care. I'm out of here!' Grabbing her handbag from beside her desk, she went out of the reception, slamming the door so hard that the square of frosted glass shattered and fell to the floor. Spinetti winced. Then he looked at me and gave me a sly wink.

'She doesn't mean it,' he said. 'She'll be back here in ten minutes. She always comes back.'

I looked at him doubtfully.

'It seemed pretty serious, this time,' I observed. 'What was it all about?'

Spinetti sighed, rolled his eyes to the ceiling.

'Money, what else?' He nodded to the coffee percolator, bubbling away on the filing cabinet beside his desk. 'Care for a cup?' he asked me.

I nodded and he got up from the desk to do the honours. I watched his pathetic attempts to construct a couple of mugs of coffee. Everything he needed was on the tray in front of him – mugs, spoons, sugar, milk – but he still managed to make a pig's ear of it, scattering sugar all over the place, slopping milk into the tray. God help Spinetti if Juliet didn't come back. As he fumbled, he outlined to me his version of what had happened.

'Things were tight last month. Something came up that I had to invest a lot of capital in. Consequently, I was obliged to ask Juliet to forego that month's wages.'

'Christ!' I could imagine with what unbounded joy such a suggestion would be greeted.

'I promised her I'd have the money today. With, I might add, a healthy bonus for her trouble. Only there's been a bit of a hold-up on that front – and what money I *did* have in the float went straight to the printers for the *Skin Flicks* posters . . .'

I groaned. No wonder Juliet had looked at me that way. I was probably lucky she hadn't embedded an axe in my skull.

'So you told her that it was *my* fault she couldn't have her money?' I muttered.

'No, not in so many words.' He considered for a moment. 'Well, sort of. I mean, the whole thing's a joke anyway. In a couple of days' time I'll have the money to pay her back, with interest. She just over-reacted.'

He finally set a mug of coffee down in front of me and I sipped at it experimentally. Coffee with milk seemed, somehow, a real luxury. I'd almost forgotten what it tasted like.

'And what was all that about the Vice Squad?' I asked.

'Oh, that.' He frowned, stirred his coffee thoughtfully. 'Well, that's who I needed the money for in the first place. The Vice Squad needed a demo video and I had to pay up front for it. Not to mention the cost of the recording studio . . .'

'What?' For an instant, I had this image in my head of a bunch of scowling, plain clothes coppers making a demonstration video entitled 'How To Apprehend Villains'. Then the penny dropped. 'They're a *rock band*!' I said.

'Well, of course, what did you . . .?' He saw what I'd been thinking and laughed delightedly, shook his head. 'No, you prannit, they're a roots reggae band with a really strong vocalist. Best voice since Bob Marley, I kid you not. They're going to be *big*. Only Juliet doesn't quite see it.'

I nodded, remembering that Juliet, in her first flush of enthusiasm as Spinetti's PA, had been talked into investing a substantial sum of her savings into the career of William K. I wasn't sure if Spinetti had ever got around to paying her back on that deal. Probably, she was still waiting for sales of William K's first CD to bring home the bacon. She didn't want to hold her breath; so far, it hadn't sold more than a couple of rashers.

'She sees the Vice Squad as a cult thing,' continued Spinetti. 'You know, kind of band that attracts big live audiences but does zilch on CD. So she's mad that I sunk so much money into them. She'll calm down a bit when they take off.'

'When are they playing next?' I asked him. 'I'll check 'em out, tell you what I think.'

'That could be a problem. They're not playing anywhere until I set up a deal for them. Pity though, I do trust your judgement on these matters. Speaking of which . . . tell me about Sepulchre.'

I glanced at him warily.

'Spike's band,' I said. 'He told me he'd sent you a demo.'

'Yeah. I only listened to a couple of tracks. Right bloody row, sounded like it'd been recorded live on a demolition site.'

'They are kind of loud,' I admitted. 'They've got quite a following though. Very dedicated crowd.'

'Yeah?' Spinetti immediately seemed more interested. 'They've invited me to this gig they're doing at the Mandrake. Think I should go?'

'Well, *I'm* going to be there,' I said evasively. 'I'm doing some "in concert" photographs for them. Hope it turns out OK, their gigs can be pretty wild.'

'Hmm.' Spinetti frowned. 'Well, maybe I should go and check them out. I don't have any heavy metal bands on my roster, yet.'

'*Death* metal,' I corrected him. 'There's a difference.' I glanced at my watch. 'Vincent, I don't want to seem pushy . . .'

'Oh yeah, sorry, I forgot.' He leaned down behind his desk and rummaged for a moment, then pulled out a large sheet of presentation board. He rested it on the edge of his desk and took hold of the cover paper between thumb and forefinger; but he hesitated theatrically and shot me a warning look.

'Now Danny, I want you to rid yourself of all preconceptions, OK? Open yourself up to this experience and appreciate the impact of it, right?'

'Right,' I said; but already I felt a sense of unease settle over me. Spinetti only ever employed such preambles when he anticipated strong opposition. 'Ready?' he asked me.

I nodded.

He hesitated a moment longer, then whipped the cover quickly upwards.

'Ta-daaa!' he said.

'Jesus Christ,' I said.

'What?'

'No.'

'Aww, Danny . . .'

'NO!'

It looked really sleazy. There's no other way to describe it. The poster was a grainy black and white photograph of the corner of a room, bare wooden floorboards littered with rubble and cigarette ends and what looked suspiciously like a couple of used condoms. Jutting into the picture was the corner of a stained old mattress that was laid out on the floor and reclining on the mattress was a piece of human flesh. I use the word 'piece' because the way it was photographed, it was impossible to identify the area of the anatomy in question. The photographer had gone close in on the bend of

159

a joint, I think – probably nothing more innocuous than the fold of skin around an elbow or a knee. But there was something incredibly lewd about the image that suggested it might just as easily have been a buttock or a crutch shot. Tattooed into the flesh in crude, black, amateurish letters were the words, *Skin Flicks. Photographs by Danny Weston*. Beneath this in smaller letters were the various other necessary details; dates, location, times. As an image it was undeniably powerful. But it seemed to be promising something decidedly unsavoury. OK, maybe photographs of a dead body wasn't the nicest subject matter in the world, but they only made up part of the exhibition. This poster seemed to be offering an exclusive opportunity to wallow in a photographic cess-pit.

'You don't like it,' observed Spinetti perceptively.

'I *hate* it,' I assured him.

'But why? It's the kind of image you'd cross the road to have a look at.'

'That may be so,' I admitted. 'But for all the wrong reasons.'

'What do the reasons matter? Provided it gets people's asses into the gallery.'

'But what would they be expecting after seeing that?' I asked, stabbing an accusing finger at the artwork. 'A good relief-massage, I should think.'

'Oh, for Christ's sake! Look, have you any idea how much it cost me to get this done at such short notice?'

'Well, that's OK. *I'll* do some posters and I won't charge you a penny for the work. How about that?'

He looked evasive.

'It's nice of you to offer, Danny but . . . well, for one thing, you won't have the time. You'll be too busy getting the actual exhibition together. And for another . . .'

'Yes?'

'The guy who did this works for a big ad agency. He moonlighted on this job. He knows about pulling the crowds in. This image will do that, I'd bet my best pair of Timberlands on it. Now, if *you* did the poster, I'm sure you'd do something good, naturally, but I doubt if it would be as *commercial*.'

'Thanks for the vote of confidence!' I snarled.

'Oh, come on, Danny! Look, I hate to come over all crass and bread-headed on you, but I've sunk a lot of money into this gig. By the time you add up the artwork and printing costs, the refreshments on the night, I'm going to be several thousand pounds worse off . . .'

'Yes, but hopefully, we'll sell some photographs, maybe get some commissions . . .'

Spinetti smiled, playing the role of Mr Reasonable to the hilt. 'Exactly my point. To recoup my investment, we'll need to sell a *lot* of work. Hence, I need to get as many punters through those doors as possible. *Ergo* . . .' He patted the poster lovingly. 'We go with this design.' He paused for a moment, then added. 'Besides, this is just a colour copy. The real artwork's already gone to the printer.'

This news was particularly galling.

'It beats me why you bothered to ask my opinion in the first place. You'd obviously decided to ignore whatever I said!'

'Don't be like that, Danny! Look, let's have some lunch and talk it over, what do you say?'

I scowled.

'You needn't think you can get round me with a flash meal,' I warned him.

'No chance of that,' he told me. 'With Juliet gone, I can't leave the office. Now let me see . . .' He leaned over and rummaged in a cardboard box at his feet. He came out with what looked like a couple of Cornish pasties in sealed plastic bags. He glanced at the instructions, swivelled in his chair to face the microwave oven on the filing cabinet behind him and slapped the pies on to the turntable. 'I keep these for emergencies,' he explained. 'Don't worry, they're long-life.'

I made a face.

'I'm not hungry,' I said. I was just saying this really, but when the office began to fill up with a foul, greasy aroma, I decided that the instinct had been a good one. Spinetti didn't seem to mind it though. He was concentrating all his energies on placating me.

'I know you think this is being foisted on you,' he said. 'And it's a drag when financial considerations have to come before aesthetic ones . . . but I honestly do feel that this decision will advance your career, no end. I mean, ultimately, we want the same thing. To see you up there with the big names in photography. Now you can plug away, year after year, gradually acquiring a reputation by word of mouth . . . or you can hit the "boost" button and take the fast lane, get there before you're staggering about with a zimmer frame. Up to you, mate.'

I glared at him. Spinetti had the knack of making everything sound so logical.

'That's just my point,' I argued. 'It's not up to me, is it? You've already made the decision on my behalf. It's the fast lane and God help us if we run into anything on the way.'

'Such as?'

I shrugged. 'Bad reviews,' I suggested.

'Bad reviews would be great for us,' he countered. 'The more scathing, the more outraged, the better. Nothing's more guaranteed to bring in the punters! Good reviews are quite useful too. But what we don't want are mediocre ones and somehow, I don't think we'll see many of those.'

The microwave pinged as if to add an exclamation mark to his sentence. Spinetti opened the door and lifted the perspex plate out of the interior. He set two steaming parcels down between us.

'Sure you won't have one?' he asked me.

'Positive. They look like they should be taken out and given a decent burial.'

I watched as he gingerly tore open one of the plastic packages and slid the pie back on to the plate. Its cardboard-like pastry had ruptured in the middle and a greyish brown blob of scalding sludge was oozing out of it. He picked up the pie in his long fingers and took an exploratory bite. He then went into a pantomime, waving one hand in front of his open mouth, whilst flipping the lump of food around with his tongue in a clumsy attempt to avoid serious burns. It struck me that if any of his ultra-cool clients ever got to see him like this, his credibility rating would plummet over night.

He pushed the plate aside and left it to cool for a while.

'How are things progressing at your end?' he asked. He appeared to have dismissed the subject of the posters, so I could only assume that there was no point in returning to it.

'I got some shots of your tattooed friend this morning.'

'He's not *my* friend!' said Spinetti, rather too quickly I thought. 'I don't even know him.'

'Oh, but I thought you said . . .'

'Just somebody I've seen dancing at Adonis. I don't know him from Adam. Turn out all right did they? The photographs?'

'I think so. Haven't had a chance to develop them yet. He was quite a find though. Tattooed from head to foot. Incredible piece of work.'

'Excellent. And what about pierced skin?'

'Well, this guy told me about a place in the Wheat Exchange that does body-piercing. I've got some free time tomorrow, I thought I might call in there, see if I can scare anything up.'

'Good man. Here, check this out!' He pulled a typed sheet from his 'IN' tray and threw it down in front of me.

'What is it?' I asked suspiciously.

'It's the people I'm inviting to the exhibition.'

I glanced down the list. All the familiar names were there: the 'unlikely' big shots – *Granada TV, BBC TV, The Guardian, The Times* – plus the more accessible local media – *Metrosound Radio, GMR, The Evening Post, Metro Magazine*. Then there were other names that stepped off into the faintly surreal. *New Musical Express? Vogue?* 'Fuck me, *Woman's Own*?' I looked at Spinetti over the top of the paper.

'OK, so it's a long shot,' he admitted. 'But if we can get them to do a "this isn't art, this is exploitation" kind of piece, we'll be laughing.'

'I really don't think that many art freaks spend their time perusing the pages of *Woman's Own*,' I muttered.

'Danny, I'm trying to explain to you, we're not just after art freaks! We want your work to get in the faces of as wide an audience as possible, right? That means dragging in Mr Ordinary and his wife, if only to get them to shout the odds about how disgusting it all is. And when they see what you've got on display, react they will. They'll be foaming at the mouth with indignation, right?'

'Right . . .'

'So they'll denounce you, call you the most evil man since Rasputin. They'll form protest groups, write stiff letters to *The Times*, they may even – if we're lucky – throw rotten eggs at your photographs. Now, the more they protest, the more all your free-thinking, trendy liberals will leap to your defence, cheque books in hand. And the closer *you* get to giving up your day job.'

I laughed, shook my head.

'You've got it all figured out, haven't you?'

''Course I have. That's my job.' He lifted the meat pie from the plate again and took a huge, wolfish bite, scattering flakes of pastry all over his desk. I looked at him and my heart was heavy. To say I had major misgivings about the whole project would have been the understatement of the century. I was by now convinced that we were headed for disaster. But like some determined cowboy who had unwittingly climbed aboard the wildest, meanest bronco at the rodeo, it seemed to me that I had no other option than to hang on tight and hope for the best. There was however one thing I could still do. I'd been putting the announcement off but now it was time to deliver my bombshell.

'Vincent, I made a decision this morning.'

'Oh yes?' He eyed me warily, sensing my determination. 'What's that?'

'The photographs of the corpse. They aren't going to be for sale. I'll show them, of course, but that's all. I don't want to be accused of profiting directly from them. Now, you can argue as much as you like, but my mind's made up on this and I'm not going to budge.'

I crossed my arms defiantly and waited for his protests. He considered what I'd said for a moment, his jaws working as he chewed a mouthful of pie. Then he nodded.

'Absolutely,' he said.

I stared at him.

'You . . . you agree?'

'Of course. I'm not a total monster, you know? I must admit, the idea had already crossed my mind. It would be in very poor taste to offer pictures like that for sale. I'm sure there'd be enough freaks out there who'd buy them, but . . . yeah, no problem.' He seemed to dismiss the idea. 'What you got planned for this evening?' he asked me. 'Friend of mine's opening a new curry house in Rusholme. I could wangle you a free dinner if you like.'

I shook my head.

'I've already got a date,' I told him.

He waggled his eyebrows at me.

'A date?' he echoed. Then added, disbelievingly. 'A woman?'

'Naturally a woman!' I retorted. I was beginning to get a complex about this. Did the idea seem *so* unbelievable?

'Anybody I know?'

I shook my head, glanced at my watch.

'I ought to be on my way,' I said. 'She'll be expecting me.'

'At *this* time?' Spinetti was clearly intrigued. 'An early afternoon appointment with a mysterious woman, eh? Must be serious.'

'As serious as it gets,' I assured him. I got up from my seat and headed for the door. 'See you later,' I said.

'Danny, about the posters,' he shouted after me. 'You do like them a little bit, don't you?'

'They're shit,' I called back over my shoulder. 'I hate them.'

'Yeah, see, I *knew* you'd come round to the idea.'

That was the thing about Spinetti. He got an idea in his head and nothing ever budged him from it. I was lucky he'd agreed with me about not selling the corpse-pictures other-wise we'd be arguing the toss for hours. Anyway, it was in the lap of the gods now. Maybe he had it all figured and it would go exactly as he envisaged, smooth as mousse through a goose. And maybe I would end up as the name on everyone's tongue.

I descended to the street, got back into my car and headed out on to Oxford Road, already running fifteen minutes late for my next assignment.

# Chapter Sixteen

I drove on to the Merton Estate with a healthy amount of trepidation. This ramshackle housing estate in the heart of Moss Side had never enjoyed a good reputation but over the last couple of years its status had sunk even lower, until it now enjoyed the kind of kudos more readily associated with places beset by war.

On the estate, crack-cocaine was now the main currency – and gangs of teenage 'bloods' fought regular battles for their respective areas of turf. Some six months back, a vicious shoot-out in a deserted flat had left several people lying dead, the youngest of them a kid of ten, who in a better world would have been out happily playing 'tag' with his mates.

Leaving a car parked in this neck of the woods – even a battered old knacker like mine – was tantamount to an invitation to steal it. The chances of spotting a policeman to whom you might report such a theft were remote indeed. The forces of law and order it seemed, had washed their hands of the Merton Estate, preferring instead to concentrate on keeping everything neatly corralled here, away from Manchester's more genteel neighbourhoods. Which was, of course, bad news for the decent law-abiding residents who still lived on the estate – one of whom just happened to be my mother.

I drew the car to a halt and sat for a moment, watching in disbelief as a couple of teenagers broke into a brand new Toyota Corolla that some maniac had decided to leave unattended. As they smashed a side window, the car's state-of-the-art alarm system kicked up an infernal trilling noise, but it didn't seem to deter the kids. One of them leaned in at the broken window and with the use of a shaped piece of metal and a casual flick of his wrist, relieved the car of its cassette player. He tucked it under his arm and walked off with it, looking for all the world like he was out for a casual stroll. He winked and grinned at me as he went by. A moment later his mate hurried after him with the stereo speakers, neatly jemmied from the back window ledge.

I told myself that the blaring alarm might at least offer my jalopy some protection, but I took all the camera equipment out of the boot and carried it with me, as I walked towards the squat, ugly, three story plaza where my mother's flat was situated. I always intended to visit her once or twice a month but for a variety of reasons, I rarely managed to keep to that schedule and inevitably, I ended up riddled with guilt because of this.

My father had been dead nearly five years now. Mother was seventy years old and not in the best of health. I'd spent most of the last five years trying to persuade her to move to a better neighbourhood. It wasn't that she couldn't afford it or anything; Dad's life policy had left her comfortably well off. But she'd lived on the estate for over twenty years, her few friends were also here and she didn't see why she should change her ways so late in life. The seemingly endless procession of pensioners on the estate who were systematically burgled, robbed or sometimes even murdered, phased her not one jot. This was her home and nobody was going to push her out of it. The only way she'd leave, she was fond of telling me, was feet first.

As you can imagine, this did no favours for my peace of mind. One of my enduring regrets was that I had failed to communicate well with my father. I had only just been getting to know him when he succumbed to a sudden and totally unexpected coronary, which had killed him in a matter of seconds. Now, I feared the sudden loss of my mother, not from a heart attack, but at the hands of some cracked-up little thug who had decided she might have money tucked under her mattress.

I moved in through a graffiti-sprayed archway and angled left to climb the stone steps beyond. Three black teenage youths were hanging out on the stairs, smoking cigarettes and waiting for something to turn up. They eyed my camera case with open interest as I moved past. I tried not to look at them too closely, not wanting to antagonise them and I thought what a shit world it was, when a grown man could find himself afraid of three bits of kids. But I knew only too well what such kids could do when they put their mind to it. A photographer friend of mine, Alan Richards, out scouting location photographs for a fashion shoot some six months back, had lost most of one ear, plus his favourite Nikon, when two kids on mountain bikes had hit him in a lightning raid. Remembering this, my fist tightened on the handle of the metal case and I told myself that if they came at me, I'd swing it straight at their heads, then run like hell . . .

Nothing happened. Maybe they sensed my intentions, maybe they just couldn't be bothered. At any rate, I made it to the top of the stairs and moved along the first floor walkway beyond. I stopped outside the door of my mother's flat and saw with a jolt of anxiety that it had been left slightly ajar. I reached out a hand, pushed it open and stepped into the hallway beyond.

'Mum?' I shouted. 'Mum, you all right?'

Silence. I examined the door, saw that the catch had been left on the 'sneck'. I released it and closed the door. Then I moved slowly along the hallway to the sitting room.

'Mum?' I called again. 'Are you here?'

I reached out to the handle of the door, aware now of a curious rhythmic 'popping' noise from within. I turned the handle and fearfully, I pushed the door open. I did it very slowly, afraid of what I might see in there.

Mum was sitting in her favourite chair, wearing her Walkman headphones. Her small grey head was moving from side to side and I realised that the popping was the sound of the drum-track on the cassette she was listening to. Judging by the level of noise, she must have had the damned thing cranked up to full volume. I set down my equipment case and moved slowly across the room into her line of vision, not wanting to startle her. But she just smiled at me and nodded, as though I'd been there all along.

'Hello dear!' she shrieked, over the volume of the music. 'I thought I was due another visit!'

I winced and reached down to turn off the Walkman. I kissed her on the cheek and pushed the earphones down around her neck.

'What on earth are you listening to?' I asked her. 'That didn't sound like Barry Manilow.'

'Oh, I'm getting a bit fed up with him. This is Septic Culture or something . . . you know, your friend Spike's group? He left it with me last time you were both here.'

'Right. I wouldn't have thought it was your cup of tea.'

'Oh, it's really rather *jolly*. Very rhythmic. Can't quite make out any of Spike's words though.'

171

*Probably just as well*, I thought. Mum was incredibly broad-minded for someone her age, but even *she* would have drawn the line at Spike's relentless diet of death, drugs, mutilation and fornication. At least, I *hoped* she would.

She was smiling up at me now, big blue eyes magnified by her powerful bi-focals and they were the eyes of a nine-year-old child, totally out of place in that aged face.

'You left the door open,' I chided her.

'Did I? Are you sure? Oh dear. Well, we'll have a nice cup of tea, shall we?'

'Stop trying to get round me. What have I told you before about securing all the doors and windows? There are *bad* people out there, Mum. It's like an open invitation to them.'

'Yes, dear, I'm sure. Now then . . .' She was getting her frail body up out of the chair, supporting herself with the walking stick she'd used ever since her hip started playing up.

'No, you stay there, *I'll* make the tea.'

'You will *not*!' she said indignantly. 'The day I can't make a cup of tea for a guest, they can dig a big hole and drop me in.'

'Don't talk like that,' I said. I followed her as she shambled determinedly towards the kitchen. At various times I'd tried to talk her into having a hip replacement operation, but such suggestions were always met with hoots of derision. 'A hip replacement at *my* time of life? Don't be silly, dear. These old bones will see me to the end of the road, don't you worry!'

Eventually we made it into the malodorous little cubby hole that was her kitchen. It wasn't her fault, she did her level best to keep it clean, but maintenance on these council-owned properties was little more than a rumour. Damp, rot and poor workmanship had taken their inevitable toll since Dad's death. He'd been a keen handyman, able to take all but the most serious problems in his stride. Needless to say, I'd inherited none of his prowess in that department; and Mum steadfastly refused to hire professionals to take care of the various shortcomings, insisting that it was the city council's responsibility and that we would simply be letting them off the hook.

This was all well and good, but it meant that she ended up living in a piss-hole and I lost sleep over the potential health-risks. I'd long nurtured a fantasy in which I won two million pounds on the football pools (unlikely, since I don't even *do* them) and bought Mum a pretty little cottage in the countryside, complete with cook, cleaner and gardener. Only even in a fantasy, Mum turned out to be stubborn. After a cursory inspection of her dream home, she would shake her head and instruct me to drive her back to her own place. That's how bad things were; I couldn't even *dream* without encountering serious opposition. What were the chances of bringing it off in reality?

I stood with my back against the rotting kitchen units and watched as Mum prepared two cups of tea. I cringed inwardly every time she slopped boiling water from the kettle in all directions. I was reminded of a similar experience back at Spinetti's office, the same clumsy hands, scattering granules of sugar and spilling the milk. But Mum was seventy years old, what was Spinetti's excuse? At last she had the two cups and saucers and the obligatory packet of digestives arranged on a tray and she allowed me to carry them back into the living room. We settled down in our armchairs to chew the fat.

'What've you been up to since I saw you last?' I asked her.

'Well, let me see now . . .' She thought for a moment, then began. 'Mrs Roberts has had a fall. Broken femur, the doctor said, she'll be in hospital for quite some time it seems. Them below have been fighting again. They started up on Sunday morning. Well, you've never heard anything like it, Daniel, the language! Between you and me, I think she's back on drugs and he's never out of the pub. It's the children I feel sorry for.' *Pause, sip of tea.* 'Poor old Jack Walters has had another stroke, the ambulance came for him late one night, we all heard the siren. I shouldn't think we'll be seeing him again, not after the last one being so severe. The young Brannigan lad got himself arrested, seems he was involved in a fight outside a nightclub in town and stabbed another youngster. Mrs Brannigan is heartbroken, she can't figure out where she went wrong. I told her, don't blame yourself, it's this flipping government! People who'd put VAT on fuel bills are capable of anything . . .' *Pause, another sip of tea.* 'Old Mrs Byrne is having trouble with her bowels again. She tries to hide it from everyone but her bedroom's right above mine and some nights, the *smell* . . .'

I sat there entranced, listening as she recounted her endless litany of sorrows. I supposed that it was the same for most people her age. Her daily experiences were largely negative ones; illness, accidents, mortalities. And naturally she talked about them, there was little else she *could* talk about, these were the events that filled her days. But somehow she managed to retain her own good humour in the face of such adversity. I doubted that I could do the same in a similar situation.

Finally, she came to the end of her current crop of disasters. She paused for breath and another sip of tea.

'And what about you, dear? What have you been up to?'

'I've been preparing for my exhibition. You remember, I mentioned it?'

'Oh, yes, I was telling Mrs Brannigan about that. Thought

it might take her mind off her Derek. The Pledge, I told her. She said she'd have to try and look in. I'm really looking forward to it.'

Now there was something I hadn't even thought about. Picture the scene if you will. You escort your frail, elderly mother out of the taxi cab and in through the imposing glass doors of The Wedge. You take her arm and help her up the marble steps to the gallery. She looks at the pictures of old age pensioners and likes them well enough, maybe even sees a few faces she recognises. And then she points to the partitioned-off central area, from which shocked-looking people are emerging.

'What's in there?' she asks innocently.

'Oh, that's just some photographs of a flayed corpse, Mum. Wanna take a look?'

No, that was going to be a bad moment, all right. In my impetuous rush to gain notoriety, I'd overlooked yet another potential thorn in the flesh.

'Well, look, Mum, this show is going to be very . . . *uncompromising*.'

'That's nice, dear.'

'No, it won't be nice at all. It will be quite . . . quite *brutal*, actually.'

'Jolly good. You show them a thing or two. You know, your father was a bit of a dab hand at photography. He took lovely holiday snaps. I always used to cut people's heads off. I don't know how it happened, I was really careful to line it up properly, but every time they'd come back from the printer with all the heads missing. Your father used to get quite cross about it. He'd say it was a waste of money, giving *me* the camera. So I mostly left it to him. A pity really, because it means that I haven't got many pictures of him. He'd be very proud of you, Daniel.'

*No, I don't think he would.* The thought flashed across my mind and I had to mentally shake myself to dispel it.

'Actually, I've brought my camera with me,' I told her. 'Thought I might take some pictures of you. Maybe use one in the exhibition.'

'Me? Oh, go on with you! With my hair in this mess? And these old clothes on?'

'That's all right. I want a natural look, anyway.' I reached over to my camera case and took out the Pentax. She immediately stopped talking and put herself in a formal pose, a forced smile on her face. 'I'm not ready yet,' I told her. 'Go on talking while I fix my settings. Did you get any joy from the council about the water tank?'

'Well, I *heard* from them, the scoundrels! They said that there are urgent priority cases to be dealt with first and I'll have to go on to a waiting list, until they can fit me in. So I told *them* they could jolly well pull their socks up and get something done. It's bad enough having no hot water in October, what will it be like when it gets really cold? I told them, I'm seventy years old, living on my own and if that's not a priority then I don't know what is . . .'

I'd flipped the time exposure to a thirtieth of a second, allowing me to shoot on the natural light that was flooding in through the room's large window, edging Mum's grey hair with a diffused silvery halo. Pretending that I was just fiddling with the focus, I shot several close-ups of her as she talked. She was sitting quite naturally now, using her small hands to emphasise every point, quite unaware of the click of the shutter, the whirr of the motor.

And for an instant there, I was no longer thinking of her as my mother. She had become an object framed in my shutter, something composed of lines and shadows and reflected light . . .

I realised what I was doing and felt a stab of guilt lance through me. It seemed to me in that instant, that I had become some kind of cold, unemotional voyeur, only able to relate to somebody when I was photographing them. Was this why I had failed to establish a warm relationship with every woman I had become interested in? Because things only existed for me when they were viewed through the lens of a camera? I thought about Julia Moreno. My first conscious act towards her had been an attempt to take her photograph . . . and how was I to explain my actions back in that railway arch on Sobriety Street? Was there anybody else in the world who would have reacted to the discovery of a corpse in the same way? I thought for a moment and decided, yes, there were people like that.

Other photographers.

'Penny for them,' said Mum.

'What?' I glanced at her in surprise.

'You seem worried. Is there something on your mind?'

'Not especially. I'm just thinking about the exhibition. You know, you really might not like what you see.'

'Of course I will, dear. If it's by you. You know, I keep all the back issues of the *Evening Post*. When my friends come round for tea, I get them out and say, "See that? My son took that snap!" Ooh, you're quite famous in these parts. Be even more famous when this exhibition opens, I shouldn't wonder.'

'You may be right,' I muttered. I pushed the idea to the back of my mind. I didn't want to think about it any more.

'Well now,' said Mum. 'What about these photographs?'

'I've done them,' I said. 'I got them while you were talking.'

'Oh, Daniel, you tinker! I wasn't even ready! I wasn't even *smiling*.'

177

I set down the camera.

'Trust me,' I said. 'They'll be fine. Now . . . shall it be the usual?'

'Yes,' she said, without hesitation. 'I always enjoy it.'

So we settled down to play 'Snakes and Ladders'. We played six times and she won every single game. She'd always been lucky like that; while it seemed to me that though I almost always took an early lead, I invariably ended up landing on the biggest, longest snake on the board and went sliding down, all the way back to the beginning . . .

# Chapter Seventeen

I got back to my place about eight PM to find that Roz was out and that the kitchen was already showing signs of slipping back into its former disrupted state. Judging by the dirty crockery and the various foil containers piled on the table she'd obviously opted for a take-away curry from Mr Bhopal's establishment downstairs, so the aroma of spices was even more pronounced than usual. My highly trained nostrils detected the presence of a vegetable rhogan josh, which must have looked a damned sight more appealing a few hours ago, before it had dried to an unappetising crust on the crockery. I broke off a piece of uneaten poppadum and chewed it without enthusiasm. I'd eaten at Mum's, her speciality shepherd's pie. She took every opportunity to feed me up and the portion she'd placed in front of me had been so gargantuan, I hadn't known whether to eat it or simply climb to the top and claim it for Britain.

A cursory glance at the television revealed that the evening was devoted to a brain-numbing selection of game shows and worthy but dull documentaries, so I decided on an early night with a good book. I found the novel that Philip Cassiday had given me and despite Geoff Greenhalge's less than ecstatic review of it, I undressed, got into bed and started reading. I was soon wishing that I hadn't.

It wasn't that the book was poorly written, quite the opposite. Cassiday was the kind of writer who was adept at putting his readers in the driver's seat, even when the destination was somewhere they would rather not go to. The book began with a queasily graphic account of the discovery of a horrific murder. In the opening chapter, the hero, an architect, was paying an unscheduled visit to the site of his latest project, a futuristic office complex. The lighting had yet to be installed, so our hero was obliged to pick his way through the rubble-littered interior with the aid of a torch. It was in this eerie setting that he chanced upon a hideously disfigured corpse, hanging by its feet from a section of recently erected scaffolding . . .

That was the point where I stopped reading. My own recent experiences had given me reason enough not to want to dwell on material of this nature: but more worrying was the awful coincidence of it. Hanging by the feet! Jesus!

Of course, it *had* to be a coincidence. How likely was it that the very day after discovering a murder I would be despatched to photograph the killer? A million to one? A billion to one? Cassiday was an odd-looking, even sinister character, but there was surely no way that he could be involved in the Sebastian Kennedy murder. And yet I could not readily attribute this to chance. The more I thought about it, the more uneasy I became. The slim, bearded man who'd been seen at Adonis, the night of the killing. Cassiday was slim and bearded, wasn't he? I thumbed back to the author's signature and the little dedication he'd written. *To Danny Weston. I'll get you back, one day!* Christ, what was that supposed to mean? At the time, I'd thought of it as nothing more than a jocular remark. Could it have a more sinister implication? Was it some kind of threat?

I told myself I was being stupid and put the book on one side. I switched off the light and tried to settle down to sleep. But I was on to a loser there. Reading the chapter had kick-started something in my unconscious. I'd read somewhere about a phenomenon called Post-Traumatic Stress Syndrome, something that often plagued people who had been in horrific or life-threatening situations. I decided that this was what I was experiencing now. My mind kept flashing back to the discovery in the railway arch. I had very clear images of the flayed corpse turning slowly as it hung from the wooden beam. Then, in what seemed like a series of photographic stills, accompanied by the glare of the flash-gun, I saw more specific pictures. Close-ups of heads, hands, feet. I began to sweat and shake like somebody with the DT's and wondered if I might be losing my mind.

The long, dreadful hours passed as I lay there sleepless and afraid. I'd hoped that Roz would come in, at least she'd be someone to talk to; but it got to midnight and there was no sound of her on the stairs. Perhaps she'd opted to stay over at Wanda's place for the night, she often did. Or was there another reason why she hadn't come home? Could something have happened to her? I became convinced that she was in some kind of danger and I kept seeing an image of Philip Cassiday, in his creepy black clothes, following Roz down a deserted street as she came out of a club, alone . . .

Somewhere in the early hours I did fall asleep, but the visions merely became nightmares, with no discernible interval. For the first time, I had the dream that would prove to be a recurring one – the dream where I am lying helpless as unseen hands remove my skin.

I woke at first light, sobbing, convinced for a moment that it had actually happened to me – that I was nothing more than a wet, bleeding mannekin, stretched out on the rumpled bed. It took a long time to convince myself that I was unharmed, that everything was as it had been the night before. On impulse, I grabbed my mobile phone and dialled Wanda's number. She answered, sounding pretty irate to be shaken out of her bed at such an unearthly hour. Yes, she told me crossly, Roz *was* there, the two of them had been out to an AIDS benefit the previous night and Roz hadn't fancied travelling home alone. Did I want to speak to her?

Before I could decline the offer, Roz's voice came out of the earpiece, sounding no happier than Wanda's had.

'Danny? What the fuck's going on?'

'Roz, I'm sorry, I was just . . . worried about you, that's all.'

'What d'you mean, worried?'

'Well, you know, with you not coming back and everything. I thought maybe . . .'

'What am I, for Christ's sake, your fucking *wife*? Of course I'm all right. And I often stay out overnight, it's never bothered you before.'

'I know. I guess it's with this Sebastian Kennedy thing. I had a bad night, I started imagining all kinds of . . .'

'Danny, have you any idea what time it is?'

'Sorry. I'm sorry.'

I hung up on her, before she could hang up on me. She would doubtless give me a hard time about this later, but that was OK. At least I knew she was alive and well and as feisty as ever.

Finally I was able to shower and dress, make my way to the kitchen for a reviving cup of black coffee (there was still no milk). Sitting at the breakfast table, I told myself that if I was going to overcome these fears, I would have to fling myself harder into my work, immerse myself in the final preparation for the *Skin Flicks* exhibition.

So I collected my camera case, put on my jacket and went out into the chill of a cold, wet October morning. With no set assignments for the day, I had decided that this would be the perfect time to go and see a man about a tattoo.

# PART TWO

We know that the tail must wag the dog, for the
horse is drawn by the cart;
But the Devil whoops, as he whooped of old: 'It's
clever, but is it art?'

Rudyard Kipling
*The Conundrum of the Workshops*


Dying,
is an art, like everything else.

Sylvia Plath
*Lady Lazarus*

# Chapter Eighteen

I found the tattoo parlour on the first floor of the Wheat Exchange, the huge, superbly tiled Victorian building that these days provides a home for the city's alternative communities. Where once respectable sober-suited business gentlemen conducted their enterprises, now a motley assortment of ramshackle shops and stalls catered for the needs of the alternative society. New Agers, new wavers, post-punks, post-modernists, Goths, crusties and various haircuts from hell all paraded here on a daily basis, searching through the second-hand records, the racks of tie-died clothing, mouldering second-hand books. Here you could buy yourself a pack of tarot cards, a water cooled hashish pipe, an army surplus water bottle, that long sought after copy of *The Eagle Annual*, 1967. More importantly, from my point of view, this was where you came when you wanted your nipples piercing.

I found *In My Tribe* tucked away between a health food store and a poster shop. The open door revealed a gloomy little waiting room within, the place lit only by the glow of a couple of satanic-looking candles. There was some rudimentary seating placed around the walls, what looked like old leather bus seats, stacked on bricks. Three of the seats were occupied by two young men and a woman, all of them clad in

Goth-style leathers, the jackets bristling with metal studs. The two men sported multi-coloured Mohicans that had been gelled up into great jagged crests, putting me in mind of Roman helmets. The woman wore her purple hair long, a thick fringe hanging like a curtain across her eyes. I wondered if she was shy but the message emblazoned on her T-shirt – Let's Fuck! – didn't suggest that she was.

The three of them eyed me curiously as I slipped into a vacant seat and set down my camera case. Maybe I didn't look the sort of person that usually frequented this joint. I occupied myself studying some of the fantasy art posters that decorated the walls, lots of bare chested, sword-wielding warriors defending swooning, big-breasted women from the attentions of various dragons, trolls and wizards.

From the other side of a closed door, I could just make out a high pitched buzzing noise, which I presumed was the sound of the tattoo needle going about its work. It actually sounded like a twenty pound mosquito swooping around in there.

One of the young men turned to his companions and grinned.

'She's really going through with it,' he observed, with evident amazement and I thought, a certain degree of pride. 'That girl's amazing.'

His male friend didn't seem so pleased about it.

'I never thought she'd do it,' he said. 'Fuck me, thirty quid it cost me. That's all I had till next Thursday.'

'Serves you right,' said the woman, unsympathetically. 'You should know by now, you don't dare Natalie to do anything. I think it's stupid. She's going to have that thing for the rest of her life. Supposing she wants to get married one day, how's that going to look to her husband? Eh?'

The two men stared at her as though she'd temporarily taken leave of her senses. Then they laughed uproariously.

'Fuck me,' said the first Goth. 'Imagine *anyone* wanting to marry Natalie!'

'It's not funny!' protested the woman. 'I mean, I've got nothing against a nice little butterfly or something. Cher's got a little butterfly, hasn't she? I mean, that's *tasteful* . . .'

'Who wants tasteful?' muttered the second Goth. 'This'll be like a statement, won't it? Like what you've got on your T-shirt.'

'Yes, but I can *change* my T-shirt.'

The first Goth shrugged.

'There's always laser surgery,' he said.

'Yeah,' agreed his friend. 'Won't cost more than a few thousand quid!'

The woman shot them a venomous look from under her fringe.

'You two really piss me off sometimes,' she said. She got up from her seat and left, leaving the men sitting there, chuckling like a pair of kids. The first Goth looked at me and gave me a wink.

'Silly cow,' he observed. He seemed to be inviting me to comment but I really didn't feel it was appropriate, so I just shrugged.

Time passed. The best part of an hour was gone and I was just thinking about giving up, when the buzzing stopped abruptly. A few moments later, the door opened and a young woman came out, looking almost like a carbon copy of her friend. Her leather jacket was slung over one arm and her right hand was tucked inside her Iron Maiden T-shirt, which I couldn't help noticing was liberally stained with blood. She looked pale and drawn, but she gave the second Goth a defiant sneer.

'Told you I'd do it,' she said. She seemed younger than her friend, maybe still in her late teens.

'Let's have a look then,' said the first Goth. 'For all we know you might just have had a tasteful butterfly.'

'Like Cher,' sniggered his companion.

The woman saw me sitting there and looked doubtful for a moment. Then she shrugged, lifted her T-shirt, pulled away a bloody rag she'd been holding against her breasts. The words HORNY BITCH FROM HELL, drawn in an ornate medieval script, rose and fell across the contours of her bust. I must have been staring because she looked at me sharply and said, 'What do you want, a fucking photograph?'

I thought about answering in the affirmative and whipping out my trusty Pentax, but her two friends were giving me the evil eye now and I doubted whether they'd see the funny side of it. So I simply turned my attention to the nearest fantasy poster, where the woman's breasts were impossibly pert and full, but unmarred by anything as ugly as the words I'd just read.

Dismissing me, the three Goths trooped out into the main area of the Wheat Exchange and I was left sitting there alone. What I had just seen had shocked me and I was beginning to think I should just go home and forget about all this. But at that moment, a man came through the open door from the tattoo parlour and I knew instantly that this must be Scott Banks.

He looked every inch the unpleasant character that Marsden had described, well over six feet tall, big and hulking, though with hard muscle rather than fat. He had a cleanly shaved head which served to emphasise his sinister appearance and as if to compensate, a thick stubble of beard. He was wearing a black, sleeveless waistcoat made from what looked like thin latex rubber, replete with a profusion of zipped pockets. His muscular arms were bare and I was vaguely surprised to note that he had no tattoos himself. He looked down at me and his dark eyes appraised me in silence for a moment.

'Didn't hear you come in,' he growled. He had a deep, gravelly voice. 'You didn't make an appointment?'

'Er, no, I—'

But he was already turning back to walk into the parlour, motioning me to follow with a flick of his bony skull. I picked up my camera case and followed him inside, finding myself in a small, airless room, dominated by a reclining leather chair of the kind more usually associated with a dentist's surgery. Beside it, the tattooing needle stood poised on the end of a tall, anglepoise arm. Banks flicked a switch on the wall and a powerful overhead lamp bathed the chair in a circle of fluorescent light.

'Sit down,' he said; and closed the door behind us.

'Well, before we go any further, I ought to explain . . .'

'*Sit* down,' he repeated, his voice harder this time and I instinctively moved to obey him. I set the camera case down beside the chair and sat looking warily at him as he perched himself on a tall stool beside me. 'Now,' he said. 'What can I do for you?'

'Er . . . well, I understand that you do body-piercing? My name's Danny Weston and I . . .'

But he had reached over to a nearby work-surface and had pulled a black-bound presentation book from a shelf. He tossed it on to my lap and the book fell open at the centre pages. I found myself looking at a close-up black and white photograph of a penis. There was a big silver ring that went right through the head of it.

I winced and couldn't prevent an expression of disgust flicking across my face. This seemed to amuse Banks no end. He tilted back his head and laughed unpleasantly.

'Yeah, that *is* a bit extreme, isn't it? But take it from me, it enhances your orgasms no end.'

'Is that right?' I thumbed hastily on to other pages, which featured the piercing of less sensitive areas – ears, lips, noses, nipples. There was one shot of a tattooed youth sporting a row of metal studs through his cheeks and another showing a woman who had a complicated arrangement of metal chains linking various parts of her anatomy together – ear to nose to nipples to belly button.

'I can pierce any part of your body,' said Banks encouragingly. 'Provided there's no bone or major arteries in the way. Had this guy in yesterday who wanted me to pierce his scrotum in several places.' He shook his head, laughed as though he'd just told a good joke. 'Funny thing, the scrotum. Very delicate part of the anatomy. You've got to be careful with it and there can be quite a bit of blood. Anyway, I fixed him up all right. Gave him a nice length of gold chain hanging from each side of it. Mind you, he isn't going to be riding a bicycle for a few weeks, know what I mean?'

He grinned at me, displaying sharp, wolfish teeth. I smiled back feebly.

'Wouldn't it be dangerous though?' I asked. 'You know, if he caught the chain in his zip or something.'

Banks fixed me with a look, one that suggested I had just asked an incredibly stupid question.

'What exactly is it you want?' he asked me. 'I usually don't pierce without an appointment but it's a slow day, so . . .'

'Oh no, I'm not interested for myself. I'm a photographer. I was wondering if I could get a few shots.'

'Photographs?' He looked suspicious. 'Photographs of *what*?'

'Of er . . . of people with pierced bodies. Like the ones in the book here only a bit less . . . graphic. It's for an exhibition, you see; and I've already photographed some of your tattoo work, so I thought . . .'

He pricked up his ears at this statement.

'How come?' he asked me. 'I mean, I don't *know* you, do I?'

'I did a shoot with an old friend of yours. Kit Marsden?'

Banks smiled coldly.

'Oh yeah? Haven't seen Kit in a long time. How's that slag doing? Still giving blow jobs in the backs of cars, is he? Still hanging around with that old queen, Joey?'

'Joey?' I raised my eyebrows quizzically.

'Yeah, you know, Joey Sparks? Kit's his bit of rough trade. That's what I heard anyway.'

Joey Sparks was virtually a household name around Manchester. An ageing drag artiste with an outrageous stage persona, he had his own club (imaginatively named Joey's Hideaway) up near Piccadilly. The club catered not so much for gay audiences but for predominantly straight ones. I'd been there once, years before and remembered that the place had the ambience of one of the old working men's clubs. It was in constant demand as a venue for hen parties, stag nights and charity events. Sparks also appeared in more mainstream roles. He did an annual ugly sister routine in pantomime and often took part in cheesy theatrical extravaganzas at the Palace Theatre.

I remembered that Marsden had mentioned a 'rich sugar-daddy' that looked after him. If that sugar-daddy was Joey Sparks, then Marsden had evidently made an astute choice.

'So . . .' Banks regarded me doubtfully. 'Kit recommended me?'

'Er . . . not exactly.'

'No, I'm bloody sure he didn't! Gave you the old sob story, I shouldn't wonder. How I used his young body to satisfy my artistic impulses, then cast him aside like an old glove.'

'Something like that.'

'He gives everyone that routine. And do you know what?' He leaned forward as if to confide a secret. 'It's absolutely true!' He laughed delightedly at his own honesty. 'I tell you what, though, he got the best deal. *He's* the one walking around with several thousand pounds worth of original art on his skin. I gave him something he could never have given himself. I made him interesting.' He seemed to consider for a moment, then added, 'I could make *you* interesting if you like.'

'No, that's all right,' I told him hastily. 'About these photographs . . .'

But he was shaking his bald head vigorously.

'Out of the question,' he said. 'Sorry.'

'They'd be on show at The Wedge,' I told him; but he looked singularly unimpressed.

'The Wedge!' He sneered. 'Listen, mate, I had a team from *Italian Vogue* down here a few weeks ago. This kind of stuff is high fashion now. They did a feature on me, photographed me at work, did pictures of some of the people I've illustrated. Actually, I phoned Kit and offered him a chance to be in on that gig, but he turned it down. Stuck up little tart, won't forgive and forget. Still, that was his loss, wasn't it?' He studied me for a moment. 'Fuck him, did you?'

I could feel my face getting hot again.

'Certainly not!' I protested, 'I'm straight!'

Banks grinned. 'Yeah, so am I. Sometimes.' He waggled his eyebrows meaningfully. 'You must admit though, he has got a perfect little tush, hasn't he? He gets dragged up, you'd never notice the difference.'

I studied my feet intently.

'I wouldn't know about that,' I said.

'Suit yourself.' Banks sighed, then clapped his hands

together. He got up from the stool and came around behind me. Before I quite knew what was happening, he was helping me off with my jacket. 'Right,' he said. 'Roll your sleeve up and pick a design from the charts on the wall – unless you want me to free-form something.' I stared at the sheets of designs pinned to the wall in front of me.

'Oh, but I didn't come here for—'

'I know you didn't.' He hung my leather jacket on a peg and came back to his stool. 'But what the hell? It's quiet today and I like to keep my hand in. So I'll give you one for free. If you like the way it turns out, you can come back and pay me the going rate for the next one. Can't say fairer than that, can you?'

'No, listen—' I started to struggle up out of the chair but he pushed me back into place with a powerful hand. 'Look,' I reasoned. 'I don't even *like* tattoos!'

'How do you know? Ever had one?'

'No, but . . . I saw that girl that was in before me? Jesus, that was horrible.'

Banks was rolling up my left sleeve now. He clearly wasn't going to take 'no' for an answer and if it came to a struggle, he was clearly going to win hands down.

He shrugged. 'Far as I'm concerned the customer gets what they ask for, every time.' He ran his fingers experimentally along my arm. 'Nice skin,' he observed. 'Like a baby's. Be lovely to work with.'

'Maybe so,' I said. 'But if you think I intend to sit here and let you tattoo me, you're very sadly mistaken.'

He gazed at me intently.

'Why? What are you afraid of?'

I couldn't believe this. That bloody question again! It seemed to me that this was all anyone had to say to me lately. Something seemed to snap inside me with an almost audible click and suddenly, I felt totally and utterly fearless. I'd show the bastards I wasn't afraid. I settled back into the chair.

'All right,' I said. 'I don't care, do it if you want to!' I scanned the charts quickly and pointed to a familiar design – a small red heart with a dagger plunged into it. Wrapped around the heart was a little scroll where somebody's name could be inked. 'That one,' I said, pointing. 'Give me one of those.'

Banks smiled. 'I call that one "old reliable",' he said. 'You'd be astonished how many people go for it.' He took some cotton wool from a pack on the bench and swabbed my arm with surgical spirit. Then he took a pack of latex gloves from the worktop, tore them open with his teeth and pulled them on to his hands. 'Got to be careful these days,' he told me. 'All kinds of nasty little buggers lurking about in people's blood.' He sat back on his stool, reached up for the needle and switched it on. It set up a high pitched whining sound and I felt myself tensing up involuntarily.

'Relax,' Banks advised me. 'The more you tense against it, the more it's going to hurt. Just accept the needle into your flesh. You *can* get to like it, you know.'

He began to work on me and I quickly doubted that I could ever get to like this. For the first few seconds, it was just vaguely unpleasant, a strange, tickling sensation that seemed to spread outwards from the point of the needle; but this was quickly replaced by a sharp stinging, like little points of flame erupting beneath the skin. As Banks worked on the design, so the feeling spread over a wider area, until I was having to grit my teeth to keep from flinching.

Banks seemed intent on his work, his eyes only inches from my skin, the tip of his tongue protruding from between his teeth.

'Relax,' he told me again. 'Pain's an illusion.'

'Yeah?' I grunted. 'Well, as illusions go it's pretty convincing. How come you don't have any tattoos yourself?'

'I do,' he corrected me. 'But they're in places that don't show. My personal exhibition isn't for public viewing, just for very close friends.'

'Who did yours? I presume you can't work on yourself?'

'A guy I knew years ago. He was a gifted artist. Specialised in tribal designs. American Indian art, stuff like that. He was the one who got me interested in the first place. Had a little tattoo parlour in Salford.'

'Isn't that where your place used to be?'

'Yeah, I took it over from Skippy when he moved away.'

'Skippy?'

'Yeah, that's what everyone called him. He was an Australian, full of nervous energy. Used to bounce around the place like a bush kangaroo. You remember the old TV programme?' He whistled a few bars of a familiar theme tune.

'Oh . . . right.' The pain was getting steadily worse and I found myself clenching my fists, digging my nails into the skin of my palms.

'Where uh . . . did he go?' I wasn't particularly interested, just making conversation to try and take my mind off the pain. 'Maybe he'd like to help with my photographs.'

Banks grinned. 'He's not exactly handy, I'm afraid. He was headed for Central America. Had this idea about going native and studying up on Aztec designs. I got a couple of postcards after he first got there but I haven't heard anything from him in years.' He leaned back on his stool, wiped the blood from my arm with a damp cloth and surveyed his handiwork. 'Coming along nicely,' he said.

'This going to take much longer?' I asked anxiously.

'Soon be done.' He went to work again, the buzzing needle

coaxing fresh agonies from beneath my skin. 'What name?'

'Hmm? Sorry, I . . .'

'For the scroll. It's usual to put somebody's name on it. You know, the one who broke your heart and all that?'

'Oh, right.' I thought about it for a moment, casting my mind back over the half dozen or so relationships I'd had in my life. They'd all been clumsy, half-hearted sorties into the mating game. In each case they'd simply fizzled out after a few weeks. No heart-breaking there. So I dismissed all the names of my previous paramours and thought back instead to an incident of just a few days ago. The way I'd felt the moment I clapped eyes on Julia Moreno. Suddenly there was no doubt.

'Julia,' I said.

Banks gave me a questioning look.

'Julian?' he asked.

'No, *Julia*. A woman's name. You got a problem with that?'

'No, I guess I just kind of *assumed* . . .'

'Look, what is this? I told you when I came in here I was a hetero!'

Banks frowned. 'Yeah, but the way you were so defensive, I thought you were lying.'

I sat there fuming. What was this, a conspiracy? Flynn had doubted my heterosexuality, Marsden had challenged it and now this bald oik had the cheek to sit there and call me a liar!

'Listen,' I said. 'Have I given you any reason to doubt me?'

'Chill out,' he advised me. 'Sounds like you've got a major hangup about it. You said you were a close friend of Kit's and—'

'No, I never said that. I said I'd *photographed* him and since I am a photographer, that doesn't seem—' A particularly fierce twinge flickered along the length of my arm and I almost scrambled up out of the chair. 'For fuck's sake,' I snapped. 'What are you doing, *skinning* me?'

He shot me a strange look – part surprise, part contempt.

'Just sit still,' he snarled. 'That kid that was in before you? She never made so much as a murmur.'

'Sorry,' I muttered. 'I'm just not very good with pain.'

'It's nearly done now. You spell Julia the usual way?'

I nodded, settled back in the chair and allowed him to continue without further protestation. It seemed to take a very long time before he was through and by then, my entire arm was throbbing. Finally, Banks sat back and switched off his instrument of torture. He gave my arm a final wipe with an antiseptic swab and leaned back to survey his handiwork.

'What do you think?' he asked me.

For the first time I examined my own arm. The simple illustration had been executed with a real deftness of touch. Julia's name was spelled out in perfectly spaced, blue-black script. As I looked at the tattoo, I felt a totally unexpected sense of pride. It was as though I'd just undergone some weird tribal initiation, a test of manhood – and this tattoo was the badge that testified to my courage. I was surprised that I felt this way. I hadn't expected to feel anything but *sore*.

'Nice,' I said.

'Keep it clean and dry,' Banks told me gruffly. 'It'll sting for a few days, that's all.'

'Right.' I lowered my shirt sleeve gingerly and getting up from the chair, I retrieved my jacket and hung it over my good arm. With an effort I picked up my camera case. 'Well,' I said. 'If you're sure I can't persuade you to let me take a few shots . . .'

He shook his head.

'Sorry. After the *Vogue* shoot, some of my regulars didn't

like the way they were depicted. Thought they'd been made to look like cranks. Maybe I'll come to your exhibition though. Specially if there's pictures of Kit. Might remind me of what I saw in him in the first place.'

'I'll send you tickets for the preview,' I said. 'The show's called *Skin Flicks*.'

Banks smiled.

'That Kit's idea by any chance?'

'The title? No, why?'

'Oh, nothing. Let's just say it's very appropriate.'

He didn't elaborate on the point and I didn't press him. By now, my arm was beginning to feel like it had swelled up to three times its normal size and I was anxious to get home. I shook Banks' hand, reflecting that under the hard-looking exterior, he didn't really seem the callous bastard that Marsden had described. As I walked out of the room, he called after me.

'Listen, give my regards to Kit, when you see him. And tell him I might come round to get my pictures back.'

It was a curious thing to say and if I'd been thinking clearly, one that would have warranted further investigation. But at the time, bothered by the pain in my arm, I attributed it to nothing more than an off-the-cuff joke.

At any rate, I stepped out into the bustle of the Wheat Exchange and promptly forgot all about what he had said. For the moment my only concern was to get home and start swallowing the pain killers. Under my shirt, a wet, red heart with Julia Moreno's name on it, was beating like a drum.

# Chapter Nineteen

The skin was peeling right off my arm. I was convinced of it and had to keep peering under the wet flannel to assure myself that this wasn't the case. Thankfully, every time I looked, things appeared to be in order. There was my latest fashion statement, a bit raw and scabby but otherwise firmly anchored in position on my arm.

I was sitting on the closed toilet in the bathroom, where I had retreated the moment I got home. I'd swallowed a couple of paracetamol tablets and ignoring Banks' instructions to keep the tattoo dry, had soaked a flannel in cold water and applied it gingerly to the affected area, at the same time marvelling at the amount of discomfort that one small tattoo could cause. I dreaded to think what the HORNY BITCH FROM HELL was going through now. Her friends were probably trying to coax her down off the ceiling.

I was sitting there, feeling pretty sorry for myself when I heard the kitchen door open and close and the sound of voices in the kitchen. Glancing up, I saw that I had neglected to fully close the bathroom door. I was just about to get up and rectify the situation when it was pushed open and Roz peered in at me.

'Oh, here you are!' she observed. 'You'll never guess who

I just met on the doorstep.' Then she mouthed something silently at me, two single syllabled words that I didn't quite catch, accompanied by a disapproving look.

Another head bobbed around the door frame. It was Spike. I quickly caught on to Roz's misgivings. He looked very strange, wild eyed and frenetic and when he spoke, his words came out like rapid bursts of machine-gun fire.

'Yo, Danny, how's it going, my man! I was on my lunch break, you know, just slippin' and slidin' and I figured, shit, why not go round and raid Danny's fridge, save myself a little dosh. Then I met Roz the Shnoz coming down the street and she said to me . . .' He finally registered that something odd was going on. After all, it wasn't every day I sat in the bathroom, stripped to the waist with a wet flannel on my arm. A puzzled expression mingled with the look of stoned bemusement he'd had a moment earlier and he moved towards me. 'Hey, Danny, you all right, man? You look kind've funny.'

'I'm fine,' I assured him.

'You don't *look* fine,' said Roz. She too came into the bathroom. 'What's that thing on your arm? You hurt yourself?'

I sighed, lifted the flannel to reveal what lay beneath.

Spike seemed suitably impressed. He grinned, nodded.

'Nice one!' he said. 'Fuck, you beat me to it. Where'd you get it done?'

'Place in the Wheat Exchange. What d'you think?'

'Sexy. Very sexy. Might get one myself. Did it hurt?'

I gave him a devil-may-care look.

'Nah. Piece of cake!'

'Piece of *shit*, you mean,' said Roz, who clearly wasn't as impressed as Spike. 'What possessed you to do a thing like that?'

I shrugged and tried not to wince at the pain this caused.

'I just fancied one,' I lied. 'You know me, Roz, creature of whim and all that. It's very fashionable. Why only the other day, *Italian Vogue* did a piece on—'

'Macho crap,' said Roz. '*Italian Vogue*, my arse!'

Spike stared at her.

'Your arse was in *Italian Vogue*?' he mumbled.

She ignored him, stepped closer. Her eyes narrowed suspiciously as she noticed the name on the scroll. Then the strangest expression came to her face. She looked shocked, dismayed. If the letters had spelled out WOMEN ARE CRAP, she couldn't have looked more unhappy.

'And just who the fuck is Julia?' she shrieked. Her voice suddenly had the shrill tones of an electric drill.

I was completely thrown by her reaction. I stared back at her for a moment before replying.

'Just somebody I met.'

'Somebody you *met*? When? Where? How come I haven't met her?'

Spike and I exchanged puzzled glances.

'I'm sorry,' I muttered. 'I wasn't aware that you had to vet all my friends before I could go out with them.'

Spike gave me a man-of-the-world look.

'Must be pretty serious, Dan-bo. The name written on your heart. I think that's cool, man, you know, I can really respect that. Who is this mysterious chick? It's like the poem says, man. "Who is Julia, what is she?" '

'I think that's "*Who is Sylvia*", actually.'

I could have done without this. I was going to look pretty foolish if I admitted she was somebody I'd met only once and talked to for ten minutes. I decided that my only hope was to keep my answers vague. 'She's just this lady I met in the course of work. She's Chilean, involved in this Mexican festival thing. We got talking and it was, you know, one of those instant attractions.'

'But when was this?' persisted Roz.

'Couple of days ago. But—'

'And you've gone straight out and had her name carved into your *skin*?'

Put like that it did seem pretty extreme.

'Well, it just kind of happened on impulse. See, I was having the tattoo and Scott – that's the guy who did it – he said there needed to be a name on the scroll and which one should he write? And hers was the first one that occurred to me.'

'That's cool,' said Spike, who was evidently operating in Beavis and Butt Head mode. 'I can relate to that.'

'It is *not* cool,' retorted Roz. 'It is fucking *Neanderthal*!'

'Yeah, that's *why* it's cool.'

'Oh shut up, Spike. Contrary to your beliefs, life is not a concept album by Judas Priest.' She rounded on me, stabbing an index finger at the offending tattoo, coming close enough to make me cringe. 'I'm surprised at you, Danny Weston! I thought you had a bit more suss than this. I never thought you were capable of something so . . . so silly.'

I bridled at this remark.

'Frankly, I don't see that it has anything to do with you.'

'It has *everything* to do with me!' she wailed, making a theatrical gesture. 'I am a woman. And that . . . that *thing* on your arm is demeaning one of my sisters!'

'I didn't know you had any sisters,' said Spike.

Roz glared at him for a moment, then decided that it wasn't worth pursuing. He was either too stoned or too stupid to comprehend. So she ignored him and kept after me.

'And what about the implications of carrying somebody's name on your body?' she continued. 'Don't you realise that's not a thing to be taken lightly? That's not a trivial matter.'

'I never said it was trivial,' I replied.

'Yes, but Danny, can't you see what I'm saying? That's something you do for somebody you're in love with.'

'So? I *am* in love with her. What's wrong with that?'

'You . . . you're in love with . . . this woman?'

'Sure. Why not?' I was just mouthing off now, throwing her own indignation back in her face: but once again, her reaction was extraordinary. For the first time since I'd met her she seemed to be temporarily at a loss for words. Her mouth dropped open and she gasped for breath. As I watched, she seemed to be deflating visibly.

'You . . . you love her?' she spluttered at last, as though she hadn't heard me the first time. 'Seriously?'

'Seriously. Look, Roz, I don't see what the problem is.'

'You wouldn't, you *bastard*!' This was yelled with such vehemence that I actually rocked backwards on the toilet seat – and I was shocked to see tears welling in her eyes. 'Well, fuck you!' she concluded. She turned and marched out of the bathroom, slamming the door behind her. I winced, then winced again at the resulting pain in my arm.

'Roz?' I called after her. 'What did I say?' But then I heard the slam of the kitchen door and the sound of her Doc Marten's clumping down the staircase. I looked at Spike in an appeal for support. 'What's got into her?' I asked him.

He grinned. 'Obvious, isn't it? She fancies you.'

Now it was my turn to let my jaw drop.

'Are you trying to be funny?' I asked him.

'Not at all. But you saw her face, didn't you? That was the classic "spurned woman" routine, if ever I saw one.'

I thought about it for a moment but couldn't take Spike's suggestion seriously. Roz Birchill . . . and *me*? Ridiculous! As far as I was aware she resented everything about me.

Why, only the other night she'd referred to me as 'sexless'. And when I'd phoned her at Wanda's she'd given me a mouthful about how she wasn't my wife or anything. 'No way,' I concluded. 'We hardly get along at all. Christ, we spend all our time bickering and slagging each other off . . .'

Spike gave me a knowing look.

'Like every married couple in the world,' he said. 'Let's face it, man, you're made for each other. And she's had the hots for you for a long time. I'm surprised you haven't noticed.'

I wasn't too impressed by Spike's apparent knowledge about the subject. The plain fact was that he was hopeless where romance was concerned and his own recent history was littered with a succession of hopeless flings and sordid one night stands that hardly put him in the Barbara Cartland stakes. In Spike's book, a relationship that lasted a week was a major success.

'You've got it all wrong,' I assured him. 'I'm not her type. For one thing, I'm the wrong sex.'

He looked momentarily baffled, then perked up as the penny gradually made its way through the layers of chemicals that were currently permeating his brain.

'What . . . you mean . . .?'

'Yes. At least, I think so. She spends most of her time hanging around with Wanda and her crowd, doesn't she? So I guess it just follows that she . . .'

It occurred to me that I was doing to Roz exactly what had been done to me over the last few days. I was making assumptions about her sexuality. I'd got pretty angry about the situation myself and maybe she'd be angry too, if she knew what I was telling Spike. So I abandoned the idea in mid sentence.

Spike shrugged. 'Well, I wouldn't be so sure, man. She did

offer to photograph your dick, right? And I couldn't even get her to *look* at mine. And you saw her just now, I thought she was going to break down in tears.'

'Well, maybe it's just that time of the month,' I ventured.

'Yeah,' he said. 'October.'

I looked at him. Whatever he was on, it wasn't doing his head any favours. He seemed to dismiss the subject of Roz and moved on to a more interesting one.

'So this Julia chick. It's as serious as you say?'

'Well, not really. I just fancy her, I suppose.'

'And she fancies you?'

'No, not exactly. I mean, I don't know yet. I hope so.' I sighed. 'Look, the truth is, this tattoo thing wasn't even planned. I went along to this place in the Wheat Exchange hoping to get some pictures of body-piercing for the exhibition. The guy there wouldn't let me do any photographs. Then he offered me a free tattoo and I said I'd have one. When he asked me which name I should put on it, hers just kind of sprang into my mind. She . . . she probably doesn't even know I exist.'

'That's too bad, man. Doomed love affair. Been there, done that, bought the fuckin' T-shirt. Still, be of good heart, because ol' Spike might just be able to help you out.'

I looked at him warily.

'Look, much as I value your advice, I suspect you may be a wee bit too stoned to make a lot of sense, just now.'

He laughed crazily.

'No, man! Not the chick-thing. I mean, I'm wired but I'm not totally out of it. Here, check this out!' He took hold of the bottom part of his T-shirt and yanked it upwards, revealing his skinny, hairless chest and something else I would never have guessed in a thousand years. 'Ta-daa!' he said.

207

Spike's nipples were pierced and he had two small, silver hoops through them.

'Christ,' I said. 'Spike, I'm shocked, I had no idea. When did you have them done?'

'Weeks ago. DIY job. Guys in the band got me drunk on tequila and did it for me. It's all the go now, you know. And it's supposed to make your sex life better. Rings through your progeny zones. I haven't had a chance to try it out yet.'

'Erogenous zones,' I corrected him. 'Still, I wish I'd known about this before. You could have saved me considerable pain. Tell you what, how'd you like to step into the studio with me? I could shoot off a few frames, might take my mind off this blessed tattoo.'

'Hey, you mean I can be in the exhibition?'

'Sure. If the pictures turn out OK.'

'They're bound to. I'm very photogenic, me.'

I eased myself up off the toilet seat, ignoring the jangling nerves in my arm. I couldn't help thinking about the irony of it. If only Spike had mentioned this to me earlier, I wouldn't even have gone to the tattoo parlour, I wouldn't have ended up with Julia's name on my arm and I wouldn't have argued with Roz. But then, I reasoned, nipples weren't the kind of thing that tended to come up in conversation.

I collected the camera case and Spike and I made our way to the studio. I started to get set up while Spike dashed about the place, following my instructions. I had him move a wooden chair and an old packing crate in front of a textured backdrop that I had mocked up as a piece of graffiti-scrawled wall. Spike had to be back at work for two o'clock so we couldn't afford to spend too long on this. I got him to lounge in the chair with his feet up on the crate. He had on a pair of imitation snakeskin shoes which I felt would photograph nicely in black and white.

'What do I do now?' he asked me.

'Well, it might be an idea to take your T-shirt and jacket off,' I told him.

'Uh? Oh yeah, right. The *nipples*.' He took off the items of clothing and slung them on the back of the chair. I moved in closer and set up the Pentax and tripod. Spike sat there twitching impatiently as I set my aperture and lights. I decided to augment the soft studio lights with a single small spot which would just pick out his right side in sharp contrast. As a final touch, I got a couple of empty beer cans from my props store and put one in his hand and one on the crate.

'Pity there's nothing in this,' he complained. 'Might relax me a bit.'

'You do seem pretty . . . agitated.' Actually 'stupid' was the word that sprang to mind but he probably wouldn't have appreciated that.

'Yeah. Must be the Zippy I took. That stuff keeps you buzzing for hours man.'

'The . . . Zippy?' I stopped what I was doing and looked at him. For an instant, I was no longer in the studio. I was back in the railway arch on Sobriety Street and the backdrop behind Spike had become a damp, mouldering stretch of wall where two words had been scrawled in Sebastian Kennedy's freshly spilled blood. I made a mental effort to wrench myself back to the comforting surroundings of the studio. 'Spike,' I heard myself say. 'What's Zippy?'

'Uh?' He looked at me blankly. 'It's just a name for this really great speed that's going around. You know, amphetamines? This stuff is really intense. I like taking it when I go up the clock tower. You get some very weird vibes.'

'Doesn't sound very safe.'

'The clock tower? Nah, it's solid as a rock.'

'That's not what I meant. Spike, who invented the nick-name? Zippy, I mean.'

He shrugged. 'That's just what we call it. That's what Dex calls it, anyway.'

'Dex?'

'Guy who deals it.'

'I see.' I reminded myself that I was supposed to be taking pictures here and began to automatically go through the process as I talked. 'Where do you know this Dex from?'

'Don't really *know* him. He turns up at our gigs with speed to sell. Probably be at the Mandrake when we play there.'

I swapped the standard lens for a zoom lens, wanting to get in close enough to pick out every detail of Spike's chest adornments – but my mind wouldn't leave the idea alone. 'This Dex character. Is he by any chance a thin guy with a beard?'

Spike grinned.

'You know him?'

I shook my head.

'And does he . . . use a lot of speed himself?'

'Yeah, he's fuckin' crazy! I sometimes think it's him we should call Zippy. He's into all this weird stuff. You know, star signs and stuff like that. First time he met me, he said he could tell straight away I was a Pisces.'

'You're a Gemini,' I reminded him.

'That's what I mean. Guy's off his head. Why are you so interested, anyway? Thinking of taking his picture?'

I shrugged. 'Maybe,' I said. I didn't know what to make of

this. Maybe it was just another weird coincidence, but I'd sure as hell check Dex out if he came to the Mandrake.

Spike, meanwhile, appeared to have remembered something he'd stored away in the carnival carousel that was his brain.

'Hey, you know what I was thinking, Danny? You should come up the clock tower with me. I can get you in, no problem! Great view from up there, you can get photos of half of Manchester.'

'Yes, maybe I'll take you up on that. I've got a new fish-eye lens I wanted to try out. Mind you, I don't much like the idea of going up there if you're smashed out of your skull.'

He gave a weird little laugh.

'You're not afraid are you?'

This was getting to be an everyday occurrence but I certainly hadn't expected to hear it from my best friend.

'I think "cautious" is the word you're looking for.'

'OK. You know I'll look after you, man. I wouldn't let anything happen to you. It's not like I'm going to push you off or anything!' Again, that shrill, manic laugh. Then he stopped, looked at me oddly. 'You're not pissed off at me, are you? About the Zippy? It's just that it's really good stuff. And there are no real side-effects. 'Cept sometimes I have bad dreams . . .'

My thumb kept punching down on the shutter release as we talked.

'What kind of dreams?'

He made a face. 'Oh, horrible. Like a slasher movie or something. A whole lot of blood and guts, you know, and me slipping and sliding about in this stuff. It's only happened a couple of times . . . but it's after I've had the Zippy and . . . maybe . . . anyway, it's worth it, man. I'd

211

go through any amount of shit for Zippy. I like the way it makes me feel . . . like I can do anything, you know?' He glanced at his watch. 'Look, it's getting late. You got what you needed or what?'

'I expect there'll be something I can use,' I said. I was feeling slightly dazed. Spike was perhaps my oldest friend but after this last, rambling confession I was having the most awful doubts about him. In all his years playing in rock bands I'd never known him to use anything stronger than draw. And why was he suddenly so anxious to get me up that clock tower with him?

'Wednesday would be a good day,' he told me, as he struggled back into his Slayer T-shirt. 'How are you fixed?'

'Uh . . . I think I'll be free,' I said mechanically.

'Nice one. Call at the Town Hall at one o'clock and I'll show you the way up. You'll love it, man, it's like being on top of the world.' He slipped into a quick James Cagney impression. 'Top of the world, Ma! Top of the world!' Then he gestured at the chair and packing crate. 'I'll bring all my friends to see it!'

'What *both* of them?' He didn't even notice I'd spoken. I accompanied him back to the kitchen and saw him out of the door. He seemed agitated now as though he'd forgotten something. 'Where was I going?' he asked me.

'Back to work,' I said.

'Oh yeah, right. Bloody clock's on the blink again. Looks like a job for Captain Insensible.'

'Be careful up there,' I told him; and I watched apprehensively as he lurched down the stairs, taking them three at a time.

Back in the studio, it was suddenly very quiet. I stood looking at a plain white backdrop and a succession of violent images seemed to flicker across it like reels of grainy old film.

Scenes of carnage in a dank, dark railway arch. Scrawled words written in blood. Something turning slowly at the end of a rope.

*What are you afraid of, Danny?*

I wasn't really sure. I only knew that I *was* afraid and more than a little bit paranoid. And I wished I hadn't argued with Roz. Maybe then she'd still be here and I wouldn't be standing alone in the gathering darkness, waiting for the night to close in.

# Chapter Twenty

That night I had one of my dreams again. It was the one in which I was a police photographer, shooting footage of the carnage in the railway arch, while Detective Inspector Flynn issued instructions. For a long time it was just the same as it had been before; a series of horrific still images, frozen in the glare of a flashgun. But when I turned to photograph the words scrawled on the wall, I registered that there had been a slight but significant change: FOR SKIPPY.

I woke in that instant, sweating and trembling, but convinced that my subconscious was trying to tell me something that my waking mind had missed. Skippy? Why was that name so familiar all of a sudden? For a moment, still dazed by sleep, I couldn't think why. Then it came to me. The tattooist that Scott Banks had told me about. The Australian who had gone off to Central America to study native art. Banks had said he hadn't heard from him in years. But what if he'd come back to Manchester? What if his years in the wilderness had driven him round the twist? What if . . .?

I realised that I was clutching at straws. Maybe the name had slipped into the dream simply because it *had* been mentioned to me. That happened sometimes.

I dragged myself out of bed and cold showered my body back to the land of the living. The chill of the water as it hit my tattooed arm jolted the last vestiges of sleep from my brain and I found myself thinking about the dreams again. They were really starting to get to me. If they went on much longer, I'd be losing my sanity, they'd be sending the big white ice-cream van and the guy with the butterfly net. I found myself wishing that there was somebody I could confide in. Usually Spike fulfilled that role, but the state he'd been in yesterday afternoon hadn't exactly been condusive to a good chat.

Once dressed, I went to have a look in my appointments diary and I didn't find much cause for celebration there, either. Only a couple of assignments pencilled in over the next month where normally there'd be dozens. Barry Summerby just didn't seem to be ringing my number these days. It was beginning to look like he hadn't forgiven me for refusing him his exclusive story. On the other hand, maybe I was just being paranoid. I'd had quiet spells before. Usually something came up.

With an empty day stretching in front of me, I decided to put in some time in the dark room. I found the exposed films of Kit Marsden and Spike, developed them and made up some contact sheets. The Marsden pictures were particularly successful, I thought. The high contrast lighting I'd used really brought out the intricate lines of his tattoos and there was an undeniably provocative feel to the poses, the way he was looking at the camera with a smouldering, come hither look.

I chose half a dozen of the best shots and did some enlargements, then hung them up to dry. I'd promised to phone Marsden as soon as I had something to show him and I decided that this was a promise I should honour. He'd asked me if I'd deliver them in person but I wasn't sure about that. I didn't know if I dared risk another face-to-face confrontation with him. Maybe I'd just ring him and get the address, put them in the post to him. A safer bet altogether.

*What are you afraid of, Danny?*

I was getting used to the voice in my head now. Maybe I already was round the twist but hadn't accepted it.

I made myself a cheese sandwich for lunch and nibbled at it half-heartedly. There was still no sign of Roz and I told myself that here was another problem that needed addressing. I didn't for one moment believe that there was anything in Spike's theory, that Roz had been harbouring a secret passion for me – and yet, how else was I to explain her outburst the previous afternoon?

With lunch finished I located the scrap of paper with Marsden's number scribbled on it, went to the phone and dialled. It rang half a dozen times before it was answered.

'Yes?'

'Kit? This is Danny Weston. I've finished your photographs.'

There was a puzzled silence, as if the man at the other end of the line was temporarily at a loss for words.

'Give me your address and I'll post them to you,' I suggested.

'Danny?'

'Yes, Danny Weston. Don't tell me you've forgotten.'

'This . . . isn't Kit,' said the voice. There was nevertheless something naggingly familiar about it.

'Oh, sorry. Well, can Kit come to the phone?'

'That would be rather difficult at the moment.'

'I see. Well, can you tell him . . . I'm sorry, do I know you?'

'Yes, Danny, you do. This is Lawrence.'

'Lawrence?' That threw me for an instant. I didn't *know*

anybody called Lawrence . . . did I? Then it struck me with an impact that made my stomach lurch. 'Inspector Flynn?' I whispered.

'Got it in one, Danny. Well remembered.'

Momentarily flummoxed, I made a few gasping noises, before I was able to construct an audible sentence.

'You're the . . . last person I expected!' I said.

'I could say the same for you. You mentioned photographs?'

'Uh . . . yes. I did a photo-shoot with Kit the other day. I promised him I'd ring when the . . . look, what's going on? Is everything all right?'

'Well, I'm not here on a social call. I think you'd better come straight over here. And bring those photographs with you.'

'But . . . I'm . . . I'm quite busy at the moment.'

'So am I. But I would very much appreciate your presence; and it would be in your best interests to attend. If transport is a problem, I could arrange to send a car for you.'

'No need. You'd better give me a note of the address.'

Another pause.

'You mean, you don't already know it?'

'No. I've never been there. Kit only gave me the number.'

'You're quite sure about that?'

'Yes. Look, what's going on? Has something happened to Kit?'

'We'll talk about it later.' He gave me an address in Chorlton and I scribbled it down. 'Be here in half an hour, or I *will* send that car for you. And don't forget the photographs.'

He put down the receiver and I stood there, totally bewildered and beginning to get a very bad feeling about this. But Flynn's instructions had been precise enough. Half an hour. I hurried to the dark room, grabbed Marsden's contact sheet and prints, slipped them into a brown envelope. I put on my jacket, grimacing at the touch of leather on my still tender left arm. Then I hurried out to my car and drove to Chorlton.

The address proved to be a three story Victorian house, converted into flats. The moment I pulled up outside, I could tell that some major shit had hit the fan. There were several police cars and an ambulance parked outside the entrance and the open doorway was fenced off with lengths of incident tape. A couple of uniformed men stood on either side of the door, looking for all the world like a pair of over-dressed nightclub bouncers. As I got out of the car and walked reluctantly towards the entrance, the shambling figure of Detective Sergeant Potts emerged from the doorway. He studied me as I walked towards him, a scowl on his face that suggested he was appraising a lowly and rather unpleasant form of insect life.

'Mr Weston,' he sneered. 'So nice of you to join us.' He gestured at the brown envelope under my arm. 'Brought your holiday snaps, have you?'

I ignored the taunt.

'Where's Inspector Flynn?' I asked.

'Upstairs, drying his nail varnish,' said Potts. He glanced at one of the uniformed men and they exchanged knowing smirks.

'I'll pass on your comments, shall I?' I said, and Potts' smug expression vanished.

'Come on,' he said; and I followed him in through the doorway. We moved along a dinghy hall and climbed a flight of creaky wooden stairs. The doors of other flats were open, the curious inhabitants peering out, trying to ascertain just exactly what was going on. We kept climbing till we'd reached the top floor, by which time Potts was red faced and out of breath.

'Wait here,' he gasped. He opened the door of an attic flat and went in, closing it behind him. I caught a brief glimpse of a lot of activity in there, people milling about as they searched the room. I waited impatiently, convinced now that something awful had happened and that whatever it was, it wasn't going to look good for me.

After a few moments, the door opened and Flynn emerged. He gave me a strained-looking smile.

'Danny,' he said. 'You do keep turning up in the oddest places.' He pointed at the envelope. 'The photographs?' he asked.

'Yes.' I handed them to him and watched as he took out the contents and scanned through them. 'Good looking chap,' he observed. 'The pictures are very accomplished, by the way.'

'Thanks,' I said. 'Look, are you going to tell me what's going on?'

'I'll do better than that,' he said, slipping the photos back into the envelope. 'I'll *show* you.'

I looked at him warily.

'I'm not sure I want to see what's in there.'

'Oh, you *don't*, Danny, I can assure you. But I'm afraid that I'm going to have to insist. I'll make it as quick as possible.'

I'd been trying not to think the worst but Flynn's grim expression told me that this was every bit as bad as it could be.

'Oh God, he's dead, isn't he?' I said.

Flynn put an arm around my shoulders. He opened the door and led me into the flat. It was a small place and seemed to be shoulder to shoulder with a mixture of plain clothes men and others wearing PVC coveralls. Everyone was wearing surgical gloves as they dusted for prints, rummaged through drawers, read letters. Potts was holding up a bra he'd found in a drawer and was making some oafish remark about it, much to the amusement of his team. He threw me a contemptuous look as I moved past him. The door to an adjoining room was open and Flynn steered me in that direction. As we drew closer, the room was lit by the glare of a flashgun.

We stepped inside and I saw that it was a bedroom. I half expected to find Kit's body stretched out on the double bed, but though the sheets were rumpled, it was empty. A man standing with his back to us turned and I recognised Dr Giles Laughton, the pathologist who had been at the railway arch. He moved aside to give me a better view of something in the corner of the room, something that a police photographer was busily photographing.

I heard a sound coming out of my mouth, a long, low moan of horror. My eyes filled with tears. If the aim of this visit was to identify the body, then it was an impossible task.

The roof sloped down in the corner of the room and an exposed wooden support beam made a forty-five degree angle with the wall. The body – I assumed it was Kit Marsden – had been tied at the wrists with a short length of rope. The arms were extended up above the head, the feet hung just inches from the floor. The beautiful illustrated skin was all gone, leaving just a mass of exposed red flesh in its place. There was a fist-sized opening in the chest cavity, through which a couple of broken ribs protruded. The beige carpet beneath the body was thick with gore. On the white-painted wall beside the body, words had been scrawled in blood: ANOTHER FOR ZIPPY.

I became aware that Flynn was studying me intently,

looking at my expression. It occurred to me then that he was wondering if I had done this; asking himself if I was some depraved monster, hiding behind a brilliantly executed display of bewilderment.

*Oh Christ*, I thought. *They are going to arrest me for this. They are going to lock me up and throw away the key!*

A cold panic swept over me and I started to hyperventilate. I couldn't stop myself. A thudding sound filled my ears and the room started to whirl around me like some grisly carnival ride, suddenly thrown out of control. My legs were turning to columns of quivering jelly beneath me. I lifted a hand to my face and swayed sideways. Flynn caught me and put his shoulder under mine to give me support. He started shouting instructions.

'He's fainted! Help me get him into the bathroom. You lot, clear out of there, give us some space . . .'

Blackness swirled through my brain and then, what seemed an instant later, a cold, wet flannel was being applied to my face. I came back to something like reality and found myself slumped on the floor of a bathroom, my head resting against a wash basin. Flynn was kneeling beside me, looking down at me with an expression of genuine concern on his face.

'Are you all right now?' he asked me.

I nodded, took the flannel from him, held it to my forehead. The room finally stopped swaying and I was able to speak.

'I'm sorry,' I muttered. 'That wasn't very manly, was it?'

'Very Isadora Duncan, if I may say so.' He handed me a glass of water and I sipped at it gratefully. 'Look, if you still feel bad, there are ambulance men outside. I could . . .'

'No, I'm fine now, really. I'm not very good with blood.'

Flynn got up off his knees and perched himself on the edge

of the bath. He studied me for a moment.

'Well, Danny, you're either totally innocent or a brilliant actor. I'm not sure which.'

'Me, an actor?' I laughed bitterly. 'The last time I was on stage was the junior school nativity play. I was the one kid singled out for bad reviews.'

He smiled thinly.

'Consider how it looks. Two killings in the space of a few days and you're connected with both of them. Even more damning, you *know* that I saw you and Kit Marsden together at Adonis – the very place where Sebastian Kennedy met his killer.'

'I'm aware of *how* it looks,' I snapped. 'But that was the first time I'd ever laid eyes on Marsden. It was the tattoos, you see. I thought he'd make an interesting subject for my exhibition.'

'Ah, yes, the infamous exhibition. I must say, I can hardly wait to see that.'

I groaned and he looked at me sharply.

'You sure you're all right?'

'Yes, thanks. Just . . . a bit dizzy, that's all.'

'Now, you claim that you've never been here before – and that you hardly knew Mr Marsden.'

'That's not a claim,' I told him. 'It's the truth.'

He pointed to the brown envelope that lay on the floor beside me.

'Yet those photographs look distinctly intimate. The young man is virtually naked.'

'How else would I photograph body tattoos?'

He thought about it for a moment.

'Point taken,' he said. 'So, you photographed him and then what?'

'Then he went home. He left me a phone number and I

said I'd ring him when I'd developed the pictures. Which I did this morning. And there *you* were.'

'And there I was. Let me suggest something to you, Danny. You were only too aware that I or some other police officer would be here. Perhaps you were the anonymous caller that tipped us off about the body. You phoned with an apparent show of innocence to establish an alibi. You even pretended not to know the address to lend your story more conviction.'

'No!' I protested. 'I can understand how you might think that, but I swear to you on my mother's grave . . .'

'Your mother is alive and well and living in Moss Side,' he told me. 'Which might sound like a contradiction in terms but . . .'

'It was just an expression,' I assured him. 'Besides, how did you know . . .?'

'I've been doing my homework, Danny. As I promised you I would. And I've discovered a likeable if somewhat hapless young man, who apart from a few teenage thrills and spills has never been in any kind of trouble in his life.'

'I must be making up for lost time,' I muttered.

'All right. This photo session. You must have talked to Marsden. I doubt that such things are conducted in silence.'

'Yes, of course we talked.'

'And this being your first real conversation, no doubt he told you a few things about himself?'

'I guess.'

'So what *did* he tell you?'

'Umm . . . that he was a cabaret artist. Did impressions of Liza Minelli, stuff like that.'

'Hmm. That would explain the fact that his wardrobe is full of women's clothing. Potts will be disappointed, he was working on a theory that there was some vengeful girlfriend in the background. What else?'

'He told me that he had a rich sugar-daddy . . .' I thought about mentioning Joey Sparks, but something made me hold back on it. 'Um . . . yes, he told me about this guy in the Wheat Exchange, the man who did all his tattoos. The two of them had something going once.'

'The Wheat Exchange, you say?'

'Yes. In fact, I went there yesterday.'

'You went there? Why?'

'Well, I thought I might get some shots . . .'

'For the exhibition. Yes, yes, silly of me. Danny, does your entire life revolve around this forthcoming show?'

'It seems to. Anyway, the tattooist – Scott Banks, his name is, he wouldn't let me take pictures and I ended up having a tattoo instead.'

'As you do,' said Flynn, with a wry smile.

'And I got talking to this Banks and he told me something very interesting. At least, I thought it was.'

'Pray enlighten me.'

'He said there was this Australian guy he'd known years before. He'd owned a tattoo parlour in Salford, right? He and Banks were close friends and then this guy decided to leave the country for Central America and he gave Banks his old parlour when he left. Kind of started him up in business.'

Flynn frowned.

'This is interesting?' he asked me doubtfully.

'Well, it gets better. The guy's nickname was Skippy.'

'So?'

'Think about it. FOR ZIPPY. How about FOR SKIPPY?'

He looked at me blankly.

'You're suggesting the killer is dyslexic?'

'No, I . . . just wondered if there could be a connection.'

Actually, hearing myself say it, it did sound decidedly half-baked. 'You see, I had this dream . . .'

Flynn seemed to get suddenly impatient with my theory.

'If we could just get back to Kit Marsden for a moment . . .'

'Wait, there's something else. This *will* interest you. There's a new drug on the streets. It's called Zippy.'

He did perk up at this news.

'Seriously?'

'Yes. It's a kind of speed-ball, I think. Amphetamines mixed with cocaine.'

'Yes, I am familiar with the term. How did you come by this information, Danny?'

Another problem. I didn't want to drop Spike into the brown stuff if I could possibly avoid it.

'It's just the word on the street. But I've heard that people can have some seriously bad dreams using this stuff. It seems to change their personalities.'

'You're remarkably well informed. You wouldn't by any chance have used it yourself?' he asked me.

'Certainly not. I don't take drugs of any kind.'

'Well, it's something we should look into, of course. I don't know about your antipodean tattooist, though. Sounds a bit far fetched to me.'

I frowned. 'I wonder, did Sebastian Kennedy have any tattoos? Maybe there's a link there.'

'What, the killer is only interested in tattooed men? I doubt it. Though by all accounts if that's the case, you'll have to watch out for yourself now. What kind of tattoo did you have?' he asked me.

'Oh just a . . . a tasteful butterfly. You know, like Cher.'

I wasn't sure why, but I didn't want him to see Julia's name on my arm. Then there'd only be a lot more questions to answer and the last thing I wanted to do was involve her in any of this. That would be my chances of romance kicked right out of the window.

'I imagine Mr Marsden's skin would make quite a trophy,' mused Flynn. 'To a man who collects such things it must be the equivalent of a tiger skin rug.'

'Not funny,' I said quietly.

'Not meant to be. No, I'll check with some of Kennedy's friends and see if there's anything in this tattoo idea; but as far as I can see, the obvious link is that the two men were gay. I believe we're dealing with a homophobic. Again we have the same ritual quality to the killing, though this time with a slight variation.'

'Oh, what's that?'

'You didn't notice the large hole in the chest?'

'Uh . . . oh yes, I'm afraid I did. What was that all about?'

Flynn frowned. 'It seems that our killer removed one of Mr Marsden's vital organs. His heart.'

'Jesus, Mary and Joseph,' I muttered.

'Quite. Must have taken it with him too. There's no sign of it anywhere in the flat.'

'Who would do a thing like that?'

'Presumably, the same kind of person who will happily remove a man's skin. That's missing too, by the way. Now . . . you said that this Scott Banks had something going with Marsden. Do you mean they were lovers?'

'I believe so. Though from what Kit said, love didn't play a very big part in the proceedings.'

'Well, perhaps I should have a chat with Mr Banks.'

I suddenly remembered something else. It shot out from my recent memory like a bolt of white heat.

'Christ!' I said.

'What now? Another revelation?'

'Could be. Most definitely, could be. Banks said something funny when I was leaving the tattoo parlour. I didn't think anything of it at the time but . . . he told me to give my regards to Kit, if I saw him. And I was to tell him that Banks might be round *to get his pictures back*.'

Flynn looked intrigued.

'I think I feel a visit to the Wheat Exchange coming on,' he said. 'Thing is, in the meantime, what do we do with you? The pathologist thinks that Marsden died in the early hours of this morning. I don't suppose there's any chance that you might have a suitable alibi?'

I scowled.

'Asleep,' I said. 'In bed. In my apartment. Alone.'

Flynn groaned.

'That's what I was afraid you'd say. Oh dear, oh dear. Detective Sergeant Potts is going to be very annoyed with me.'

'You're . . . you're letting me go?' I had hardly dared hope for this but I saw to my relief that Flynn was nodding.

'Oh, I still don't think you had anything to do with the killings, Danny. At least, not directly. Your little performance in the other room drove away any shreds of doubt I might have had. No, I think you've either been involved in a freakish, million to one coincidence, or . . .'

'Or what?'

'Or that you are somehow linked to these two killings. I don't mean in a conscious way. It's something unwitting, something we can't identify yet. I'm sure it was simply chance that caused you to find the first body, but the odds on this one seem too long. I believe that in due course, we'll discover that the second murder was anything *but* a coincidence.' He made a steeple out of his hands and tapped his fingertips against his lips, something I was beginning to recognise as an habitual gesture. 'One thing I'm certain of. Whoever, or whatever this Zippy is, that's the key to the whole thing. If we can crack that one, then the fabric of this case will start to unravel.'

'And in the meantime?' I asked him.

'Go on with your life, Danny. But stay alert. I'll be doing everything possible at my end, but if you see or hear anything that might be of interest, I want you to contact me. All I ask is that you be scrupulously honest and tell me everything you know.'

Again I felt the stirrings of guilt deep inside. There were things I hadn't told him, things I couldn't bring myself to say. I masked my expression by mopping at my face with the flannel. Then I got to my feet, supporting myself by leaning my weight on the wash basin.

'How do you feel now?' he asked me.

'OK, I guess. Do you mind if I go?'

He shook his head, then picked up the photographs.

'I'll hang on to these for a while, if I may. I presume you've still got the negatives?'

'Yes . . . actually, I was wondering about that. I did those shots for the exhibition and I was really pleased by the way they turned out. Would there be any problem with showing them now that . . .?'

'Now that the subject is dead? That's entirely a matter for your own conscience, Danny. There's certainly nothing in the law that would oppose it. And as I said before, they *are* remarkable photographs.' He got up from the bathtub and opened the door. We walked through the bathroom and I tried not to look at Marsden's corpse, hanging like a butcher's shop carcass in the corner of the room. I knew that I'd be seeing that self-same image in my dreams for many nights to come.

We walked quickly out to the lounge and I pushed my way through the press of people, making for the exit. Potts looked at me incredulously as Flynn escorted me to the door. We went out on to the landing and I hesitated a moment, looking down the staircase. It seemed a long way down.

'Don't forget, Danny. Stay in touch,' said Flynn; then turned in surprise as Potts came out of the lounge, an indignant expression on his face.

'You're never letting him go!' he protested.

'Ah, Sergeant, if only all my officers were so perceptive! Yes, I'm letting him go. Do you have a problem with that?' Clearly the bad feeling between the two men had gone way beyond the formalities of being polite to each other.

'Have you taken leave of your senses? He's mixed up in this, somehow, he *has* to be! You're not telling me you fell for that little prima donna routine, back there? He was faking it.'

'I think not, Sergeant Potts. And I'm sure I needn't remind you that I am still leading this inquiry.'

'Yes, but . . . you could at least let me take him in for questioning. I'd soon get a confession out of him.'

'I don't doubt that for a moment – regardless of whether he's guilty or innocent. Besides, I've already questioned him myself and I'm perfectly satisfied . . .'

'You're not down south now, you know,' interrupted Potts. 'We have our own ways of doing things up here. Happen you'd be better advised to take a bit more notice of them.'

'Why, Sergeant Potts . . . you wouldn't by any chance be *threatening* me, would you?'

'Me, Sir?' Potts made an expression of exaggerated innocence. Then he turned away and strolled back into the flat. Flynn shot me a world-weary look.

229

'You see how things are, Danny. Not everyone is as convinced of your innocence as I am. For both our sakes, I hope the next time something like this comes up, you have the foresight to provide yourself with a decent alibi.'

I looked at him. 'The next time?' I murmured. 'You think there's more of this to come?'

He didn't answer that, just stood there looking at me with a sad expression on his face. I shrugged and went down the stairs, not wanting to think about the possibilities of it. I just wanted to get out of this awful place and go home.

Out in the car, sitting behind the wheel, I felt a wave of raw emotion wash over me and fresh tears welled in my eyes. I had barely known Kit Marsden; he had passed through my life with the brief glare of an emotional skyrocket, but the impact he had made on me was enough to justify me grieving for him. I knew then that I couldn't sit idly by and leave everything to the police. I would have to motivate myself, start looking for some answers. Banks had given me a vital piece of information that I had chosen not to pass on to Inspector Flynn and this seemed the logical place to start.

I needed to talk to Joey Sparks.

# Chapter Twenty-One

'Joey's Hideaway' wouldn't have won any prizes for interior design. I had last been here some years ago, a guest at a friend's stag night and so far as I could tell, it hadn't changed one jot.

It was essentially a big, rectangular space with the straight run of a bar at one end and the large stage at the other. In between, arranged around a postage-stamp-sized dance-floor were maybe a hundred formica tables complete with bum-numbing wooden chairs, many of which were already occupied by the evening's punters. As I bought myself a drink at the bar and searched out a vacant table, I was 'entertained' by what must have been the support act, a hyperactive young Barry Manilow lookalike with sculpted hair, dayglo teeth and a silver lurex jumpsuit.

The act consisted of him belting out a string of hit singles from the seventies and eighties, to an enthusiastic karaoke backing. In between numbers he'd slip in a few tired jokes about Irishmen and his mother-in-law. His singing voice wasn't much to write home about but he had bags of confidence and knew how to get the audience on his side. Somebody from a large stag party heckled him at one point and he rolled his eyes at the ceiling.

'Ooh, that makes me feel nostalgic,' he told the audience.

'I remember when I had *my* first glass of Babycham . . .'

This got him an enthusiastic round of applause and seizing the initiative, he went into a energetic version of *Delilah*, getting the audience to clap along and join in on the 'why, why, why' parts.

I wasn't much in the mood for singing along and instead, I took the opportunity to study the audience. Apart from the usual selection of stags and hens, who seemed to have been ghettoised at long, trestle tables off to stage left, most of the audience was made up of working class married couples. The men had their jackets off and shirt sleeves rolled up as they slugged their way through pint after pint of best bitter. The women sported permed hairdos and were chain-smoking kingsize fags, most of them drinking Bacardi and Coke. It always struck me as ironic that Joey Sparks, as unashamedly gay and camp as a row of tents, should attract such a conservative audience.

The support singer culminated his act with an overly dramatic rendition of *Without You*, giving the echo lots of elbow on the high notes in an attempt to disguise the fact that he wasn't quite reaching them. He finished to rapturous applause and did several low bows which threatened to tear the seat out of his jumpsuit. He could probably have justified doing an encore, but chose instead to slip into the role of Master of Ceremonies. He stepped back up to the microphone and for some reason, adopted an oily American accent.

'Lights!' he said – and a powerful spotlamp lit the wings to his right. 'Music!' he roared and a Hollywood epic style brass fanfare blared. 'And now, Ladies and Genital-Men, the star you've all come here to see! Direct from his engagement at Caesar's Palace . . . Stockport! Star of the erotic movie, 8½ . . . months! The man who put the *cock* into cocktails, the *dick* into dictaphone and the *tit* into titillation! Would you welcome, barely alive on stage, Manchester's very own killer queen . . . Joeeeeeey Sparks!'

The resulting applause nearly brought the roof down. The glitter-suited singer exited stage left and Joey Sparks entered stage right, wearing an even more glittering lamé ball-gown which scintillated in the glare of the follow-spot. He strode confidently centre stage, head back, hips swinging like a fashion model. Then he executed a perfectly timed trip on his platform stilettos and went into an ungainly, bandy-legged stumble, which brought gales of laughter from the audience. Sparks flung out a hand and grabbed the microphone stand, apparently in an attempt to stop himself from falling down. He stood there for a moment, surveying his public sternly. 'Bog off,' he said at last.

Again, everyone laughed uproariously. This was Joey's catch phrase, something he resorted to whenever he was in need of a sure-fire response. It wasn't exactly witty, it was something in the way he said it, revealing the common-as-muck Salford slag lurking behind the trappings of respectable affluence.

It was immediately apparent that Sparks was no spring chicken. His face was deeply lined and grizzled beneath the plastered make-up. He was tall and leggy, an effect heightened quite literally by the platform stilettos and the blond, beehive wig that seemed to be in danger of igniting under the spotlights just above his head; but his bare arms were running to flab and his once lissom figure now had a pronounced pot-belly that no girdle would ever completely disguise.

His years in the business had not softened him any. Joey's act had always stemmed from the 'theatre of outrage' and his targets were the very people who'd paid good money to see him. Standing up there and looking down at his public, he set about coldly and mercilessly taking the piss out of them. A bald-headed man at one of the front tables was asked to place a handkerchief over his skull. 'The reflection's dazzling me,' announced Sparks, to much amusement. He went on to say that in his experience, bald men usually had small penises and spent some time discussing the subject with the man's wife, who certainly didn't seem shy about commenting on her husband's physical attributes. Joey indicated a young man at the next table who had shoulder length hair. 'Now I bet *he's* hung like a donkey,' he observed.

At another table a woman in a boldly patterned print dress was alleged to have 'the dress sense of Elton John and a slightly less convincing wig' while her friend really came in for it. 'Ooh, what's up with her, she's got a face like a bulldog licking piss off a nettle!'

Next up, Sparks performed a spoof version of an old Beatles song. 'I wanna hold your gland!' he wailed, in a barely passable baritone, at the same time performing a suggestive routine with a pair of pink marraccas that looked exactly like a woman's breasts. By this time, members of the audience were virtually falling off their chairs with mirth.

With barely a pause for breath, Sparks was into the next segment of the act, another exercise in ritual humiliation. Various people were pulled on to the stage – those who had birthdays or wedding anniversaries, the would-be brides and grooms from the various stag and hen parties: while Sparks took on the persona of a game-show host and made them take part in a series of puerile games. The most obvious of them was when the women were made to get on their knees and had to eat peeled bananas that were clutched between the legs of a row of smirking males. This should have been merely infantile but Sparks kept up a string of perfectly timed comments that ensured the laughter didn't flag.

'Ooh, I can see you've done that before! Yes, slow down, dear, you're supposed to stop once you get to his trousers! By God, look at the gob on her, you can see she's had a few of those in her time! That reminds me, I must write to my mother . . .'

The giggling contestants were awarded packets of condoms as prizes for their efforts and were sent back to their seats. The lights dimmed as Sparks slipped into a more reflective mood.

'Joking aside,' he said. 'I want to take a little time to thank some very special people. The people who've made all this possible, who keep coming back to my little club night after night. I mean, of course, you, the public, my wonderful, wonderful fans. God bless you from the bottom of my heart, I love each and every one of you.'

I'd been waiting for a pay-off punchline but it never came. Instead, in a moment of absolutely sickening sentimentality, the music swelled and Sparks launched into a melodramatic version of *The Wind Beneath My Wings*, waving his arms as if he was really trying to achieve a vertical take-off. I sat there in disbelief. Maybe the act had been the same the last time I was here but I was probably lying drunk under a table by this time of night and had missed the finale. When the song finished, an even weirder thing happened. As the music played a strident reprise, Sparks descended from the stage to greet his fans. He moved amongst them like some ageing monarch parading before his subjects, shaking hands, blowing kisses. Everyone was suddenly up on their feet, clapping and shouting, some of them even *crying*, for Christ's sake, quite overcome by the emotion of it all – except that it was so phoney, so manipulated, I couldn't believe that anyone was falling for this routine.

And then it was all over. With a last theatrical bow, Sparks headed back up the steps to the stage and out through the wings.

'He doesn't do encores,' a middle-aged lady at the next table told me. Perhaps I'd had a puzzled expression on my face or maybe she sensed that I was not one of the 'regulars'. At any rate, the entertainment was clearly over and the punters got stuck into the serious task of consuming copious amounts of alcohol.

I waited a decent interval then went in search of Joey Sparks. It was easier than I'd anticipated. I flashed my business card at a bouncer who seemed happy enough to direct me to his boss' dressing room. After the rapturous reception he'd just had, I'd expected to find Sparks beseiged by adoring fans, but this wasn't the case. I found the door with the discrete gold star on it and when I knocked, it was the voice of the great man himself who bade me enter.

I opened the door and looked into the small, shabby room. Sparks was in there alone, seated in front of a well-lit mirror. He had changed out of his gown and put on a bathrobe. His wig now resided on a polystyrene bust on the dressing table and I noted that his real hair was dyed an improbable shade of auburn. He was in the act of removing his make-up with handfuls of cold cream. He peered at my reflection in the mirror and raised his pencilled eyebrows.

'What can I do for you, dear?' he asked. His voice was softer, less abrasive than his drag *alter ego*.

'Danny Weston,' I said. '*Evening Post*.' This was admittedly misleading but not exactly a lie. At any rate, he seemed pleased enough to talk to me.

'Come on in, pull up a pouffe. Like a drink?' He gestured to a half empty bottle of gin on his dressing table, standing amidst the paraphernalia of cosmetics and grease paint.

I shook my head. 'That was quite a show you put on,' I observed. 'You had them eating out of your hand.'

He smiled. 'Well, we're old friends,' he said. 'Some of them have been coming to see me for donkey's years. What I said out there, about loving each and every one of them. You probably thought that was just showbiz, didn't you?'

I shrugged. 'Well . . .'

'It's the God's honest truth,' he assured me. 'They're the ones who've put me where I am today. Without them, I'd be nothing, I'd still be back at the biscuit factory, stacking boxes.' He made a face, took a sip of his gin and tonic. 'They're the people who bought me my Rolls Royce and my house in Wilmslow. Of course I love them.'

'I can see how you'd be *grateful*,' I admitted. 'But love and gratitude aren't quite the same thing, are they?'

He studied me for a moment, perhaps realising that I didn't sound like a hack from the *Post*.

'What exactly did you want?' he asked me. 'It can't be another interview, I was only talking to one of your lot the other day. Look, you don't mind if I carry on removing my make-up?'

'Of course not . . .' Now I was here, I was suddenly unsure of how to continue. I watched Sparks in the mirror as he stripped away the mask that gave the illusion of being a woman. 'It's not exactly official business. Look, there's no easy way of saying this, but . . . I understand you were a friend of Kit Marsden.'

He hesitated in the act of removing a false eyelash and turned to look at me over his shoulder. He seemed suddenly wary.

'Kit? Yes, I know him. What's he been up to now?'

Unfortunately he'd missed my use of the past tense.

'I'm afraid you'll have to brace yourself for some bad news. Kit's dead.'

He kept staring at me as realisation gradually dawned in his eyes. Then he gasped and his whole body slumped, as though he'd been punched hard in the stomach. For a moment, I thought he was going to tumble right out of his chair. I was on the point of going to his assistance when he recovered himself a little. He raised his head to look at me and I could see that his eyes were brimming with tears.

'How,' he whispered fearfully. 'It . . . it wasn't drugs, was it? He messed around with them for a while but he told me he'd kicked it.'

I shook my head.

'He was . . . he was murdered. They found his body this morning, in his flat.'

'Murdered?' Sparks tried the alien-sounding word and his voice was dead, expressionless. 'You're . . . you're sure?'

'Yes, there's no doubt. He was . . . it was a very violent death.'

'Oh God.' Joey fumbled for a packet of cigarettes on the dressing table and lit one up with shaking hands. Then he took a large gulp of gin and tonic. 'I don't understand,' he whispered. 'You're not a policeman. How come they haven't contacted me?'

'I don't think they know about your . . . relationship. At least, not yet. I was only aware of it myself because Scott Banks told me.'

'Banks?' His eyes narrowed and a look of disgust came to his face. 'What's that slag got to do with this?'

'I don't know. Maybe nothing. The thing is though, the police are sure to be questioning him about the murder – and it's possible your name will be mentioned. I suppose I just . . . wanted you to hear about it from me, rather than from the police.'

'I see. That was thoughtful.' Sparks attempted a smile but only managed a grimace. 'You're a friend of Kit's then?'

'Not exactly. I only met him a couple of times. I took some photographs of him. That's what I do for a living.'

'And Banks? Where does he fit into this? Kit wasn't seeing him again, surely? I warned him, you know, several times. I told him to stay away from that maniac. It'll only end in tears, I said. That boy's got a screw loose, he's sick in the head . . .'

I held up my hands in an attempt to calm Sparks down.

'As far as I can tell, he hadn't seen Banks for months. I just happened to meet them separately, through my line of work.'

'So . . . who do they think did it?'

'It looks pretty much like it was the work of the same man who killed Sebastian Kennedy. There were . . . certain similarities.' I didn't want to have to go into detail.

Sparks shook his head.

'Well, I read about that, of course, but . . . Kit, *dead*? Murdered. Jesus, I told him he was mixing with the wrong crowd. But you couldn't ever tell him anything, oh no, he thought he knew it all. And now look what's happened to him. Oh Christ!'

'When did you last see him?'

'A couple of weeks ago. He called around to try and borrow some money. A thousand pounds he wanted, wouldn't say what it was for. I figured it was to buy drugs and I was very reluctant to give it to him. But he talked me round in the end. He always managed to talk me round.'

'Was it to buy a drug called Zippy?'

Sparks looked baffled.

'I don't know what he took. That scene doesn't interest me in the least. Actually, he said he wanted to invest it in a film he was making.'

'A film?'

'Yes, he was doing quite a bit of video work. It was his latest thing. I didn't ask too many questions about it, he always felt I was prying. He said he'd pay me back with interest. Not that the money mattered.' He slugged down the rest of his drink and refilled the glass with neat gin. His hands were shaking so badly, he slopped half of it on to the dressing table.

'Do you know if Kit was connected with Sebastian Kennedy in any way?' I asked.

'They worked together a couple of times,' said Sparks. 'Or so Kit once told me.'

'Really.' I was intrigued by this piece of information. 'But . . . forgive me, that doesn't figure. Kennedy was a highly respected theatre director. Kit was . . . no offence, but he just did a drag act, didn't he?'

'I know that!' snapped Sparks irritably. 'Who do you think taught him everything he knew? And there's nothing wrong with drag acts, let me tell you!'

'Of course not, I didn't mean to imply . . .'

Sparks sighed, shook his head. 'I'm sorry, I didn't mean to shout . . . I . . . I only know what Kit told me and as a rule, he chose to tell me precious little. He used to . . . you know, tease me sometimes, tell me about all the younger men he'd been involved with. A couple of months ago, Kennedy was featured on a local news report. Kit and I were watching it back at my place and he just suddenly turns around and says, "See him? I've worked with him!" Naturally I asked him to explain but he wouldn't tell me any more. I can see him now with that smug, infuriating smile on his face. Sometimes he used to make me so mad . . .' He stopped suddenly, as though realising that what he was saying could easily sound incriminating. 'It can be like that when you really care for somebody,' he told me. 'They have you running round in circles, jumping through hoops, but still you go crawling back for more punishment.'

He buried his face in his hands and began to cry, big, ragged sobs coming out of him now. I sat there uncomfortably, wondering if I should leave – but after a few moments he made an effort and got his emotions back on a tight leash.

'It was the same with that Scott Banks,' he whispered. 'Kit was always comparing me to him. *Oh, Scott does this, Scott does that*, like he was somebody to aspire to. But the truth of it is that slag used Kit something cruel, leaving him was the best thing he ever did. I used to say to him, "I know you'll get fed up with me sooner or later and go looking for somebody more your own age. I don't mind what you do, so long as you keep away from that Banks." He's violent, unpredictable. Capable of anything.'

'Including murder?' I asked.

'It wouldn't surprise me, not for one moment.'

I considered this. If Banks was the killer I was fairly confident that Flynn would rumble him soon enough.

'You said that Kit was running with "the wrong crowd". Did you mean anyone in particular?'

Sparks shook his head.

'Kit was no angel,' he said. 'He was mixed up with all kinds of people, real street-trash some of them, rough trade. He seemed to have a fascination for them. I used to warn him that a man in my position couldn't risk being associated with the kind of weirdos he hung around with. I kept threatening to dump him. But when it came to the crunch, I just couldn't bring myself to do it.' He laughed bitterly, shook his head.

'No fool like an old fool. Isn't that what they say?'

'So you can't think of anyone, besides Banks, who might wish him harm?'

'No, I'm afraid I . . .' He paused, looked at me sharply. 'Look, just what exactly is your interest in this? You say you're not a policeman, but you're asking an awful lot of questions.' His eyes narrowed suspiciously. 'For all I know you're one of his bits on the side! Is that it? You were involved with Kit too?'

'No. Like I told you, I only met him a couple of times.'

'Well then, he must have made quite an impression on you.'

'Yes, it's fair to say that.' A short silence descended on the room. Sparks just sat there looking at me and I felt that he was waiting for some kind of explanation. It was hard to know where to start. 'I don't even know why I came here tonight,' I told him. 'Out of respect, I suppose. All I *do* know is that up until a few days ago my life was all fine and hunky-dory. Then the Kennedy murder happened and suddenly the rug was snatched out from under my feet. In the space of those few days I've seen two corpses at very close quarters and it seems . . . in some way that I can't figure, that their deaths are connected to me. I feel like I'm falling and I don't have a clue where I'm going to land. I don't sleep much and when I do I have these horrible nightmares. I feel like I'm on the verge of losing my mind. I need answers, Joey! I need an explanation. Now, you've already said that there's some kind of link between Kit and Sebastian Kennedy. Was Kennedy connected with Scott Banks in any way?'

Sparks shook his head.

'Not that I know of. But you've got to remember, the Village is a very close community. Everybody knows everybody else. If somebody gets a rash, twenty people end up scratching. I'm sorry, but I really don't think I can tell you any more than that.'

I sighed, nodded.

'Well look, for what it's worth, I'm sorry about Kit. From what I know of him he seemed a remarkable person.' I got to my feet. 'One thing. I'm fairly certain that Banks will direct the police on to you. He was happy enough to tell me all about your relationship with Kit. If they do show up, I'd appreciate it if you didn't tell them I've been here to see you. They might not be too happy about it.'

Sparks nodded.

'Leave it to me,' he said. 'I'll give 'em an act. The show must go on and all that. Actually, I'm grateful for the warning. It will give me a chance to prepare a story.'

I looked at him inquiringly.

'A story?'

'Well, yes. It might sound mercenary but I've got my career to think of. I'll have to tell them that I haven't seen Kit in months. There's no way I'm going to be dragged into this business, shit sticks whether you're innocent or not. Don't misunderstand me. I loved that boy, but he's been nothing but trouble . . . and there's nothing I can do for him now.' He stubbed out his cigarette and immediately lit another one. 'Those photographs you mentioned? I'd love to see them sometime.'

'Well actually, they were intended for an exhibition I'm doing. But maybe now, after what's happened . . .'

'Oh no, you go ahead and use them. Kit would have wanted that. That boy was so vain. Beautiful and vain . . .' He was losing control of his emotions again. Fresh tears were welling in his eyes and his bottom lip was trembling as he struggled to hold on to his composure. 'He loved to be the centre of attention. The star of the show . . .'

That did it. He broke down again, burying his face in his hands, his shoulders shaking uncontrollably, the sobs tearing themselves out of him in a frenzy of grief. I stood there for a moment, wishing there was something I could say. But there was nothing that would make any impression on the kind of torment that Joey Sparks was experiencing now.

So I let myself out of the room, pulling the door gently to behind me. The sounds of his tears followed me along the corridor as I made my way to the exit and up the stairs to the dark silent street beyond.

# Chapter Twenty-Two

After yet another troubled night, plagued by terrifying dreams, I slept late and finally crawled out of bed around eleven o'clock, painfully aware that I was beginning to look and act like something out of a zombie movie. I shuffled to the bathroom and examined my reflection in the mirror. A gaunt face peered mournfully back at me.

'Hear the one about the photographer who *snapped*?' I asked myself and laughed manically.

On impulse, I found a razor and an ancient can of shaving foam. I lathered up my face and set about shaving my beard off. I told myself that if the mysterious hirsute killer carried out any more crimes in the neighbourhood at least nobody could say that he looked like me. After the drastic deed was done, I stared at my reflection doubtfully. I'd had the beard so long, I'd forgotten what my face looked like without it. Decidedly odd, I thought, but it was too late to worry about that now. I showered and dressed, then went to the kitchen to prepare an unappetising breakfast of dry toast. In addition to no milk, the kitchen now boasted a total absence of butter or margarine. I badly needed to visit a supermarket and promised myself that I would organise a shopping expedition, soon.

There was still no sign of Roz. I was pretty sure that she'd be at Wanda's again, but didn't dare try phoning her. She'd only give me another earful and I really didn't feel up to dealing with it today.

After two mouthfuls of toast and a cup of tap water, I felt ready to go out and greet the day. I picked up my camera case, put on my jacket and went down to collect my car from its regular parking spot. I set off for the Town Hall, where I'd arranged to meet Spike for our ascent up the clock tower. I hoped to God he was in a more coherent state than the last time we met.

On the way, my mobile phone trilled and I was obliged to drive one handed while I answered it. Maybe it was Barry Summerby with an assignment, I thought.

'Danny? It's Lawrence Flynn.'

'Oh, hello.' My disappointment must have been audible.

'You were expecting somebody else?'

'No, that's all right. What bad news have you got for me, this time?'

'You mustn't assume that I only ever bring bad tidings, Danny; though I'll confess this isn't particularly encouraging. I talked to your friend Scott Banks this morning.'

'Not *my* friend,' I assured him – and immediately thought there was something familiar about my denial. I'd heard somebody else adopt a similar, dismissive tone recently. But who? And about whom? 'What did he have to say for himself?' I asked.

'Precious little. But the chat was enough to convince me that he's not the most pleasant character in the world. He was far from amused by the fact that you'd put me on to him.'

'Great,' I said glumly. 'So no doubt he'll be round to rearrange my face, any minute.'

'Oh, I don't think he'd risk causing any trouble, not after

246

the grilling I gave him. The thing is, he came up with a fairly convincing explanation for his remark about "getting his pictures back". It seems when he and Marsden went their separate ways, Marsden appropriated some framed illustrations that Banks had done. It was those he was referring to.'

'And you believe that?'

'Well, it checks out. The pictures are right there in Marsden's flat, autographed by Banks. Plus he has a very good alibi for the night in question . . . which I might add, is a damned sight more than you've got.'

'Yeah, tell me about it,' I muttered.

'There are three people prepared to say that he was at a dinner party in Whalley Range on the night in question. He stayed over because he was too drunk to drive.'

'I see.'

'As for your Zippy/Skippy theory, I'm afraid it's a non starter. Banks claims that he hasn't seen the elusive Aussie in years. After some prompting, he dug out an old photograph of Skippy, who turned out to be a tubby, balding chap with very few teeth in his head. Hardly the slim, dark, bearded man we've been looking for. The man who resembles you.'

'Not any more,' I mumbled.

'Sorry, come again?'

'Never mind. Did Banks tell you anything else of interest?'

'Nothing, I'm afraid. It seems we're as much in the dark as ever we were. Anyway, I'll keep you posted. Ciao!'

He hung up. It looked as though Banks had decided not to mention the Marsden–Sparks connection and for the moment at least, I saw no reason to tell Flynn about it. Confirming that there was some kind of link between the two victims was doubtless important but I couldn't tell Flynn what I had discovered without dropping Joey Sparks head first into the shit; and for some reason, I was reluctant to do that. For one thing I was convinced that he was innocent of any involvement other than being Marsden's sugar-daddy. And from what he'd told me, he'd already been through enough grief on that score.

I found a parking spot outside the G-Mex centre, locked up the car and walked past the Midland Hotel. Crossing the street, I angled left towards Albert Square and then hesitated as I got the distinct feeling that I was being followed. I glanced back over my shoulder but the other pedestrians I could see seemed perfectly innocuous and I decided my imagination was getting the better of me. I walked on across the intricately cobbled, tree-lined square and went in through the hallowed portals of the Town Hall. I stood in the gloomy, cavernous interior, looking around. Despite the early hour, the huge building seemed to absorb all the light. Tall marble columns rose up on either side of me to support the intricate tracery of the Gothic roof.

Typically, there was no sign of Spike. He'd told me he'd meet me 'by the entrance' and I'd assumed that he meant this one, the main doors off Albert Square – but it occurred to me now that there were in fact four entrances to the building and that Spike could have been referring to any of them.

I turned right and began to traverse the interior, my shoes clumping hollowly on the beautiful mosaic tiled floor. There didn't appear to be many people about and after the bustle of Albert Square, the place seemed downright deserted: but up ahead of me by the opposite entrance, I could see a small information desk with a uniformed man sitting in front of closed-circuit TV screens. I started to head towards him. To my left, a magnificent circular staircase in smooth granite led up and down, to higher and lower floors. To my right was the large open chamber known as the Sculpture Hall, where a collection of rather ugly busts and statues were arranged in front of tall leaded windows. This area too looked deserted as I moved past.

Suddenly, I heard the sound of footsteps behind me and I glanced over my shoulder, expecting to see Spike grinning a welcome – but there was nobody there. The acoustics in the place must be deceptive, I told myself and I continued on towards the enquiry desk. But again I heard footsteps and this time, as I turned, I glimpsed movement. I froze in my tracks, hardly believing what I thought I'd just seen – a black cloaked figure slipping out of sight, behind the cover of a huge marble statue. It had been too brief a glimpse to establish if the figure was male or female, but it seemed such an eerie image that my heart leapt into my throat. I stood there, waiting, expecting to see the figure emerge from its place of concealment, but it didn't. Puzzled and more than a little bit afraid, I took a cautious step forward.

'Hello?' I said – and my voice seemed to echo on the empty air. No answer. This was ridiculous. Had I imagined that there was somebody there? Was my constant state of anxiety giving me hallucinations now? No, I was sure I had seen somebody . . . and as if to confirm this, I heard a gentle rustle of movement from behind the statue.

*What the . . .?*

I was beginning to feel very frightened now and I tightened my grip on the handle of the metal camera case. I reminded myself that there was a security man less than thirty yards away and I glanced over my shoulder towards the information desk: only to see that the man's seat was now conspicuously empty. It was a bad moment. For an instant there, I was on the point of running for the nearest exit, screaming for help. Then I started as I heard a low cough from behind the statue. I turned back to face it and took another hesitant step forward.

'Who's there?' I demanded. Still no answer but whoever it was, they *must* have heard me. It occurred to me that it might be Spike, playing silly buggers. God help him if he was, because this wasn't the least bit funny. 'Look, you arsehole,' I said, trying to sound forceful. 'I know you're there. Now are you going to come out or do I come round there and fetch you?'

Silence.

*OK, if that's how you want it . . .*

Fear was suddenly replaced by anger. I'd had enough of this shit. I began to walk purposefully towards the statue, holding the camera case out in front of me, ready to strike hard at whoever was waiting for me back there. I was only a few steps away from the statue when a figure glided out from behind it, coming straight at me. I lifted the camera case above my head, then registered that I was looking at an elderly nun, carrying a Berlitz guide book. I could also see the ancient hearing aid she wore in one ear. She gave me a startled look and hurried off in the direction of the exit. I stood there dismayed, feeling like a complete and utter pillock.

'I'm terribly sorry,' I called after her. 'I didn't mean to . . .'

A hand settled on my shoulder with a suddeness that made my heart thud. I gave an involuntary yelp and whipped around, swinging the camera case like a heavy, metal club. Luckily, Spike's reactions were quick enough to allow him to jump back out of harm's way. The corner of the case missed him by about three inches.

'Jesus!' he exclaimed. 'What's the matter with you?' He stared at me for an instant. 'And what happened to your beard?'

'Fancy creeping up on me like that!' I protested. 'You scared the shit out of me!'

Spike gave me a puzzled look. His long hair was tied back in a neat pony tail and he had forsaken the familiar jeans and leathers for a navy blue boiler suit.

'You need to chill out,' he observed. 'You're as jumpy as a frog on a hotplate. And why were you talking to that statue?'

'I wasn't,' I snapped. 'I was talking to *her*.'

I pointed towards the exit where the diminutive nun was making her escape on to the streets. 'I thought she was following me,' I concluded.

Spike laughed. 'Why would a nun follow you?' he asked.

'Never mind. Look, Spike, I'm feeling very jumpy today, OK? I had to look at this flayed body . . .'

'Yeah, I know. That still bothering you, is it?'

'No, this was a second body.'

'Another one? Shit, what's going on?'

'I wish I knew. This was the guy from Adonis. You remember, the one with the tattoos? I'd done some photographs of him only a day or so earlier.'

'Fuck.' Spike pondered this information for a moment. He looked perplexed. Then he eyed me nervously.

'Danny, I'm not being funny or anything but is it safe to be hanging around with you?'

'What do you mean?' I asked him irritably.

'Well, you took Sebastian Kennedy's photograph once, didn't you? And then he got murdered. Now this guy with the tattoos . . .'

'So?'

'Well . . . you took *my* picture. For the exhibition and all that? So, maybe . . .'

I stared at him. Could it really be as simple as that? It seemed so blindingly obvious and yet, it hadn't occurred to me that this might be the answer . . . that somebody was killing the people I photographed. Almost instantly, I discounted the idea. In my time at the *Post* I must have photographed literally *hundreds* of people. For a killer to work his way through that lot, even at the rate of several a day, it would take years to accomplish. No, it had to be more complicated than that.

'Look,' I said, 'I'm sure you've got nothing to worry about on that score. It's . . . it's probably just a coincidence.'

'You don't believe that,' he said quietly. 'You don't believe it any more than I do. Something heavy's going down and you're involved in it.'

I considered what he'd said. For Spike, it was a pretty astute observation.

'It would seem so,' I admitted.

'And you've got no idea at all how you fit into this thing?'

I shook my head, then glanced meaningfully at my watch. I really didn't like discussing this subject.

'Look, hadn't we better get this guided tour under way? Time's moving on.'

'Yeah, OK. Sorry, man.'

Spike turned and strode towards the circular staircase. I followed with my camera equipment, glad to note that Spike was a good deal more 'together' than he had been at our last meeting.

'You've decided to stay straight today,' I observed.

He gave me a sheepish grin.

'Yeah, sorry about the other day. I was blitzed. I'm going to have to cool it with the Zippy thing.'

We reached Level Two and Spike immediately led me around to the next flight.

'The bad dreams you mentioned. Did you have any that night?'

'Umm . . . yeah, I did.' He grimaced. 'Really horrible, it was.'

This wasn't the answer I'd been hoping for but I pressed on with the questions.

'Like the other ones? A lot of blood?'

'Yeah, like I said, I'm going to have to lay off it for a while. It was *too* real . . .' He glanced at me sharply. 'Why are you so interested?' he demanded.

'Uh . . . oh, I was thinking about trying it myself, but er . . . I don't think I'll bother. Sounds a bit scary.'

'Not as scary as you without your beard! What made you do it, man?'

I shrugged. 'Just fancied a change,' I lied.

We stepped out on to Level Four. Spike turned away from the staircase and led me along a wide corridor. A short distance down it he stopped by a small wooden door set into the left-hand wall. He took an old iron key from his pocket and inserted it into the lock.

'I'm the only one in the building who's allowed to carry this key,' he told me proudly. He unlocked the door and pushed it open, revealing a narrow stone staircase, spiralling upwards. 'Hope you've got stamina, Danny! It's a long way to the top!'

We began to climb, clockwise, Spike leading the way, me following on his heels, encumbered by the heavy camera case. The opening was only just wide enough to accept our bodies and the steps themselves were worn and slippery from decades of use. After just a few moments, I knew what it must feel like to be a cork as it is slowly screwed from the neck of a bottle. After a few minutes, we passed a small wooden doorway that Spike told me led out across the roof of the main building. I took a moment to get my breath back and we continued on our way, seeming to climb for ages before we found our next respite.

We reached a point where the tower opened up into a

windowless chamber beyond the staircase. Spike beckoned me inside and indicated a great slab of complicated machinery against one wall. Much of it was clearly ancient – cogs and wheels, levers and belts; but there were newer additions, digital displays and rows of switches and buttons, boxed behind perspex screens.

'That's the new electrical timing system,' said Spike. 'Funny thing, the clock never went wrong in its life till they installed that gizmo. Now it's hardly ever right.' He turned and motioned me to follow him with a flick of his head. We left the chamber and recommenced our journey upwards. A glance through a small slit window we passed on the way showed me that we were already very high up, but Spike assured me that we still had a long way to go.

Our next rest came when we reached the bell-ringing chamber. We emerged into a small square room. A huge metal spindle rose up through the floor and the walls on four sides revealed the translucent backs of the huge clock-faces. Spike, doing his 'official guide' routine informed me that each clock face was sixteen feet in diameter. He also indicated strategically placed ladders that allowed some brave individual – presumably him – to climb up and adjust the hands if necessary. Up above, the roof began to narrow into the spire and a series of bell ropes hung down to where we were standing.

'If the Queen or the Prime Minister died tomorrow, they'd send me up here to pull on these bell ropes,' Spike told me. Big responsibility that.'

'It must be,' I said. I peered apprehensively up through the timbers above our head.

'That's as high as we go, is it?'

'Yeah, come on. You'll shit when you see the view!'

We started up the final leg, the staircase now seeming even

more claustrophobic. Spike was scrambling up the steps like a mountain goat and I could only struggle along in his wake, my heart thudding in my chest. I had the distinct impression that the tower was swaying backwards and forwards as I climbed and a brief glimpse out of another slit window revealed nothing more substantial than empty sky.

Suddenly, I heard the sound of a bolt being drawn up ahead of me and as I rounded the turn, I saw Spike disappear out through an open doorway. A welcome blast of fresh air chilled my face and I followed him into the weak haze of October sunshine. I found myself standing on a narrow stone balcony which was affixed to the side of the steeple. There was a parapet at about chest height and without thinking, I leaned forward to look over it.

It was the first time I'd ever understood people who suffered from vertigo. While I'd never been particularly comfortable with heights, they hadn't bothered me unduly until now. But this . . . this was something else entirely.

I looked over the sheer drop and my eyes focused on the point where they expected the ground to be: then they were obliged to forget that and refocus a good fifty or sixty feet lower down. My stomach lurched and I had the distinct impression that my testicles were shrinking in on themselves, till they seemed to be the size and temperature of two frozen peas. It occurred to me that the little moving dots travelling across the patchwork quilt of the city were *people* – and that the slightly bigger dots were *cars*. As I stood there, stunned, I had the impression that the stone balustrade was crumbling away beneath my feet . . .

I snatched a breath and stepped smartly back, slamming up against the wall of the steeple behind me. Spike was leaning nonchalantly on the parapet, gazing calmly down at the ground one hundred and eighty feet below. As I watched in silent dread, he spat over the edge and the blob of phlegm went whirling into space. He turned and looked at me.

'You all right?' he asked.

I nodded, hoping my face wasn't as grey as it felt.

'No problem,' I gasped. 'I'll just . . . get my camera out,' I crouched down and unlatched the metal case with shaking hands. I removed the fish-eye lens from its cover and attached it to the body of the Pentax. Then I straightened up very slowly, looped the strap around my neck and edged carefully back to the parapet. Spike had taken out a pack of cigarettes and was lighting one up.

'One good thing about being up here,' he observed. 'The no-smoking policy is very hard to enforce!' He laughed gleefully and I responded with a feeble smile. I got the camera to my face and lined it up on a familiar-looking street stretching away below me. The convex lens gave the straight lines of perspective a pleasing curved effect. My hands threatened to shake again but I managed to talk them out of it and went dutifully about the task of taking some photographs, moving along the stretch of balcony, getting as many different views as I could.

After a few minutes, I'd managed to curb my terror and had replaced it with a sensation of mere dread. I couldn't quite rid myself of the notion that this ancient edifice might fall apart at any minute, a notion I mentioned to Spike.

'Don't worry,' he assured me. 'This old dump is as safe as houses. They knew about building, them Victorians!' As if to prove the point, he turned his back to the parapet and vaulted himself up on to it. He sat there, grinning at me.

'Spike,' I murmured. 'I'm not sure that's a good idea . . .'

'Chill out,' he advised me. 'I come up here every day, man, it's no big deal.'

I turned aside and noticed a small wooden doorway at the far end of the balcony.

'What's in there?' I asked.

'That's where Big Abel lives,' said Spike, hopping down and crushing out his cigarette beneath his shoe. He led the way along the balcony and unlatched the wooden door. We went inside the conical tower and I stood looking around. I was surprised by the general decrepitude of the interior, particularly by the astonishing amount of graffiti, most of it football orientated, that appeared to be sprayed, inked or carved into every available surface.

'This is terrible,' I said. 'Isn't this supposed to be a listed building? Look at all this vandalism.'

Spike shrugged.

'I know what you mean. But the only other people who come up here are the steeplejacks. Most of them are young football supporters and there's nobody to tell them not to do it, right?'

'Yes, but you'd have thought they'd have a bit more—' I broke off as I noticed a large SEPULCHRE ARE ACE carved into a wooden hatchway. Spike gave me an embarrassed smile.

'Well, at least it's not a football team,' he said.

The centre of the tower was dominated by a structure of ancient wooden beams, upon which the gigantic blue-green bronze bell rested. I wasn't too happy to note that much of the supporting woodwork was riddled with rot and that here and there, metal girders had been shoved into position to provide a little extra stability.

'Weighs eight-and-a-half tons,' announced Spike, sounding for all the world like a professional tour guide. 'He's six foot high, seven-and-a-half feet wide and he was installed in 1882.'

I frowned. I hoped to God that the remaining beams could be relied on to go on supporting such a colossal weight. If they collapsed it wouldn't be hard to envisage the giant bell crashing down through the flimsy wooden floor and on through all the levels until it hit the ground. I removed the fish-eye lens, snapped on a telephoto and took a couple of shots pointing up into the apex of the roof. Then moving across to the other side of the chamber, I nearly tripped over the bell ringing mechanism. I studied it with interest. It seemed unbelievably primitive. A metal lever jutted upwards through a ragged hole in the wooden floor. Through a pulley at the top of the lever, a length of metal cable ran downwards to the clock mechanism and upwards to a horizontal beam that ran alongside the base of the bell. This end of the cable was attached to the handle of a large wooden mallet, which in turn, was mounted on a simple fulcrum device. Even as I watched it, the cable began to tighten, pulling the lever back a short distance.

'Shit,' said Spike. 'He's gonna strike the half hour. Cover your ears!'

I got my hands up just in time. The lever cocked back and the mallet hinged forward, striking the bell with a sonorous roar. Even with my hands clamped hard over my ears, the volume was extraordinary. The mechanism struck a second time, the new din building on the dying echoes of the first. It seemed to take ages for the sound to die away. Spike went into a knockabout routine, his version of the Hunchback of Notre-Dame, hunching himself over and stomping around the tower like a maniac.

'The bells made me deaf, you know!' he lisped.

I ignored him and fired off a few more shots of the interior. I doubted that I would be able to use them in the feature I was planning but I was just putting off the moment when I'd have to walk back out on to the balcony.

Now Spike clambered up a short stretch of ladder to examine the wooden mallet which appeared to be attached to the steel cable with strips of gaffer tape.

'Only fixed this the other day,' he announced. 'And this is where I'll have to stand to make Abel strike thirteen!' He scowled, thought for a moment. 'Funny, isn't it?'

'What's funny?'

'Well, this clock and everything. It's like a symbol, ennit? Of the city and all that. But it's just rotting away up here, bit by bit. When this place was built it was the bees knees, man, people came from all over the country to have a decko at it. Now look at it. I mean, if they cared anything about it, wouldn't you think they'd spend a few bob fixing it up?'

I wasn't quite sure who 'they' were but perhaps it wasn't important. I could see his point.

'Somebody will have to start a charity,' I said.

Eventually I could put it off no longer and we stepped back out on to the balcony. Steeling myself, I walked to the parapet and looked over. With a little foreknowledge it was surprising how much better I handled it. This time I was merely apprehensive instead of terrified. I figured that with application, it was a fear I could eventually conquer. Wouldn't take more than four or five years . . .

'Race you down!' yelled Spike, lunging for the door but I happily let him go to it. I collected my camera case and followed him at a more sedate pace, stopping to bolt the door behind me. Then I started down the long spiral, turning anti-clockwise this time. For a while I could hear Spike's footsteps thudding ahead of me but then the sounds faded and I was left alone, moving downwards in the half light and those narrow stairs that seemed to go on for ever and ever . . .

# Chapter Twenty-Three

That afternoon, Roz came home. No excuses, no explanations, she simply walked in the door, announced that she quite liked my new clean-shaven look and asked if we had anything decent for dinner.

I was so glad to see her I rashly announced that I had just been about to set off for the supermarket. Roz offered to come with me, which was absolutely unheard of in my experience. I took her up on her offer before she could change her mind and the two of us embarked on a voyage to Kwik Save, looking for all the world like a happily married couple doing our weekly 'shop'.

We came back to the unprecedented luxury of milk in our coffee and butter on our toast and suddenly, the world was a more agreeable place. Roz seemed a changed person. Whatever had happened to her during her absence, it had been some kind of healing experience.

I spent the next week or so doing the final preparations for the exhibition. This largely consisted of me dry-mounting blown-up photographs on to display board. To give Roz her due, she proved to be very helpful with this; and even Spike pitched in, borrowing Sepulchre's Luton van to help me ferry the larger pictures around to The Wedge.

Vincent Spinetti, meanwhile, was doing his utmost to whip

260

up a media frenzy for *Skin Flicks*. Walking through town one day, I saw that a major bout of flyposting had taken place overnight and that the sleazy image I had hated on sight, now appeared to be affixed to every non-movable surface. I hoped to God that Spinetti hadn't done this off his own bat. There were only a couple of established firms that handled bill-posting in these parts and there was fierce competition between them. Independent operations were simply not tolerated.

Flynn rang me a couple of times, just to say that his investigation was getting nowhere fast. His only option was to wait for something to break. Not for the first time, I asked myself why he had chosen to confide in me. It was hardly official police policy, but then Flynn was no ordinary policeman.

The date for the *Skin Flicks* exhibition loomed – and the closer it got, the more apprehensive I felt. But it was useless to even think about pulling out now. Both Spinetti and myself had too much riding on it.

One evening, the three of us – me, Roz and Spike, were mounting up the last pictures, the shots of Sebastian Kennedy's flayed corpse. I'd chosen to make these blow-ups myself, not wanting Trevor Bird and the staff at Photolab to catch wind of what I was doing. To achieve the size I'd wanted, I'd been obliged to lay my ancient enlarger down on its side and project from a distance on to large sheets of photographic paper pinned to the wall. Developer and fixer were then painstakingly applied by spraygun. It had been a hit and miss technique but I was very pleased with the results. Both Roz and Spike assured me that I was doing the right thing by exhibiting the pictures. They didn't see anything wrong in it, though they were both fairly sure that it would be misunderstood.

'Great art is rarely appreciated in its own time,' said Spike gravely. 'I mean, look at Black Sabbath.'

Roz laughed. Since her return, she even seemed to be more tolerant of Spike.

'Right,' she said. 'And look at Modigliani.'

'Who are *they*?' asked Spike.

'Italian heavy metal band,' I told him. 'Surprised you haven't heard of them.'

'Oh, Modigli*ani*!' said Spike. 'Yeah, sure, I think I saw them on the box, the other night.'

Roz and I exchanged conspiratorial grins.

The phone rang and I answered it.

'Hello, Daniel?'

I recognised my mother's voice instantly. She was the only person in the world who called me that.

'Hi, Mum, what's up?'

'Well, I'm sorry to bother you so late, dear, but I'm really in a bit of a quandary at the moment.'

'Oh, what's the problem?'

'Well, there's this man in the house . . .'

I felt a coldness gathering in my stomach.

'What man?' I asked her.

'I don't know, dear, he won't say.'

'You . . . you've let a stranger into the house?'

'I couldn't help it, Daniel, he pushed past me at the door and sat down in my chair. He keeps talking to me but I can't understand a blessed thing he's saying. Between you and me, I think he's had too much to drink.'

Alarm bells started going off in my head.

'Mum, phone the police, now!'

'That's just the thing dear. I don't know the number. He's gone to use the toilet, that's the only reason I managed to phone you. I know it's a nuisance, but do you think you could come over? I want to go to bed . . .'

'Mother.' My voice was hoarse with fear now, enough to make Roz and Spike stop chattering and look at me. 'What . . . what does this man look like?'

'Well . . . he's really rather scruffy. He has long dark hair. And a beard. He . . . oh wait, Danny, I think he's coming back. I'd better go now . . .'

'Who are you ringing? I told you not to ring anybody!'

The voice, though some distance from the phone, was clearly audible. It sounded like the voice of a maniac.

'This is my house!' I heard my mother protest. 'You can't just come in here telling me what to do!'

Then the phone went abruptly dead, as though the lead had been yanked from its socket.

I stood there, horrified. My skin seemed to crawl with apprehension and I had the awful sensation that the room was getting smaller, the walls crowding in on me. I dropped the phone and turned to look at the others. They could see from my expression that something was horribly wrong.

'My mother,' I said. 'Some maniac's broken into her home . . .'

That was all I needed to say. The next minute the three of us were out of the door and running to the car, as if our lives depended on it. But it was my mother's life I was more worried about. Spike dived into the back and Roz slid into the passenger seat, beside me. I got the engine running and took off in a reckless U-turn, narrowly missing a concrete bollard. I drove down to Piccadilly, jumped a red light and headed off in the direction of the Merton Estate.

'We should call the police,' said Roz.

'Yes, good idea,' I agreed. Then cursed, as I realised that in my hasty departure, I'd forgotten to grab the mobile phone. 'Too late to go back for it now,' I said.

'Maybe we could stop at a call box,' suggested Spike.

'No way! We can't afford to lose the time. He could be doing anything to her, right now.' This thought goaded me into stamping down hard on the accelerator and we screeched around a tight bend at sixty miles an hour, the offside wheels momentarily losing contact with the tarmac.

'Fuck, man!' I heard Spike hiss in my ear. 'You're gonna kill us!'

'I'm going to kill *him*!' I retorted. 'If he's harmed so much as a hair on her head . . .'

'Easy.' Roz put a hand on my knee and squeezed gently. 'You can't be sure. There might be a perfectly ordinary explanation.'

*Yes*, I thought. *It isn't necessarily the killer*.

And logic told me that too. The murderer was somebody who got his kicks from killing homosexual males. What could he possibly want from a seventy-year-old woman? But I couldn't help thinking about Spike's theory. That people I photographed soon wound up dead. And not so very long ago, I'd photographed Mum, hadn't I?

By the time I'd reached the outskirts of the Merton Estate, I'd nearly killed us all several times over. I slewed the car to a halt in a layby and the three of us clambered out. I led the way at a brisk run. We went through an archway and pounded up a flight of unlit stone steps, tripping and stumbling in the darkness. Up at the top, we raced along the elevated walkway beyond and finally arrived at the door of my mother's flat. I couldn't see any lights on inside and I hammered at the door frantically with my clenched fist. It seemed to take ages for the call to be answered but finally, the door opened and there was Mother, looking perfectly all right.

'Daniel!' she beamed. 'Now that *was* quick! I hope you

weren't driving recklessly, you know you don't get there any faster if you do that. Oh and you've brought your friends with you! How lovely!'

We stepped into the hallway and I glanced around, baffled.

'Where's this man you told me about?' I asked.

'Oh, him. He's in the front room, dear. But you won't get a lot of sense out of him, I'm afraid. Now, I'll put the kettle on and make us all a nice cup of—'

'Just a minute, Mum.' I motioned Spike to follow me and we walked down the hall. I hesitated a moment, before pushing open the sitting room door. I stepped warily into the room.

The man was sitting in Mum's armchair, staring at me. He was a big, shabby guy in a heavy black overcoat. He had greasy, shoulder length hair and a matted, unkempt beard. I noted that there was a crust of dried blood on his forehead and even from this distance I could smell whisky on him. I felt immediately that this wasn't the killer I'd anticipated, just some poor, bewildered dypsomaniac who'd temporarily lost his bearings on his way back from the pub.

'Can I help you?' I asked him.

'I don't know,' he said and gave me a bug-eyed look. 'Are you trained in psychiatry?' He had a refined accent that was badly slurred by alcohol. I moved closer.

'Look, I don't know what you're doing here but . . .'

'Hah! That's rich!' he interrupted me. 'You don't know what *I'm* doing here? I don't recall inviting you into my flat.'

'*Your* flat?' I glared at him. 'What are you talking about? This is my mother's place.'

'Don't be ridiculous! I live here. Have done for years. Look, here are my identity papers.' He pulled a sheet of paper from his pocket and handed it to me. I examined it. It was an advertising handout for a new health club and gymnasium.

'Look,' I said. 'I'm very sorry, but if you don't leave now, I'll phone the police and have you forcibly removed.'

'Be my guest,' he said, motioning to the coffee table where the phone usually resided. Only it was no longer there.

'What have you done with the phone?' I asked him wearily.

'I've eaten it,' he said.

'I seriously doubt that. Where have you hidden it?'

'That's for me to know and you to find out. Phones are dangerous objects. They have powerful electro magnets in them. Magnets send messages to the brain that can give you *lesions*.'

'Look, it's getting late and my mother wants to get to bed.'

'In *my* flat?' The man looked positively outraged. 'I'll have you know I don't approve of that kind of behaviour.'

'OK, that does it. Spike?'

'Here, man.'

'Help me escort this gentleman off the premises, will you?'

'Sure thing.' Spike stepped forward to assist. I took hold of the bearded man's wrists and eased him to his feet. Then I got him moving towards the door. Spike stuck close to us in case he needed a little more persuasion. At first, I thought I'd have no trouble evicting the intruder, but then he stopped and gazed thoughtfully at the room's large windows, over-looking a small balcony at the rear of the building.

'See them windows?' he said.

I looked at them, puzzled.

'Yes?'

'I'm going to chuck you right through them,' he told me.

This was a very bad moment for me – because despite the fact that he'd announced his intention in a quiet, calm voice, at that same moment I'd somehow sensed the power in his big arms and had realised that he was quite capable of carrying out his threat.

'Now listen,' I pleaded. 'There's no reason to get—'

That was when he kneed me in the bollocks, doubling me over with a gasp of pain and causing me to let go of his wrists. Through watering eyes, I saw his right fist rising towards my chin and somehow I managed to duck under the blow. There was a meaty thud as his knuckles connected with Spike's jaw. Spike reeled backwards and went down like a sack of spuds, colliding with the coffee table and snapping all four of its legs like matchsticks. He lay there stunned and groaning as the bearded man turned his attention back to me.

'Now,' he said, advancing on me threateningly. 'I think I know you, don't I?'

I shook my head feebly but he ignored that.

'Of course I do. You're the man who shot John Lennon, aren't you? You're the man who keeps UFO's on his allotment. You're the man who dips goldfish in sawdust and sells them as Kentucky Fried Chicken!'

I retreated from him, one hand held up in submission, the other cradling my bruised testicles which were sending flickers of pain through my central nervous system.

'You're a fucking nutter!' I said.

'*I'm* a nutter? That's rich! At least I don't go round evicting innocent people from their homes.'

'For the last time, this is *not* your home!'

'You're just trying to confuse me,' he said. 'But I know this is my place. There's my boxing trophies.' He pointed to my mother's modest display of Capo Di Monte figurines on the nearby sideboard. 'I was heavyweight champion of Barnardos for three years running,' he told me proudly.

'They used to call me "The Hook". Would you like to find out why?'

'Uh uh,' I said. 'No, I really don't think so.' I took another step back and my buttocks connected with the wall. I had nowhere left to retreat to.

'I once hit this kid so hard, he was in a coma for weeks,' he said, dreamily. 'Then he died. That's why I stopped boxing. I didn't *want* to, you understand, but they said it was for the best. They'd look at me and there was something in their eyes. It was fear. They were afraid of me because I was the best at what I did. But this boy died, you see. They said it was his brain. Got slammed around inside his skull like a couple of pounds of mince meat in a tin box. That was the hook, did that, see? A killer punch they said it was.'

I nodded grimly.

'Well then, you . . . you wouldn't want that to happen again, would you?' I whispered.

He thought about it for a moment, then smiled vacantly.

'Oh, I dunno,' he said. 'Might be fun.' He drew back his right fist to the shoulder.

*Oh, Mary, Jesus and Joseph! He's going to—*

And that was when Roz appeared at the man's side. She grabbed him by the wrist in some kind of complicated hold and with what looked like ridiculously little effort, she ducked under his grasp, twisted the arm behind his back and jammed it up behind his shoulder blade. The man's eyes bulged in pain and surprise.

'Oww!' he roared. 'Leggo, you bitch! You'll break my arm . . .'

'If necessary,' Roz assured him. 'Unless you leave, now.'

'All right, all right . . .' The man was up on his tip toes in a vain attempt to minimise the pain. The whole thing looked vaguely surreal. Roz was about half his size but he was absolutely helpless. I told myself that I'd never take the piss out of her self-defence classes again.

'Open the front door, Danny,' said Roz calmly. 'The gentleman is just leaving.'

'Right.' I scuttled out of the room, still bent over double from the pain in my crotch. As I passed the open door of the kitchen, I could see my mother, happily preparing tea and biscuits, oblivious to what was going on.

'Everything all right, dear?' she asked me.

'Under control,' I croaked. I unlatched the front door and turned back to see Roz propelling the intruder bodily along the corridor.

'Oww!' he bellowed. 'Stop it, you cow, you're hurting me!'

'Tough,' snarled Roz. She pushed him out through the open door and frog-marched him for some distance along the walkway beyond, before releasing him. I followed warily, afraid that once free he might turn on her. Instead, he just stood there, rubbing his injured arm. His bottom lip was trembling and he looked as though he might be about to burst into tears.

'Not right,' he complained bitterly. 'Could have done me serious damage.'

'You want serious damage?' Roz adopted a Bruce Lee fighting pose. 'It can be arranged, no problem.'

The man backed off a couple of steps.

'Fascist,' he grumbled. 'You ever heard of "Care In The Community?" ' Roz didn't answer him so he turned and began to walk away. He moved down the staircase out of sight, but a few moments later, we heard his disembodied voice echoing up the stairwell. 'Assault!' he roared. 'An innocent man, in his own home, set upon by three young thugs! Near broke my bloody arm, they did!'

'Shut the fuck up!' yelled a voice, from one of the flats.

'People are trying to sleep in here.'

'Here, I know *you*!' yelled 'Mr Beard'. 'You're the man who puts Dettol in my porridge!'

Roz glanced at me, shook her head.

'Jesus,' she exclaimed. 'Are you OK?'

I nodded. 'Just bruised bollocks and wounded pride,' I told her. 'You were amazing though. You really saved my skin back there. Thanks.'

She blushed, made a dismissive gesture.

'Just a very basic Aikido move,' she assured me.

'Are you kidding? That guy was like the Empire State next to you.' I took a step towards her, then felt a twinge of pain go through my groin. I had to make an effort not to grab hold of my testicles. 'Maybe I should come to those self-defence classes myself,' I said through clenched teeth.

Spike came limping slowly along the hallway, looking rather dazed. He had the makings of an impressive bruise on his jaw.

'Where'd he go?' he muttered.

'To his own home, I hope,' I told him. 'You all right?'

'Uh, yeah. No problem.' Spike drew himself upright and spat through the open doorway. 'Dude caught me with a lucky punch, that's all. I wasn't quite ready for him. But if I see him again . . .' Another shout echoed up the stairwell and, startled, Spike took an involuntary step backwards. 'Yeah, well . . . I'll go and help your mum with the tea,' he concluded. He headed back towards the kitchen.

Roz took a few more steps towards the stairs.

'You not coming in?' I asked her.

'I just want to be sure that he's gone,' she said. 'Don't want him coming back after we've left, do we?'

'We can dig out the phone and ring the police, if you're worried. Anyway, I think he's learned his lesson.'

'Maybe.' She frowned. 'He'd been drinking.'

'Yeah, I could smell it on him.'

'People like that shouldn't be allowed near drink,' she said. 'He'll be on all kinds of medication. You mix that with alcohol and you've got yourself a walking time bomb. The next thing you know, he'll go off the deep end and kill somebody.'

I looked at her. There was something in her voice that spoke from experience. I didn't say anything. I had the feeling that there was something she wanted to tell me. There was a long silence, broken only by the distant bellowing of the bearded man.

'My father was just like him,' said Roz, quietly.

This was a revelation. In all the time I'd known her, Roz had never mentioned her parents, had always changed the subject whenever they came up.

'Your father?' I prompted her.

'Yeah. That *bastard*.' She somehow managed to load the word with a hatred that went way beyond its actual meaning. 'He made my life hell for fifteen years – my mum's for a lot longer than that.' She walked across to the wooden balustrade and stared down at the weed-pocked forecourt below. I moved to stand beside her. We saw the man emerge from an archway and go weaving unsteadily across the flagstones, throwing a long, angular shadow in the moonlight. He was muttering to himself now. He saw us watching him and threw a crude two fingered gesture at us before disappearing down an alleyway.

'Thursday was his day,' said Roz. 'Dole day, of course. He'd cash his cheque around lunchtime and then head up to the social club to meet all his old cronies. Mum and me would dread him coming home that night. He wouldn't arrive back till he'd drunk away every penny of it. No

thought of giving Mum anything for the house-keeping, it all
went down his neck. I can remember sitting there with Mum
on a Thursday night, waiting for the sound of his key in the
door . . . knowing it would start the moment he got in.'

'He . . . he would hit you?'

'Not me. My mother. He used her as a punching bag all
her life. He'd beat her and swear at her and . . . that night,
always on the Thursday night, he'd make her . . . you
know . . .'

I put a hand tentatively on her shoulder. She didn't shrug it
off.

'Later, he became a manic depressive. He was convinced
that me and Mum were trying to poison him. Wouldn't eat
any of the food we'd prepared. And he'd say things . . .
crazy things. Make out that Mum was having it off with every
man in the street . . .' She laughed bitterly. 'I wouldn't have
blamed her if she had; but the truly tragic thing about it is
that she took everything he dished out and never fought back
once. Not once.' Roz looked at me in baffled despair and I
saw that her eyes were filling up with tears. 'I used to pray
that the evil bastard would die, so we could both be free of
him, so that Mum could have some life of her own, you
know? She deserved to have *something*. But he even took
that away from her in the end.'

I stared at her.

'You're not saying that he . . .'

'Oh no, he didn't murder her. Not officially. It was suicide.
See, when I was around sixteen, I started staying at friends'
houses on Thursday nights. It was just so wonderful not to
have to go through that bloody weekly ritual.' I looked at her
hands where they were gripping the wooden rail of the
balustrade and her knuckles were white. 'I . . . I should have
realised that I'd left Mum alone with it. Alone with her

fear. One night, she was just sitting there waiting for the sound of his key in the door and she must have got too scared . . . so scared that she started popping pills, one after the other. Paracetamol. It doesn't take many. By the time Dad got home she . . . she was long dead. Me, I was round at my mate's house. Watching telly. Eating chocolate. Having a really good time . . .'

Her voice cracked and her shoulders began to move as the tears came in earnest.

'Oh, Roz,' I said. 'I'm sorry. I had no idea . . .'

I stepped closer and took her in my arms. She pressed her face against my chest and sobbed out her anguish.

'I should have been with her, Danny! I should have *protected* her. I could do that for her now, but it's too late. It's far too late for her . . .'

She gave in to the tears for a moment and I just held her, reaching up one hand to stroke her hair. It seemed weird to be this close to Roz, weird but oddly reassuring. When she had quietened down, I asked about her father.

'Is he dead too?'

She shook her head.

'No. At least, I don't think so. He was institutionalised after Mum's death and I just got far away from there. For all I know he's still in the mental hospital in Blackburn – or maybe he's walking around like that guy just now. I don't know or care what his situation is. All I know is if he ever comes near me, I'll kill him.'

'You don't mean that,' I said.

She pulled away from me then and gave me a scornful look.

'Of course I mean it,' she retorted. 'What would you know?'

'Nothing,' I admitted. 'It's just the kind of thing you're

supposed to say. Roz, I wish you'd told me about this before. I mean, no wonder you're . . .'

'What?' she asked me defensively. 'A dyed-in-the-wool crank? A *man-hater*?'

'I wasn't going to say that!' I protested.

'No, but you were going to *think* it. I know how people perceive me. Well, let me tell you, I don't give a fuck what people think. And if I'm wary of the male species, I've got every reason to be.'

We sensed movement behind us and saw Spike emerging from the kitchen, carrying a tray of tea and biscuits.

'Hey, come on you two. Tea's up!'

Roz nodded. She wiped her eyes on the sleeve of her jacket, then went to step past me; but I put a hand on her arm, restraining her a moment.

'Look,' I said. 'Thanks for sharing that with me.'

She shrugged, made a dismissive gesture.

'You probably have enough on your plate, just now.'

'Still, it's good to talk,' I said. 'We haven't done enough of that in the past. And thanks again for saving my neck. You're a good scout, Birchill.'

She smiled and it was great to see that. It seemed to transform her whole face.

'Come on,' she said. 'Let's get that tea before it goes cold.'

We stepped into the flat, closing the door behind us.

# Chapter Twenty-Four

On the morning of the exhibition preview, I woke feeling refreshed and ready to take on the world. The feeling lasted about ten minutes and was replaced by an attack of the jitters that had me shaking in my boots.

I got a call from Mum. She told me that she'd come down with a bad cold and regretted that she wouldn't be able to make it to the opening. I had mixed feelings about that but had to admit to myself that the relief outweighed the disappointment. She'd be able to catch the show later, when I had a better idea of how people were reacting to it. I told her to dose herself up and to call me when she felt able to make the trip into town.

On the face of it, things were beginning to look up. I hadn't suffered a nightmare for the best part of a week and Barry Summerby had phoned with a couple of *Evening Post* assignments which I'd be very grateful for if I failed to sell anything from the exhibition.

Vincent Spinetti had persuaded me to set the prices high – *ridiculously* high, I thought, but he had argued that it was a mistake to make your prices too competitive. A hefty price tag, he insisted, helped to convince buyers that they were getting something worth having. So the original signed prints were set around five hundred pounds each; (I'd originally suggested fifty) with limited edition runs of copies set at two hundred and fifty quid a throw. I hoped to God Spinetti knew what he was doing.

In the kitchen, last night's dishes had been washed and stacked and there was a note from Roz informing me that she'd gone into town to do 'a bit of shopping' and that she'd catch me later. The changes in Roz Birchill over the past week or so had been extraordinary. She seemed to have somehow transformed herself into a polite, helpful, sincere individual who, more often than not, was great fun to be with. Some cynical part of me anticipated a pay-back somewhere down the line.

I breakfasted on scrambled eggs, toast and milky coffee and after washing the crockery, decided to follow Roz's example and take myself off for a stroll. The time would surely pass more quickly if I was in motion.

It was a cold, but sunny, October day. The air held the mysterious bonfire smell that seems to appear as the nights shorten towards Halloween. A lot of the shop windows already had ghoulish displays on show; mannekins dressed as witches and vampires and Frankenstein monsters. I reflected that one of my upcoming assignments was at the city museum, where they were putting on an *El Dia de Muerte* exhibition to tie in with the *Viva Mexico* festival, currently gearing up for its big finale at the end of the month.

In the city centre, I couldn't seem to look in any direction without seeing a *Skin Flicks* poster and I wondered if Spinetti was laying it on a bit thick. Actually, I hadn't seen him since the day the artwork had arrived and our two phone conversations since had been brief and business like. He always claimed to be too busy to see me in person, but had given me his promise that he'd left tonight free in his diary.

'I'll be right there with you, mate,' he'd assured me and I

was relieved to hear it. The thought of fielding the event on my own was not something to relish.

If I'd hoped to run into old friends in town, I was disappointed. I hung around in the city art gallery for a while but even their sublime collection of Pre-Raphaelites failed to engage my interest and after a mere glance through a seemingly endless procession of Turner watercolours, I grew listless and was soon back on the streets. I thought about calling in at The Wedge but decided against it. I'd been working there till late the previous night, adding the finishing touches and it now seemed like bad luck to show my face again until show time.

So I wandered into a small coffee shop in the Royal Exchange and ordered a *cappuccino*. Looking around for a vacant seat, I finally spotted somebody I knew. It was Juliet Fleming, Spinetti's former PA. At the same instant, she glanced up and saw me. The smile she gave me was dutiful rather than genuine, but nevertheless, I carried my cup across to her table and asked if the seat opposite her was taken.

'You can see it isn't,' she replied testily, but waved me into it. She was dressed in a sharp pinstripe two-piece and had an expensive-looking leather briefcase beside her chair. She looked every inch the upwardly mobile young business-woman and I told her so. This time her smile seemed a little warmer.

'I've just been for an interview,' she told me, with a conspiratorial air. 'Another PA's job. Think I did OK, too.'

'That's great.' I stirred a lump of sugar into my coffee. 'So you've decided against going back to Spin International?'

'Most definitely. How's Vincent managing without me?'

'Not good,' I told her. 'I've only spoken to him on the phone but he told me that he's had a couple of temps who haven't shaped up too well. He did say that if I saw you, I was to ask if you would reconsider . . .'

'Forget it,' she said. 'Not interested.'

'You seem adamant,' I observed.

'Let's just say I had my eyes opened to the realities of working for Vincent Spinetti.' She studied me for a moment. 'It's your show at The Wedge soon, isn't it?'

'Very soon. As in, *tonight*.' I sipped at my coffee. 'Look, Juliet, Vincent told me . . . well, that he'd used some of your wages to help finance the exhibition. I want you to know I had no idea about that. When he told me, I felt awful.'

She shrugged.

'That's all right. I'm not surprised he didn't tell you.' She looked at me meaningfully. 'I'd be willing to bet that there's quite a few things you're not aware of.'

'What's that supposed to mean?' I asked her.

'Don't get me wrong, Danny. I've got no axe to grind with you. I've always thought you were a nice bloke. Maybe *too* nice. Frankly, I don't think you should be working with Vincent, because however he may seem on the surface, underneath he's anything *but* nice.'

I smiled. 'Oh, come on. If I had a fiver for every time I've heard somebody bad-mouthing Vincent . . .'

She laughed at me.

'Well there you go!' she said. 'That's exactly how he gets away with it. You see, essentially, Vincent is a charmer. Guy could charm the birds down from the trees, isn't that right? He certainly charmed the pants off me for a couple of years.' She glanced at me sharply. 'Metaphorically speaking.' She lifted her coffee cup in both hands and stared into it thoughtfully. 'You know what Vincent reminds me of? A beautiful garden in the summer, nourished, colourful, well-tended. But you go into any garden and turn over a few stones. Just see the dark, squirmy things that come wriggling out.'

I scowled.

'I don't think it's fair to talk like this behind his back.'

She laughed again, putting down her cup so she could clap her hands in apparent delight.

'You see, he's charmed you too. Automatically you spring to his defence! That's his gift, Danny. That's the secret of his success. And it's not that you're unbelievably naïve. I've seen it done to so many intelligent people – myself included.'

I glanced quickly around the interior of the coffee shop. It wasn't busy and there were few people who might overhear us.

'Look, if you've got a specific allegation to make . . .'

She grimaced.

'Not my place to do that, sunshine. But you remember that business over my wages? How it was invested in other projects?'

'Yes, Vincent told me all about that.'

She looked surprised.

'Really? What did he say?'

'That there'd been a cash-flow problem and that all the money he did have had gone into making a promo tape and video for the Vice Squad.'

Juliet glared at me.

'What?' she protested.

'Yes, he said that he really believed they'd make it big, but you thought they'd only ever have a cult following. You were mad that he'd sunk your money into a band that you didn't like.'

'A band?' she murmured.

'Yes, the Vice Squad. A reggae band, I think Vincent said. He reckons they've got a great—'

I was interrupted by a burst of manic laughter from Juliet. She was laughing at a volume that turned heads at the other tables and for a moment there, I thought she was actually going to fall off her seat.

'You believed that?' she cried. 'Oh, correction, Danny, *correction*! Maybe you are *unbelievably* naïve!' She pounded the table with the flat of one hand, making our respective cups and saucers rattle. Finally, she got herself under control. 'Listen to me, Danny,' she said. 'Vincent has a quick tongue and a way of selling a story to the gullible but . . . next time you see him, you just ask him about the videos, OK?'

'Videos? What videos?'

'Oh no, that's all I'm saying. Next time I see you, no doubt you'll be able to tell me exactly what his explanation was. I can hardly wait!' She seemed to remember something and glanced at her watch. 'Got to be moving,' she announced. 'Things to do.'

'Wait,' I said. 'You can't leave it like this.'

'Oh yes I can,' she retorted. 'I wouldn't want to be accused of sticking a knife into poor Vincent's back, now would I? So I'll just let you work it out for yourself. And then we'll see if you still think he's Mr bloody Wonderful.' She picked up her briefcase, got up from the table and headed for the door. She hesitated in the entrance for a moment and glanced back at me. 'Good luck for tonight,' she added. 'I hope the end justifies the means.' And with that she stepped out into the street and was swallowed up in the crowds of people moving around the arcade.

I sat there with the rapidly cooling dregs of my coffee, pondering what Juliet had said. Clearly she had it in for Spinetti, but was that really so surprising after what had happened? And was there any more to it than met the eye?

That stuff about videos, for instance, seemed easily explicable. Spinetti had contacts in the bootleg trade and always knew where to get a pirate copy of the latest blockbuster; but it hardly made him Professor Moriarty, did it? Was it this Juliet was referring to – or something else?

At any rate, I resolved to ask Spinetti about it later that night. It was a bad time to be having serious doubts about my manager. Glancing at my watch, I saw that it was fast approaching time for me to head home and prepare myself for the evening.

Back at my place, I shaved, showered and dried myself. I put on the new Matinique suit I'd bought only a few days earlier, three hundred quid squandered on a beautifully cut two-piece in charcoal linen, plus another fifty notes on a flame red raw cotton shirt by Jigsaw. I was examining myself dubiously in the wardrobe mirror when there was a soft rap on my bedroom door. Roz looked in and gave me an encouraging grin.

'Hey, looking *good*!' she exclaimed. She came into the room, nodded appreciatively, her arms behind her back. 'Give us a twirl,' she said.

I did a parody of a male model on a catwalk.

'What do you think?' I asked her.

'Not bad. It still needs something though.' She brought her arms out into view and I saw she was holding a small, neatly wrapped package. 'I picked this out for you,' she said. 'Hope you like it.'

Bemused, I unwrapped the package. It contained a white silk tie, hand-printed with charcoal and red designs. For a moment, I wondered how she'd managed to get something that matched so perfectly. Then I remembered that I'd modelled the outfit for her a few nights earlier and had debated whether or not it needed a tie. She'd assured me that it didn't and now I understood why.

'It's brilliant,' I told her. 'Thanks, Roz, that was really thoughtful of you.'

'You're sure you like it?' she asked warily. 'I mean, I kept the receipt in case you wanted to change it . . .'

'Are you kidding? I love it. And I'm amazed that you took such trouble on my behalf.'

She shrugged.

'Just my way of saying "sorry", really. I treated you badly for a while. I knew I was doing it but somehow I just couldn't help myself. You're too easy-going, Danny. You invite people to use you and they can't resist it.'

'Somebody told me today that I was unbelievably naïve. Do you think that's true?'

'Well, you always look for the best in people. I don't know if that's good or bad. Here, let me help you with that.'

I'd been struggling to do up the tie but she managed it easily. As she tightened the silk around my neck I was momentarily surprised by the strength in her hands.

'I bought it from that ethnic shop off Newton Street,' she told me. 'The designs are Aztec. This one here is Quetzalcoatl, the Feathered Serpent. That one's Mictlantecuhtli, the Lord of the Dead . . .'

I smiled. 'How is it you know so much about them?' I asked.

'Oh, just one of my many night classes.'

'Well, however you pronounce the names, they make the perfect finishing touch. Thanks, Roz.' Impulsively, I leaned forward and gave her a peck on the cheek, something I wouldn't have dared to have done a couple of weeks ago. She flushed a little but seemed perfectly happy with the gesture. 'Will I do?' I asked, spreading my arms.

'You look sharp. Go and knock 'em dead, kiddo.'

'I'm going to walk into town,' I told her. 'In case I need a few fortifying snifters. I'll er . . . I'll see you later.'

'Yeah, see you. Break a leg!'

I let myself out and nearly did exactly that when I missed my footing on the stairs. I steadied myself and continued at a more cautious pace, making it on to the street without major mishap. It was six o'clock, already dark and the relative warmth of the day was shot through with the advancing chill of winter. I stood there for a moment and felt like turning on my heel and going right back inside, climbing into bed and pulling the covers up over my head.

*What are you afraid of, Danny?*

A good question. Gritting my teeth and thrusting my hands into my pockets, I set off to walk to The Wedge, for what promised to be a very eventful evening.

# Chapter Twenty-Five

I arrived at The Wedge a good half hour before the advertised starting time. Deep down, I knew this was a mistake, that I'd only get nervous standing around waiting for things to happen, but somehow I just couldn't help myself. On paper the cool way to handle it would be to turn up an hour or so into the proceedings, suitably well oiled from a session down the pub. I would then insult a few journalists, make a few profound statements about 'my art', drink several bottles of wine and finally go to sleep under the refreshments table, smashed out of my brain.

But there wasn't a cool bone in my body. I was, by nature, a worrier. I would be the one skulking unhappily in the corner of the room, nursing a glass of wine, straining to overhear everyone's observations about my work, constantly seeking reassurance from my friends.

I pushed through the glass doors of The Wedge and climbed the steps to the first floor gallery. Beside the swing doors, a giant blow-up of the *Skin Flicks* poster left little doubt as to the kind of material that a visitor might expect to find within; and a warning in bright red print had been attached to the door:

PLEASE NOTE
 SKIN FLICKS IS AN ADULT ORIENTATED EXHIBITION

WHICH INCLUDES IMAGES THAT MAY SHOCK AND
DISTURB.

THE MANAGEMENT ACCEPTS NO RESPONSIBILITY FOR
ANY OFFENCE CAUSED.

CHILDREN UNDER THE AGE OF SIXTEEN WILL NOT BE
ADMITTED UNLESS ACCOMPANIED BY AN ADULT.

I frowned. This approach seemed to have more in common
with a seaside waxworks exhibit than a serious art show. I
wasn't sure if the notice had been put there at the gallery's
insistence or whether it was a bit more of Spinetti's razzle-
dazzle showmanship coming to the fore. I suspected the
latter.

I went into the gallery. Everything looked to be just as I'd
left it the previous night. The giant black and white blow-ups
were picked out by strategically placed spotlights. In the
centre of the floor space stood the octagonal partitioned off
area containing the Sebastian Kennedy pictures. I saw that
another of the warning signs had been placed beside the
entrance, so at least nobody could claim that they hadn't
been warned.

Up at the top end of the room, a large refreshments table
had been set up, and I saw Spinetti putting out bottles of
wine and glasses. He was dressed in a sharp, pearl grey suit
with a contrasting Liberty-print waistcoat. He glanced up as I
approached and gave me a discouraging look.

'Sorry, mate, we don't open till seven-thirty. If you'd like
to come back . . .' He paused, looked at me more intently.
'Danny?' he said. 'Jesus, I didn't recognise you, you look so
smart.'

'Thanks a bunch,' I said. 'So how do I usually look?'

'No offence, mate, but you've had that beard as long as I
can remember. You look so much . . . *cleaner*.' He reached

out and felt the lapel of my jacket between thumb and forefinger. 'Very nice,' he observed. 'I bet this didn't leave much change out of four hundred notes. *Love* that tie!'

'Oh, just a couple of old rags I threw on,' I told him. I glanced around the big, empty gallery. 'Do you suppose anybody will turn up?'

'Sure they will.' He slapped me heartily on the back. 'Come on, what say we have a drink, get you loosened up a bit?' He grabbed a corkscrew and a bottle of red. 'You can tell me what you think of this stuff. Got hold of a job lot of Bulgarian plonk, didn't I? Cost me nearly fifty pence a bottle, so it'd better be good!' He pulled out the cork with a flourish and filled a couple of glasses.

I sipped at mine and decided that even at fifty pence a bottle the wine was seriously overpriced. But I didn't tell Spinetti that. Actually, I didn't need to. The look of disgust when he tasted his own drink suggested that he had no misconceptions on that score.

'Jesus,' he said. 'Rat piss and vinegar. Still, it's strong enough. Couple of glasses of this and they'll be putty in our hands.' He smiled, glanced at me. 'So, how you feeling? Nervous?'

'Like a long tailed cat in a room full of rocking chairs,' I told him. 'I'm beginning to wish I'd never got into this.'

Spinetti made a dismissive gesture.

'You'll be fine. Just keep thinking about the money we're going to make.'

I frowned. 'Speaking of money, I bumped into Juliet Fleming today . . .'

'Yeah?' Spinetti perked up at this news. 'Hey, tell me she wants to come back to me, please! Those new girls have been no use whatsoever. They keep quitting on me after a day or so, can't take the pressure.'

I shook my head. 'Actually, she was chasing another job.'

'Shit.' He looked cross for a moment, then seemed to resign himself to the news. 'Oh well, these things happen. How is she?'

'OK. She said something funny though.'

'Really?' He stepped closer, eyebrows raised as though expecting a good joke.

'Not so much funny as *odd*. Something about you.'

'Go on, spit it out.'

'Well, we were talking about that new group of yours. The Vice Squad?'

'Oh, er . . . right . . .'

'She seemed to think that was hilarious. She made out that it was just some line you'd spun me. Then she said that you weren't such a nice guy as you seem and that if I needed proof, I should ask you about your videos.'

Spinetti nodded.

'I see,' he said.

'So?'

'So what?'

'Well, I'm asking.'

He took a sip of wine, then gave me a hurt look.

'You're saying you don't trust me?' he murmured.

'No, of course not. It's just that Juliet told me to ask.'

Spinetti put down his glass and took out his cigarettes. He extracted one, placed it between his lips and lit it with his brass Zippo. He inhaled smoke, blew it out again.

'And if Juliet had told you to ask me about some child sex murders, I suppose you'd do that too?'

'God, no, of course not. Look Vincent, it's no big deal. Forget about it if it bothers you.'

He sighed, shook his head.

'I'm sorry, I shouldn't get angry. That's one thing about

Juliet that always got up my nose. Her "holier than thou" attitude. Look, what it is, right, she doesn't like the way I spend my leisure time.'

I smiled.

'Wouldn't have thought you got much.'

'I don't. But when I do, I like to spend it watching adult movies. You know, *unlicensed* stuff. Stag movies . . .' He moved his hands about looking for a suitable description, then had a brainwave. 'Skin flicks,' he said. 'Nothing very artistic. Bunch of women and men in your basic kit-off scenario. Guys with big dongs shagging the backsides off insatiable women wearing stockings and suspenders . . . your basic heterosexual fantasies.'

I was somewhat surprised. I had never thought of Spinetti getting off on stuff like that – but then I had never really thought about his sexual interests full stop.

'Surely that isn't Juliet's business,' I said.

'Amen to that! She was round my house once and I must have left one of these films in the video recorder. She happened to press the "play" button and she didn't like what she saw. Which is fair enough of course, but . . . well, it doesn't make me Hannibal Lector, does it? Still, you know Juliet. Right-on feminist, save the whale, all men are rapists.'

I considered this statement. Juliet had never struck me as that type at all. A career woman, most certainly, but a hardline feminist?

'Surely there must be more to it than that?' I reasoned. 'The way she was talking about you, it was like genuine *hatred*.'

Spinetti sighed again. He lowered his voice, leaned closer as if to confide a secret.

'Let me tell you something about Juliet,' he said. 'Ordinarily I wouldn't talk about somebody behind her back but . . . well, she did draw the first blood. The thing is that for a long time, she had the hots for me.'

'Get away!' Now this *was* a surprise.

'Straight up. She made it really obvious too. It was a drag because like I told you, she was the best PA I'd ever had. And she was letting this . . . infatuation get in the way of our professional relationship. In the end, I just had to tell her straight that I wasn't interested. After that, she had it in for me in a big way. When she found out about the videos, she used it as an excuse for me not fancying her. Convinced herself I was some kind of weirdo. You know how it is, Danny. A woman spurned . . .'

'Right,' I said, not wanting to admit that my experiences of spurned women were very few and far between. 'Absolutely.' I gulped down my glass of wine and refilled it. The taste seemed to improve a bit if you persevered.

'So naturally I'm cursed now whatever I do,' explained Spinetti. 'Perhaps her leaving like she did was the best thing that could have happened. Who knows? All I can say is, the picture looks a lot different when you've got all the facts.' The swing doors of the main entrance opened and a young gallery assistant poked her dreadlocked head into the room.

'Shall I open up now, Mr Spinetti? I realise it's early but there's quite a crowd waiting downstairs.'

'Why not?' he called back to her. He gave me another encouraging slap on the back, almost causing me to choke on a mouthful of wine. 'Right Danny, if you've finished with the interrogation, I think we'll get this show on the road. It's time to present you to your adoring public.'

'Right,' I said feebly; and reached once again for the bottle of wine.

# Chapter Twenty-Six

An hour later, everything was buzzing.

I think even Spinetti was astonished by how many people had turned up. The spacious gallery was packed shoulder to shoulder with punters and press. Many of the former were of course, familiar faces, but a good fifty per cent were people I'd never seen in my life.

By this time I was on my sixth glass of wine. I was slightly sozzled and consequently, the interior of the gallery was fast becoming a blur of jabbering faces. More often than not, they were jabbering in my direction. I jabbered back and everyone seemed happy.

Every so often Spinetti would appear with a journalist in tow whereupon I would be obliged to answer a series of stupid questions. How had I happened to photograph the flayed body? Did I think it was a valid subject for an art exhibition? Wasn't I simply exploiting a tragedy to my own materialistic ends? I gave them the answers I had rehearsed beforehand and they dutifully wrote it all down.

Then there were the photographs. It's a well known fact that nobody hates having their picture taken more than somebody who takes photographs themselves. I seemed to do an endless series of shots posed in front of one of my less controversial pictures and it seemed strange to be on the other side of the lens for a change. 'Look menacing,' they kept telling me and I began to understand why Philip Cassiday had got so pissed off with the process. I would just stand there, hands in pockets, scowling furiously into the lens; and whenever a session was over, I would creep back to the refreshments table to replenish my drink.

There were a lot of familiar faces here tonight. I noticed Spike and the four skinny, leatherclad Muppets that comprised his band, gathered around the 'nipples' portrait while Spike excitedly held forth on his new career as a photographic model. A short distance away, I could see Roz, looking surprisingly fetching in a red cord mini-dress, listening attentively while big Wanda pontificated about the meaning of one of the 'tattoo' poses. Across the room, I could see Trevor Bird and his girlfriend, Mo, staring thoughtfully at the portrait of my mother. As I watched, Mo was making some acid remark and I could almost imagine her saying, 'I bet *she's* not with an agency!'

Somebody tapped me on the shoulder and turning, I found myself looking into the glowering, bearded face of Philip Cassiday. The horror writer was dressed in his familiar black gear and he looked, if anything, even more sinister than I remembered him.

'The pictures in the partitioned area,' he said. 'Are they genuine?'

'Absolutely.' I'd anticipated a condemnation from him, but Cassiday had other things on his mind.

'I'm told they aren't for sale,' he complained. 'But they'd be the perfect thing for my new study.'

'Er . . . well, I'm afraid I . . .'

'Come along now, let's not beat about the bush. I'll pay a thousand each. I need four.'

I gulped. This was double the cost of the other prints.

'I can't sell them,' I told him. 'It wouldn't be right.'

Cassiday interpreted my reply as an attempt to push the price up. 'Very well,' he said wearily. 'I'm prepared to go to two thousand pounds each, but for that much, I'll expect an exclusive edition.'

I winced. It wasn't going to be easy turning down that kind of money, but I was a creature of principle, damn it.

'I'm sorry,' I said. 'Surely there must be something you like amongst the other stuff . . .'

He made an impatient noise and turned away. I saw him pushing through the crowds towards Spinetti who was currently talking to a sober-suited Joey Sparks. As I watched, a gallery assistant was applying sold stickers to some of the photographs of Kit Marsden. Sparks caught my eye and gave me a sad smile. I smiled back. My impulse was to go over there and tell him I'd do him some copies for nothing, but Spinetti would have blown a gasket; and besides, Sparks was allegedly one of the richest men in Manchester. A few hundred quid would be nothing to him.

Now Cassiday accosted Spinetti and started talking excitedly to him, pointing back at me and then pointing at the enclosure. Spinetti looked inquiringly towards me, eyebrows raised and I replied with a curt shake of the head. Spinetti shrugged regretfully and conveyed the information to Cassiday, who seemed affronted. He turned away and marched straight out of the exit.

'Hello, Danny.' The familiar Brummie accent cut into my thoughts. Geoff Greenhalge had a peculiar expression on his face, as though he had just discovered a dead mouse in his bread bin.

'Oh, hi Geoff. Been here long?'

'Long enough. I've just paid a visit to your little Chamber of Horrors, over there.'

'Oh right. What did you think?'

'Think?' Greenhalge gave me a look of pure contempt. 'I was sickened,' he said. 'I can't believe you've sunk so low.'

'Steady on, Geoff. Do the words "pot" and "kettle" mean anything to you?'

'Eh?'

'Well, weren't you the one who was nearly foaming at the mouth trying to get that Death-Skin-Horror-Victim story?'

'Yeah, well it's obvious now why you didn't want to say too much about it. But a news story is one thing, Danny, this is quite another. It's despicable what you've done. That's not *art*!'

'Oh, so you're the big authority on it now, are you?'

'I know when I'm being exploited,' he assured me. 'And for integrity, this one's on a level with a snake's belly. Furthermore, since Alex Wyndham Jones is on holiday, I've been assigned to write the review for this fiasco. You can bet it won't be complimentary.'

'Ah well, I'm sorry you feel that way about it. In my defence, I can only tell you that my reasons for displaying those pictures are strictly honourable.'

'Yeah? I bet that's what the carnival boss said about the Elephant Man!'

He moved away and I told myself that if Spinetti's theory was right, Greenhalge would be giving us the biggest plug we could possibly ask for.

I looked back in Spinetti's direction and saw that he was now chatting with Don Lynch who had made a big effort for this event and was wearing his best clothes; a tattered navy blue blazer that looked like it was coming apart at the seams, and a pair of half-mast cavalry twill trousers. He was holding a plate piled high with chicken legs and sandwiches and was chomping his way through them as he talked, putting Spinetti

in serious peril of being peppered by flying crumbs. Actually,
I hadn't realised that the two men knew each other, but then
I shouldn't have been surprised. Spinetti seemed to have
connections with just about everybody in the city.

Roz wandered over accompanied by the black-clad, glowering hulk that was Wanda.

'Wanda wanted to have a quick word with you,'
announced Roz brightly. I tried not to quake in my boots. I'd
only recently recovered from my last little peptalk from
Wanda. I looked around for moral support, just in time to
see Spinetti going out of the exit doors. I forced a smile and
set my back against the wall as Wanda closed in for the kill.

'We've just been looking at the flayed corpse pictures,'
growled Wanda.

'Ah, yes, well . . .'

'They're quite brilliant, Danny. By far the best thing
you've ever done.'

I nearly laughed out loud in surprise.

'You . . . you *like* them?' I croaked.

'Like them? They're masterful! I love the way you've
subverted the genre.'

'Subverted the . . .?'

'The way you've entered an arena that traditionally
exploits women and confounded everyone's expectations.'

I looked at her blankly.

'I hadn't realised,' I said.

'Oh, you're just being coy! Come on, Danny, I can see
where you're coming from! A naked man, stripped in the
most extreme sense of the word and – I love this – actually
hanging *upside down* . . . to point out of course, that you're
literally standing the world of pornography on its head!'

I gave a hollow laugh.

'Ah, you . . . you spotted that, did you?'

'Well, naturally! Furthermore, I love the sequence of images with the tattooed man, cavorting and prancing like the conventional image of the blonde bimbo. More importantly perhaps, the images of *real* women have a dignity and a sense of power to them. You can be sure that I'll be telling all the sisters to come along and support this. It's frankly streets ahead of your previous work.'

I smiled sweetly.

'What, that old "penis-driven shit?" ' I couldn't resist the dig but she didn't even seem to notice it. She strolled away to continue browsing.

'You've made a hit there,' observed Roz. 'Actually, I can't believe what she just said. What a load of old tosh!'

We shared a laugh and I found myself thinking yet again, how nice it was to see Roz in such rare good humour.

'What's happening about *your* exhibition?' I asked.

She shrugged. 'Oh, I think we've decided to kick that one in the head. We're going to try and come up with something less problematic. Actually, I've got a few new proposals, I wondered if I could sound you out on them sometime?'

'Well sure, why not? We could—' I broke off in surprised delight as I recognised a beautiful face on the other side of the room. It was Julia Moreno. She was standing all by herself, studying a photograph. She was wearing a short, red silk dress and she looked absolutely incredible. 'We'll talk about it some time,' I concluded dismissively. 'Excuse me, Roz, there's somebody over there I really must speak to . . .'

I left Roz and pushed my way through the crowd to Julia's side.

'Hello again,' I said. She favoured me with a smile.

'Ah, hello!' she said. 'I was beginning to wonder if I had the right exhibition.'

'This is it. I'm really glad you came.'

'Oh, I'm enjoying it, really.' She sipped at her glass of wine, then glanced nervously over my shoulder.

'Something wrong?' I asked her.

'I don't know. That woman is staring at me.'

I glanced in the direction she indicated and saw Roz looking daggers at us. She turned quickly away and pretended to study the nearest picture.

'She is your girlfriend?' asked Julia.

'What, Roz? Good heavens, no! She's just my photographic assistant.'

Julia looked unconvinced.

'She has the look of a girlfriend,' she insisted.

'No, honestly. She's just a bit nosy, that's all. Ignore her.' I made an attempt to change the subject. 'So, what do you think of my work?'

'It's fascinating, Mr Weston.'

'Please, call me Danny.'

'Yes, of course. Some of the images are very shocking . . .' She pointed towards the partitioned area up ahead. 'Visceral, uncompromising . . . but undeniably powerful. You do not shy away from controversy and this is a quality I admire. My older brother, Pablo, had this in common with you. He was not drawn to beauty but to images that could shock and horrify.'

'Sounds like a man after my own heart,' I said. 'But I noticed you used the past tense.'

A pained expression came into her dark eyes.

'He is one of *los desaparecedos*,' she said. 'The missing. He was arrested by the secret police shortly before I left Chile. He was only eighteen and had just started work for a student newspaper. I have never heard anything of him since that day.'

'Christ, I'm sorry.' Instinctively I reached out a hand and

placed it on her arm. 'I should have realised.'

She shook her head.

'How could you be expected to know? It happened years ago, when I was little more than a child. But I kept an image of him alive in my head. I admired him tremendously and I think that is why I have always felt a strong attraction to photographers.'

I tried not to break into a sweat when she said this. It occurred to me that I'd been waiting all my life for a beautiful woman to say something like this to me. Now that one had, it seemed too good to be true. I found myself waiting for the cruel disclaimer tacked on the end. But happily it never came.

'Funny thing,' I said. 'After we last met, I realised I didn't even get your phone number. I asked around and nobody seemed to know anything about you.'

'I keep myself to myself,' she said. 'I feel safer that way.'

I frowned. 'But why?'

'You couldn't understand. Somebody who has come from my background feels that there is danger in information. When the Pinochet regime was at its height, there were people who went round finding out all the little details, just so they could betray you to the secret police. Such an experience makes you cautious. When I first came to this country, I was afraid to go out of my room most of the time. And even now, such habits die hard. There are still those who are on the lookout for people like me. Ones who have slipped the net.'

'After all this time? Surely not.'

'Believe it,' she said.

'So, how did you come to end up in Stockport, of all places?'

'I was sent to stay with my aunt who still lives there. My

parents stayed on to look for my brother and they too disappeared a few months later.' She saw me wince and was quick to reassure me. 'You mustn't feel bad. It was all a very long time ago.'

'Yes, but Jesus, your whole family? Are there no other brothers or sisters?'

She shook her head.

'I am all alone now.'

'Well how come you're not on the electoral register?'

Her eyes narrowed suspiciously and I felt like biting my tongue off.

'You have been checking up on me?' she murmured.

'Yes. No! Well, kind of . . . I really wanted to see you again and I didn't know what else to do. I'd tried the phone directory. A journalist friend of mine had a copy of the register. But there were no Moreno's listed in the Stockport area.'

Julia gave me a cool look.

'Be careful, Mr Weston. You will make me think that you are one of those people who are always asking questions. And then I will not like you any more.'

'Well, surely it wouldn't hurt to give me your phone number? Then I wouldn't have to go trawling through all that paperwork.'

She gave me a curious little smile.

'I'll think about it,' she said. 'Now, tell me about your photographs. This one for instance.' She pointed to the portrait of my mother. 'This one has great integrity. I feel like I already know this woman.'

'That's my mother,' I told her.

'Ah, I should have guessed. You have her eyes. She looks so natural, so relaxed. How do you achieve this look?'

'It's easy. You take the picture without them realising it.

The worst thing you can do is tell somebody to smile. They say that the camera never lies. What it *does* is accentuate things. If the subject is a little bit stiff and uncomfortable when you release the shutter, he's going to come out looking like a showroom dummy. If he's bored, he'll look comatose. So you have to make people feel comfortable. You engage them in conversation, make them forget that the camera is even there. You give them confidence to be themselves and you never, *never* ask them to smile.' I was giving Julia my standard 'I am a camera' shtick but she seemed to be going for it.

'So it is . . . almost like a seduction?' she murmured.

I nearly choked on a mouthful of wine, but just about managed to get away with it.

'In some ways,' I admitted. 'You know, I'd love to photograph you sometime.' Emboldened by alcohol, I reached out a hand and traced my index finger down the curve of her cheekbone. 'People probably tell you this all the time, but you're very beautiful.'

'And you are kind. But I do not have this trust of the camera you speak of. My brother was taken because of the images he captured on film. Somebody did not like the truth of his pictures. And maybe I'm a little afraid that those same people might see my photograph and know where to come looking for me.'

'But that's all in the past, surely? Nothing could happen to you now.'

'Don't be so sure. Besides, for those of us who lived through the junta, the fear will never be over. It is something we live with every day of our lives.'

I was casting around for an appropriate reply when I saw Spinetti pushing his way through the crowd towards me. I hadn't noticed him coming back in.

'Ah, there you are,' he said.

I introduced Spinetti to Julia. He shook hands with her and I noted the way he appraised her with a quick flick of his eyes, a gesture that told me, yes, she was every bit as beautiful as I thought.

'I think we'll have a few more photographs in a minute,' Spinetti told me.

'What, *more*? We've already done loads of them. How are we doing, sales-wise?'

'Not bad. But we'll be doing better before the night's over,' he added mysteriously. 'I'll just go and rally the men with the cameras.' He gave me a sly wink and moved off in the direction of the refreshments table, where several members of the press had congregated. I turned back to speak to Julia and found that she'd moved on to the next photograph in the sequence, the first of the Kit Marsden pictures. I hurried after her.

'Another of your seductions?' she asked me playfully. The shot in question showed Marsden standing with his arms spread wide in an appealing gesture. There was no mistaking the look of sexual invitation in his eyes. 'This man wanted to make love to the photographer,' said Julia, with surprising candour. 'Did he?'

'No,' I assured her. 'That was almost the only time I ever met him. He's dead now.'

'Dead?' She raised her eyebrows and looked at me.

'Yes. He was murdered just over a week ago. You probably read about it in the papers . . .'

She frowned, shook her head.

'What a terrible coincidence,' she observed grimly.

'I'm not sure it is a coincidence,' I told her. 'But look, this is getting depressing. Let's talk about something more cheerful, shall we?'

'Why not?'

'How about having dinner with me sometime? Tomorrow night. I know this great Nepalese restaurant in . . .'

But she was gazing over my shoulder now with a troubled expression on her face and I suddenly realised that the lively hubbub of conversation in the gallery had died abruptly to a polite murmur. I turned and saw a lot of black uniforms coming through the door, followed shortly by the familiar figure of Detective Inspector Lawrence Flynn. He stood for a moment looking around the room, grim-faced. Then he spotted me and made his way over. He didn't have to push his way through, the crowd seemed to part magically in front of him.

Meanwhile I was experiencing a simultaneous dropping sensation in stomach and jaw. He'd joked about coming to the exhibition, but I certainly hadn't expected him to turn up tonight. And the proliferation of uniformed men in the room suggested that he wasn't making a social call.

'Danny,' he said, with a curt nod of his head. 'I've just been the recipient of some rather disturbing news.'

'Oh?' It wasn't much of a reply but it was all I could summon up under the circumstances.

'I received an anonymous phone call informing me of the fact that a certain Danny Weston was exhibiting horrific photographs at The Wedge gallery. The caller thought them likely to deprave and corrupt the public. He claimed that they included photographs of a flayed corpse? I hope you're going to tell me that I've been the victim of a hoax.'

'I . . .' For a moment only, I considered trying to bluff my way out of it. Then I realised that the game was up. In a weird kind of way it would be a relief to have the matter taken out of my hands. 'Over there,' I mumbled. I pointed to the partitioned area.

Flynn looked at me sadly. His expression was more than anything else, that of a betrayed man.

'Shame on you,' he said quietly. 'I thought we were being honest with each other.' He waved a hand at his men. 'Take all the pictures from the enclosure,' he told them. The uniforms moved to follow his instructions, shouldering their way through the crowd. I could only stand there shame-faced.

'Look,' I said. 'I never mean't to deceive you. It just . . . it just kind of happened.'

'Did it?' He gave me a pitying look. There was a sudden flaring of flashguns and glancing up in surprise, I saw that Spinetti had marshalled his press photographers and was instructing them to record this incident from every conceivable angle. The cops were coming out of the enclosure now, struggling to carry the huge blow-ups and the cameramen were snapping away, while Spinetti paced around like a meglomaniac movie director, shouting instructions.

The crowd was beginning to catch on to what was happening. They started to hiss and boo the police. After a few moments, with some encouragement from Spinetti, they were clapping their hands and chanting in protest, their voices getting louder by the second. 'Pigs! Pigs! PIGS!'

Flynn surveyed the scene for a moment. Then he gave me a cold smile.

'Well, Danny, looks like your little stunt is bearing fruit, doesn't it?'

'What are you talking about?' I protested. 'You don't think I had anything to do with this? An anonymous call, you said. Somebody who was here earlier and was offended by what he saw.'

Flynn studied me intently for a moment. Then he shook his head, sighed.

'Oh I doubt that, Danny,' he said. 'I doubt that very much.'

'But I don't understand. What . . .?'

The penny dropped. I looked around for Spinetti. There he stood, leading the chanting, a wolfish grin on his face. You could almost see the pound note signs flickering in his eyes. I remembered that he'd left the gallery only a short time ago. There were public phone boxes on the ground floor. Realisation hit me like a clenched fist in the chest. Now it was my turn to feel betrayed. My eyes filled with tears.

'Vincent,' I said. 'Oh no.'

And of course it all made sense. Having told him that I wasn't prepared to sell the corpse photographs, he'd thought of a better way to use them – to generate enough publicity to put a mention of this exhibition into every newspaper in the country. It was brilliantly executed but utterly heartless. Worst of all, he'd neglected to consult me.

I turned back to Flynn with an apology on my lips but he was clearly in no mood to hear it; and the look of cold contempt he gave me, struck me dumb.

'I may be in touch about this,' he warned me. 'There could be the little matter of withholding evidence – not to mention offending public decency.'

The last couple of photographs were being carried out of the door now. Flynn followed his men out of the room, as the chants of the crowd dissolved into a burst of triumphant applause. But I was almost oblivious to it. I crossed the room towards Spinetti. He was grinning at me for all he was worth, his hands raised above his head like some champion boxer. I felt like throwing a few punches myself but was prevented from doing it when he threw his arms around me in a fierce bearhug and began to waltz me around the room. I struggled to break free.

'Let go of me, you bastard!' I snarled.

He stopped what he was doing and stared at me in dull surprise.

'What's up with you?' he yelled. 'We just pulled off the publicity stunt of the decade!'

'No,' I snapped. '*You* pulled it off. You didn't even have the good grace to tell me what you were planning to do!'

'Oh, you'd have fucked it up, Danny. No offence, mate, but you would.' He twisted me around to look at the crowd. Now that the police had left they were virtually beseiging the gallery staff as they signalled their desire to purchase the remaining work. 'See that?' Spinetti whispered in my ear. 'That's just the start. Now they'll buy anything you do as fast as you can produce it. I smell a sell-out tonight!'

'So do I,' I assured him flatly. I struggled free of his grip and started walking towards the exit.

'Danny!' he shouted after me. 'Don't be an arsehole! This is it, man! They *love* you!'

'Get stuffed!' I yelled back at him. I pushed through the swing doors as a battery of cameras recorded my hasty departure. I could almost see the next day's headlines. POLICE STOP SICK 'ART' SHOW! God but I'd been a dummy. I'd let myself be used, fucked over good and proper by a man I had always regarded as a close friend. Telling myself that it was all for my benefit was scant consolation.

Halfway down the stairs, I found Julia waiting for me. I hadn't seen her leave the gallery. She stepped close to me and placed a hand on my shoulder.

'Are you all right?' she asked me. 'That was terrible.'

'I'm OK,' I told her, but I didn't sound very convincing, not even to myself.

'I have my car outside,' she told me. 'I can give you a ride home, if you like.'

She was looking up at me and the nearness of her, the smell of her perfume, the warmth of her body, all conspired to make me lose my head. I took a chance and tried the John Wayne thing. I just kind of grabbed her, pulled her to me and kissed her full on the lips. She didn't struggle or try to push me away. In fact, after a few seconds, she responded, just as I'd dreamed she would, just like Maureen O'Hara used to when the Duke took her in his arms. We held the position for quite some time and finally, I had to pull away and come up for air. Julia stood there looking at me. Her face was flushed and she was breathing rapidly, as though she was excited. Then the door at the top of the stairs opened and I saw Roz standing there, staring down at us in silent accusation.

'Danny?' she said.

'Come on,' whispered Julia. 'Let's get out of here.' She slipped an arm through mine and led me down the stairs to the exit.

# Chapter Twenty-Seven

The next thing I knew, we were in Julia's car, a rather flash Toyota Corolla, and we were driving fast through the darkness in the direction of my place. I was in a state that could most politely be described as 'turned on'; and Julia too, seemed almost breathless with excitement. We didn't talk much as we drove. Occasionally I muttered curt directions and my voice sounded hoarse and clumsy to my own ears. I simply wasn't used to having this effect on beautiful women.

The happenings back at The Wedge had already acquired a misty, dream-like patina. I realised that I should be filled with righteous indignation over what had happened but the prospect of making love to Julia – I was certain it would happen once we arrived at our destination – had over-shadowed recent events and I already felt distanced from them. No doubt there'd be time to rake over those particular coals later.

Julia took one hand off the wheel and grabbed my right wrist. She transferred my hand to her thigh and it was as though a jolt of pure electricity flickered through my finger tips. She glanced at me and the look of open invitation in her dark eyes prompted me to go further. Slowly, I slid the hand beneath the hem of her silk dress and upwards, past the smooth tops of her stockings to the warm, silk covered V of her groin. I began to move my fingers up and down in a rhythmic motion. She moaned softly, opening her legs wider to accommodate me. Her panties began to moisten under my touch.

Thankfully, we soon reached my regular parking spot and we were able to embrace, our mouths kissing hungrily, her warm tongue coaxing shivers of excitement out of me. Her hands moved down to my crotch, exploring the hardness there. She pulled away a little and her eyes seemed to devour me in the half light of the illuminated dashboard.

'Let's go inside,' she whispered.

I nearly fell out of the car in my haste to do as she suggested. I led her across the street to the entrance, fumbling for my keys as I approached. I managed to get the door open and we stepped into the gloom. Switching on the light I led her up the flight of stairs to my apartment.

I unlocked the entrance door and we walked into the kitchen. Closing the door, I turned to face her and immediately she moved against me, her mouth finding mine in the darkness, her hands beneath my jacket, tugging impatiently at the buttons of my shirt. Now the anxieties started. It was so long since I'd done anything like this, I was afraid I might have forgotten how. My throbbing penis, however, was trying to assure me that it knew exactly what to do. I reached up to undo the buttons of Julia's dress and my hands encountered the delicious shock of her naked breasts beneath the silk.

'The bedroom?' I gasped. Her breath was hot against my face.

'What's wrong with right here?' she asked. She pushed me to the floor and came down on top of me, her open mouth on mine, her tongue probing. Then she was pulling at my jacket, fumbling awkwardly in the darkness to get it off me. Next the shirt, tearing off several buttons in her impatience, but I was past caring about that. She eased back so that she could sit astride me and her hands reached out to remove my glasses. Everything receded into a gloomy blur.

'Now Danny,' she whispered. 'We're almost ready.' She started to undo my belt buckle and I began to seriously wonder if I wasn't going to come before I'd so much as entered her.

'Julia,' I whispered. 'I want to—'

'Shhh.' She placed the fingers of one hand against my lips and slid the others beneath my trousers, coaxing me to full erection. 'I'm going to—'

That was as far as she got. That was when the door opened and the kitchen light clicked on. Julia gave an oath in what sounded like Spanish and she scrambled up off me. I fumbled around on the floor for my glasses. After a few moments I found them and put them on. Sitting up, I swivelled around to look towards the door.

'Ooh, sorry,' said Roz, 'Was I interrupting something?'

I glared at her.

'Roz,' I spluttered. 'What are you doing here?'

She gave me an indignant look.

'What do you *think* I'm doing? I *live* here!'

'Yes, but . . . well, you can see we're . . . busy, surely?'

Getting to my feet, I glanced apologetically at Julia. She had turned away and was hastily buttoning up her dress, covering up those perfectly formed breasts. I tried not to groan.

'Odd place for it, the kitchen,' observed Roz airily. 'Isn't the bedroom more appropriate for such shenanigins?' She stepped past me to the worktop and switched on the kettle.

'Anyway, don't mind me, I'll just make myself a cup of coffee.'

'Roz, for Christ's sake, give me a break!' I was doing my utmost to maintain my dignity and failing badly. It occurred to me that to have got back here this quickly, Roz must almost certainly have leapt into a taxi and followed us home.

'You must be Julia,' I heard her observe. 'I'd like to say that Danny's told me all about you, but he hasn't really. You're a bit of a dark horse, aren't you? I mean, if it wasn't for the tattoo, I doubt that you'd even have come up in conversation!'

'Tattoo?' Julia looked at her blankly.

'Yes, don't tell me he hasn't mentioned it.' Roz took me by the wrist and turned me around so that Julia could see the illustration on my other arm. She stared at it in dull surprise, her mouth slightly open. 'Danny seemed to think it was an enormous compliment to you, but I've always felt that there's something distinctly sleazy about body art. What do you think?'

'It was a spur of the moment thing,' I blurted. I felt like I had to say something. Julia was just staring at the tattoo as though it contained some kind of obscene message. I felt so uncomfortable under her gaze that I went to retrieve my shirt and put it on, started buttoning it up with clumsy fingers.

'So how long have you two been an item?' asked Roz.

Julia did her level best to force a smile but her eyes flashed with anger.

'We only recently met,' she said dismissively. 'We hardly know each other.'

'Roz, isn't there something else you should be doing?'

Roz looked at me blankly. 'No, I don't think so,' she said.

I turned to Julia.

'We'll go to my room,' I suggested.

'Oh no, don't go off on my account.' Roz moved back to the kitchen table and sat down. 'Let's all have a coffee and get better acquainted, what do you say?'

I looked at her. I couldn't believe she was doing this.

'Roz,' I said quietly. 'Could we have a word in private?'

'Oh, there's no need for secrets, Danny. Let's be civilised about this. Julia, tell me *all* about yourself. That's a charming accent you have. Spanish, is it?'

'I'm from Chile,' muttered Julia, who now looked like she wished she was somewhere else – *anywhere* else.

'Oh really, what part? That's a place I've always wanted to visit. Lived in this country long, have you?'

'Many years.' Julia scowled at me. 'I think it's best I go.'

'No,' I protested. 'Roz was just leaving, weren't you?'

Roz did an elaborate pantomime of looking puzzled.

'But, Danny, I only just got here.'

I came the closest I'd ever come in my life to hitting a woman. It was only with the greatest effort that I managed to restrain myself. By now, I was a seething pool of frustration. What's more, I could see that Julia had inevitably jumped to the wrong conclusion. She'd cast Roz in her mind's eye as the wronged wife, returning home to find her man about to cheat on her.

'This is not how it seems,' I told her. 'It's like I said, Roz is just my assistant . . .'

'Who happens to live with you,' said Julia, coldly. 'That's very convenient.'

Well, yes, she *does* live here but . . . that's all. Nothing goes on between us, we're not . . . involved in any way. Roz, tell her, for God's sake!'

'Tell her what, Danny?' Roz fluttered her eyelashes in an exaggerated display of innocence. 'That we have an open relationship? That we allow each other our little indiscretions?'

I stared at her, goggle-eyed and open-mouthed. If she'd struck me in the face with a wet fish, I couldn't have been more flabbergasted.

'What the fuck are you talking about?' I gasped.

'I think I've heard enough,' said Julia. She snatched up her handbag from the floor where she had dropped it and started for the door.

'Wait!' I cried. 'It's just a wind-up, Julia. I don't know why she's saying that, she . . . she must have gone mad or something.'

'Yes, *do* stay, Julia,' enthused Roz. 'We can swap notes about Danny. I could even give you a few pointers. Things he likes, stuff like that . . .'

That did it. Julia was out through the door and halfway down the stairs before I even had a chance to react. Then I was scuttling pathetically after her, doing my damnedest to salvage a disastrous situation.

'Julia, please, listen to me! It's not true, I swear, I don't know why she's saying these things! Look, please don't go off like this, we need to talk.'

She rounded on me, a look of dark fury on her face.

'Go back inside and talk to your woman,' she advised me.

'She's not "my woman" . . . she's a . . . a fucking head-the-ball, that's what she is. A fruitcake!'

Julia opened the outer door and stepped into the night. I followed, pleading with her, but she wasn't having any of it. Roz had stitched me up, good and proper.

'Look, I don't even have your phone number,' I said. 'If you go like this, I've no way of contacting you.'

'Good,' she snapped. 'That suits me just fine.' She unlocked her car door and got in behind the wheel. 'I thought you were different,' she told me quietly. 'But you are just like all the rest of them. A filthy liar.' She slammed the door in my face and turned the ignition, kicking the engine into life.

'Julia!' I shouted. 'For God's sake, will you listen to me?'

But the car took off at speed with a shriek of burning rubber, leaving me standing there in baffled rage. I watched the Toyota's tail lights disappearing down the street. Then turning away, I stormed back across the road, up the stairs to the apartment. I was now only inches away from committing a particularly bloody homicide. I stalked into the kitchen, where I found Roz unconcernedly making a drink. I stood there glowering at her while I tried to get my temper under control.

'Coffee?' she asked sweetly.

'You know what you can do with your coffee,' I snarled.

'Charming.'

'Roz, you've pulled some idiotic stunts in your time but this one has to take the bloody biscuit. Just what the hell did you think you were playing at?'

Roz glanced at me disdainfully.

'Saving your bacon, that's what.'

'Saving my . . .' I shook my head. *She's gone mad*, I decided. It was the only possible answer. She'd completely taken leave of her senses. 'What are you talking about?'

'I'm talking about Miss Fancy-Knickers, back there. Miss Too-Good-To-Be-True. I don't know what her game is but it smells like three-month-old haddock if you ask me.'

I staggered over to the table and flopped down in the chair that Roz had just vacated.

'Excuse me,' I said. 'I don't want to seem incredibly thick or anything, but could you, in words of three syllables or less, explain to me what you're on about?'

Roz spooned coffee into two mugs and added boiling water.

'I can't explain exactly,' she told me. 'It's just that something is so obviously *wrong*. You can't see it because you've got a hard-on for Miss Hot Chile Pepper, but I ask you. A fancy piece like her chasing around after a bit of old rough like you! Hardly credible, is it?'

'What is so unbelievable about that?' I demanded.

'Oh, come on, Danny, it's obvious! She's some kind of gold-digger. She's realised that you're about to make it big and she wants a piece of the action.'

I laughed bitterly at this remark.

'Roz, did you see her clothes? The car she drives? Does she really strike you as a woman who's down on her luck?'

'Appearances can be deceptive. For all you know, her software company just went to the wall and that fancy car's being repossessed first thing tomorrow morning . . .'

'*What* software company?'

She rolled her eyes upwards. 'I was just theorising. All I can say is she's the kind of woman who under normal circumstances, wouldn't look at you twice.'

'Oh thank you. Thanks very much.'

'So the way I see it, I saved you from a sticky end.' She brought the coffee cups over to the table and set one down in front of me. 'You'll thank me for it one day. God knows what might have happened if she'd had her wicked way with you.'

'That's just the point!' I snapped. 'She's beautiful, Roz, one of the most drop-dead gorgeous women I've ever seen . . .'

Roz sniffed disdainfully. 'She's OK, I suppose.'

'Couldn't you . . . couldn't you at least have waited until she'd *had* her way with me? Christ, we were that close to doing it. That close!'

Roz sipped at her coffee.

'Well, I'm sorry, but if you set so much store by a mere sexual encounter . . .'

'There was nothing *mere* about it!' I roared. 'She's a Latin Love Goddess, for Christ's sake! And she wanted me, Danny Weston, the man who's been without it for so long my condoms have all passed their sell-by date. I was about to get the lay of my life. She was going to bonk my brains out!'

'That wouldn't take long,' observed Roz, uncharitably.

'Hah hah, very funny!'

'And there's another thing. You noticed when I asked her about Chile. She was very vague about her homeland.'

'Can you blame her? You were giving her the third degree. Besides, it's none of your business where she comes from. None of this is any of your business!'

'Calm down. All I'm saying is, she acts like someone with something to hide.'

'And you're acting like a jealous wife.'

Roz stared at me for a moment. Then she threw back her head and laughed.

'Don't be ridiculous!' she said.

'Well how else am I supposed to explain your behaviour? That's certainly the conclusion that Julia jumped to – and most definitely the one you intended to give her.'

'Yes, but . . . I was just looking out for you, that's all. I wouldn't want to see you taken for a ride. God knows, you're so bloody useless, anybody with half a brain cell could do it. But it's not like I *fancy* you or anything.'

'Isn't it? Spike reckons you do.'

'Spike?' She sneered. 'Oh well, he's an authority, isn't he? The man who did for romance what *Psycho* did for showers!'

'So you're denying it then?'

'Of course I'm denying it. Wishful thinking, if you ask me.'

'No, Roz, quite the opposite. You're most definitely *not* my type. In fact, I'd go so far as to say that if we were ever stranded together on a desert island, you'd be in no danger whatsoever!'

She scowled.

'There's no need to be hurtful,' she protested.

'Hurtful? I could be hurtful, all right. The way I feel at this minute, I could happily put you across my knee and give you a good spanking.'

'You could *try*,' she admitted. 'But I guarantee you'd wake up down at Accidents and Emergencies. Typical male reaction to assume that you have the physical advantage. I could break every bone in your body.'

I remembered how Roz had dealt with Mum's intruder and reflected that this was probably an accurate statement.

'Well, all things considered it's been the perfect end to a perfect day,' I observed. 'Thanks for everything.' I turned on my heel and with as much dignity as I could muster, I went to bed. I told myself that maybe I'd wake up in the morning and find that it had all been a bad dream.

But the bad dream that was waiting for me that night was the by-now-familiar scenario of death and bloodshed: with another slight variation. I was back in the railway arch, wandering around with my torch and my camera. I caught sight of the flayed corpse hanging by its feet and I lifted my torch to illuminate the ghastly upside-down head. In the lurid glow of the torch beam, I saw my own face peering sightlessly back at me.

# Chapter Twenty-Eight

The next morning at nine o'clock, I was awakened by the shrill bleeping of my telephone. I struggled out of bed and went to answer it.

'Morning, maestro. Seen the papers yet?'

Spinetti's voice sounded unbearably enthusiastic for such an early hour and for a moment, I considered slamming down the phone on him. But I decided that I should at least give him a chance to explain himself. Spinetti however, seemed more interested in crowing about his latest scam.

'We got a front page photo-caption in the *Mirror* and the *Sun*! And nearly every other paper has carried the story. Listen to this! POLICE STEP IN TO BREAK UP SICK 'ART' SHOW! Or how about this one? ART IS DEAD! OFFICIAL! I tell you mate, some people would kill for this kind of exposure . . . oops, sorry, no pun intended. Now, the *Guardian*'s been on the blower this morning, asking if they can blag an interview and I think I've lined up a photo shoot with *Esquire*, we've just got to discuss the details . . . Danny, you still there?'

'Yes,' I said. 'Only I haven't decided if I'm still talking to you.'

'Oh, come on mate, don't be like that! I understand that you were a bit pissed off with me, but it was all for your own good. You didn't have to go running off. What happened to you, anyway?'

I thought about the events of the previous evening and had to suppress a groan.

'Don't ask.' I said.

'Who was that fabulous bit of totty you had in tow? I noticed she'd vanished too, so I assumed you were making full use of your new celebrity status.'

'*Don't ask*,' I said again.

'All right, point taken. I'm not one to pry. Anyway, we just about had a riot at The Wedge after you'd gone. Unbelievable! We sold all the original prints and I've got dozens of orders for limited editions. And that was just the preview! I'm heading down there shortly, see how things are shaping. You coming with me?'

'No, I have a photo-assignment this morning.'

'What, for the *Post*?' he sneered. 'You don't want to bother with that, mate, you've got enough advance orders to keep you employed for months. You've just gone into a different league.'

I sighed.

'It would be very unprofessional to let them down at such short notice. Besides, I . . . I still haven't made up my mind about what happened last night. Part of me feels like washing my hands of the whole sorry business.'

'Are you shitting me? Don't be silly, this is just what you've always . . . Oh hang on, I've got a call on the other line. Jesus, I've got to get myself an assistant!' There was a pause and I faintly heard his voice talking into the other mouthpiece. 'Hello, Spin International, Vincent Spinetti speaking. Yes, that's correct. Of course we can talk. Can you hold for a moment, please?' Then he was back on the line, sounding excited. 'Danny, got to split. That's *GQ* magazine, sounds like they're interested in a feature. Look, try and call in at The Wedge this afternoon. We'll talk about it over drinks.'

'Vincent, I don't think . . .'

But he hung up on me. I shuffled to the bathroom to wash and shave. The assignment was for ten o'clock at the Manchester Museum. I was to meet a Dr Hulce, Curator of Archaeology, who would show me around the *El Dia de Muerte* exhibition. In a way, I was glad to have something to do. At least it would stop me from brooding about recent disasters. There was no sign of Roz and I assumed she'd gone back to her former lazy ways, but that was just as well. Anything I would have to say to her this morning was going to sound pretty terse.

I drove down to Oxford Street, parked up in a vacant spot and lugged my camera case into the Museum. The reception-ist directed me up to the first floor where Dr Hulce was waiting to meet me. On the face of it, he looked pretty much the part, a small bespectacled man in a scruffy tweed suit. His long, wiry grey hair stuck up from his head like an explosion in a mattress factory and a garish silk handkerchief protruded from his breast pocket in a vain attempt to give him an air of flamboyance. He seemed pleasant enough though, beaming seraphically up at me as he shook my hand.

'Excellent,' he observed. 'Right on time. This way please.' He had a cultured accent that marked him as a native of some unidentified region of the south of England. He led me towards an ante room on the first floor. Above the door, a huge poster depicting a grinning skull welcomed visitors to *El Dia de Muerte*.

'We've tried to give the room the ambience of a Mexican street carnival,' Dr Hulce told me, as we went inside. 'We wanted people to experience what it must be like to be in

318

Guadalajara on The Day of the Dead.'

They'd done a fair job of it. Visitors walked along a central aisle and on either side, simple market stalls were laden with all kinds of traditional artefacts in a multitude of vibrant colours. There were piles of sugar skulls decorated in bright icing with a series of Mexican sounding names. There were little plaster models of capering skeletons making off with alarmed-looking peasants. Here were a selection of tiny cardboard models depicting entire funeral ceremonies, crêpe paper priests and altar boys gathered around an open coffin, containing a brightly coloured candy corpse with two black dots of liquorice for eyes. Behind the coffin was a square frame where a photograph of the recently departed could be inserted but which for the moment, held the image of the current Prime Minister. I glanced at Dr Hulce inquiringly and he gave me a sheepish grin.

'Couldn't resist it,' he said. 'Wishful thinking I suppose.'

We moved on, while I took in all the other images on offer. Wooden and metal crosses, plaster saints and wholesome-looking madonnas, lanterns and streamers and huge fire-crackers that seemed to be merely waiting for somebody to put a light to them. A hidden sound system provided a background of *mariarchi* music, the recorded sounds of children laughing, dogs barking, street vendors calling out their wares in Spanish. It was the next best thing to being there.

It was only a shame I wasn't photographing this for the colour magazine. Black and white film would hardly do the subject justice. Nevertheless, I set down my case, took out my camera and an appropriate lens, then snapped on an electronic flash.

'Right, Dr Hulce, let's have you standing over here to begin with,' I said.

He looked surprised.

'Oh, I didn't realise you'd be wanting *me* in the pictures,' he said. 'I'm afraid I'm not very photogenic.'

'We like to get the human touch,' I explained. 'And I'm sure you'll be fine. Here . . .'

I posed him in front of a full-sized plastic skeleton, and dangled one of its bony arms over his shoulder. I asked him to look startled, reflecting that it shouldn't be difficult for him, since this appeared to be his usual expression. He did his best to accommodate me and we moved up and down the aisle, trying different poses. I had him stand behind a stall like an avuncular sweet shop owner dispensing grisly treats. I had him looking suitably thoughtful as he presided over one of the mini funerals. Unlike many academic types, he seemed to enjoy himself enormously and after fifteen minutes' work, we had some suitable shots in the can. As a final option, I even persuaded him to put on a huge straw sombrero and pose with a pair of skull-shaped maracas.

'You don't think this is a bit frivolous?' he murmured.

'It's just an option,' I assured him; though part of me felt convinced that inevitably, this would be the shot that Barry Summerby would go for.

'So, what do you think of our little show?' Dr Hulce asked as I was putting away the camera.

'Weird,' I said. 'But very inventive.' I pointed to the ranks of ghoulish artefacts. 'They're all little works of art, aren't they?'

'Absolutely,' enthused Dr Hulce. 'Extraordinary imagery, isn't it? Gleaned from a heady mixture of Catholicism and pre-Christian beliefs, of course.'

'These people must be obsessed with death,' I observed.

Dr Hulce frowned. 'The idea is to celebrate not so much death itself, but the cheating of death by those who remain *alive*. In that respect it's an affirmation of life. Every child will eagerly buy a candy skull with his or her name on it and eat every scrap, thus showing that they do not fear their own death. In many ways it's a remarkably healthy approach to the subject.'

'I suppose. But what makes a race of people so ghoulish?'

Dr Hulce smiled.

'Well, you must remember that they're descended from the Aztecs, one of the cruelest empires in history. These were people who thought nothing of flaying a man's skin from his body simply in order to ensure a better harvest. Why, it's only . . .' He broke off as he saw the expression on my face. 'I say, are you all right? You've gone quite pale.'

I wasn't surprised to hear it. The sudden mention of flaying had all but stopped me in my tracks.

'Uh . . . yes, I'm sorry, it was something you just said. That business about flaying? That's er . . . something I'm quite interested in, actually.'

Dr Hulce raised his bushy eyebrows.

'And you were just saying that the Mexicans were ghoulish!' he observed.

'Yes, it's just that . . . that certain things have been happening around Manchester lately and . . .'

'Things?' He gave me a puzzled look.

'I can't really tell you any more. It's a police matter, actually. But . . . well, I know this sounds silly . . . could you tell me a bit more about it? Or perhaps recommend some books . . .'

Dr Hulce frowned, glanced at his watch. Then he smiled, shrugged. 'I'm sure I could spare you fifteen minutes. Actually it's a pet subject of mine. Tell you what, we'll go up to the Ancient Civilizations floor. We've a whole exhibit about the Aztecs.' I collected my camera case and he led the way out of the room and up a couple of flights of stairs. I hadn't visited the museum for years, but I recalled that there was an impressive collection of Egyptian artefacts here. One of my first assignments for the *Post* had been to photograph a newly acquired mummy, complete with sarcophagus. The lined and wizened face of the embalmed corpse had given me the heebee-jeebees and every time the flash had gone off, I'd got the distinct impression that the damn thing was winking at me.

Dr Hulce led me into a large room filled with glass cases, wall paintings and a scale model of a step pyramid. He stood for a moment, unsure of where to start.

'Is it just the flaying you're interested in?' he asked me.

'Yes and er . . . they did human sacrifices, didn't they?' Maybe I was grasping at straws here but the whole thing seemed to be making some kind of sense to me. I thought about all those slim bearded men who'd been standing about at the *Viva Mexico!* reception. Flynn had spoken about the perturbing ritual nature of the murders. Maybe it was nothing and yet . . .

Dr Hulce brought me across to a large glass case filled with vicious-looking stone knives and primitive statues.

'Here's the chap who was indirectly responsible for all the flayings,' he announced cheerily; and he indicated a round stone mask with a strange bloated expression. The eyes were two inverted crescents, the mouth had a curious circular ridge around the lips and the prominent ears had large round rings hanging from them. I was immediately struck by a sensation of familiarity. I'd seen this mask somewhere else, quite recently, I thought – but I couldn't for the life of me remember where.

'He looks a charmer,' I observed.

'That's Xipe Totec,' said Dr Hulce; and alarm bells started going off in my head.

'Zippy who?' I gasped.

'No, that's *Xipe*,' he said; and pointed to the spelling on the display card. 'Xipe Totec. It means "Our Flayed Lord." '

'But it's *pronounced* Zippy!' I insisted.

He frowned. 'Well, at a push. More of a "shh" sound really.'

'So he was some kind of god, was he?'

'Yes, one of the four creator gods of Aztec mythology. A fertility deity really, identified with the spring and new growth. He's also connected with suffering and self-mutilation. You see the round ridge around the mouth? He's depicted here actually wearing the skin of a sacrificial victim. If you look closely, you can still see traces of red on his face, the colour that was always associated with him . . . for very obvious reasons.'

'So . . . this would actually *happen* to people? Their skins would be uh . . . removed?'

'Oh absolutely. Huge numbers of them, usually in the spring. Sometimes they were captives taken in war, but often they were people who'd been specially picked for death. It was considered an honour to be chosen and for the year beforehand, the victim was treated like a king, indulged in everything he wanted. Food, drink, women.' He waggled his eyebrows like an upper crust version of Groucho Marx. 'Must have been a very pleasant final year. When the time came, he was bound and carried to the top of a step pyramid.' He indicated the model off to our left. 'He was held down across that stone altar you can see, a priest hanging on to each limb and he was expertly skinned – sometimes while he was still alive, though more often than not, the priests would first cut his heart out and burn it on a

323

fire as an offering to Xipe Totec.'

'They . . . cut out the heart?'

'That's right. Afterwards the flayed body would be thrown down the steps of the pyramid. A priest would wear the victim's skin for up to twelve days. Must have stunk to high heaven by then, I should think.'

'And this was all to make sure that the crops would grow?'

'Mostly. Of course, the ritual might also be carried out as a punishment for people who'd transgressed in some way. Wearing the skin of the victim would be a way of absorbing all the powers that the dead person had possessed in life, a way of gaining absolute dominance over him. It's a fascinating subject, if somewhat morbid. You know, I had a particularly promising student who was preparing a paper on that very topic. It was abandoned unfortunately but the opening chapters were quite . . .'

'How difficult would it be?' I interrupted him. 'To remove somebody's skin, I mean?'

He gave me a worried look.

'Extraordinary question,' he said.

'Yes, but just supposing I wanted to do it to somebody.'

He shrugged.

'Well, I dare say it's a skill like any other. Given the right tools and a certain degree of application, I've no doubt that anything can be accomplished. It would simply take practice. And a good deal of time, I should think. You know, some of the ancient texts actually describe the various ways of doing it. Sort of Aztec DIY manual.'

'Hmm.' I nodded. 'Well thanks, you've been a great help. Would it be OK if I took some photographs in here?'

'Surely.' He glanced at his watch. 'I'm afraid I have to be getting off to a class now. I hope I've been some kind of help with your er . . . interest.'

'Well you've certainly given me food for thought.'

'And when can I expect to see the piece?'

'Piece? Oh, the article! It'll be in the next few days, I expect.' I'd almost forgotten the reason I was there in the first place. 'You've already spoken to a reporter, I take it?'

'Yes. Frightful bearded chap with a Birmingham accent. A Mr Greenhouse?'

'Ah yes. That's Greenhalge, actually,' I tried not to smile. 'Should be right up his street, this lot. He's rather fond of the grotesque by all accounts.' I shook hands with Dr Hulce and he left me to it. I got the camera out again and took a couple of shots of the mask. Again I got the distinct impression that I'd seen it somewhere before. I warned myself that maybe this didn't mean anything: and yet, the Zippy/Xipe angle seemed too strong to ignore. Then I told myself I was being ridiculous. Could the two victims really have been sacrificed to a centuries old Aztec god? It seemed a totally outrageous idea but I had reached the stage where I was prepared to consider just about anything.

From the glass cabinet the awful bloated mask gazed serenely back at me with its dead, crescent shaped eyes and I became suddenly aware of how horribly quiet it was in this room of ancient, dusty relics. I seemed to be the only person in there. All in all it was a relief to pack up my equipment and escape to the noisy bustle of the streets.

# Chapter Twenty-Nine

On the way back to the car, I passed a street vendor selling the early edition of the *Evening Post*. A display board teaser ad, written in ugly black felt tip pen announced the day's lead story: LOCAL MAN IN SICK 'ART' SHOCKER!

Breaking the habit of a lifetime, I purchased a copy, then retreated to a safe distance and ducked into a shop doorway to read all about me. There I was on the front page in lurid colour. The photograph showed me standing open mouthed in surprise, while behind me an impassive police officer made off with one of my exhibition pieces. Laughably, this had been tinkered with by the *Post*, who were clearly too nervous to show one of my 'banned' images: so it had been painted out by the printer and the policeman now appeared to be making off with a large black rectangle. The accompanying prose held few surprises:

Police were called to the prestigious Wedge Arts Centre last night, after an anonymous tip-off revealed that Manchester-based photographer, Daniel Weston, aged 32, was exhibiting a series of photographs of a dead body, thought to be that of recently murdered Theatre Director, Sebastian Kennedy. Twelve pictures were seized and removed by the police and the exhibition was allowed to continue without them; though it appears that the show still includes photographs of another murder victim, who died only a few days after the pictures were shot. Mr Weston was not available for comment, but his manager, Vincent Spinetti, 31, defended his client's right to exhibit the photographs. 'Art should be a mirror on society,' said Mr Spinetti, at the show's opening night. 'We live in violent times and Mr Weston has chosen to reflect that.' He added that the X-rated pictures were only a small part of the exhibition, provocatively entitled 'Skin Flicks' and he advised all art lovers to come to The Wedge and judge for themselves. (See review, page 31.)

Geoff Greenhalge's review had been given a lot more prominence than it would normally have received – there must have been some pretty frantic rejigging of the presses late last night. It occupied nearly half a page and was basically a long-winded condemnation, peppered with insults. The last paragraph pretty much summed up his thoughts on the matter:

I would advise anyone thinking of going to this evil, manipulative travesty of a show, to think again: even without the despicable corpse-shots of the late Sebastian Kennedy, there is still plenty here to offend decent sensibilities. Some particularly sleazy studies of an almost naked, heavily tattooed man, would seem more at home in a back-street massage parlour than in a respectable art gallery – and they too, it transpires, are pictures of a dead man. The subject was murdered within days of the photo session. It seems that the contemporary arts are rapidly sinking into a cesspool of exploitation. How low must we sink before somebody calls an end to it?

Oh, he was pissed off all right: but what got up my nose was that at no point in the proceedings did anybody have the guts to mention that this depraved, demonic Daniel Weston character had for several years been a regular contributor to the *Evening Post*. Oh, no fear of that! That would be a bit too close to home, wouldn't it? Well, stuff them. I decided there and then that I had just done my last job for the paper – though if I was truthful about it, I seriously doubted that my services would ever be required again.

Dejectedly I rolled up the paper and shoved it into my pocket. Then I went to collect my car, made the short drive down to The Wedge and parked outside Oxford Road station. I walked out of the car park, rounded the corner and stopped dead in my tracks. The glass doors of The Wedge were open and a long queue of people extended out of them. The queue went around the side of the building and when I followed it, I saw that it continued for a length of some sixty yards down Oxford Street.

I scratched my head. There must be something special on, I told myself, something I hadn't heard about. Maybe Martin Scorcese was paying a surprise visit, handing out free tickets to his latest *magnum opus*. Jesus, he'd have to be handing out twenty pound notes to get this kind of reaction.

Bypassing the queue, I went through the doors into the foyer and found myself in a contemporary version of Dante's *Inferno*. A couple of harrassed-looking workers in trendy black and white 'Wedge' sweatshirts were doing their level best to keep the restless queue in order. At the same time, they were attempting to organise the dozens of other people who were there to book cinema tickets, use the bar or who had just wandered in to see what the fuss was about. To my amazement, I saw that sure enough, the queue went on up the stairs in the direction of the first floor gallery. I started to walk in that direction and one of the Wedge staff, a girl who didn't look as though she was out of her teens, shouted after me with a voice that had all the subtlety of a klaxon.

'Hey, you! Where are you going?'

I turned back to look at her.

'*Skin Flicks?*' I muttered.

'What's the matter, can't you see there's a queue?'

'Er . . .' I moved closer to confide a terrible secret. 'Actually, I'm Danny Weston.'

'Uh?' She looked at me blankly for a moment. She was a skinny, pale girl with a shaved head and large gold rings through her eyebrows. Her pipe-cleaner legs were encased in black stretch ski-pants and culminated in a huge pair of Dr Martens. For some reason, I kept thinking of the comedian, Max Wall.

'Er . . . Danny Weston,' I repeated, pointing to a nearby poster. She was looking at me blankly. 'The photographer?'

Then her eyes seemed to refocus and she gave me a very weird look. It was composed of equal parts awe and disgust. Awe, I suppose, because she was in the presence of somebody who had managed to entice hundreds of people along to a photography exhibition. And disgust that I turned out to be this plain, scruffy guy with glasses.

'Sorry,' she muttered. 'It's frantic. We're only letting them in two at a time. Have to wait for two others to come out, first. Fire regulations, you see. Bloody jam-packed up there.'

'Oh right.' I was hearing it but I still couldn't quite believe it. 'Is er . . . is Vincent Spinetti about?'

'Yeah, he's in the gallery trying to arbitrate.' She made it sound like a political war was being waged in the gallery.

Perhaps it was. 'Never seen anything like it,' she told me. 'Not in all the time I've worked here.'

This would have been more impressive if she'd been an old timer but since she looked like she hadn't been out of school more than a few months, I took it with a large pinch of salt.

'Well, I'll go up,' I said. 'You're doing a good job.'

She gave me another look which seemed to invite me to stick a large object up my own backside, so I left her to it. As I climbed the stairs, I was aware of the queue of punters examining me as I passed by.

'That's *him*!' I heard somebody whisper.

'Nah, he's better looking than that.'

I kept walking but halfway up the stairs, a hand reached out and tugged at my elbow. I turned and found myself looking at a couple of Goths, one of either sex, both wearing scuffed black leathers. They looked to be in their early twenties, though it was hard to tell behind all the hair.

'Hey, you're Danny Weston!' said the young man, as though I hadn't actually been aware of it. 'We saw you in the paper.'

'Yeah, in the paper,' echoed the girl, smiling shyly out from behind a shaggy black fringe. She was wearing black lipstick and nail varnish which gave her the look of a rather plumper version of Morticia Addams.

I smiled back, uncomfortably aware that some kind of response was anticipated.

'Uh . . . yes, it's me all right,' I assured them.

The young man extended a hand to shake. 'Keef,' he said. He jerked a thumb at his companion. 'Debs.'

I shook her hand too.

'Saw you in the paper this morning,' said Keef, as though he suspected I might not have heard him the first time. 'Said to Debs, "fuck, Debs, we gotta go and support this guy". We think what you're doin' is great, man. Fuckin' A.'

'Yeah, fuckin' A,' agreed Debs.

'Why?' I asked them. It didn't seem an unreasonable question but it clearly took them by surprise. They both gave me vacant looks, before Keef came up with some kind of an answer.

'Well . . . it's the truth, ennit?' he blurted. 'It's like . . . well, what art *should* be about, right? But the minute anybody tries showin' what it's like . . . what it's *really* like, *they* wanna come and sweep it all under the carpet, don't they?'

I wasn't sure who 'they' were but maybe it didn't matter. Keef was just getting up a head of steam.

'S'like Charles Manson, right? I mean, why's he still in jail, man? It's not as if he killed anybody! And you know, Guns 'n' Roses record one of his songs, right, and all this shit comes down from on high. But Charlie just wanted to be a rock n' roll star, you know? He wanted to be one of the Monkees!'

'Yeah, he *auditioned*,' added Debs.

'I'm sorry,' I said. 'I don't quite see what—'

'It's just like they swept that one under the carpet, right?' explained Keef. 'Like they swept Brian Jones' murder under the carpet, the My Lai massacre, Jim Morrison, Nostradamus, you name it! They just took a bloody big broom and . . .'

'Brushed it under the carpet,' concluded Debs, helpfully.

My brain reeled from the hopeless task of trying to follow the logic of this argument. It also occurred to me that Keef almost certainly hadn't been born when any of these events took place. Maybe he was older than he looked. Nevertheless, I decided that Keef and Spike ought to get together for a long chat one of these days. Now *that* would be some conversation.

'Anyway,' concluded Keef, proudly. 'It's a show of solidarity, man. We think what you're doin' is *cool*.'

I gazed at him thoughtfully. He looked like your average, brain-scrambled Sisters of Mercy fan. I seriously doubted that he'd ever seen the inside of an art gallery before.

'What would you say if I told you that this whole thing was a cheap publicity stunt?' I asked him. 'Designed to get you up off your arse and in through these doors.'

A slow, stupid grin spread across his face, revealing a broken tooth in the top row.

'Fuckin' A,' he said.

'Yeah, brilliant,' agreed Debs.

'You wouldn't be angry?'

'No, man, why should I? Way I see it, you got to use whatever you've got, right?' He nodded at the long queue stretching down the stairs behind him. 'And if it *is* a stunt, it worked,' he added. 'That's cool.'

'Was it a stunt?' asked Debs.

I shook my head. 'It wasn't *meant* to be,' I told her. I moved on up the stairs. At the door of the gallery, a harassed young man was arguing loudly with the couple at the head of the queue.

'And I'm telling *you*, you've got to wait till a couple of people come *out*! It's regulations!' He turned to look at me as I approached and for a moment, was about to make the same mistake as his associate downstairs; but at the last moment, he recognised me and opened the door just enough to let me pass. As I went in, I heard shouts of protest behind me and the young man trying to explain that it was OK since I was the photographer.

'Tell him to get to the back of the queue anyway,' I heard

somebody mutter, uncharitably.

The gallery now resembled the world's largest phone box. For once, 'pressing the flesh' was more than just an expression. It was solid, wall-to-wall people in there and it was only with extreme difficulty that I managed to make my way across the room to Spinetti. He was standing in a corner, chatting animatedly with a middle-aged man in a sober grey business suit. He had longish white hair and a flamboyant goatee beard. He seemed somehow familiar to me though for the moment, I couldn't place him.

As I struggled over to them, Spinetti glanced up and noticed me. 'Ah, here's the man himself!' he exclaimed. 'Danny, there's somebody here I'd like you to meet.' He grabbed me by the shoulder and virtually propelled me forward until I was standing face-to-face with the bearded man. I was obliged to shake hands with him. 'I'm sure you know Sir Gareth Parker,' said Spinetti. 'The owner of *Metrosound Radio*? We've just been discussing the possibility of a commission.'

'Er . . . Mr Parker,' I muttered. 'Yes, of course I know of your er . . . reputation.' I neglected to mention that what I'd heard hadn't been particularly good. He was generally thought of as a *nouveau riche* entrepreneur, who'd made a packet from a series of dodgy deals in the property market and had subsequently bought himself into independent radio, a business he had no real aptitude for. There were many who claimed that he'd ruined *Metrosound*, sanitising it by stamping out the popular late night talk shows they used to run, in favour of safe, bland, top forty programming. There'd been some kind of trouble at the station shortly before the axe fell, a DJ had got himself mixed up in some weird goings on. Parker was reputed to have bought out the guy's contract, then skipped off to his villa in Spain until the heat died down.

More recently, his name had come up in connection with a live radio interview featuring black gangsta-rap star Bobby C Cooper, whose uncompromising language had caused considerable embarrassment to *Metrosound*. Parker had gone to the unprecedented lengths of banning not just Cooper from the station but *all* black rap artists, an action that was regarded by many as out and out racism.

Frankly, Parker was the last person I'd have expected to show interest in somebody like me.

'Mr Weston, it's a pleasure.' Parker gave me an oily grin and I immediately felt a sense of mistrust spark up inside me. He had the face of a wolf, long, grizzled and distinctly untrustworthy. 'You're doubtless familiar with our offices in Piccadilly?'

'Yes, I've driven past them a few times.'

'Then you'll almost certainly have noticed a series of plate glass windows up on the first floor. For as long as I can remember, we've used them to display giant colour photographs of our resident DJ's. But it's beginning to look distinctly tacky. I thought perhaps you might be able to come up with something more . . . 1990s?'

I frowned. 'I don't do celebrity photographs,' I warned him.

'Oh no, I wasn't thinking in those terms at all, I'd want something quite different. Something that reflects the diversity of *Metrosound*. Mr Spinetti and I have been discussing some ideas, but I think it's up to you to come up with your proposals . . . and of course, a price.' He gave me an oily smile. 'I'm not expecting such undeniable flair to come cheap.' He took a business card from his top pocket and handed it to me. 'At any rate, if you're interested, you can give me a buzz some time and we'll talk in more detail.' He nodded to Spinetti and moved off, shouldering his way through the crowd.

'Jesus,' muttered Spinetti. 'You can write your own ticket now, mate. When people like Sir Gareth Parker come sniffing around after you . . .'

'I don't get it,' I said. 'I thought he was Mr Safe As Houses. He'd normally run a mile from controversy like this.'

Spinetti frowned. 'Well, he's not stupid, either. The ratings at *Metrosound* have taken a severe tumble recently and the word is that it's Parker's programming that's caused the slide. See, they're doing fine on their Gold wavelength, lots of nostalgia for ageing rockers. But it's their slick, FM channel that's hitting the skids. Parker's probably seen the headlines this morning and come down to check out the action. Then he's noticed the fact that a lot of people in the queue are in the sixteen to twenty-five age group. You're riding on a youth ticket, Danny and he's hoping that if he gets you on board, a bit of it might rub off.'

I scowled.

'Yeah, well I chatted to a couple of my young fans on the way in here,' I told him. I shook my head. 'A pair of sad cases. The lights were on, but there was nobody home.'

Spinetti shrugged.

'What, you want us to check their qualifications at the door?' He gestured to the press of people all around us. 'Look at this place, it's a *phenomenon*, that's what it is. There's a list of orders as long as *War and Peace* and they're still coming thick and fast.'

'Mostly thick,' I added gloomily, thinking of Keef and Debs. 'It's like Charles Manson, man. I mean, he didn't kill anybody, right?'

Spinetti gave me an odd look.

'What are you on about?' he asked me.

'Forget it. Look, I still haven't made my mind up about you. There's part of me that feels like hauling off and planting one on your nose. We've known each other a long time, Vincent, how could you go behind my back like that?'

'Because I knew I could pull this thing off. If we were standing in an empty gallery now, I could understand you being hacked off, but just look at this place! Picasso doesn't get crowds like this!' He glanced self-consciously around and put a hand on my shoulder. 'Look, we can't talk here. Let's go down to the bar and celebrate. They've put a bottle of Moët on ice.'

'Yeah? Who's paying for it?' I asked ungraciously and he gave me a slighted look.

'That's not fair,' he said. 'Come on, we can talk better over a drink.'

Reluctantly, I followed him back out of the gallery and down the stairs. I saw that Keef and Debs had progressed a few steps closer to their goal. As I moved past them they greeted me like a long lost friend. 'Fuckin' A, man!' said Keef and I smiled inanely at him.

'What does that actually *mean*?' I asked Spinetti, once we were out of earshot.

'No idea. I think it's a compliment though.'

We located a vacant table in the bar, where we had a clear view of the long queue plodding silently up the staircase. Spinetti snapped his fingers and one of the bar staff hurried over with two glasses and the bottle of Moët in an ostentatious ice bucket. Spinetti filled the glasses and savoured his drink before sipping at it. Then he smacked his lips loudly.

'Oh yes,' he said. 'You could get used to this.'

I sipped at my own drink. It was cold and quite delicious. What's more, I reflected, it was possibly the first drink that

Spinetti had ever bought me. Things must really be looking up.

'Listen,' I said. 'I don't want to seem ungrateful to you. I mean, I do appreciate that you put a lot of work into this. You took a big gamble and obviously it's paid off brilliantly, but . . . well, I think you should have been straight with me. I thought our relationship went a bit further than manager and client.'

'It does, Danny, honestly. And I realise that I should have levelled with you. It won't happen again.'

'You promise?'

'Cross my heart, mate. From now on, everything that happens regarding this exhibition, you'll be the first to know. Listen, I've got stuff lined up for you that you won't believe . . .'

'Never mind about that,' I interrupted him. 'You've got this way of slipping out of a situation, Vincent. You just start talking about money and you figure everyone will shuffle happily along in your wake. But this isn't about money, it's never been about that. It's about *trust*.'

Spinetti glared at me.

'Look, what do you want, blood? I've already said I'm sorry . . . though I'm not entirely sure what I'm supposed to have done. Sorry for making you the hottest news in Manchester? Sorry for kick-starting your career into a whole new league?'

'There you go again! Making me feel that I should be grateful that you went behind my back!'

He sighed, topped up the glasses.

'Look, it's history now, OK? What happened, happened, I can't change that. But face it, I've given you exactly what you wanted. You've got the city at your feet.'

I shrugged.

'Well then, why doesn't it feel any good? Why do I feel like something's wrong. Like I passed an exam, only I cheated?'

He laughed.

'It hasn't sunk in yet, that's all. But you look at that.' He pointed at the seemingly endless queue. 'That's the start of a new life. You can kiss goodbye to hack work at the *Post*.'

'That reminds me.' I took the crumpled newspaper from my pocket and showed him Geoff Greenhalge's review. He laughed delightedly.

'Well, you can see that's frightened *loads* of people away,' he said. 'Pompous little git, he's given us the best plug we could have asked for.'

'Hmm. But it's definitely burning bridges time. I hope I never need to go back to these people for a job. After this little débâcle, they probably wouldn't give me the time of day.'

'Don't worry, sunshine. Vincent Spinetti predicts that after tonight, your hack days are well and truly over.'

I looked at him, puzzled by the remark.

'After tonight?' I muttered. 'What's happening tonight?'

'Don't tell me you've forgotten! It's that gig at the Mandrake. Your mate's band? Didn't you tell me you were doing the photographs?'

'Tonight?' My spirits sagged. 'Oh great. Just what I need. The photo-assignment from hell.'

'What, you're saying they're not worth checking out?'

I thought of Spike and how much was riding on this gig.

'Er . . . no . . . I guess I'm just tired. Didn't get much sleep last night.'

Spinetti nudged me suggestively.

'I'm not surprised! Where did you scare that Julia up from, you dark horse!'

'Oh, just around and about,' I muttered, and drained my glass of champagne.

'That's the spirit!' he said, refilling my glass. 'We'll get a couple of bottles of this inside us and you'll soon feel as good as new.' He lifted his own glass in a toast. 'To *Skin Flicks*,' he said. 'And all who sail in her!'

His enthusiasm was as infectious as ever. After a few minutes, I'd forgotten that I was ever angry with him. The two of us sat there getting steadily more inebriated and ahead of us, the queue of people kept moving slowly up the long flight of stairs. I reminded myself that it was *my* work they'd come to see; and I wondered why I didn't feel good about that. I should have been elated, but what I actually felt was a powerful sense of foreboding. No good would come of this. Success earned in this way would somehow backfire on me.

I told myself not to be stupid. Maybe Spinetti was right. It just hadn't hit me yet. It took time for these things to sink in. Meanwhile, we had the Moët and the long afternoon ahead of us, so when the first bottle was gone we ordered another and after a while, I was able to drown my misgivings in a cheery tide of alcohol. And the people kept coming to *Skin Flicks*. By closing time, the queue was a lot shorter but still a queue. By then I was fairly drunk. Spinetti, who seemed to hold his alcohol better than me, was moving with that exaggerated care that habitual drinkers adopt to show that they're still in control. We reeled out of The Wedge and across to my car, to get the camera case out of the boot.

'Maybe we should take a rain check on this,' said Spinetti, looking doubtfully at me as I weaved my way back up Oxford Street.

'Danny Weston, intrepid photographer, never lets a

customer down!' I announced grandly. 'Besides, if this is going to be my last proper assignment, I intend to make a good job of it.'

Spinetti rolled his eyes.

'Conscientious to the last,' he observed. 'Saint Danny.'

I laughed and we moved unsteadily up the street, in the direction of the Mandrake and the night's entertainment.

# Chapter Thirty

I'm in this rock n' roll version of hell and I can't seem to concentrate on the simple task of taking pictures, something I should be able to do with my eyes shut. Well, not exactly, but you get the general idea.

I'm crouched on the front section of a narrow stage with a monitor blasting in my right ear and just behind me, the five members of Sepulchre are midway through their set, pounding out a gut wrenching version of *Bring Out Your Dead*. That would be easy enough to handle if it wasn't for the blitzkrieg of lighting effects, smoke bombs and dry ice that they've chosen to accompany tonight's show.

Every time I lift the camera up to my face, the lights seem to change: a deep blue gives way to a violent yellow glare, a soft red switches abruptly to the electric white flicker of strobes. Just when I think I've got a good shot lined up, I'm enveloped in clouds of noxious white smoke that billow periodically from under the drum rostrum. I've given up trying to take readings, I've just set a general exposure and I'm hoping for the best. The other problem of course, is that I'm three parts pissed and my reactions aren't everything they should be. Furthermore, the various members of the band seem reluctant to remain in one place for more than a second at a time, apart from Kenny, the drummer, who resembles the many-armed goddess Kali as he hammers at the mountains of drums, cymbals and gongs that tower all around him.

Johnny, the bass player and Steve, the guitarist, seem to feel it incumbant upon themselves to dart backwards and forwards like nervous whippets, one moment standing open legged and thrusting their groins at the audience, the next performing bizarre leaps and pirouettes like leather clad ballet dancers. Jacko, the keyboard player is virtually lost to view, I can just make out the nodding mound of his head, behind banks and banks of keyboards. And Spike . . . well, Spike's giving it everything he's got tonight and what he appears to have got is a bad case of St Vitus' Dance, since he is flinging himself around the stage like a hyperactive dervish. One moment, he's draped around the mic stand, bellowing incomprehensible lyrics into what must be the world's biggest PA system, the next he's leaning over the front of the stage to commune with the hardcore members of Sepulchre's following.

The audience are every bit as lively, particularly down at the front of the stage, a sea of thrashing hair and flailing limbs, gorgon-like in the strobes. Every so often, somebody manages to clamber up on to the boards, where they perform the strange ritual known as stage diving, launching themselves on to the heads of their comrades, then thrashing about like stranded fish before sinking to the floor out of sight. It's a small wonder they aren't trampled in the crush.

Peering across the heads of the audience, I can see the little static island of light that is the mixing desk, out in the very midst of the crowd. It's like a castle besieged on all sides by an army of restless Goths. Ron, the big, silent roadie stands poised at the controls, watching with an expression of emphatic boredom on his face. Beside him, I can see

Spinetti, arms crossed, surveying the proceedings impassively. He's almost certainly the only person in the room who's wearing a suit and for the moment, it's impossible to tell what he thinks of the performance. But if general audience reaction is anything to go by, this is an impressive show.

Actually, even I have to admit that Sepulchre are sounding better than I remember them. They've evidently rehearsed hard for this and though the numbers they play are simple, three chord affairs, the rhythm section is as tight as the proverbial bumblebee's arse. The result is that for once, the band are not so much lumbering along as rocking on all pistons.

I focus in on Spike who's standing, arms raised, in front of the mic and just as I'm about to press the shutter release, the song ends with a series of synchronised explosions, one of which goes off only a few feet away from me, scaring me half to death. I probably end up getting a pretty good shot of the tobacco stained roof of the Mandrake.

'Fank yew!' I hear Spike yell, over the applause. 'Fanks a lot! We're gonna do a little fing for you now that we fink you're gonna like. It's called *Blood Sacrifice*!'

There are shouts of recognition from the diehards down the front. This is Spike's solitary foray into theatrical rock, which has him prowling dementedly around the stage like a poor man's Alice Cooper, making threatening gestures with a prop knife. The number always culminates with him committing 'suicide' (the knife has a retractable blade) and spewing a mouthful of fake blood over the front row. It's corny as hell but the fans seem to go for it in a big way. It starts with Steve performing a long, noisy improvisation on the guitar, using a variety of effect pedals to make the musical equivalent of World War II bombers attacking

Dresden. Spike meanwhile, collects his knife from the drum rostrum and begins to prowl.

I'm glad to see that he appears to be relatively straight tonight. During the sound check, he's introduced me to Dex, the man who has previously supplied him with 'Zippy'. I am somewhat relieved to note that Dex is nothing like the slim, bearded man that Spike described. He has a beard, right enough, a greying ZZ Top affair, but he also has a balding head and probably weighs a good eighteen stone. His full length leather trenchcoat gives him a somewhat sinister appearance but in conversation, he turns out to be an affable bloke with a pronounced Geordie accent, who tells me that he's stopped dealing that particular drug after customers reported some worrying side effects. From now on, he assures me, he'll confine himself to draw, acid and straight speed. I don't know if I'm supposed to be reassured by this information, but I have at any rate crossed him off my mental list of suspects. Besides, I have my Aztec theory now and though on paper, it seems decidedly surreal, it certainly measures up better than my two previous leads.

Steve's guitar finally quits its histrionic squealing and launches into a familiar riff. The other instruments add flesh to it, the drums, bass and keyboards locking into a tight, urgent 4/4 rhythm. Glancing down at the audience, I see them respond instantly, as though they've been jabbed with an aural cattle prod, rows of shaggy heads jerking up and down to the beat. Spike stalks along the front of the stage, making stabbing motions at the faces in front of him, giving them his best bug-eyed leer. It's meant to be menacing but always makes me want to laugh. One young man scrambles up on stage to give Spike a brief hug, before turning away and flinging himself back into the crowd. I twist around to try to get a shot of the kid's thrashing body and that's when my attention is caught by somebody way over at the back of the hall. A slim, bearded man is pushing his way through the audience towards me.

Why do I notice him in such a large crowd? It's hard to explain but he stands out instantly. Perhaps it's because he's not dressed at all like a Sepulchre fan. He has on a set of military overalls, olive green, loose fitting. There's a generous sized hood which is pulled up over his head, a draw cord pulled tight so that it frames his face in a circle. He's wearing black leather gloves, which also seems distinctly odd in a sweat-pit like this. And what I can see of the dark, bearded face, fills me with a sudden rush of anxiety. This is what I expected Dex to look like. The Identikit picture that Flynn showed me of the man who was seen at Adonis, the night Sebastian Kennedy died. The man who looked rather like me before I shaved my beard off . . .

> *The candle flame is burning low*
> *as figures round the altar go!*
> *Sacrifice! Sacrifice!*

Spike's bellowed lyrics burst from the monitor beside me in deep echo, almost making me jump out of my skin. I whip back to look at him and he's draped around the mic again, the prop knife held above his head. As I turn back to look for the bearded man, the strobes flick on, reducing the audience to a collection of Chaplinesque marionettes and for a moment, I cannot place him; but then I see him, he's much closer now, shouldering his way through the crowd, his glaring eyes fixed intently on something ahead of him. I look in the direction indicated by his eyes and I see that he is angling left towards the mixing desk and that he seems to be looking at Spinetti . . .

> *The crimson path it calls your name,*
> *you gibber like a man insane,*
> *Sacrifice! Sacrifice!*

Spinetti is watching the show, intent on what's happening on the stage. He doesn't see the bearded man approaching him. I stand there, helpless, knowing that there's no way I can get through the crowd to him in time. I raise my arms and shout at the top of my lungs but the sound is lost against the tumult of music blasting from the stage. Now the bearded man is reaching inside his coat, the strobes transforming the fluid motion into a series of staccato jerks . . .

> *The priests bring in their victim now,*
> *she's naked like a fattened sow,*
> *Sacrifice! Sacrifice!*

Spinetti turns his head and sees me waving frantically at him. He gives me an amused smile, it must look funny in the strobes and he raises a hand to wave back in comic semaphore. I point straight at the bearded man and try desperately to mouth to Spinetti that he should turn around, but he simply raises his eyebrows quizzically. It's like a chilling version of the old pantomime favourite, 'Behind you, behind you!' But Spinetti is still looking straight at me and as my panic mounts, I see the bearded man's hand emerge from under his coat. The strobes pick out something in his fist, something that glints wickedly . . .

> *The naked blade it tastes her pain,*
> *it rises and it falls again,*
> *Sacrifice, sacrifice, sacrifice!*

And I do the only thing I can do, I snap the camera up to my face and I power off a series of shots as the bearded man's arm rises; and through the viewfinder now, I see Spinetti somehow sense a presence behind him. He turns slow, slow in the strobes and then flings up his own arm as the bearded man's fist descends in a series of stabbing motions and then something connects with Spinetti's forearm. I see the fabric of his jacket tear and a crimson spray spurts down his chest. His face contorts in a mixture of surprise and agony and he falls backwards against Ron, the roadie, who is knocked off balance by the impact, the two men disappearing behind the mixing desk in a tangle of flailing arms and legs. The bearded man stands there for a moment, uncertain whether to follow up the attack or to turn and flee.

And in that instant, I throw myself off the stage into the crowd, intending to go after the killer, not even thinking about the fact that he's armed. But the idiots in the front row mistake my actions for a spot of impromptu stage diving and I find myself being lifted up above their heads. I am kicking and cursing as I am passed by unseen hands back over the audience like some unwanted article. At last, their interest wains and I am allowed to slide down into a void where I connect heavily with the floor, lose my footing and fall over.

For a moment, I'm in a state of total panic as I scramble about on hands and knees through a forest of denim clad legs. A boot catches me a glancing blow in the ribs and somebody's heel narrowly avoids crushing my fingers. The camera still trails uselessly around my neck. I manage to get myself upright and I stand there, looking around in a kind of daze. I've lost my bearings for a moment: but then I spot the lights of the mixing desk and I start to slam my way towards it, throwing people aside in my haste to get across to Spinetti.

The bearded man is nowhere to be seen. I register this as I run around the mixing desk to find two figures slumped on the floor. Spinetti appears to be covered in blood and for a moment, I'm convinced that he's dead but as I stoop to touch him, he sits upright and I can see that the extent of the damage is a long, bloody cut down the back of his forearm. Ron is sitting up too, looking vaguely stunned by the unexpected turn of events. The music still rocks on at maximum volume, Spike is chanting now, '*Sacrifice! Sacrifice!*' and the entire audience seems to be joining in with him.

Spinetti grimaces, gritting his teeth as he attempts to stem the flow of blood from his lacerated arm. I reach into his pocket for his mobile phone, he's going to need urgent attention. I glare at Ron and make a slashing motion with my finger across his throat. He nods, understanding me. He gets to his feet and with one practised action, slides the master volume control to the off position, cutting the noise of the band to a fraction of its former volume.

As I stand up, I see that Spike has just plunged the fake knife into his stomach and is in the act of spewing up blood, a mixture of Kensington Gore and water, surreptitiously swigged from a container in his shirt pocket, drenching the first couple of rows in crimson spatter. Then the band realise that their volume has gone and they exchange puzzled looks, begin to lurch to an ungainly halt. Kenny has his head down and keeps hitting the drums for several beats before he realises that he is performing unaccompanied. He stops and sits there, looking blankly around.

Spike shields his eyes with the flat of one hand and stares

out towards the mixing desk, a look of impotent fury on his face. His mouth and T-shirt are liberally stained with crimson and the handle of the knife jutting from his belly looks faintly comical.

'What the fuck's going on?' he yells.

A good question, but there's no time to answer it. I'm too busy using Spinetti's phone to dial 999.

# Chapter Thirty-One

It was the early hours of the morning and we sat in the little cubicle in Accident and Emergencies, waiting for the police to arrive. Spinetti was on the bed, his arm heavily bandaged from wrist to elbow. The cut had required forty stitches and he'd been given tablets for the pain. Though still drawn and pale, he seemed to have recovered a little from his shock and was now complaining loudly that his best suit was ruined beyond repair.

Spike sat shamefacedly in a corner. He'd insisted on accompanying us in the ambulance and had almost been rushed off to a treatment room himself, when staff had caught sight of his gore-splattered T-shirt. He kept apologising profusely to Spinetti and I got the distinct impression that his contriteness was prompted not so much by his concern for Spinetti's health, as his fear that the incident had kiboshed his chances of acquiring a manager for the band.

'I can't understand it,' he said, for perhaps the fifteenth time. 'We never get violence at our gigs. Never. All right, maybe the odd punch-up, now and then, but this . . .' He shook his head in despair. 'I mean, we're anti-violence, man. You just have to listen to the lyrics.'

This struck me as a bit rich, considering the song that Sepulchre had been playing when the knifing incident had taken place, but I refrained from commenting on it.

'This was more than just a random attack,' I told Spinetti. 'That guy came right through the crowd for you. I tried to warn you but you didn't catch on. Christ, if you hadn't turned around . . .' I thought for a moment. 'What *did* make you turn?' I asked him.

Spinetti looked puzzled, as though trying to remember.

'I think it was . . . the smell,' he said.

'What smell?'

'Must have been the guy who attacked me. He had the worst body odour problem of all time.' He tried to adjust the position of his arm and winced. 'Fuck, what were those pain killers they gave me? Aspirins?'

'You want me to call a nurse?'

'No, I'll be all right. Wish those bloody flatfoots would hurry up though. I just want to get home to bed.'

'I mean, it's not like we're one of those bands who provoke violence,' muttered Spike. 'We've never been into that. Jesus, I'm a member of Greenpeace!'

Spinetti gave Spike a look that suggested he might be safer if he shut up. Spike got dejectedly up out of his chair.

'Maybe I should go fetch some coffee,' he said.

'Good idea,' I told him. 'I need to have a private word with Vincent, anyway.'

'OK.' Spike trudged resignedly out through the curtained entrance and Spinetti and I exchanged glances.

'The guy who attacked you,' I said. 'It was the same man who killed Sebastian Kennedy and Kit Marsden. I'm sure of it.'

Spinetti laughed nervously.

'Don't be ridiculous,' he said. 'Why would he go for me?'

'I don't know. Maybe because of the exhibition. Us showing pictures of the body like that . . .'

351

'No way.' Spinetti shook his head and grimaced at the pain it caused him. 'Just some nutter with a grudge.'

'No, Vincent. I saw the Identikit pictures, this guy was the spitting image.' I patted the camera case by my feet. 'I also think I managed to get a photo of him. Don't know what the quality will be like, but hopefully it'll be enough to make an ID from.'

'Great,' muttered Spinetti. 'We'll be able to include it in your next exhibition.'

'I was wondering . . . . you're sure you haven't got some kind of connection with Kennedy and Marsden? Business dealings, something like that?'

'Of course not!' The denial was a little too indignant, I thought; and I remembered a similar reaction from him when I'd assumed that he and Kit Marsden were friends.

'But you must admit, Vincent, it was you who put me on to Marsden in the first place. It seems a mighty big coincidence that—'

'That's exactly what it is!' he snapped. 'A coincidence. And I don't want you mentioning it to the police when they turn up. It could get me in all kinds of trouble if they think we were linked in some way.'

'I'd say you're in pretty bad trouble already,' I told him. 'Jesus, Vincent, somebody just tried to kill you! Don't you think you should tell the police everything you know?'

'What's the matter with you? There's no connection. I saw the tattooed guy dancing at some clubs, that's all. And I'd never even heard of Sebastian Kennedy until I read about him in the papers.'

This struck me as particularly unlikely. Kennedy had been a well known figure on the entertainment scene and Spinetti had always prided himself on knowing everybody who was anybody in Manchester.

'This just doesn't add up,' I said. 'Why do I get the distinct impression that you're hiding something from me?'

'Will you get off my back?' he growled. 'Look, I'll get enough of the third degree from the cops. I don't need it from you as well.'

We lapsed into a gloomy silence. After a few minutes, Spike returned with three paper cups full of tepid coffee.

'I didn't know what everybody took,' he muttered. 'So I got two with sugar and one without.'

Spinetti plumped for the one without and we sat there, sipping our drinks. The more I thought about his behaviour, the stranger it seemed. Why should he be worried about being linked with the dead men, unless he had something to hide? It occurred to me now that several people had tried to warn me that Spinetti was a dodgy character. Up till now I'd been his most loyal defender, leaping in without hesitation to lend him my support. But he'd recently demonstrated how devious he could be over that business with the exhibition. Maybe it was time I stopped being so trusting and started viewing the world with a more cynical eye.

The curtains parted and Detective Inspector Flynn stepped into the cubicle. He surveyed the three of us wearily, then gave me a sardonic smile.

'Mr Weston,' he said coldly. 'You do keep popping up in the oddest places, don't you?'

I noticed the formal use of my surname and deducted that he was still pissed off with me.

'Well,' I said. 'At least this time I have a good alibi. I was standing on stage in front of hundreds of witnesses when it happened. And I'm pretty sure that the attacker was your mysterious bearded man.'

'Really?' He frowned. 'Well I've just come from the Mandrake. We've several people who've given us conflicting descriptions, everything from a short, dark midget to a seven foot albino.'

'I can do better than that,' I assured him. 'I think I got a photograph.'

Flynn gave me a sharp look.

'Such a flair for capturing violence on film,' he observed. 'You could make a whole career out of that.'

'So I'm told.'

'Yes, well, I'll trouble you for the film, then. The *correct* film, if you don't mind.'

'It's colour stock. There's a lab I use in Ardwick, if you like I could get them done for you tomorrow . . .'

Flynn shook his head.

'I'll organise it myself if it's all the same to you. Who knows where the resulting pictures might end up? The Tate Gallery, I shouldn't wonder.'

I winced. 'Well, if you feel like that about it . . .' I went to my equipment case and started rewinding the spool of film from the camera. Flynn transferred his attention to Spinetti.

'So, Mr Spinetti. I must confess, when I heard about your little *contretemps*, my first reaction was to assume that this was another of your publicity stunts.' He regarded Spinetti's bandaged arm with a raised eyebrow. 'But I imagine that's taking things a little too far, even by your own extraordinary standards.'

Spinetti scowled.

'Very funny,' he muttered. 'You'll excuse me if I don't shake hands.'

Flynn looked at him thoughtfully for a moment.

'Mr Weston suggests that the killer of Sebastian Kennedy and Kit Marsden has now come looking for you. Why would that be, do you suppose?'

'Haven't the foggiest.' Spinetti shrugged. 'Anyway, I'm

not convinced it *is* the same man. Just some bloody lunatic if you ask me.'

'Oh, so being attacked with a knife is an everyday occurrence in your line of work is it?'

'There's people queuing up to stab you in the back, if that's what you mean.'

'I shouldn't be at all surprised,' said Flynn.

'Yeah, well, you've seen the punters in that club. It was probably just one of the weirdos that *his* lot attract.' He nodded at Spike.

'That's not fair!' protested Spike. 'I told you, we've never had anything like this before.'

Flynn turned his head to look at Spike.

'And you are . . .?'

'Spike Hughes. Lead singer with Sepulchre. We headlined the gig tonight.'

'I see.' Flynn surveyed Spike thoughtfully, taking in his mop of hair, his stained T-shirt, his torn jeans. 'And would I be right in assuming that you're a . . . heavy-metal band?'

'*Death*-metal. There's a difference.'

'Yeah,' said Spinetti. 'A very dangerous difference. This guy was prancing about the stage with a knife when it happened. Is it any wonder that some nutter took it into his head to have a go at me?'

Spike's jaw dropped open in surprise; and I too was astonished that Spinetti should have picked up on this point. He'd made no mention of it before. Flynn frowned.

'So you're suggesting that this . . . death-metal band somehow encouraged the attack?'

'There's a lot of sad people out there,' Spinetti told him. 'Impressionable kids. They see an idiot like him waving a knife in their faces and they get crazy ideas. Probably went

355

for me because I was wearing a suit. Image of authority and all that.'

'That's bollocks,' said Spike angrily. 'Besides, I thought you were there because you wanted to manage us.'

'You must be joking! I went along as a favour to Danny. I wouldn't touch your band of no-hopers with a barge-pole.'

What was going on here, I asked myself. A favour to me? That wasn't the way I remembered it. Spinetti had seemed quite keen to go to the gig and I knew perfectly well that he'd never let his own musical tastes get in the way of signing a hot property. No, he was using this as a way of shifting suspicion from himself.

'I must say, I find this all a bit rich from a man who quite happily put pictures of a dead body on public display,' observed Flynn. 'This sudden concern for the city's youth does you proud, Mr Spinetti. It just seems a little late in the day.'

'It wasn't a kid who attacked you,' I reminded Spinetti. 'I'd say late twenties, early thirties. Hardly an impressionable age.' Spinetti flashed me a look that asked me whose side I was on, but I wasn't going to stand by and let Spike be blamed for this. 'The band have been doing that number for years,' I told Flynn. 'There were never any problems before. Besides, the attack was planned. I saw the guy right at the back of the crowd, he pushed his way through to get to Vincent. It wasn't a spur of the moment thing.'

'Oh, it was no ordinary stabbing,' agreed Flynn. 'Not if the weapon is anything to go by. We found this in the middle of the dance-floor. Nobody would admit to owning it and it does appear to have fresh blood on the blade.' He reached into his pocket and took out a plastic bag, containing what looked like an ornamental dagger. He held it out so I could see it better.

The blade was made of smooth black stone, knapped to a jagged but razor-sharp edge. The wooden handle was carved in the form of a kneeling warrior figure, dressed in what looked like a feathered cloak. The figure was decorated with small pieces of coloured stone, turquoise, black and yellow. As soon as I saw it, I knew that I'd recently seen something very similar. In a glass case in the city museum.

'Aztec,' I said.

Flynn glanced at me.

'I beg your pardon?'

'It's an Aztec knife. Oh, I don't mean a genuine historical artefact, but it's definitely made in the same style. Take it to Dr Hulce at the museum, I'm sure he'll confirm that.'

Flynn looked intrigued.

'So where does this sudden knowledge of archaeology come from?' he asked me.

'I was at the museum on an assignment the other day. And this Dr Hulce happened to mention flaying. Well, I asked him some questions and he came up with some pretty interesting answers. He told me . . .'

Flynn held up a hand to silence me. Then he looked at my two companions.

'Gentlemen, I think that will be all for now. I'm sure you'd both like to get back to your respective homes. If you'd be so good as to leave your addresses with the officer outside, I'll be able to contact you if necessary.' He looked pointedly at Spinetti. 'And if you'd like me to assign somebody to keep an eye on you for a few days . . .'

'Don't bother,' Spinetti told him flatly. 'I can take care of myself.'

'Yes, but Mr Spinetti, if your attacker is who we think he is, surely you . . .'

'I told you. There's no connection between me and those

two people. Far as I'm concerned it was just some spaced-out whacko who was feeling pissed off with the world.'

Flynn sighed.

'If that's how you feel about it . . .'

'It is.'

'Then I can only wish you a safe journey home.'

Spike and Spinetti realised that they were dismissed. Spike got to his feet.

'I'll wait for you in reception,' he told me.

Spinetti was having trouble getting up off the bed. He extended his good arm in Spike's direction.

'Give me a hand, will you?' he said.

'You can fuck right off,' Spike told him testily, and quickly strode out of the room. I obliged instead.

'Thanks,' he said. He glanced towards the doorway. 'Touchy sort, your mate.'

'Hardly surprising under the circumstances. I think he was floored by your er . . . critical assessment. How will you get home?'

'I'll hop in a taxi.' Spinetti gave Flynn a scornful glance. 'I'll leave you to have your little chat,' he announced: then he gave me an altogether more meaningful look. *Don't drop me in it*, the look seemed to say. He went out through the doorway.

Flynn stared after him for a moment.

'Curious,' he said. 'Wouldn't you have thought that a man who'd been so viciously attacked would have been grateful for a little back-up? Or is it that he has other reasons for not wanting a close police presence?'

I didn't answer him, so he moved across to the bed and perched himself on the edge of it.

'Now then, Danny, you've come up with another of your little theories, have you?'

I felt vaguely cheered that I had suddenly been promoted to 'Danny' again. Flynn was clearly a fickle sort.

'Yes, I have. But I think you'll like this one. It holds a lot more water than my previous attempts.'

'I'm all ears,' he assured me.

'OK. There's an old Aztec god called Xipe Totec. That's XIPE, but it's pronounced with a Z, more like Zippy.'

Flynn gave me a doubtful look.

'Oh, now look,' he said.

'No, hear me out! The name means "Our Flayed Lord". A very powerful god to the Aztecs. Every year, men were sacrificed to him to ensure a good harvest. Their hearts were cut out and they were flayed. I'm pretty sure that the heart was removed with a special stone knife, like the one you have there. You see the carved figure? That's what's called an Eagle Warrior, I think.'

'October is hardly harvest time,' Flynn reminded me.

'OK, I know there are some rough edges. But think about it for a moment!' I ticked off the points on the fingers of my left hand. 'Flaying, hearts cut out, stone knives . . . there's got to be something in all that. It's surely worth talking to Dr Hulce?'

Flynn shrugged.

'I suppose it can't do any harm.'

'Good. There's one other thing. You're no doubt aware that there's this big Mexican festival going on at the moment?'

'Absolutely. I have a ticket for the Halloween Ball.'

'Me too. Well, I went to the festival launch, met all the people associated with it. There's more slim, dark, bearded Mexican's in that party than you could shake a stick at. Supposing one of them has a screw loose in his head, thinks he's a reincarnation of an Aztec priest or something . . .'

Flynn gave me an amused look.

'Don't laugh,' I warned him. 'It really isn't that funny. I've heard of weirder cases. You have to admit that the first killing happened virtually the day after the Mexicans arrived. You see, the whole thing is building up to this Day of the Dead party. There's an exhibition at the museum, it's chock full of skulls and coffins and stuff like that. Maybe one of the visitors is treating the whole thing a bit too literally.'

Flynn shook his head in apparent admiration.

'I have to hand it to you, Danny. That's some story you've put together. Have you ever thought of writing fiction?'

'Don't dismiss it,' I warned him. 'I'm serious about this.'

'Hmm. Well . . .' Flynn paused for a moment, looked suddenly thoughtful. 'Tell me about Mr Spinetti,' he said. 'Is he gay?'

'No,' I replied, without hesitation. 'Quite the opposite, actually. A bit of a ladies' man.'

'Hmm. That's the impression I got. Which rather piddles all over my theory about the killings being homophobic. Are you aware of any links between him and the previous victims?'

I shook my head.

'I asked him about that. He said not.'

Flynn glanced at me sharply.

'But you doubt his word?'

'No, not exactly. Let's just say that I . . . I have no evidence to the contrary.'

'Something doesn't seem right?'

'I don't know. Vincent is a friend as well as my manager. I wouldn't want to say anything that might make him look bad.'

Flynn sighed. 'That's the trouble with you, Danny. You're Mr Nice Guy. The problem is that you're surrounded by

people who aren't anything like as nice. Take your Mr
Spinetti, for example. Would it surprise you to know that
he's had several previous brushes with the law?'

I shrugged.

'I wouldn't know anything about that,' I said.

Flynn reached into his coat and pulled out a small notebook. He flipped it open and read from the contents.

'London, September '83. Charged with attempting to pass
off forged traveller's cheques. Served a three month custodial
sentence. January '85. Indecent assault on a sixteen-year-old
girl, but got off when the girl suddenly dropped all charges.
The word was she was scared off by threats of bodily harm.
March '85, accused of running a house of ill repute in
Fulham. Case dropped on insufficient evidence. Oh, now
here's a good one, July '85. Accused along with three other
men of raping a young woman . . . what I believe is referred
to as a gang-bang. He did six months inside for that one and
shortly afterwards, he moved to Manchester, where ever
since, he's managed to keep his affairs just on the right side
of legal. Or at least, so far as we know.'

'That's not fair,' I blustered. 'All that stuff was in the past.
People *can* change for the better, you know!' But I had to
admit to myself that this news had shocked me. I'd had no
idea about Spinetti's past misdemeanours and it made me
feel very differently towards him.

'My only point is that you should perhaps be a bit more
careful about the people you put your trust in. And not just
Vincent Spinetti. What about that little photographic assistant of yours. She's had a few brushes with the law too.'

'Roz? I don't believe it!'

'Oh, it's true enough. Nothing too startling. She was mixed
up with an animal rights campaign group a couple of years
ago. Some members thought they were making a perfectly

valid point by poisoning chocolate bars in supermarkets. She was one of the ones that slipped through the net. Oh, and there was the little matter of GBH. That would have been only a few months before she came to live with you.'

'What are you talking about?'

'She was arrested for beating up an elderly gentleman. Apparently she's a bit of a martial arts expert. You can see that in her dancing, mind you. It's all in the leg movements . . .'

'Hang on a minute. You're telling me that Roz beat up an old man? What utter crap!'

'It's a fact, I'm afraid.' He consulted his notebook again. 'Fractured tibia, a couple of broken ribs, broken collar bone . . . the officers attending the incident told me that they were appalled by the severity of the old man's injuries. Put him in hospital for several weeks. He didn't press charges though.'

'How come?'

'Apparently he was her father. He'd traced her to her previous address and had gone round to try and borrow some money off her. It would seem that there was some bad feeling between them over the suicide of Miss Birchill's mother. She's never mentioned that to you?'

'She has . . . well, some of it anyway. I didn't know about her beating up her old man, though. Christ.'

'Christ, indeed. One of the fascinating things about an investigation like this, is that you get to find out all the little secrets. It rather appeals to the voyeur in me.' He sighed. 'I'm going to miss it,' he said.

'Miss it? You're planning to leave the police?'

'I doubt if I'll have much choice over the matter. It seems that this city isn't quite ready for a police officer with my particular sexual preferences. I've detected sinister rumblings in the background. Could be better to jump before I'm pushed.'

I stared at him. 'It's a mystery to me how you ever wound up on the Force,' I told him.

'Oh well, obviously I haven't always been quite so open about it. For years, I kept it scrupulously hidden. It's only over the last year or so that I've decided it was time to come out of the closet. The revelation caused a bit of a bombshell back in London and frankly, that's how I came to be here in Manchester. I suspect that whoever had me transferred was exercising a certain degree of malice in sending me to this particular location. Though it's been rather amusing watching the reactions. Our own dear Detective Sergeant Potts is a good case in point. The man can hardly bear to be in the same room at me. When I stand near him, he *scratches*. I really ought to be preparing to make a fight of it but . . . the truth of the matter is, I feel I'm rapidly losing my vocation.'

'I thought only priests did that.'

He smiled.

'Coming to Manchester has opened my eyes a bit. It's brought out a certain . . . flamboyant streak in me. There's a quality to the clubs here that's been a revelation. I shouldn't be at all surprised if I decided to investigate some other line of work, before very much longer.' I must have looked worried, because he continued. 'Naturally, I'd want to see this case through to a suitable conclusion. Unthinkable to quit at this stage. Just when it's getting interesting.'

'Interesting in what way?'

'I think our killer is getting reckless. The two previous killings were carried out in the utmost secrecy. This latest attempt took place in a crowded club in front of hundreds of potential witnesses.' He took the spool of film from his pocket and examined it. 'He even allowed himself to be photographed. When people get reckless, they eventually make a mistake. That's when we catch them. At any rate, I'll get this developed and we'll see what we've got. I trust you remembered to take off the lens cap?' He slipped the film back into his pocket and glanced at his watch.

'Anyway, it's late and I think I've covered everything. I'll let you get off home. But Danny, about your Mr Spinetti. If I were you, I'd seriously start looking for another manager. And you might want to think about acquiring the services of a more placid photographic assistant. One who does night classes in macramé, rather than Kung Fu.'

'Thanks for the advice,' I said. 'And you'll take that knife to Dr Hulce?'

'I certainly will. First thing tomorrow. We'll see if he can shed any light on the matter. It promises to be an education. Goodnight, Danny.'

'Goodnight.' I picked up my camera case and went out of the cubicle, down the corridor to reception, where I found a disgruntled-looking Spike slumped on a plastic chair, his head in his hands. 'Cheer up,' I told him. 'It might never happen.'

'It already has,' he moaned. 'We lashed out a fortune on that gig. Decent PA, lights, pyro-bleedin'-technics. Wanted to make a showcase out of it, didn't we? Now I've got to go back and tell the guys that Spinetti ain't gonna sign us. Jesus, they'll kill me . . .' He realised what he'd said and shook his head. 'Sorry, man, I didn't mean . . .'

'Forget it,' I said, slapping him on the back. 'Anyway, maybe you had a close escape.'

'How's that?' he asked me, getting to his feet.

'I'll tell you about it on the way home,' I promised him: and we wandered out into the night to look for a taxi.

# Chapter Thirty-Two

The next morning, after a late breakfast, I walked into town to collect my car. It was a crisp, clear day, sunny but shot through with the unmistakable chill of advancing winter. The events of the previous night seemed somehow unreal, a vivid hallucination brought on by my alcoholic over-indulgence: but I knew that it *had* happened and was only too aware that the violence was getting closer all the time. I had hardly known Sebastian Kennedy and had only just been getting to know Kit Marsden. Now a close friend had been subject to a vicious assault. How much closer would the violence get before all this was over? I was beginning to get very frightened.

I didn't know what to think about Flynn's revelations concerning Spinetti and Roz. I'd tried phoning Spinetti before I left the apartment that morning, but his answerphone had been on and I'd just asked him to contact me. Roz hadn't been at home last night and there'd been no sign of her this morning, either. I'd finally concluded that she'd had her own reasons for not telling me about the final run-in with her father. It was hardly likely to be something she was proud of.

As I approached The Wedge, I saw that it was just opening up for business and that a small queue had already formed at the entrance, more eager punters lured by Spinetti's publicity stunt, ready to gawp at a series of pictures that ordinarily, they wouldn't have crossed the road to look at. It seemed to me now that my photographs were merely an irrelevence. It could be anything up there on display – tins of baked beans, random splashes of gravy on white table-cloths, house bricks, used condoms, empty crisp packets. The punters weren't coming to see the pictures for their own intrinsic value but because of the outrage with which they were associated.

I was beginning to feel totally depressed about the whole sorry business and though I tried to tell myself that my work was still as good, bad or indifferent as it had ever been, I couldn't help feeling that I had been cheated somehow. On paper, I was fronting a resounding success. In my heart, I felt like a quack in a medicine show, a complete con artist.

As I trudged around the front of the building towards the station car park, a familiar voice called out to me.

'Hey, Danny! How's it going?' Turning, I saw Trevor Bird hurrying towards me. He was wearing a tweed overcoat and a long red scarf was wrapped repeatedly around his neck, making him look more like Billy Bunter than ever. He grinned wildly and jerked his thumb at the queue of people making their way into The Wedge. 'Now there's a sight to warm the cockles!' he observed.

'Yeah,' I said, without enthusiasm. 'Great.'

Trevor looked puzzled.

'I was just going in for a second look,' he told me. 'I've got a few days off work, so . . .'

'I should have thought one look was enough,' I told him. 'Besides, haven't you heard? The police confiscated the Kennedy pictures.'

'I know that, I was *there*, remember? Saw you shooting off with that nice looking piece, you sly dog you! Anyway, that doesn't matter. They weren't the best stuff in the show, not by a long shot.'

'You . . . you don't think so?'

Bird shook his head.

'It's the portraits I like the best. The old people? They're a knockout! I love the way you've done those, the character just seems to shine out of every pore. And some of those inner city landscapes are superb, too. God, Danny, what I wouldn't give to have your talent.'

'Oh, no,' I protested. 'You're kind, but—'

'Really, mate, I mean it. Me, I'm just fumbling along trying to discover some kind of style, but you've got such an *eye*, Danny. That's a rare gift.' He waved a pudgy hand in the direction of the queue. 'Oh, most of them are only here because of all that crap in the papers, I know that. But if they just bother to open their eyes and *look*, they'll see plenty to justify them going.'

I felt distinctly cheered by this unprompted recommendation – cheered and rather touched. Other photographers were generally very grudging with their praise. It occurred to me that I'd been guilty of looking down on Bird in the past and that wasn't really fair. He was a decent sort who'd always had the highest regard for what I was trying to do.

'Thanks, Trevor,' I said. 'I really appreciate that. Look, er . . . what are you working on at the moment?'

He scowled.

'Oh well, I've been trying to do that portfolio for Mo. I keep telling her when we get the chance to use that studio of yours, we'll be able to put together something really special. I expect you're snowed under after the success of *Skin Flicks*.' I smiled. I was in a better mood now and feeling decidedly magnanimous.

'Not at all. How does today suit you?'

'Today?'

'Sure. The studio's standing there empty and I've got nothing planned. I could help you rig the lights if you want.'

Bird looked at me and for a moment, I thought he was going to start crying.

'Really?' he asked me. 'You're not pulling my leg?'

'Of course not. I told you, once the exhibition was out of the way . . .'

'Danny, that would be *brilliant*!' Bird almost danced a jig of delight right there on the pavement. 'I just need to nip back home and pick up my gear. Mo's on half day, I could pick her up on the way back . . . take me maybe an hour or so . . .'

His enthusiasm was infectious and I couldn't help smiling.

'Yes, well, take your time,' I told him. 'I'll be there all afternoon, so there's no problem. You can work as long as you like, go through the night if you want.'

'Oh, Danny, Danny, I owe you one for this! I'll just . . . I won't be . . . I'll see you later!' He turned and hurried off in the direction from which he had come.

I unlocked the car, climbed inside and drove back through town to my regular parking spot. I told myself that it would be a genuine pleasure to help him with his photographs, to work on something with no ulterior motives whatsoever. I just hoped he could persuade Mo to keep her clothes on for a change.

I let myself in through the entrance door and immediately became aware of a powerful cooking smell that, unusually, was coming from upstairs, rather than Mr Bhopal's take-away. I climbed the stairs, unlocked the kitchen door and stepped warily inside. The kitchen was full of steam and Roz was standing at the cooker. She was wearing a striped apron and was stirring a large pot of something that was bubbling and steaming on the hob. She glanced up at me and smiled pleasantly, which immediately put me on my guard. Then she went on with what she was doing. I closed the door behind me and went over to stand beside her. This was not an everyday occurrence. Far from it. In fact, when I thought about it, I couldn't ever recall seeing Roz cook anything more complicated than toast.

'Expecting company?' I asked her.

'He just arrived,' she assured me. 'I hope you're hungry.'

'Er . . .' I glanced cautiously at the contents of the pot she was stirring and was instantly reassured. It looked like chilli, an old favourite of mine. 'Yes, I *am* feeling peckish.'

'I just thought I'd try and make amends for the other night,' she explained. 'We got a little bit heated, didn't we?'

'Oh, that's OK.' My God, I *was* feeling magnanimous today, ready to shrug off a bitter argument with a gesture of dismissal. 'It was just one of those things, really.' I took off my jacket and slung it over the back of a chair. Then I moved back to the stove, rubbing my hands in a show of anticipation. 'I *love* chilli,' I told her.

'Actually, it's a spaghetti sauce,' she said.

'Yes, of course, I knew that! I was just going to say that if there's one thing I like more than chilli, it's a good spaghetti sauce.'

'Of course, if you'd rather have had chilli . . .'

'No, no, it looks terrific, honestly.'

'It's my own recipe. Roz's spicy spaghetti surprise.'

'Oh yeah? It smells great.' I leaned forward to inhale the contents of the pan. 'Looks delicious,' I said.

Roz had now brought a large pan of salted water to the boil and was folding strands of fresh spaghetti into it.

'Basically, it's a bolognese sauce but with extra garlic and my own mixture of spices. Whole chilli peppers, tobasco sauce, cayenne, paprika, cumin, stuff like that. My mum taught me to make it when I was a kid and I've kind of adapted it a bit over the years.'

'Terrific,' I assured her. 'And I must say, this is a pleasant surprise.'

'Didn't think I could cook, eh?'

'No! I mean, yes. That is, I didn't really know whether you could or not. But since I've never actually seen you do it, I suppose I just kind of assumed . . .'

She shook her head, adopted a grave expression.

'I've let myself get into some terrible habits,' she muttered. 'But that's all going to change from now on. I'm turning over a new leaf.'

I felt like saying that I was glad to hear it but I resisted the impulse. It almost certainly would have been misconstrued, the equivalent of me saying, 'thank God for that, you've been crap so far!'

I watched as Roz dipped a spoon into the sauce and lifted it to her lips. She looked thoughtful, then handed me the spoon. 'It might need a bit more chilli powder,' she observed. 'What do you think?'

I took the spoon from her, scooped up a dollop of sauce and lifted it to my mouth. My first reaction was that if anything, it was actually a little bit *heavy* on the chilli but, ever the diplomat, I opened my mouth to tell Roz that it was just perfect.

That was when the culinary equivalent of a thermo-nuclear device exploded on my tongue. My mouth became the entrance to a miniature blast furnace, I could almost visualise my tongue blackening and shrivelling within it. My eyes filled with moisture and I felt the skin of my face redden to a beetroot shade as my temperature galloped up the scale. The compliment I had intended to give emerged as a formless croak of pure agony.

Then I was rushing past Roz to the sink. Frantically grabbing the nearest receptacle, a large teacup, I filled it with cold water and gulped down the contents in indecent haste, almost imagining that I could hear the pronounced hiss of steam as the liquid made contact with the spice-blasted surface of my tongue. At last, I was able to construct a short sentence.

'My goodness, that's . . . that's got quite a kick, hasn't it!'

Roz regarded me coldly.

'You don't like it,' she observed.

'Not at all! I *love* it. I was just taken unaware, that's all. I mean, I didn't expect it to be quite so hot.'

'It's meant to be hot,' she said tonelessly. 'It's spicy spaghetti surprise. The surprise is that it's *hot*.'

'Absolutely.' I considered getting another cup of water but decided it would be laying it on a bit thick. I couldn't help wondering how I was going to get through an entire portion of the stuff but I'd have to cross that bridge when I got to it. 'It's delicious, really. Only, the thing is, everyone has a different tolerance to spices and—'

'You don't like it,' she said again, with an air of glum finality. 'Nobody *ever* likes my cooking.'

'Oh now, I only said—'

'I bet *she* can cook, can't she?'

'She?'

'Julia. I bet she can cook.'

'Er . . .' I was somewhat thrown by the abrupt change of subject. 'I really wouldn't know. She's never—'

'Oh yes, sure, I can see it now! Miss bloody Perfect, of *course* she can cook! She's a Latin American Delia Smith!' She lifted the pan up and slammed it down again for emphasis. 'Why not, she has everything else going for her, hasn't she? The long black hair, the long brown legs! Perfect teeth, perfect tits, the kind of looks you'd *kill* for . . .'

'But . . . I thought you said she wasn't that good looking!'

'Of course I said that, you idiot! What was I supposed to say, that she was beautiful? What did you call her? A Latin love goddess?' She directed a scornful look in my direction. 'Nobody ever called me a love goddess.'

'Oh, but that was just a figure of speech . . .'

'What do you know?' she asked me. 'You've no idea what it's like to be second best all your life!'

She seemed to be getting angrier by the moment.

'Roz, don't be silly. Nobody said you were second best.'

'You didn't have to.' She looked tearful now as she gazed down at the two bubbling pans on the stove. 'I should have known it would turn out like this,' she muttered. 'The way it *always* turns out. What was I trying to do, for God's sake? Who was I trying to kid?'

'Roz?' I murmured: then had to duck as with a quick motion, she snatched up the pan of sauce and flung it in the general direction of the sink. The contents splattered messily up the wall above the worktop. I stared at them in dull surprise for a moment, before turning back to face her. 'Roz, for Christ's sake!' I reasoned. 'Nobody said that it was—' But then I was dodging the potentially lethal contents of the spaghetti pan. Scalding water splashed across the floor and a few strands of spaghetti wrapped themselves around the light fitting above my head, but most of it joined the sauce in the sink in a ghastly approximation of the finished meal.

Roz seemed to have lost her cool in a major way now. She was stamping up and down the small kitchen, her hands gesturing as she snapped out a series of curses at the world in general.

'Always the same,' she snarled. 'Nobody thinks I'm capable of doing anything. Ever since school, the same. You're hopeless, Birchill, you'll never amount to anything, can't cook, can't sew, can't spell! But I'm a capable person, I *can* do things! Then *she* comes along. Miss bloody Moreno. What's her game, eh? What's she up to? And how come I'm the only one that can see there's something wrong?' She whirled around to stare at me imploringly. 'She's not right for you, Danny. She'll hurt you! You mark my words, she'll chew you up and spit out the pieces.'

'Roz, for God's sake, stop it!'

I stepped forward and grabbed her shoulders in an attempt to calm her down and that was when she hit me with the back of one hand, a fierce swipe that rocked me back several steps, slamming me against the work surface behind me. I stepped in some stray spaghetti and almost slipped, had to throw out one hand to support myself. I crouched there, temporarily stunned, looking warily at Roz. She was staring wildly back at me, her chest rising and falling as she tried to catch her breath, her hands bunched into fists. For an instant, she looked like some wild animal about to pounce.

Then her expression softened a little and she stared down at the reddened knuckles of her right hand, as though surprised to see what she had done.

'Oh, Danny,' she said. 'I . . . I didn't mean to—'

But I was in no mood to listen to her excuses. Now I'd got over the shock of being struck, my own temper was rising and I had to struggle to keep my voice calm.

'Roz, I think it's best that you leave, as soon as possible. This clearly can't go on.'

She stared at me, then flinched as though I had actually struck her.

'Leave?' she whispered.

'Yes, please. The sooner the better.'

'Oh, but . . . but . . .' Her jaw began to tremble and fresh tears welled in her eyes. 'I didn't . . . I didn't mean . . .' She gestured helplessly at me. 'Danny, I'm sorry.'

'I'm sure you are. And so am I, Roz, but we can't go on like this. It's got so I don't know what to expect from you next. If you hate me so much, then—'

'Hate you?' She looked at me for a moment, then laughed bitterly. 'Is that what you think?'

'How am I supposed to know *what* to think? One minute you can be as nice as pie, the next . . .' I waved my hands in exasperation. 'God knows I've given you every opportunity to mend your ways and just when I think we're starting to get somewhere, you pull some stupid stunt. Like the other night when Julia was here. I mean, what was that all about? What was I supposed to make of it?'

'Oh, you fool.' She shook her head in apparent disbelief. 'What do you suppose it was all about? I love you, you pillock!'

I opened my mouth to give a suitably terse reply but the effect of this last statement was much the same as a mouthful of Roz's spicy spaghetti – and even more surprising. I just stood there like a complete goon, my mouth hanging open, one finger pointing at the ceiling for emphasis.

'You . . . you *love* me?' I gasped.

But she was turning away with a groan of despair, pulling off the striped apron and flinging it aside. She opened the kitchen door and running out on to the landing, almost collided with a bemused looking Trevor Bird who was just lugging his camera case to the top of the stairs. Roz shoved past him and went pounding down the staircase.

'Roz!' I yelled: and started after her.

'Danny?' muttered Bird, peering uncertainly into the spaghetti-splattered interior of the kitchen. 'Mo wasn't at home, so I . . .'

'Sure, sure, come right in!' I yelled. 'The studio's at the far end of the corridor.' I grabbed my jacket and pushed past him. Looking down the stairs, I saw the exterior door open and close as Roz pushed out on to the street. 'Just help yourself to anything you want, Trevor, I'll be back in a bit.'

'But Danny, I just . . .'

'Can't talk now, Trevor! See you later!'

I dashed down the stairs, jumping them three at a time. There was no way I could let it go at that. '*I love you, you pillock!*' she'd said. OK, so it wasn't the most romantic declaration of all time, but no woman had ever said anything remotely like that to me in my entire life. I wasn't about to let her get away from me; at least, not until she'd given me a full explanation.

Doing a fair impersonation of an Olympic runner I pushed through the outer door and ran out on to the street. I glanced right and left, then spotted Roz some distance away, running down Oldham Street towards the city centre. Taking a deep breath, I set off in hot pursuit.

# PART THREE

What is commonly called love, namely the desire of satisfying a voracious appetite, with a certain quantity of delicate white human flesh.

Henry Fielding
*Tom Jones*

There is no fear in love; but perfect love casteth out fear.

*John* 4:18

# Chapter Thirty-Three

I finally caught up with Roz in Piccadilly Gardens. I found her sitting on a wooden bench, getting her breath back while she stared blankly at the flocks of hopeful pigeons, foraging around her feet in their never-ending quest for crumbs.

By this time, I was fairly out of breath myself. I moved across to the bench and flopped down beside her. We didn't speak for at least ten minutes, we just sat there, watching the pigeons who were slowly cottoning on to the fact that we had no food for them. One by one, they fluttered off to seek sustenance elsewhere.

I kept glancing at Roz, but her gaze was fixed straight ahead, a fierce expression on her face. I thought about saying something to her but in her present mood, it wouldn't have been wise. She'd probably have hit me again. So I decided to leave it to her to break the silence.

Finally, after what must have been a good fifteen minutes, she muttered something under her breath and I was obliged to turn my head and look at her.

'Come again?' I said gruffly.

She scowled at me.

'I said, "I made a right mess of that one, didn't I?" '

'I don't know about a mess. You certainly surprised me. I mean, that was about the last thing I expected.'

She gave a tut of irritation.

'How could you not have noticed?' she asked me. 'I mean, wasn't it obvious?'

'It most certainly was *not*!' I assured her. 'In fact, I was under the impression that you hated my guts.'

She laughed at that.

'My God, you don't see anything, do you? Even Spike had a clearer idea of what was going on. Christ, even Spike!'

'Yes, but there you go. When I told you what Spike had said, you laughed it off, said it was ridiculous.'

'Of course I did!' She gave me a scornful look. 'What was the alternative?'

'Well, the truth might have been refreshing.'

'Oh yeah, and have you *gloating* about it.'

'I wouldn't have gloated. Why would I gloat?'

'I don't know.' She glared furiously at a last, hopeful pigeon who seemed to have convinced itself that we were holding out on it. 'I'm . . . I'm a bit confused by all this. I'm not usually so . . . so soppy.'

'*You're* confused! Jesus, what about me? I was convinced that you were . . .'

She glanced at me.

'That I was what?'

'That you were a . . . well, a lesbian.'

She laughed bitterly.

'You kill me,' she said.

'Well, what was I supposed to think? I mean, you spent all that time hanging out with Wanda and her cronies and . . . and every time I said anything halfway nice to you, you virtually jumped down my throat. You . . . you even said I was *sexless*!'

'Classic self-denial. I should have thought anybody could have seen through that.'

'Oh well, excuse me for being so thick!'

There was another long silence. The last pigeon gave a dismal flap of its wings and whirled off to join its mates, who had just found a little old lady with a whole sliced loaf to dispose of.

'So, how long?' I asked Roz, after an interval.

'How long *what*?' she snapped.

'How long have you . . . had feelings for me?'

'Bloody ages,' she complained, as though it was a major imposition to be in love with somebody. 'God knows I didn't want to. I couldn't stop myself . . . look, what are you laughing at? It isn't funny.'

'Who's laughing?'

But she was clearly unconvinced by this.

'Oh, I'm sure it's all a great hoot, isn't it? Roz Birchill, lovesick sap. Making a complete fool of herself over some worthless bloke who doesn't care a fig about her.'

'Now why do you say that? Why do you assume that I don't care about you?'

'Because that's how it always is.' She lifted her feet up on to the bench and cradled her knees in her arms. 'I'm just not fanciable, that's all.'

'What nonsense! Of course you're fanciable.'

'No.' She was shaking her spiky head in contradiction. 'Believe me, Danny, I have no misconceptions about myself. It's always been like that, ever since school. My mates were fanciable, they had blokes chasing them all over the place. I was the one the lads wanted "as a friend". Somebody they could knock about with, tell dirty jokes to, arm wrestle with.' She tilted back her head a moment and stared up at the sky, as though trying to puzzle it out. 'Julia Moreno is fanciable,' she said. 'There's a woman who can inspire a man she barely knows to carry her name about on his skin. I couldn't inspire

381

a man to wear my name on his *hat*.'

'Why are you so hard on yourself?' I protested. 'Roz, you are a very attractive person. At least, you can be when you put your mind to it. You have a nice figure, clear skin, a terrific personality, when you allow it to show . . .'

'Oh yes, wonderful! Great. The consolation prize for not being fanciable. "Oh, but Roz, you have a wonderful personality!" Which actually translates as, "sorry Roz, but I don't really fancy you!" '

'It does not! You must have a very low self-esteem if that's what you think.'

'But it's true, isn't it? You don't fancy me, do you?'

'Well, I—'

'Do you?'

'Jesus, I don't know! I've just got over the notion of you not being a lesbian. There's . . . there's absolutely no reason why I shouldn't fancy you. I need time to think about it, that's all.'

Roz sighed. She crossed her arms on the top of her knees and rested her chin on them.

'It wasn't meant to be like this,' she observed to the world in general. 'I mean, I didn't want to have to push you into a corner. What I really wanted was . . .' She hesitated, looked vaguely disgusted with herself.

'What?' I prompted her.

'No, it's just too soppy!'

'Go on, tell me.'

'Well . . . what I sometimes wanted was for you to just take me in your arms and . . . hold me, like . . . like . . .'

'John Wayne and Maureen O'Hara?' I ventured.

She nodded.

'That kind of thing,' she agreed glumly.

I shook my head in bewilderment. I had terrible trouble

visualising that. All I could see was me trying it and Roz hitting me. This reminded me of something.

'Why didn't you tell me about your father?' I asked her. 'About how you beat him up?'

She gave me a shocked look.

'How did you—?'

'Flynn told me. He said you put your old man in the hospital for several weeks.'

She nodded gravely.

'It was before I moved in with you,' she said. 'He was let out of the home he'd been staying in and somehow he tracked me down. He wanted me to give him money for drink. When I refused, he started slagging off Mum, telling me how she'd always been a whore, how she'd been having it away with everyone in the street behind his back. It was a filthy lie and he knew it, he just wanted to hurt me. And he succeeded. I saw red. I don't even remember hitting him. It was like I blacked out and when I came round, he was lying there all busted up.' She looked at me defiantly and I saw that her eyes were filling with tears. 'But I don't regret it, not for a moment. He had that coming to him for years.' She paused to wipe her eyes on her sleeve. 'I have a lot of bottled-up rage in me, Danny, I'm aware of that. And for years, every man I ever met seemed to be a milder version of my old man. But you're different, I know that. I'm sorry I hit out at you, back there. I promise I'll never do it again.'

There was another long silence while I absorbed this information.

'Look,' I said. 'Clearly I've been wrong about you. And now I know how you feel, maybe . . . maybe something will materialise. Who knows?'

'You don't want me to move out?'

'No, of course not. I said that in the heat of the moment.'

'And Julia?' she asked fearfully.

'What about her?'

'I know you think it's just jealousy on my part . . . but . . . she's not right for you, Danny. She couldn't make you happy, not like I could. You see, I know that deep down, we're like *that*.' She crossed the index and second finger on her right hand and held it out to show me. 'We're alike you and me, mostly because we're so different.'

'Uh . . . right.'

'No, don't just agree with me! I know you think that's the standard hippie bullshit, but it's more than that. Sometimes you meet somebody and you *know* . . . you just know that deep down, you were made for each other. That's you and me.'

It was weird hearing Roz come out with this Mills and Boon stuff, it was almost as though she'd undergone some schizophrenic transformation. I was beginning to feel decidedly uncomfortable with it.

'Listen,' I said, 'since we missed out on lunch, why don't we go somewhere and have a meal? My treat.'

She looked at me hopefully.

'What, just the two of us?'

I glanced around.

'I don't see anybody else, do you?'

'You mean like a proper date?'

'Sure, why not? We could walk down to Chinatown, have a nice lunch, maybe a couple of beers.'

Roz smiled. 'I'd like that,' she said. She seemed to consider for a moment, her brow furrowing as though she was worrying about something. 'Danny, I want you to know that it's not because of the exhibition or anything, your career taking off. I'm not a gold digger. I've felt like this for a long time, pretty much since I moved in with you.'

I shook my head.

'I just wish I'd known,' I told her. 'I had feelings about you, too.'

'When?'

'After you first arrived. I used to . . . you know, think about you a lot. At night.'

She laughed, shook her head.

'You're just saying that!' she protested.

'No, Scout's honour. I really felt that way. But then when I seemed to be getting nowhere with you, I suppose I just suppressed it. Now you tell me that it's OK to feel like that about you and I'm *confused* . . .' I trailed off. What was worrying me now was something that I couldn't bring myself to mention. Yes, I had once had strong feelings about Roz – but after all the time spent brushing my emotions under the carpet, I didn't know if I could rekindle the flame.

Then there was Julia to consider. Though it seemed that Roz had effectively seen her off, there was still a part of me that hoped against hope that my mysterious Latin lady would resurface sooner or later. Not for the first time, I asked myself why love had to be so bloody complicated. Anyway, one thing at a time.

'Come on,' I told Roz. 'We'll try the Woo Sang. They do a—'

I broke off as I caught sight of a familiar shaved head, jutting up from the screen of shrubs in the central sunken gardens below us. Scott Banks was turned away and he was talking animatedly to another familiar figure.

Joey Sparks looked angry. The two men were clearly having a heated conversation though from where I was sitting, I couldn't make out a word of what was being said. Banks turned aside to light a cigarette and I could see that he had an unpleasantly smug expression. He turned back and blew a cloud of smoke into Sparks' face. Sparks said something and punched his right fist into the palm of his left hand, for emphasis. Then he turned abruptly away and strode quickly across the square towards the tram stop in front of the Plaza. Banks gazed after him for a few moments, then he too turned and swaggered off in the other direction.

I asked myself what was going on there. Sparks had told me that he hadn't seen Banks for ages, that he wanted nothing to do with him. Could it be that Sparks was not as innocent as he seemed? Had my attempts to keep his name out of the mud been misdirected? I decided that another visit to Joey's Hideaway was most definitely on the cards . . .

I suddenly realised that Roz was talking to me. She was saying something about how she'd normally insist on 'going Dutch' for the meal, but since she'd come out without her money, she'd make an exception this time and let me pay. As we got up from the bench, she looped her arm through mine and I was once again struck by the strangeness of the situation. Roz Birchill and *me*? Surely not? And yet . . . and yet wasn't there something incredibly pleasurable about the situation? After all, this wasn't some woman I'd just met at a club or a bar; this was an old friend, somebody I knew quite a bit about already. There would be none of the awkwardness normally associated with a first date and we wouldn't have to waste time asking about all those dumb things that you felt obliged to ask a stranger. I had every reason to suppose that this could be the start of something very special.

With high hopes and a light step, Roz and I set out for Chinatown and our second attempt at lunch. I just hoped it would be less dramatic than the first.

# Chapter Thirty-Four

Somewhere between the crispy Won Ton and the Singapore noodles, I decided that yes, Roz was still very fanciable.

It didn't take long to convince me. Now that she'd divested herself of the sullen, sneering persona that I had been so familiar with for so long, it was a relatively easy matter to find myself desiring her. She was a changed person that day, warm, funny, articulate, appreciative. We sank a couple of Chinese beers with the starters and that helped things along no end. By the time the main course arrived, we were getting on like the proverbial house on fire.

For the first time since she'd mentioned her unhappy childhood, Roz really opened herself up to me. Instead of the hard-faced, quarrelsome creature I'd always encountered, I discovered instead a shy, neurotic kid with very low self-esteem who had somehow learned to hide it all behind a tough, cantankerous exterior. Her tendency to argue was, she told me, a defence mechanism, every bit as studied as the Aikido classes she regularly attended. She told me that whenever the mechanism was activated, she was aware that she was doing it and hated herself for it; but when she was in that certain frame of mind, she was simply unable to stop herself. She was willing to change, she assured me; and she had decided that the key to it all was the need for a fruitful relationship.

'Basically, I'm sexually frustrated,' she told me, within earshot of an elderly male waiter, whose eyebrows arched comically at the news. 'I'm not exactly a virgin or anything like that . . . but it's been a very long time for me, over a year.'

I almost said 'snap', but at the last instant, my stubborn male pride prevented me from doing so. Instead, I just nodded sympathetically and tried to look like somebody who was in and out of other people's beds every other night.

Roz told me that it had been the appearance of Julia that had finally galvanised her into making her feelings towards me more obvious. She said that she'd suddenly realised that if she didn't do something about it now, she might lose the opportunity once and for all. Her recent visits to Wanda had been attempts to seek the great one's valued advice on matters of the heart.

'I was driving her nuts with it,' Roz explained. 'Finally, she suggested I should make a nice meal for you. She said that was the only sure-fire way to a man's heart.'

*What the hell would she know about it*? I couldn't help but wonder; and I couldn't quite picture Wanda as some kind of alternative agony aunt. It struck me that it was just possible that Wanda had herself experienced Roz's spicy spaghetti surprise and had been counting on it to effectively put paid to any romance between the two of us. But perhaps I was being uncharitable. Still, it all seemed to have worked out nicely in the end.

After the meal, I paid the bill and Roz and I sauntered in the direction of home. We started off with our arms linked but by the time we'd reached the top of Oldham Street, we actually had our arms around each other. I remembered that Trevor Bird was working in the studio but told myself that Roz and I could easily let ourselves in and creep to my room without major upset: and judging by the way Roz was nestling her head against my shoulder, I had every reason to suppose that she would be amenable to the idea.

I unlocked the outer door and we started climbing the staircase. Halfway up, I responded to a sudden impulse and decided it was now or never. I paused, took Roz in my arms and kissed her. For an instant, she seemed to freeze and I anticipated disaster. But then she relaxed a little and responded enthusiastically, slipping her arms around my waist and her tongue into my mouth. It was going to be all right, I told myself.

I took her hand and hurried on to the top of the stairs. The door to the apartment was open, but I didn't give it a second thought, intent as I was on more pressing matters. I remembered a similar scene with Julia only a short time ago but told myself that this time, nothing was going to interrupt. I stepped into the kitchen, pulled Roz in after me, then pressed her back against the door to kiss her again.

But as I leaned towards her, her expression changed dramatically. Her eyes widened in shock, her mouth dropped open in a gape of sheer horror and she made a sound, a grunt of what could only be interpreted as disgust. For a moment, I had the distinct notion that she'd gone schizo on me – that any second, she was going to drop into Bruce Lee mode and deliver a good kicking. But then I realised that she wasn't even looking at me. She was staring at something over my shoulder.

I turned and started so violently that the air was jolted out of my body with an 'oof!'. I also stepped instinctively backwards, colliding with Roz and inadvertantly slamming her against the door.

A face was peering into the kitchen, around the edge of the open doorway that led to the hall. Oddly, the face was down at floor level, resting on one cheek, but it took me some moments to recognise it as belonging to Trevor Bird. He was lying in the hallway, his glasses hung skew-whiff on his face and behind the thick lenses, his eyes were staring blankly up at me. What was infinitely more horrible was the fact that he appeared to have two mouths. From the first, his tongue lolled obscenely. From the second, a crescent shaped slit in his throat, copious amounts of blood had flowed and fanned out in a wide pool of rapidly congealing crimson.

A long, silent moment creaked by while I stood there staring down at him in dismay. Then I managed to produce a short sentence.

'Trevor, oh Jesus!' I gasped. I pulled myself together enough to run over and drop down on my knees beside him – but it didn't take an expert to realise that there was absolutely nothing I could do. I put a hand on his cheek and it was already cold to the touch. I recoiled in horror and I just kneeled there, looking at him as I tried to control my breathing, the breath jolting out of me in a series of shallow gasps.

'Who the fuck is it?' gasped Roz. She was still standing with her back to the door, as though afraid that he might get up at any moment and come after her.

'It's Trevor,' I said and realised that meant nothing to her. 'Trevor from Photolab. He was using the studio today. He asked if he could . . .'

'Shh!' Roz lifted a finger to her lips and gestured over my head into the hallway. 'I thought I heard something.'

I listened intently and felt a shiver of pure terror ripple

along my spine from neck to groin. Now I could hear it too. Hoarse, gutteral breathing coming from somewhere down the hall.

'There's somebody here!' whispered Roz.

A surge of anger coursed through me. I gestured her to silence while I looked frantically around for a weapon. Getting shakily to my feet, I grabbed a large kitchen knife from the draining board, wincing as metal scraped against metal. Holding the thing out in front of me, I turned, stepped gingerly over Bird's body and began to advance cautiously down the hallway. I'd taken maybe three steps when I suddenly felt hands on my shoulders and I nearly jumped out of my skin; but it was only Roz, who had hurried forward to back me up. I was grateful for her presence and simultaneously amazed that she hadn't just made a run for it. Clinging together and quite terrified, we moved forward.

We took three faltering steps then froze again. The open doorway of the bathroom was to our left and we realised now that the sounds were coming from in there. It was slow, tortured breathing and to my ears, it sounded barely human. My mind ran riot with grisly images of what I might find in there and part of me wanted to just turn and run, but somehow I talked myself out of it. I hefted the knife and turned to peer around the door frame.

The interior of the bathroom came into view. I saw that the shower curtain was pulled across the bathtub and I realised that the sounds were coming from behind it. As I looked, I thought I perceived the faintest trace of movement through the translucent curtain.

I glanced at Roz. She gave me a frantic look, her eyes wide, her mouth set in a tight grimace of fear. I swallowed hard and moved towards the doorway, placing my feet with great care, cringing at every creak of a floorboard. I placed my right foot on the firmer surface of the tiled bathroom floor, then my left. Roz stayed with me and now we were inside the room, moving slowly closer to the bathtub. The breathing sounds seemed horribly amplified in here. I held my own breath as Roz and I covered the last few feet and now I was being assailed by awful doubts.

What did I think I was doing, for Christ's sake? Would I have the guts to plunge the knife into whoever was hiding behind that curtain? Trevor Bird had been murdered. Whoever was hiding in here would kill me too without a moment's hesitation. But when push came to shove, was I prepared to do the same to him? Supposing I wasn't. Supposing I simply stood there like a lemon while he came at me with whatever weapon had made that vicious gash in Bird's throat?

Sweat broke out all over me and I found myself wishing that I'd simply got the hell out of there when I had the chance. Too late to worry about that now, I decided. I extended a trembling hand towards the curtain but was intercepted by Roz. She shook her head urgently, then indicated to me that *she* would pull back the curtain, thus leaving both my hands free to grapple with the intruder. I nodded and large beads of sweat dripped from my forehead. I squared up to the bathtub and raised the knife to head height, watching as Roz cautiously reached out and gripped the edge of the shower curtain. She glanced at me again and I nodded. Then she whipped the curtain aside.

There was an ear splitting shriek and I caught a glimpse of something big and pink; but before I could react, a prodigious strength slammed me full in the chest. I reeled back under the assault, lost my footing and fell. The tiled floor connected with my shoulder-blades, driving the breath out of me and the knife slipped out of my grasp, skittering away across the floor. Then the screaming face was pressed against mine, sharp red nails were tearing at my throat and there was an impression of soft nakedness against me as I struggled to push off a crushing weight . . .

Only then did I realise that it was Mo, stark naked and hysterical with fear.

'Help me!' I gasped, and Roz leapt in to try and pull Mo off. There was a brief struggle, that under different circumstances would have seemed farcical. Then we managed to drag Mo over to a corner of the room and sit her down on the floor. Roz grabbed a towel and draped it over her while I tried to calm her down.

'Mo, it's all right. It's OK, it's Danny. You hear me, it's Danny!'

For a moment I thought she'd lost it completely. She was trying to tear at my face with her nails and I was obliged to hold both her wrists, while she struggled. Then realisation came into her eyes and she slumped back against the wall with a groan.

'Thought you were *him*!' she sobbed. 'Coming back for me . . . like he came after Trevor . . .' Now she burst into tears, burying her face in her hands, her whole body shaking with the unspeakable terror of the situation. I realised that the tortured breathing had been the result of her vainly trying to control her mounting fear. For all my supposed stealth, she had clearly heard every step.

'Phone the police,' I told Roz. 'Ask for Detective Inspector Flynn and tell him to get round here, *now*!'

Roz nodded, hurried grim-faced out of the bathroom. I put a hand on Mo's shoulder and she shrank from my touch.

'What happened?' I asked her. 'I didn't even know you

were here.' Her reply came in a series of staccato half-sentences, punctuated by bouts of hysterical sobbing.

'Trevor left me a message . . . told me to meet him here . . . soon as I got back. We were going to do some glamour shots. He was setting up and . . . I came in here to . . . to undress. I heard the buzzer go downstairs . . . Trevor must have thought it was you . . .' Tears were flooding down her face at the recollection. 'A man went past the door . . . towards the studio. He didn't see me.'

'Mo, did you catch a glimpse of his face?'

She nodded. 'Beard. He had a beard . . . I thought he was a friend of yours or something . . . then I heard sounds. In the studio. Fighting. I looked out of the door and . . . Trevor was coming towards me. On his hands and knees. And his throat . . . his throat . . . oh God, his throat . . .' She became hysterical again, shaking her head and screaming and I had to slap her face to calm her down again.

'Tell me,' I demanded. She gazed at me blankly for a moment, then continued.

'I could see Trevor was finished,' she gasped. 'Didn't know what to do. I could hear the man in the studio. Smashing things. Yelling. I was afraid. I ran to the bath and pulled . . . the curtain, I pulled it closed and prayed he wouldn't find me. And I could hear Trevor by the door . . . awful sounds. Choking his life away . . . I was afraid . . .'

'Of course you were. What happened then?'

'I could hear him . . . the bearded man . . . moving around. Going from room to room. Like he was looking . . . looking for something.' She lifted the edge of the towel to wipe at her eyes. 'He came . . . right past the bathroom door . . . he . . . I swear, he stood there for a while . . . and I thought . . . but no, he moved. He moved on and then it was quiet for a while. But I . . . was still afraid to come out. Then I heard other sounds. Thought it was him. Coming back for me.'

'Christ,' I muttered. 'We must have just missed him.'

Mo raised her gaze to mine. She looked at me imploringly.

'Trevor?' she whispered.

I shook my head, confirming what she must already have known.

'I'm sorry,' I said.

'But, why?' she whispered. 'Why him? He wouldn't have hurt a fly. He wouldn't . . .'

'I know,' I said. I patted her hand. 'The bearded man. Did you notice anything else about him?'

'I only saw him for a moment!'

'Yes, but . . .'

Her eyes widened as though she'd just remembered something.

'There was a smell. A bad smell. When he was standing by the door, even through the curtain I could . . . smell him and it was like . . . death. He smelled like death.' Her face crumpled into an expression of disgust. 'He was talking to himself . . .'

I looked at her sharply.

'Could you make out what he was saying?'

She shook her head, stared at me.

'Do you know him? Do you know who it was?'

'No,' I told her: but in reality I felt that I was beginning to know him, better than I cared to. Then something else occurred to me. There was surely no way that Trevor Bird could be involved in any of this. That left me with one inescapable conclusion. The killer had come here looking for me. By a mere accident of timing, he had found Bird instead. That was a very bad moment for me. I'd wondered how close the violence was going to come before this was over and now I knew the answer only too well. I was also marked for death. I remembered the dream I'd had, seeing my own face in the glare of the torch beam and the short hairs on the back of my neck began to stand up, one by one.

Roz appeared in the doorway.

'The police are on their way,' she told me.

We settled down to wait.

# Chapter Thirty-Five

Lawrence Flynn looked uncharacteristically tired and haggard. He seemed to have aged ten years in the brief time that I had known him. I knew how he felt.

It was late evening now and the mass invasion of my apartment was finally over. The uniformed men, the pathologist, the forensic investigators had all packed up their equipment and gone home. Bird's body had been zipped into a plastic bag and ferried up to the city morgue. Mo, fully dressed now, had been driven to the police station to make a statement and from there was to be taken to her mother's house, where she still lived. The bloodstains in the hall had been photographed, fingerprints had been dusted for – (Roz and I had been fingerprinted too in order to eliminate our dabs, but it looked as though the killer had been wearing gloves anyway). Roz was currently in the kitchen, giving a statement to Detective Sergeant Potts, who had not exactly endeared himself to her by calling her 'darling' or 'sweetheart' every time he spoke to her. Flynn and I were sitting in the devastation of my studio. The killer had done a pretty thorough job in here. Shelving had been knocked over, expensive equipment destroyed and every drawer in the place had been upended, as though the man had been frantically searching for something.

Whatever his intentions, he'd neatly put paid to my photographic career for the immediate future. I was glad I had good insurance cover and could only pray that there wasn't some sneaky clause that excluded damage enacted by an angry psychopath. But these considerations paled into insignificance when I considered what had happened to Bird. Though logic told me I couldn't be held responsible for what had happened, there was still a part of me that felt guilty about it. If I'd been there helping him with the lights as I'd promised, maybe I'd have been able to help him. Maybe he'd still be alive.

'What do you suppose our mysterious assailant was looking for?' Flynn asked me, glancing around at the debris.

I shrugged.

'I haven't the faintest idea,' I told him.

'This is merely an idea off the top of my head, but do you suppose it could possibly have been the negatives?'

'What negatives?'

'The series of pictures that you shot in the railway arch? I take it you still have the negatives somewhere around the place?'

In all the confusion, I hadn't even thought about that.

'It's the most likely explanation,' I admitted. 'Though why would he want them?'

'That's the question that I keep asking myself.' Flynn gestured at a couple of upended drawers, the contents scattered all over the floor. 'It's quite obvious that he was anxious to find something; and I can't think of anything else you would have that could conceivably interest such a man. Can you?'

I shook my head.

'Let's see if he found them,' I suggested. 'They're in a special place.'

I got up and walked to the far corner of the room. Against one wall, a piece of loose floorboard could be prised up to reveal a little cubby-hole beneath. The negatives and the contact sheet that went with them were still safely tucked away in there. I pulled them out and carried them back to Flynn.

'Maybe it's best if you hang on to these now,' I told him. 'They seem to have caused nothing but trouble.'

He unfolded the contact sheet and scanned it thoughtfully.

'I don't recall there being so many pictures in the exhibition,' he said.

'I didn't use them all. Just the dozen or so that I thought were the best.'

'Hmm. I don't suppose you'd happen to have a magnifying glass?'

'Somewhere . . .' I was obliged to get down on my hands and knees and root around in the chaos of scattered equipment, before I found what I was looking for: a small, folding eye-glass magnifier that had escaped being smashed. When I stood up again, I saw that Flynn had set the overturned desk back on its legs and had laid the contact sheet flat on it. I found him an anglepoise lamp that was still working, plugged it in and set it up for him. He opened the eye-glass and started examining the rows of tiny black and white frames, one after the other.

'What are you looking for?' I asked him.

'A reason for the killer to want these negatives,' he said. 'Other than the obvious.'

'The obvious?'

'As a rather grisly memento of an enjoyable night's work. After all, he could hardly risk coming to your exhibition to *buy* a print. Somebody might have recognised him.'

'Those prints weren't for sale anyway,' I said: and then

Philip Caveney

remembered something. 'Jesus,' I muttered.

Flynn glanced up at me.

'Something occurs?' he asked me.

'Yes. There's this guy called Philip Cassiday. He's a horror writer, lives locally. I photographed him once . . .'

'And he's not been murdered yet? You're losing your touch.'

'Very droll. Anyway, he's an odd character, a *bearded* guy as it happens. He was at the exhibition on the opening night and he was very keen to buy some of the Sebastian Kennedy pictures, told me he wanted them to decorate his new study.'

'Charming. Fed up with Laura Ashley, is he?'

Despite the grimness of the situation, I couldn't help smiling.

'The point is, despite me telling him that the pictures weren't for sale, he was very pushy. Offered me two thousand quid a throw, well over the odds. Anyway, I turned him down.'

'Danny, I'm impressed. You're obviously a man of integrity.'

'Listen, will you? When I turned him down, he was angry. He walked right out of there without saying another word.'

'I see. And you think he could be our man?'

'I don't know what to think any more. If you'd asked me a week ago, I'd have said no way. Now . . . even Ronald McDonald looks suspicious to me.'

'Ronald McDonald? Do I know him?'

'Forget it. Listen, I meant to ask you, did you talk to Dr Hulce?'

'I did, just this morning. Very interesting chap. He confirmed what you said about the stone knife. A contemporary copy of a traditional Aztec obsidian dagger. A very high quality replica weapon. The professor tells me he's seen

400

similar items on sale in Mexico City. They usually have blunted blades to prevent any unfortunate accidents but this one had clearly been sharpened recently.'

I held out my hands in a gesture of appeal.

'Well surely that settles it,' I said. 'It's got to be one of our Mexican visitors. Who else would be likely to have such a weapon? You're going to have to question them all.'

Flynn glanced up from the contact sheet and made a face.

'It's not quite as simple as that, I'm afraid. Those people are honoured guests in the city, I can't go charging in there like a bull in a china shop. It's going to have to be handled with discretion.'

'What, you mean like Trevor Bird was handled? Fuck the diplomacy! Get in there and arrest the whole bunch of them.'

'Oh yes, that would go down beautifully with the city council wouldn't it? No, it has to be done carefully. What I *can* do is try to keep the individual members of the group under low-key surveillance. But even that's a tall order. As I understand it, there's over eighty of them. I really don't have the manpower to cope with something like that. Besides, I'm not at all sure if we wouldn't be barking up the wrong tree. I have some evidence of my own that . . . hello? What's this?'

I stepped nearer to the table and he indicated the last shot on the reel, the stretch of wall with the words FOR ZIPPY scrawled on the bricks.

'Well, you can see what it is,' I told him.

'No, what's *this*?' The tip of his finger indicated a tiny smudge of grey and white amidst the black shadows at the corner of the frame. I studied it with the eye-glass but it was still indistinct, a seemingly random splash of reflected light. I seemed to remember now, that when I took the photograph, I'd glimpsed a momentary flash of something off to the left of the writing, but had forgotten about it when the camera started rewinding itself.

'This is too small to make out any detail,' I said.

'Can you enlarge it?'

'Well . . .' The cursory glance I've given the darkroom earlier had suggested that most of it had escaped serious damage, but I was hardly in the mood for playing detective at the moment.

'If it's a problem, I'll get our own lab boys to sort it out. But that's going to take a bit of time. I've got a strange feeling about this . . . what they refer to in all the best movies as "a hunch".'

'All right, let's see what we can do.' I picked up the pack of negatives and started towards the darkroom. 'It's probably nothing,' I warned him. 'Just a bit of reflected light.'

'Let's have a look anyway,' he said. 'Put my mind at rest.'

It took a little while to set up. Flynn came in with me, watching the process in silence. I located the correct strip of negative and got it into the enlarger. I selected a sheet of high contrast paper, in order to make the most of the interplay between shadow and light. Then I focused in on the corner of the frame, enlarging and re-focusing until the blob of grey filled the whole of the sheet. At this scale, it began to look more like something solid, though it was still impossible to say what. I exposed the paper and transferred it to the tray of developer, rocking it to speed up the process. The image began to materialise. At first, it didn't look like anything, just a sea of grainy dots, like static on a badly tuned television. Then the shadows around the lighter section hardened up and all at once, the image seemed to solidify and leap right out of the frame. I felt a jolt of pure fright stab into me.

'Fuck!' I said. I was so stunned I almost let the picture go on developing past its optimum point: but then I recovered and quickly transferred the print to the fixer.

'Well, well,' said Flynn. 'What do you know?'

We could see now that the blob of grey was a misshapen shard of fly-blown mirror, propped against the wall to the left of the scrawled words. Dimly reflected in it was a bearded face, half obscured by shadow, the eyes grotesquely lit by the flare of the flashgun as it was reflected from the glass. The man must have been crouched some distance away from me, his back to the opposite wall. The expression was one of dull surprise as though the killer had realised in that instant that his face might just have been caught on film.

'He was there,' I whispered. 'He was there the whole time. He *saw* me shoot those photographs . . .'

'That explains a lot,' said Flynn. 'We were puzzled by the seemingly random nature of the events. Clearly they weren't random at all.'

'But how could he have got out of there without me seeing him? I was standing right out front of the building . . .'

'Don't you remember? We found a broken window at the back of the arch. He must have escaped while you were waiting for the police to arrive. Afterwards, it would have been a relatively easy matter for him to trace you.'

'But . . . he wouldn't have known me from Adam. I could have been anybody.'

Flynn shook his head.

'You were a walking advertisement that day, Danny. I seem to recall you were wearing a baseball cap with the *Evening Post* logo prominently displayed on it. It wouldn't take a Sherlock Holmes to decide how to track you down. A few enquiries to your place of work and some idiot would almost certainly tell him where to find you. Besides, with all the recent publicity about the exhibition, he'd have to be blind not to have read about you or seen your picture in the papers.'

I nodded. The more I thought about it, the more it made sense. Automatically, I removed the print from the fixer and pegged it on the line to dry.

'So . . . what do we do now?' I asked him.

'Well . . . with this new information, we're in a much stronger position.'

'How do you mean?'

'We know that you're a potential victim. The killer has tried for you once and we've every reason to believe that he'll try again.'

'Oh, great. That's good to know.'

'The point is, Danny, it will make my life a damn sight simpler. Instead of attempting to keep eighty Mexicans under surveillance it will be so much easier simply to keep an eye on you. When our bearded friend makes his next attempt on your life, we'll be there to arrest him.'

I didn't like the sound of that, not one little bit.

'So you're fairly confident he *will* try again?'

'Yes, I think so. Oh, I don't suppose he'll try and get to you here, he'll assume that this place will be under surveillance now. But somewhere soon, when you're out and about, he's going to make a play for you. And that's when we'll get him.'

Hold on a minute,' I said. 'Supposing you're a bit late stepping in? I don't want to seem overly critical but your success rate on this case hadn't exactly been brilliant, has it?'

'A tad unfair, I think. Obviously, we haven't had this kind of information before, we were blundering about in the dark. Now we've a little illumination to work by.'

'So the plan is, a SWAT team follows me everywhere I go?'

He chuckled.

'Hardly. That would be guaranteed to frighten our man off. No, I think I'd like to handle this one personally. I'll keep some backup just a phone call away, naturally, but for all intents and purposes it'll be just you and me. Actually, I think we'll make a good team. A kind of Starsky and Hutch for the nineties. I might even break out my flares.'

'It's easy for you to be so flippant,' I snapped. 'You're not the one who's a potential target.'

'Forgive me, Danny. But believe me, I think this is our best course of action. So . . . what have you got planned for us tonight?'

I looked at him.

'Actually, I was planning to go to a little place in town. It's called "Joey's Hideaway".'

Flynn looked interested.

'Yes, I've heard of that. A drag club, isn't it?'

'That's right.' I wondered if I should go on bluffing it out, then decided I'd kept enough secrets from Flynn. I had a vested interest in telling the truth now. It was my life that was on the line. So I told him all about Joey Sparks and his connection with Kit Marsden; and how I'd seen the ageing drag artiste arguing with Scott Banks in Piccadilly Gardens only hours earlier. As a finale, I informed him of something else that I'd learned from Joey Sparks; that Kit Marsden claimed to have 'worked' with Sebastian Kennedy. Flynn listened with a long-suffering look on his face. When I'd finished talking, he shook his head and gave me a scornful glare.

'It would have been rather nice if you'd seen fit to tell me some of this earlier,' he said. 'I've been trying to find a connection between those two myself.'

'Well, I appreciate I should have said something. The opportunity just didn't arise . . .'

'You know, Danny, it strikes me at this moment that you are a very duplicitous person. I've always attempted to be open with you but since the first moment we met, you've spent most of your time concealing facts from me.'

'Oh now that's a bit extreme.'

'I wouldn't say so! I just wonder how many other items of information you're hiding.'

'Oh look, it's not like that. It's just . . . well, I didn't want to drop Joey Sparks in it. The fact is, I felt kind of sorry for him. He's just a sad old queen and Kit Marsden was taking him for everything he had. He's got nothing to do with any of this.'

'Oh and you know that for a fact, do you? You're such a brilliant judge of character that you can make these assessments simply by chatting to people for five minutes? Well let me tell you something, Danny, in my experience people are rarely what they seem to be. So I think I'll accompany you to this club tonight and have a few words with Mr Sparks myself.'

I sighed.

'If you must.'

'Oh, I practically insist. I particularly want to talk to somebody who can shed a little more light on Kit Marsden.'

'Bit late in the day for that, isn't it? After he's dead.'

'If he *is* dead.'

I stared at him.

'What are you talking about? Of course he's dead. We both saw the body, didn't we?'

'Oh, we saw *someone's* body . . . but we're still trying to make formal identification. We were able to confirm Sebastian Kennedy's identity by comparing dental records. But so far as we can discover, Mr Marsden was one of those irritating creatures who appears never to have visited a

406

dentist or a doctor. Obviously, our enquiries continue but . . .'

I interrupted him impatiently.

'But why would you have reason to suppose it *wasn't* his body? You . . . you said something about new evidence you'd found.'

'Indeed I did. And I'd like you to note that I am not the sort to keep information to myself.'

Flynn reached into his jacket pocket and brought out a brown envelope. He opened it, removed several colour prints, then handed the top one to me. I recognised it as one of the pictures I had taken in the Mandrake, a blurry amateurish shot of the crowd. There in the midst of a sea of out-of-focus faces, was the bearded man, his arm upraised to strike down at a startled-looking Vincent Spinetti. Flynn indicated the man's raised arm, at a point where the action had caused the sleeve of his jacket to pull back from the wrist. The flesh appeared to be multi-coloured.

'This area looked interesting,' he said. 'I asked one of our technicians to enlarge and enhance it.'

He handed me a second photograph, an enlargement of the gloved hand and arm. Whoever had enhanced the image had done a pretty good job. I could see now that the dagger in the gloved hand was the same type of stone knife that had been found on the Mandrake's dance-floor; and that below the wrist the man's skin was intricately tattooed in full colour. The image was of a dragon's head, the mouth open to reveal a forked tongue.

'This has to be the work of the artist who tattooed Kit Marsden,' I said. 'It's the same style.'

'More than just that,' Flynn assured me. He handed me a third photograph, a detail from one of the black and white shots I'd taken of Marsden, for the exhibition. 'We got this from one of the prints we confiscated. You see, the arm is up in almost the same position; and the images are identical.'

I saw that he was right. The same dragon's head, the same forked tongue. And beside it, just as in the colour photograph, the start of another image, what looked like the tip of a bird's wing curling around to the underside of the wrist.

'Then . . . you think . . .?'

'I find it highly unlikely that a tattoo artist would reproduce the exact sequence of images twice over, on two different people. This kind of work is supposed to be unique, isn't it? Until we have a positive ID that the body we found in Marsden's flat is his own, I'm inclined to think that he's still alive . . . that he supplied a flayed body to throw us off his trail . . . and that *he's* the killer we've been looking for. The fact that there also appears to be a connection between Marsden and Kennedy only lends weight to the argument.'

'But . . .' I pointed to the face of the character in the photograph. 'He doesn't look a bit like Kit Marsden.'

Flynn nodded.

'I've thought about that. Didn't you tell me the man was an actor of sorts?'

'So he said.'

'Well then, wouldn't he be adept at using stage make-up? That could very easily be a false beard. He could darken his skin, change the shape of his nose, all manner of things. Maybe it's time we stopped judging everything at face value and started looking a little deeper.' He clapped a hand on my shoulder. 'We'll start tonight,' he said. 'With Joey Sparks.'

# Chapter Thirty-Six

That evening Flynn drove me into town to pay an un-announced visit to 'Joey's Hideaway'. Before leaving, he assigned a couple of plain clothes men to keep a watch on the entrance to the apartment. Roz was in there alone and I wanted to be sure she was in no danger.

We arrived at the club at about seven o'clock. The place was busy, the foyer already filling up with its nightly intake of exhuberent stags and hens. Flynn flashed his ID at the man in the box-office and we were not asked for the price of admission. Ignoring the main concert hall, I led the way around the back and we went straight to Joey's dressing room; but tonight we found our way blocked by a beefy-looking minder in an ill-fitting tuxedo. He had close cropped ginger hair and a face that appeared to have been pummelled into its current shape by years of fist fights.

'Can I help you?' he asked, in a non-too-welcoming tone.

'We just wanted a quick word with Joey,' I said.

'Sorry fellers. Joey's due on stage for the first set in ten minutes, you'd best wait till the interval.'

'He'll see us,' said Flynn; and he flashed his ID a second time. The big man looked at it blankly for a moment, then shrugged, told us to wait. He went into the dressing room, closing the door behind him. A few moments later, he reappeared and ushered us inside with a flick of his cropped skull.

'Keep it brief,' he warned us. 'Joey doesn't like to keep the punters waiting.' He moved off down the hall, his hands in his pockets, a dismissive sneer on his ugly face.

We stepped inside and found Sparks sitting in front of his mirror, putting the finishing touches to his make-up. Unlike the last time I'd talked to him, he was in full drag, right down to the glittering ball-gown and outrageous beehive wig. He appraised me in the mirror for a moment, then fluttered his false eyelashes and smiled.

'Oh, it's you,' he said. 'I thought Duncan said something about the police?'

'This is Detective Inspector Flynn,' I explained, motioning to my companion. 'He er . . . he'd like to ask you a few questions.'

'I see.' Sparks gave me a disapproving look, as though he felt that I'd somehow betrayed him. Then he turned his swivel chair around to face Flynn and regarded him thoughtfully. 'You're young for a Detective Inspector,' he observed. 'I meet a lot of coppers through my work for the Police Benevolent Fund.'

Flynn didn't comment. 'Mind if we sit down?' he asked.

''Course not.' Sparks ushered us to a couple of vacant chairs with a wave of his hand. I noticed that the long false nails were painted shocking pink. 'Now, gents, I'm a bit pushed for time,' he said. 'You had some questions?'

'That's right. I want to talk to you about Kit Marsden.'

Sparks sighed and glared at me.

'Sorry,' I said. 'I tried to keep your name out of it but . . . it's just got very complicated I'm afraid.'

'Well, I suppose I knew it would come to this sooner or later.' Sparks reached for a pack of cigarettes, extracted one

and placed it carefully between his red-painted lips. He lit up
with a gold lighter and tilted his head back to blow a cloud of
smoke towards the ceiling. Then he looked at Flynn. 'To tell
you the truth, Inspector, I really don't know any more than
I've already told Danny here.'

Flynn smiled sweetly.

'Forgive me, Mr Sparks, but I don't believe a word of that.
Marsden was your lover, wasn't he? And I'd say it's in the
nature of an older man to keep a close eye on a young lover.
The situation breeds a certain paranoia.'

'Does it indeed?' said Sparks irritably. 'Expert on the
subject, are we?' He reached out a hand and refreshed his
gin and tonic from a bottle on the make-up table: but he
didn't offer us a drink. He was trying to appear cool and in
control, but I noticed that his hand shook slightly as he raised
the glass to his mouth. 'So where shall we start?' he wanted
to know.

'Perhaps you'd like to begin by telling me what you and
Scott Banks were talking about in Piccadilly Gardens yesterday.'

'Ah . . .' Sparks looked momentarily surprised. Then he
shrugged. 'I told him it was stupid meeting in such a public
place, but he insisted. Kid thinks he knows it all. Told me to
meet him there to discuss a little business proposition.'

'Let me take a wild stab,' said Flynn. 'He was trying to
blackmail you?'

Sparks laughed bitterly. 'Naturally. Money is the only
thing people like him are interested in. Scott very charmingly
pointed out that when he'd talked to the police recently, he'd
neglected to mention my relationship with Kit. He said that if
I wanted it to remain a secret, it would cost me ten thousand
pounds.'

Flynn winced.

'What was your reaction?'

'I told him I'd think about it. He said not to wait too long, because he'd quite happily drop me in it.'

'Did he say what the money was for?'

'He gave me some crap about opening a more upmarket tattoo parlour in the city centre. Frankly I didn't believe a word of it. Little toe-rag would have spent it on drink and drugs in a few weeks and been back for more. Actually, I'm rather glad you've turned up. I'd more or less made up my mind to pay him. Now I'll have the pleasure of telling the vindictive little bastard to shove his threats where the sun don't shine.'

'Quite.' Flynn changed tack a little. 'Now, you told Mr Weston here that Kit Marsden claimed to have "worked" with Sebastian Kennedy. You told him you didn't know what that work entailed but I think you were lying. Care to elaborate?'

Sparks shook his head and his beehive wobbled alarmingly. He lifted a hand to pat it back into place. Then he took a large gulp of his gin. The ice cubes rattled against his teeth. When he lowered the glass I saw that the rim was marked by lipstick.

'Look,' he said, 'I have a high public profile. If I tell you anything, I'll want your assurance that you'll keep my name out of this.'

Flynn spread his hands in a gesture of helplessness.

'I'm afraid such an assurance isn't mine to give, Mr Sparks. But at this stage of the game, I think you'd do best to concentrate on saving your own skin . . .' He glanced at me. 'If you'll pardon the expression.'

Sparks seemed merely puzzled by the remark. After a pause, he seemed to resign himself to his fate and he started to talk.

Well, they say you shouldn't speak ill of the dead,' he murmured. 'But . . . Sebastian Kennedy wasn't exactly what he seemed to be. As I'm sure you're aware, he had quite a reputation around the city. He moved in respectable circles, knew all the right people. There was however, another side to him. A side he kept well hidden.'

'Which was?'

'He made movies, Inspector. Not the sort designed for public consumption. They were made for people with, shall we say, special tastes?'

'Porn flicks?'

Sparks scowled.

'Yes and no. That is, they were not what your average punter would expect in an under-the-counter skin flick. These were more . . . exotic. Mostly they featured transvestites with a lot of S and M and bondage thrown in for good measure. They were exclusively male and aimed at a gay clientele; and, I might add, they were also very lucrative.'

'Did you ever see one of these films?'

Sparks nodded.

'Kit brought some of them round, usually the ones he'd acted in. I can't say I approved of them. I found them distinctly tasteless. The last one I saw was – what do you call it . . . a *snuff movie*? Kit was pretty excited about it, the way he was going on you'd have thought he'd got a part in *Lawrence of Arabia*. He insisted on the two of us watching it.'

'Can you remember anything about it?'

'Well, there wasn't much of a story to it, as you can imagine. A couple of people having explicit sex, one of them a transvestite. Then I think Kit comes in and kills the "man". Only make-believe, of course, though it certainly *looked* real enough. I had to pretend to Kit that I'd

413

enjoyed it, but to be honest I couldn't stand to watch any more after that. Give me a good old Judy Garland, any day of the week.'

I remembered now how Marsden had told me that he was used to acting in front of video cameras. Clearly this was what he had been referring to.

'So Kit appeared in a lot of these films?'

'Quite a few, I'd say. Half a dozen, maybe.'

'How did he meet up with Kennedy?'

'Oh, it was at some club or other. Kit loved to dance, he was a fabulous mover. From what I've heard, Kennedy had quite a clique that went everywhere with him. He would recruit people who he thought would be right for a particular picture. I remember that Kit told me that Kennedy had acted in a couple himself. He was a good-looking boy and he liked to cross-dress; but then he started getting success in respectable theatre and he got nervous that his films might somehow get into the wrong hands, spoil his chances in the respectable world. After that, he restricted himself to directing.'

'Do you think . . . is it possible that Kit and Kennedy might have been . . .?'

'Lovers? Oh, I shouldn't be at all surprised. Kit was no angel. But if anything had happened between them, he certainly didn't tell me about it. He'd have been out on his ear if he had. That boy knew which side his bread was buttered.'

'And where were these films screened?'

'Mostly, there was a network, people passing the videos out to various friends for home consumption; but the rental wasn't your usual three quid for the night, more like fifty notes. I believe there were some screenings at private cinemas, some of them in Manchester, but Kit told me they went all over the place – London, Glasgow, Birmingham – wherever boys and *femmes* come out to play.'

'Who else was involved? You know any names?'

Sparks looked reluctant to go further.

'Look Inspector, why bother with all this? Kennedy is dead now, Kit's gone . . . the whole thing is history.'

Flynn's face remained impassive.

'Names, Mr Sparks. I can just as easily have you down to the police station on a more official basis.'

'All right, all right. Let me think now . . . there was some sleaze-ball photographer with a studio in town. They used his place to film a couple of the pictures. Not gay himself but happy to take the work. Horrible scruffy-looking fellow with bad teeth. He was at your exhibition on the opening night, Danny.'

'Don Lynch,' I said, flatly.

'Yes, I think that was the name.'

I wasn't too surprised by this information. Lynch had told me he was making videos that time I'd been round to his studio with Philip Cassiday. He'd even asked if I wanted to invest in his latest production. Now that I knew there was a video connection it was easy to put two and two together.

'And where did the money come from?' asked Flynn. 'I take it even crummy movies like that need a substantial budget.'

'Yes, well Kennedy put up some of the costs himself. But the bulk of it was bankrolled by a chap called Steve Asher. He was always billed as executive producer.'

'Any idea where we might get in touch with him?'

Sparks smiled.

'Ask Danny here. The two of them are friends.'

'I beg your pardon?' I glared at Sparks. 'Who did you say?

Steve Asher? I've never heard of him!'

Sparks rolled his eyes towards the ceiling.

'That wasn't his real name, naturally. But you *do* know him. I was only talking to him at your exhibition. Claimed to be your manager . . .'

It was like being struck in the face. I sat there, staring at Sparks open mouthed.

'Vincent?' I whispered. 'Vincent Spinetti?'

'Is that what he calls himself? I only met him the once before, at a club in town, when I was there with Kit. "Asher" was boasting to me about how he was using his bands and so forth to finance the pictures. He was doing pretty well out of it by all accounts. Again, I got the impression he wasn't interested in that kind of thing himself. He just saw it as a way of making buckets of money. Here, are you all right? You've gone as white as a sheet.'

I've no doubt he was right. I just sat there open-mouthed, wondering how I could have been so blind, so stupid. People had tried to warn me about Spinetti and I'd just sailed blithely along, trusting him because he was a friend and friends never shat on you, did they? Now I understood what Juliet Fleming had been so angry about. '*Ask Vincent about the videos*,' she'd said; and when I'd followed her advice, he'd simply fed me another of his slick little stories, as he led me along by the nose. There was no band called the Vice Squad; and I couldn't help wondering what proportion of the profits from *Skin Flicks* were earmarked to be invested in his next seedy little epic. I realised that Flynn was looking at me and I shook my head, fighting back the tears of humiliation.

'I didn't know,' I told him. 'I swear to God.'

'I can see that,' he said. 'I suspected that your Mr Spinetti was crooked but even I underestimated him. It might be an idea if we paid him a visit in the not-too-distant future.'

I nodded.

'Oh, we'll visit him all right,' I said.

Out in the concert hall, they were playing Joey Sparks' signature tune. Then somebody knocked on the door.

'Well, gentlemen, you can see I'm a bit pressed for time,' said Sparks. 'If that about covers it for now . . . ?'

Flynn nodded.

'You've been very helpful, Mr Sparks. I'm obliged to you. And I *will* try and keep your name out of this. I'll also be calling on our friend Scott Banks. He won't be making any more demands on you, I promise you that.'

'At least that's something,' said Sparks, glumly. 'Ah well, if you gentlemen will excuse me, it's time to *change*.'

I was just about to point out that he already was changed, but I'd misunderstood. Sparks got to his feet and drew himself up to his full height. As he stood there, he went through an inexplicable transformation. The whole process took seconds, but it was one of the most extraordinary things I've ever seen, something to do with his posture, the expression on his face, the way he held his hands. One instant he was merely a man in women's clothes. The next he was a woman. I glanced at Flynn and saw that he was sitting there fascinated by what we were observing.

Then with a theatrical flourish of his hand, Sparks strode towards the door and swept majestically out of the room. We waited, listening to the exuberant applause as he walked out on stage. A few moments later, we heard his amplified voice booming through the building in a stirring rendition of *I Am What I Am*.

Flynn seemed to come out of some kind of reverie.

'Astonishing,' he said. He got up from his chair and

417

glanced at his watch. 'Well, let's not waste any more time. What say we go and find your manager? I imagine there are a few things you'd like to say to him.'

I nodded. Later, I'd have plenty to say, but for the moment, I felt incapable of uttering so much as a word. The expression 'gob-smacked' had never seemed more appropriate. So I simply followed Flynn, out of the dressing room and along the corridor to the exit. The strains of Joey Sparks' song followed us all the way up to the street.

# Chapter Thirty-Seven

We drove across town in the direction of Portland Street. It was still only seven-thirty and I knew there was a good chance of finding Spinetti still in his offices. Failing that, we'd be required to head out to his house in the suburbs of south Manchester.

I rode in silence most of the way, brooding on the information that Joey Sparks had just given us. At that moment, I could gleefully have murdered Spinetti and walked away a happy man. I was furious with him, but more than that, I was angry with myself. A familiar criticism that friends often made of me was that I was too easy going, too trusting. In the past, I had laughed it off, telling them that it was better to be that way than to be an eternal cynic. Now I seriously doubted that I'd be able to trust anyone ever again.

'It must have been a shock for you,' observed Flynn, as we swung around Piccadilly Gardens. 'Finding out like that.'

I laughed bitterly.

'To tell you the truth, I feel like a complete jerk. Vincent played me for a sucker all down the line. What really gets my goat is that I should have seen it coming.'

'Don't be so hard on yourself, Danny. You're a trusting

sort. That's a rare commodity these days. Something to be cherished.'

'Think so?' I gave him a hard look. 'It just means I'm available for anybody to take advantage of. Or at least, I *have* been up till now. I'm going to change.'

'Change . . .' Flynn looked thoughtful. 'How nice that would be. To simply change everything about yourself. Like our friend Mr Sparks back there. Did you see that transformation he pulled off? Quite extraordinary.'

'Just a trick of the trade, I suppose. He has to get up there night after night and convince people that he's a woman. I suppose the first person he needs to convince is himself.'

'Yes. But it's opened my eyes, Danny, I don't mind telling you. He's living proof that if you don't like yourself the way you are, you can be somebody else.'

I glanced at him. In the light of the dashboard, his face had a serene quality.

'Don't you like yourself?' I asked him.

'Not particularly. It seems to me now that I've been living a lie for more years than I'd care to admit to. Maybe I shall change too. Who knows?'

We turned on to Portland Street.

'Now, where are these offices?' he asked me.

'Just up here on the right . . .'

I ducked my head to look up at the first floor of the old red-brick building and saw that there was a light on in Spinetti's office. The street-level entrance door was standing open.

'Looks like we're in luck,' I said. 'Pull in over there.'

Flynn brought the car to a halt and started to get out of his seat but I put a hand on his arm, restraining him.

'Do me a favour, will you?' I asked him. 'Give me ten minutes alone with him.'

He looked doubtful.

'Oh, I don't know about that. In your present ill-humour, you might . . .'

'Don't worry. I'm not going to attack him. At least, not physically. I just want the chance to talk to him face-to-face. I want to hear what he has to say for himself, without having to hear him tailor it for your benefit.'

Flynn still didn't like the idea.

'It's most irregular, Danny. Supposing he escapes?'

I pointed to the main doors of the building.

'The only way out is through here,' I told him. 'You can wait right in the foyer. Look, just ten minutes. I'll never ask you for anything again.'

He smiled thinly.

'Do you suppose I could have that in writing?' he asked. 'It seems to me I'm always bending the rules for you.' He looked at me for a moment and then sighed. 'Oh, very well, ten minutes. Then I'm coming up.'

'Thanks. I owe you one.'

'You owe me *several*,' he corrected me.

We got out of the car and crossed the pavement to the entrance. Flynn looked around for a few moments, evidently less than impressed with his scruffy surroundings. He positioned himself at the bottom of the stairs and glanced at his watch.

'Ten minutes,' he reminded me, as though I might already have forgotten.

I started up the long flight of stairs. As I climbed, I glanced over my shoulder and saw Flynn gazing up at me, his face strangely white in the glare of the fluorescent lights.

Emerging on to the first floor, I caught the familiar smell of coffee, mingled with a greasy unappetising odour of cooked meat. Clearly Spinetti was still living on microwaved junk. I moved towards the door of the outer office, opened it and looked inside. The room was empty but through the recently repaired frosted glass of the inner office door, I could see light and more puzzlingly, a shifting, billowing whiteness, as though somebody was flapping a bedsheet on the other side of the glass.

I moved towards the door and the smell of food became more intense. I was vividly reminded of the stink of donner kebabs from Aphrodite's Charcoal Pit, a smell that for obvious reasons now had bad associations for me. What the hell was he cooking in there? Whatever it was, it had been left in too long. I put a hand on the door knob and hesitated a moment, peering through the glass at the shifting whiteness, puzzled and more than a little bit afraid now. I thought about going back to the staircase and shouting down to Flynn but decided against it. Nothing was going to deprive me of the pleasure of telling Spinetti exactly what I thought of him. I'd make him wish he'd never been born . . .

I opened the door and a wave of thick white smoke spilled out at me, enveloping me in an acrid, throat-searing cloud. I coughed, thrashed my arms about in an attempt to dispel the smoke. Peering through watering eyes into the inner office, I caught a brief glimpse of Spinetti sitting in his chair, slumped forward over his desk, seemingly unconscious. Behind him, I saw the illuminated front of the microwave from which the smoke was billowing. Something was going around and around on the turntable.

'Vincent, for Christ's sake, wake up!'

Concern had instantly replaced anger. The idiot must have fallen asleep and left his supper cooking. I snatched a breath and plunged into the room, stumbling blindly towards the window at the back of it. My foot snagged on a trailing telephone lead and I stumbled, nearly fell. I could dimly make out Spinetti's hunched shape to my right and told myself that he must have been overcome by smoke. I thrashed upright again, dragging a tangle of phones and a fax machine to the floor with a crash. My eyes were watering now and I seriously doubted that I could hold my breath any longer. I groped forward, hands outstretched like a blind man. I kept expecting to reach the window long before I actually did. Then at last, my hands touched against the cool glass surface and I scrabbled to find the catch.

My fingers encountered metal and I managed to slide it back with an audible click. Then I was lifting the ancient sash window to admit the cold night air. Smoke billowed out into the street like the coils of a huge snake. I gratefully gulped down a couple of lungfuls of air and turned back to survey the room.

The microwave was still throwing out more smoke from the ventilation grills on its roof.

*Idiot, you should have turned that off first!*

Now I was blundering back to the infernal machine, trying to examine the control panel with the two watering slits that were my eyes. I located the 'off' button and hit it. The machine gave a loud beep and the door sprang open, throwing fresh clouds of smoke into my face. I reeled back with a curse, grabbed a handful of papers off Spinetti's desk and started fanning the air frantically with them.

'Vincent, for Christ's sake wake up!' I yelled; but there was no reaction.

Gradually, the smoke was beginning to dispel as more of it spilled out of the open window. I ran back, took in some more clean air and turned to assist Spinetti. For all that I hated him, I wasn't going to leave him to asphyxiate; but his total lack of movement made me wonder if he hadn't already succumbed to smoke inhalation. I'd have to pull him to the next room, see if I could remember how to administer mouth-to-mouth resuscitation. I grabbed him under the arms to lift him out of his seat and that was when I saw that the top of his desk was thick with blood. I let go of him with a gasp of shocked surprise and he flopped backwards in his chair, revealing a chest that had been slit open from throat to belly, a gaping vertical opening from which broken ribs and ragged folds of muscle protruded. He was staring up at me blankly, a furious scowl on his face. He seemed to be saying, '*How could you let this happen to me*?'

The yell that burst out of me must have been audible all across Manchester. What seemed like seconds later, Flynn was hurrying into the room, taking in the scene with a shocked expression on his face. I turned away from Spinetti's corpse and only then saw the words scrawled on the wall in front of me: ZIPPY SAYS . . . HE HAD NO HEART TO LOSE!

'Sweet Jesus,' I heard Flynn say. His voice was muffled and I saw he was holding a handkerchief up to his face. 'That smell . . .'

The last clouds of smoke were dispersing from the interior of the microwave and I could see what had been cooking. At some point it must have exploded, splattering the white interior with scraps of flesh and tissue – and though it was shrivelled and blackened by too much cooking, it was still unmistakable.

*They cut the heart out and burned it on a fire*.

Dr Hulce's words came back to me as I stood there, staring into the bloody oblong of the microwave. I felt my gorge rise but somehow I managed to talk myself out of throwing up. Flynn walked over to me and I heard him take a sharp intake of breath. Then he put an arm around me and guided me out of the room into the outer office. I slumped down in the leather chair with a groan of despair and buried my face in my hands.

I was only dimly aware of Flynn phoning in for his army of technicians. The tears were welling up and despite everything I had thought and said about Spinetti, I cried for the friend I had lost, one way or another.

# Chapter Thirty-Eight

I was getting used to this scenario and the problem was I really didn't want to. Here I sat in Vincent Spinetti's outer office while in the next room, Monty Python's Forensic Circus was in full swing. Lights, camera, finger-print powder!

It was becoming like some ghastly TV gameshow that I couldn't get away from – or one of those irritating mazes that you visit at a stately home, where you wander in and can't find your way out. I didn't have the least idea how I'd become mixed up in all this and I didn't have a clue how to extricate myself from it: I only knew I wanted it to be over.

And I had to remind myself that Spinetti was dead. A man whom I had thought of as a friend as well as a business associate. Someone who had guided my photographic career and who had fulfilled his promise to make me the name on everyone's lips. Someone who I had imagined I knew so well; but clearly hadn't known at all . . .

I'd finished crying for him some half an hour ago. My feelings of compassion had been replaced by a cold, hard numbness. I told myself that what had happened to him, he'd doubtless brought on himself. But what had been my crime? Why was it that I also had to go in fear for my life?

I heard Flynn's voice in the next room, talking heatedly with Detective Sergeant Potts.

'And I'm telling you that you're quite capable of handling this. I have other matters to attend to!'

'The Chief Constable won't like it, Sir.'

'I don't give a damn what the Chief Constable likes or doesn't like. I have very good reasons for leaving you in charge and I'll thank you not to question my judgement. Now carry on!'

A pause then.

'Yes, *Sir*.'

'Oh, and Potts?'

'Sir?'

'Has anyone ever told you you've got a disgusting case of halitosis?'

A stunned silence ensued. Then Flynn strolled in from the next room and stood for a moment, leaning against the door frame.

'Feeling better?' he asked me.

I nodded.

'I've assigned Potts to handle the scene of the crime,' he told me. 'I don't think we should hang around here.'

'What do you mean?' I asked him.

'Well, I was thinking about the other name Mr Sparks gave us. Don Lynch? Where would we find him, I wonder?'

I frowned, tried to engage the various cogs and gears that powered my thinking mechanism. I felt like I was waking up from a long sleep.

'Don Lynch . . . he's got a studio in Ancoats . . . his flat is just above it. But look, you surely don't think . . .?'

'At the moment I'm thinking dark and dangerous thoughts. It's now quite apparent what our killer's motive is. He's going after everyone that has some connection with these video nasties. Now, unless he's also planning to hack his way through the focus puller, the best boy and the man

427

who made the coffee, it seems to me that this Mr Lynch is the only other person we know of who's standing directly in the line of fire . . .' He considered for a moment. 'Apart from yourself of course.'

'Look,' I said, 'I hope you don't think that I've got anything to do with all that.'

'*I* don't,' Flynn assured me. 'But it seems that our killer does. And you'll remember that Sparks told us that Mr Spinetti boasted that he was using some of the earnings from his talent roster to finance these sleazy videos. It could be that some of your earnings were earmarked to help with the next production. And maybe . . . just maybe, the killer thinks that he was doing that with your blessing. He believes you're a member of the team.'

'Christ,' I said. 'Do you think that could be the answer?'

'It's only a guess, but it's an educated one. And at this moment in time, I can't come up with anything better. At any rate, I don't think we should be hanging about discussing it. Unless I'm very much mistaken, this Don Lynch character is in very real danger of joining the rest of the bunch down at the city morgue. Come on, you can give me directions.'

He led the way out of the inner office and down the stairs to the exit. We stepped out into a cold, late October night, our breath clouding on the air. We climbed into Flynn's car and drove off in the direction of darkest Ancoats. I glanced at my watch. It was a little after eight-forty-five and already we seemed to have packed enough bad experiences into one night to last a lifetime.

We pulled up outside Focus Studios just before nine PM. I couldn't see any lights on inside. We got out of the car and walked across to the main entrance. I rang the intercom buzzer and waited for a few minutes, before ringing it again.

'Doesn't seem to be anybody home,' I muttered.

'Keep trying,' Flynn told me.

I tried for ten minutes without success.

'Maybe he's down the pub,' I ventured hopefully.

'Maybe.' Flynn sounded doubtful. He reached into his breast pocket and took out his wallet, removed an American Express card.

'That'll do nicely,' he quipped.

'You're not going to break in?' I protested.

'My dear chap, a breath of wind would open a door like this. Not much on security, our Mr Lynch, is he?' He inserted the card into the gap in the door and with a neat flick of the wrist, he had it open. 'You're my witness, Danny. We found the door ajar.'

I frowned.

'I've got a bad feeling about this,' I told him.

We stepped inside and Flynn wrinkled his nose at the smell of dust and decay in there.

'Ugh! Not much of a housekeeper, is he?' He found a light switch and flicked it on. Lynch's office door stood open. The room was empty. On the scarred surface of the table, a huge ashtray full of cigarette butts stood next to a couple of half empty coffee cups, one of which was growing a ring of green mould.

'Charming,' muttered Flynn. We moved on down the hallway and reached the staircase up to the flat. We peered up the stairs but the place was in darkness.

'Well, if he's up there, he's keeping very quiet,' I said. Turning back, I noticed a strip of light escaping from under the closed door of the studio.

'How come we didn't see that from outside?' whispered Flynn in my ear.

'It's the studio. There aren't any windows.'

'Follow me.' To my surprise, Flynn reached into his jacket

and pulled out a pistol: a big, squat automatic. I had never been a supporter of the proposal to arm the police – until now.

'You must know how to use that?' I asked stupidly.

He gave me an irritable look.

'Of course.' He held the pistol out in front of him, two-handed.

'Maybe we should just leave,' I said nervously.

'What, and miss all the fun?'

Flynn led the way forward again and I winced as the ancient floorboards creaked beneath our feet.

'Here goes nothing,' said Flynn, with a calmness that both surprised and infuriated me. He reached out to push the door of the studio open with his foot. It swung silently back on well oiled hinges and there was a moment of deep, impenetrable silence, during which he seemed to be counting: then he stepped decisively into the room. I heard him stifle a curse.

'What is it?' I whispered fearfully.

'We're too late,' he said. 'There's been a massacre in here.' I stepped through the door and looked in the direction he was indicating. Then despite everything, I found myself laughing with relief. Flynn gave me a strange look. He must have thought I'd cracked under the strain.

'It's all right,' I assured him. 'It's been here for ages.'

He was pointing to a white paper backdrop with bright red stains splattered across it. I could hardly believe it was still here, it seemed like years ago that I had done the shoot with Philip Cassiday. It was proof positive that Focus Studios really were in deep financial trouble.

'But it's still wet,' protested Flynn.

'No, it only *looks* wet. It's gloss paint. Non-drip gloss, actually. I had a bugger of a job getting it on there in the first place.' I moved past him and walked into the studio to stand beside the backdrop. 'I painted it myself.'

'Danny, there's no way that could be paint!'

'Sure it is. That horror writer I told you about? Philip Cassiday. This was for his benefit.'

'You're . . . sure?'

'Yes, look!' I reached out a hand to touch the paper. It felt damp to the touch. I took my hand away and examined my fingertips. They were red. Puzzled, I prodded the surface of the paper with my index finger and it sank to the knuckle into wetness: simultaneously I became aware that the paper was bulging towards me, as though something heavy was resting against it on the other side. Then the paper tore raggedly in a vertical line with a soft, glopping noise as the weight overcame the paper's precarious resistance. A face from my worst nightmare burst through the backdrop and came lurching straight at me.

Somehow I had the presence of mind to step aside and the body struck the floor with a heavy thud, only inches from where I was standing. I stared down at it in shocked silence. The head was twisted to one side and I noticed with a twinge of dull surprise that Don Lynch had something sticking out of his mouth, an oblong of black shiny plastic. It was a video cassette and it appeared to have been pushed down his throat lengthways, the size of it distending his mouth so much that the corners had torn bloodily open to reveal his back teeth. Blood had soaked into the front of his shirt and from there had transferred itself to the paper backdrop.

I turned back to the ragged hole the falling body had made and could see now, the narrow alcove in the wall where Lynch's corpse had been propped, with only the thick paper backdrop to hold it in place. I noticed too the bloody words

431

scrawled on the wall above the alcove: ZIPPY SAYS CHOKE ON IT! ONE MORE.

Flynn stepped forward and stood there looking down at the corpse, a grim expression on his face.

'Don Lynch, I presume,' he muttered.

I didn't answer him. I was still in shock and still staring at the writing on the wall. Lynch, it seemed, had been the penultimate victim: and I was only too well aware of who was next in line.

*What are you afraid of, Danny?*

The voice in my head asked its habitual question: and at long last, I knew the answer.

# Chapter Thirty-Nine

I had expected that Flynn would phone in our latest finding from Lynch's office but he didn't. Once we had recovered from our fright, he took his handkerchief and forcibly removed the video cassette from the body's mouth, having to wrench and tug to release it from the grip of those tightly clenched teeth. I couldn't bear to watch so I stood off to one side, my face turned away.

'What are you doing?' I asked him. 'I thought you weren't supposed to touch anything.'

'What I'm doing, Danny, is . . . cutting through the . . . bloody red tape,' grunted Flynn. 'My God, how did he manage to force this thing . . . all the . . . way in?' He gave a last pull and the cassette came free with an obscene sucking sound that made my stomach heave. 'It's obvious from the look on his face this is what killed him,' observed Flynn. 'We've already got a team hard at work on one murder, we can't hope to get anyone up here for an hour or more. And at the moment, I'm more interested in watching this video.'

'Great,' I said. 'I'll go out and get a six-pack and a Chinese take-away, shall I?' The moment I said it, I regretted it. The thought of Chinese food – indeed, the thought of *any* food, made my gorge rise and I had to walk away and sit down for a while. I tried to get my breathing under control. After a few moments, Flynn came over, wiping the worst of the gore from the cassette with his handkerchief.

'I hope this is playable,' he said. 'All that blood might have gummed up the works.'

'Please,' I murmured.

'Sorry. You feeling queasy again?'

'How do you think I feel?' I snapped. 'Half of the people in my phone book have been killed tonight!' It was a ridiculous exaggeration but I was very scared and very angry. I made an attempt to get a hold of my mounting terror. 'You think the video might be important?' I asked.

Flynn shrugged.

'For all I know it's a pirate copy of *Terminator 2* . . . but there must be some reason why this particular one was chosen. CHOKE ON IT, the message says.'

I nodded grimly.

'It also says something about ONE MORE. No prizes for guessing what that means.'

'Hmm. I'd love to offer reassurance and say that it can't possibly mean you, but . . . I rather suspect that it can and does. All the evidence points to it.'

'Thanks,' I said. 'You've been a great help.'

'I understand it can't be the best feeling in the world. Let's try and take your mind off it, shall we? Lynch was a film maker of sorts, so presumably there must be the appropriate viewing equipment somewhere?'

'Through here,' I said. I got wearily to my feet and led him into the adjoining editing suite. Flynn stood in the doorway of the filthy little cubby-hole, looking around in disbelief.

'If I'd known it was going to be like this, I'd have worn overalls,' he complained. He moved to the tiny television and video set up and switched on the screen. Then he pushed the video cassette into the slot and searched around for a remote control. He found it on a worktop and picked it up between thumb and forefinger, as though he suspected it might contaminate him. Next to it was the dried and shrivelled remains of a half-eaten cheese sandwich.

'Good God,' he said, with a look of disgust. 'Lynch must have been a direct descendant of Miss Haversham. This place hasn't seen a duster in years.' He indicated a couple of tubular metal seats. 'May as well make ourselves comfortable, I suppose.'

We sat down, though 'comfortable' was hardly the appropriate description. Flynn pressed the 'play' button. The video player made an alarming screeching noise and for a moment I thought it was going to blow up: but then the inner mechanism corrected itself and the film show began. There were no credits as such, just a title, plain white lettering on a black background. SUBMISSION.

There was a fade-up on to a rickety-looking four poster bed, the same one that still stood in a corner of Lynch's studio. It had a black silk cover thrown across it and behind it, the background consisted of a pair of blue velvet curtains that ran to the edges of the frame. We were clearly not talking a Stephen Spielberg production here. After a few moments, a good-looking woman strolled into view and lay down on the bed, a tall, slim brunette with straight, shoulder-length hair. She was heavily and rather severely made up and was wearing a clingy red silk dress, black stockings and high-heeled shoes.

'I thought Joey Sparks told us there were no women in these films?' I muttered.

Flynn nodded.

'That's what he said.'

'Well, you're not telling me that's a transvestite?'

'I'm not telling you anything.'

'But what do you think?' I asked him.

'I think she's beautiful,' he replied.

'Yes, OK: but I mean, is it a man or a woman?'

He shrugged, looked at me.

'Who cares?'

'I'd like to know, OK?'

Flynn shook his head.

'You miss the point, Danny. At this moment that person is undoubtedly a woman: just as Joey Sparks was a woman when he went out on stage earlier on. The fact that there might be a penis somewhere in the equation is immaterial.'

'It might be immaterial to you . . .' I began; but broke off as a man sauntered into the frame, his back to the camera. He was dressed in a white tuxedo and was carrying a couple of glasses of champagne. He moved around the bed and sat beside the woman and for the first time, we saw his face in profile.

'Jesus!' I said. 'That's *him*!'

'Who?'

'The killer . . . the . . . the man I photographed at the Mandrake . . .' I grabbed the remote control and waited till the man turned full face to the camera. Then I pressed the 'pause' button and froze the image, so we could study it in more detail.

'There's definitely a resemblance,' admitted Flynn.

The man had a dark complexion and a neatly-trimmed beard and moustache. His brown eyes had a smouldering quality to them and though I had only caught a glimpse of Spinetti's attacker at the Mandrake, I felt that the likeness was marked.

'It's the same man,' I insisted. 'The guy from the railway arch. Or his double.'

'Let's move on,' said Flynn impatiently.

I pressed 'play'. Now there was some rather banal dialogue. The woman had a soft, husky voice, the man a pronounced accent. It sounded to my ears like a Latin American voice and I wondered again about the visitors from Mexico. The woman was called Lola, the man Jorge. Jorge begged Lola to allow him to make love to her. She told him that she had a terrible secret and that anyone who discovered that secret had to pay a price. Jorge assured her that he was willing to pay any price for just one night of love. Then the pair of them leaned closer to kiss.

'That's the talking over with,' observed Flynn. 'Now for the action.'

Sure enough, the young man put down his champagne and was taking the woman in his arms. He was kissing her passionately, fumbling with the buttons on her dress.

Then as if to avoid the slow, awkward removal of clothing, there was a dissolve; and now the man was totally naked, the woman stripped down to a white silk basque and panties. The man lay on the covers, his head thrown back in ecstasy while the woman sat astride him working on various parts of his muscular physique with her lips and tongue.

I haven't seen many stag movies in my life and the ones that I *had* seen had nothing on this. For one thing, the quality was good, it seemed to have been shot on High 8 and was undoubtedly a first generation copy. There was no background music, which gave it a distinctive quality feel. And it was very, very explicit. As the tape progressed, 'Lola' went through just about every sexual position ever invented and it was obvious from Jorge's flushed and ecstatic face that there was no faking involved.

I started to feel embarrassed and I have to confess, just a little bit turned on. I felt the same way I'd felt when I was a

kid, sitting there with my parents when people on the TV
started snogging each other: I felt like I wanted to be either
on my own or somewhere else.

I glanced guiltily at Flynn. He seemed to be transfixed by
the film, he was leaning forward, resting his chin on the
knuckles of his hands, studying every move with an expression of intense concentration. He might just as well have
been watching a serious drama.

Now came the moment that settled all the arguments.
Jorge had reached down a hand to Lola's panties. He pulled
the white silk aside to reveal an erect penis. He did a pretty
convincing double-take and for a moment, it looked as
though he was going to recoil in horror. But then he seemed
to accept the situation and went on with what he was doing
with even more enthusiasm than he had shown before.

'Lola's secret,' muttered Flynn.

'Well,' I said. 'There you are. Whatever he is in his mind,
he's still a man where it counts.'

'Hmm. And a strangely familiar one, wouldn't you say?'
Flynn pressed the pause button, freezing the 'woman's' face.

'Familiar?' I said. 'I . . . don't think so.'

'Oh yes, Danny. You've even photographed that face, for
the *Evening Post*.'

'I have?'

'Yes.' He got up and stepped over to the screen, used his
hands to block out the long black wig 'You'll have to use
your imagination. Remove the hair, the lipstick, the eye
shadow . . . and unless I'm very much mistaken, that's
Sebastian Kennedy.'

'Jesus,' I said. 'I think you're right!' Now that it was
pointed out to me, I could see it; and I remembered how
Joey Sparks had mentioned that Kennedy had appeared in a
couple of the earlier films, before he'd panicked about being

recognised. 'Hey, isn't this the one that Sparks told us about? The one that Kit appears in?'

'We'll soon know.' Flynn moved back to his seat and pressed 'play'. The action continued. Now Jorge had got to his knees and Lola was going down on him, bringing him very close to orgasm. Jorge had his head thrown back and he was breathing fast and shallow, his arms flung out in a crucifixion pose. Behind him, the curtains parted suddenly and Kit Marsden stepped out from cover, a cruel smile on his face. He was naked too, showing off his intricate tattoos to the camera. In his hands, he held a large transparent plastic bag.

He came silently up behind Jorge and stood there for a moment, observing the man's ecstatic writhing. Marsden had a look of anticipation on his face, as though he was savouring the moment; then with a sudden movement, he jammed the bag over Jorge's head and pulled the edges tight around his throat. Through the layer of plastic, Jorge's face seemed to register genuine surprise shortly before it was contorted out of shape by the tight plastic. His mouth opened in a silent scream and he began to struggle, throwing up his arms in a helpless attempt to claw at his attacker; but Marsden simply grinned mirthlessly and increased his pressure on the edges of the bag, the plastic biting deep into the tanned skin of his victim's neck. Jorge's breath began to fog the inside of the bag, making it difficult to see his face. Through all this, Lola kept right on doing what she had been doing; and an instant later, a shudder went through Jorge's body as, despite the horror of his situation, he came violently into Lola's mouth.

It struck me now that there would have to be a dissolve or a cut – there was simply no way the actor could hold his breath any longer. But with a sense of mounting horror, I realised that the action was continuing. Lola sat up, licking her lips, a malevolent grin on her face. She rolled aside and lay there, watching calmly as Marsden finished off the victim, continuing to apply a powerful pressure. Jorge's struggles became weaker by the moment, his hands clawing feebly at thin air, his chest rising and falling in a desperate attempt to find some oxygen. Now Marsden put one knee against the small of his victim's back and forced his head down on to the black silk covers. He gave a final wrench and Jorge's head snapped sideways in what had to be a killing stroke.

I sat there stunned, hardly able to breathe myself. I was hoping against hope that now they might fade or cut from the scene: if they did, maybe there was still some hope that it was an illusion.

But no. In a chillingly cruel act, Marsden reached across the bearded man's sprawled body and began to kiss and fondle Lola, putting his tongue into her mouth. Lola reached out to throw her arms around Marsden's neck and now another sex scene was played out over Jorge's still body.

'For fuck's sake,' I gasped. 'That was all one take, he—'

'I know,' said Flynn. 'Sparks said it was horribly realistic. I don't think he appreciated just how real it was.'

We watched numbly as the picture faded out on the image of Marsden and Kennedy kissing passionately beside the corpse on the bed. There was a brief credit sequence, where we learned that the part of Lola was played by Lola Vasquez, Jorge by Jorge Delgado and that 'The Assassin' was played by Victor Scott. Amongst the equally fictitious technical credits I was saddened to note that the Executive Producer was one Steve Asher – Vincent Spinetti's alias.

Flynn switched off the television and turned back to me with a look of revulsion.

'There's our killer's motive,' he said quietly. 'Revenge. It's somebody who discovered the truth about that murder and has set out to eradicate everybody who was involved.' He pressed the eject button and removed the video cassette.

'But I don't understand,' I told him. 'That was the same guy. The man we've got photographs of. If you want, we'll get the pictures and compare them . . .'

'It *can't* be him,' argued Flynn. 'This film was obviously made some time ago, certainly before the killings began.'

'OK, then . . . maybe he didn't die. Maybe he recovered and came after the people who'd done that to him.'

'No way. That man was dead. I've seen enough deaths in my time on the Force to know when there's no chance of survival. That last wrench broke his neck, for God's sake.'

'It . . . it could have been a fake. Jesus, they can do anything in movies these days . . .'

'Come on, Danny, who are you kidding? That wasn't *Alien* we were watching. It had a budget of thousands of pounds, not millions: and the main scene was shot in one take. They can do some extraordinary special effects these days but one thing they haven't managed yet is to find an actor who can hold his breath for over ten minutes.'

'Then . . . then what . . .?'

'Well, I refuse to accept a supernatural explanation. People simply don't come back from the dead in order to avenge their own deaths. Nice idea, of course, but strictly for the movies. So . . .'

'So?'

'My guess is that the fellow you photographed was a relative of the man we just saw murdered. A brother, maybe.'

I pulled a face.

'Oh, come on now . . .'

'Yes, I know it seems far-fetched, but it's not impossible. People do have brothers, don't they? I'll tell you what, it seems more likely than your theory about a reincarnated Aztec priest.'

I frowned, nodded.

'But you heard his accent, didn't you? He didn't come from Salford, that's for sure.'

'No, he sounded Hispanic to me. South America, maybe.'

'Or Mexico?'

'Yes, maybe . . .' Flynn paced about the room for a moment, thinking it through. 'My only regret is that the . . . scum that made this film have already been brought to account for their actions. I'd like to have seen them suffer for what they did.'

'I'd say they suffered, anyway,' I told him. 'And frankly life imprisonment seems like a holiday camp next to having your skin removed, layer by layer.'

'Good point. I can't condone that, obviously. The law's the law, Danny, and it has to be observed. But it's hard to sympathise with their fate once you know the full story.' He tapped the video cassette he was holding. 'They must have all known about it, every one of them. I don't believe that the killing was a spur of the moment thing. They planned the death of that young man, coldly and mercilessly. Worse, they filmed it for their own entertainment . . . and probably for the entertainment of other, carefully chosen customers. It rather gives me mixed feelings about our killer. Up until now, I've thought of him as some sick deviant. Now I see that it was his victims who were the deviants.'

'So you think he's some kind of . . . avenger?'

He laughed bitterly.

'Somewhat melodramatic term but I can't think of anything more appropriate. I'd say he's a man who has discovered evil and in attempting to take his vengeance, has slipped over the edge into madness. And he's very nearly finished his

442

self-appointed task.' Flynn studied me thoughtfully. 'You saw the words back there: ONE MORE. He has to mean you, Danny. He's tried once, he surely isn't going to give up now.'

Flynn was making me even more nervous than I already was. No easy task.

'So . . . what are we going to do?' I asked him helplessly.

'We're going to draw him out. From now on, it's going to be the old music hall song. *Me and My Shadow*. Wherever you go I, or a member of my team, is going to be right with you. But we're going to keep a polite distance. It mustn't be obvious what we're doing or the chances are he'll never show his hand.'

'I really don't like this,' I told him.

'There'd be something very wrong with you if you did. But it seems the logical way to continue. Not much chance of him trying to get to you at the apartment, he'll realise we've got that covered now.' He thought for a moment. 'What are your plans for the next couple of days?'

I shrugged.

'Well, tomorrow night's Halloween. I had been planning to go to the masked ball at the Town Hall . . . but obviously that's out of the question now.'

'You mean the *El Dia de Muerte* thing?' he asked.

'Yes, but . . .'

'No, Danny, you *must* go to that!' He seemed suddenly animated, excited at the idea. 'If anything is going to draw him out, that will. Think about it, the Day of the Dead! It will be the ultimate symbolic act, taking out his last victim on All Soul's Night . . . especially if you're right about the killer being a Mexican. He'll see this as the perfect opportunity to get his full score . . .' I gave him a sharp look and he smiled sheepishly. 'Sorry, I could have put that more tactfully.'

'Yes, you bloody well could! Supposing something goes wrong?'

'Nothing *can* go wrong. Just think of me as your fairy godmother. Yes, Danny, you *shall* go to the ball!'

I shook my head. His flippancy seemed particularly ill-placed, but then it was easy for him. He wouldn't be the one with his balls on the line.

'You know, call me an old fuddy duddy, but I really don't feel in the party mood.'

'Don't worry, Danny, I'll be there right alongside you.'

'I thought you said that would frighten him off.'

'Ah, but you see, it's perfect. He won't be able to recognise me, will he?'

'How come?

'Because I'll be in a mask and a costume, dummy, just like everybody else there.'

I thought about that for a moment.

'But er . . . *he'd* be in a costume too, wouldn't he?'

Flynn looked momentarily thrown, as though he hadn't thought about that: and I got a very bad feeling about the whole idea.

'No problem!' he assured me. 'I'll simply station some men at the main entrance. As every guest arrives they will be asked to take off their masks and show their faces. We've got two perfectly good mug shots to work from, so the chances are we'll nab him before he even gets close to you.'

I frowned.

'I don't know,' I murmured.

'Danny, what else are you going to do? Hide yourself away in that apartment of yours and spend every day praying that you don't get an unexpected visitor? This will be your chance to end it. Trust me, I know what I'm doing.'

I sighed.

'I suppose I've got no other choice,' I said.

'Actually, I'm really looking forward to it,' said Flynn enthusiastically. 'It appeals to my flair for the dramatic. I must find myself an appropriate costume.'

I gave him a scornful look.

'So long as you don't forget that you're supposed to be keeping an eye on me,' I growled.

'Danny, I shall place your safety even above my very own. Why, if anyone so much as tries to lay a finger on you . . .' He held open his jacket to show me the holstered pistol. 'Glock 9mm,' he said. 'A real stopper.'

I didn't know how to take this. Right in front of my eyes, Flynn seemed to be transmuting into Dirty Harry.

'Anyway,' he said. 'I think now we'll phone this one in and see about getting that team over here. Not that I think for one moment they'll find anything useful.' He glanced at his watch. 'After that, I see no reason why we shouldn't get you home. We've made some real progress, even if it is a bit late in the game.'

He went out of the studio and down the corridor to Lynch's office to make his call, leaving me sitting there looking at the blank television screen, a very worried man. I tried to be positive about what he'd said. Maybe he was right about the Halloween Ball. Maybe the killer wouldn't be able to resist it. If so, by tomorrow night it would all be over.

# Chapter Forty

Flynn dropped me off outside my apartment in the early hours of the morning. We sat in the car for a moment and he pointed out the blue Ford Escort parked just across the road from us.

'Two trusted police officers,' he told me. 'They've been keeping this place under constant surveillance since your visitation yesterday. Wait here a moment, I'll go and have a word with them.' He got out of the car and strolled across the road. The Escort's driver's window slid down and Flynn leaned in to have a chat with whoever was inside. Then he nodded and came back, climbed in behind the wheel.

'Nothing to report,' he told me. 'Your lady friend is in there, she turned off her lights about half an hour ago.'

'My *assistant*,' I corrected him. I don't know why I said that, it seemed important. I opened the door of the car and climbed out, aware of my breath fogging on the air. Winter was definitely on its way. 'What are you going to do now?' I asked him.

'Off home to get some shut-eye. But don't worry, my friends there will keep watch through the night. I'll be back to take over from them tomorrow lunchtime. We've checked out the building, there really is no other way he could get in to you. Try and get some rest.'

I nodded. I walked across to the entrance, reaching into my pocket for the keys. I unlocked the door and switched on the interior light. Flynn did a U-turn and waved briefly as he drove away. I climbed the stairs to the apartment and unlocked the entrance door. Switching on the light, I stepped into the kitchen. Everything seemed normal. I didn't bother with coffee or food, simply went down the hall to my room. After the frantic happenings of the day I felt exhausted and ready for sleep. I stripped off my clothes, flung them into a corner and crawled into bed. I took off my glasses and set them down on the bedside cabinet. Then I closed my eyes and turned on to my side.

But it took me a long time to get to sleep: my mind swarmed with a succession of horrific images, recently remembered scenes of death and mutilation. Finally, just before dawn, I did manage to fall into a kind of shallow slumber: and then what seemed like only a few minutes later, I opened my eyes with a start, aware that the door of my room had just opened.

I lay there, staring up at the ceiling, not sure if I was really awake or still dreaming. It was morning now and a pale light was seeping in through a gap in the curtains. I sat up a little and saw that a figure was standing by the open door of my wardrobe: then it turned and came slowly towards me. Without my glasses it was just a dark shadowy blur with a pale round moon for a face.

'Who's there?' I gasped. I groped on the bedside cabinet for my spectacles and put them on. The world swam back into focus just as the figure stepped into the rays of daylight coming in the window. I saw with a jolt of terror that the intruder had a hideous white skull for a face. The black empty eye sockets regarded me balefully, the clenched teeth were set in a mirthless death-grin. As it came forward, it extended a hand towards me . . .

I screamed and jolted upright in bed, slamming my back up against the headboard. The figure hesitated as though startled and then reached up a hand to pull away the death mask.

'Roz!' I gasped.

She was looking down at me with an apologetic smile.

'Sorry, Danny, I didn't mean to frighten you . . .' She considered this statement for a moment. 'Well, obviously I *did* mean to give you a scare, but not that much of one. You nearly screamed the place down . . .'

I sat there, trying to get my breathing back under control.

'For fuck's sake, Roz, what were you . . . what were you thinking of? You scared the shit out of me!'

'I'm sorry.' She came over and sat beside me on the bed. 'I just picked up your costume for the ball. I got you a skeleton outfit.' She indicated a black stretch outfit with white bones printed on it, hanging from the door of my wardrobe. 'I guess I just didn't think . . .'

'I'll say you didn't bloody think! After last night, it's a wonder I didn't die of a heart attack.'

She looked puzzled.

'Last night?' she murmured. 'What happened last night?'

I stared at her for a moment.

'We found Vincent,' I told her. 'Dead. He was . . . he'd had his heart cut out.'

'Oh my . . . Vincent Spinetti? Why would anyone want to . . .?'

'It's a long story,' I told her. 'We also found a guy called Don Lynch. He was dead too.'

She shook her head.

'I don't think I know him,' she told me.

'A photographer. I worked with him sometimes.'

'Jesus, Danny, what's going on? All these people . . . I don't understand. What's happening?'

'It's quite simple,' I told her. 'People who knew Vincent are being killed. And I appear to be next in line for the chop.'

She frowned.

'Which explains why we've still got a car full of cops camped out on the doorstep. A couple of them even followed me into the town when I went to pick up the costumes . . .' She looked down at the skull mask in her hands. 'I suppose this means we won't be going tonight?'

I shook my head.

'Flynn wants us to go. He thinks the killer will follow me there. The plan is that the cops will get to him before he gets to me.' I pulled my knees up to my chest and wrapped my arms around them. I was starting to tremble at the prospect of it.

'Oh God, I chose a fine time to pull a practical joke on you, didn't I? I'm sorry, Danny, I'm a stupid mare sometimes.'

'It's all right.' I made a desperate attempt to change the subject. 'Where's your costume?' I asked.

'The one I wanted was still out. I've to go back for it this afternoon.'

'Yeah? What is it?'

'A surprise. I'll show it to you later . . . hey, are you all right?'

'I'm fine.'

'No you're not. You're shaking.'

'I'm cold, that's all.'

'Then we'll have to try and warm you up, won't we? Here, move over.'

'What?'

449

Before I could stop her, she'd pulled aside the duvet and was sliding in next to me.

'Er . . . Roz, I don't know if I'm up to this at the moment.'

'Up to what? We don't have to do anything more than cuddle. Not if you don't *want* to.' She kicked her shoes off and pulled her legs under the covers. Then she snuggled up and put her arms around me.

'But I . . . I haven't got any clothes on!'

'So I see.' She lifted the covers with an elbow and looked down at me. She raised an eyebrow. 'You don't look so depleted to me,' she observed.

This was true. The mere touch of her warm body against mine was arousing. After all, it had been over a year, if you didn't count the interrupted foreplay I'd recently experienced with Julia Moreno. So before I really knew what was happening, Roz and I were kissing and then I was helping her to remove her clothes and the next thing I knew we were making love. No, that's not exactly what we were doing, not that first time anyhow. Having sex is what we were doing: frantic, exciting, uninhibited sex. And it was absolutely brilliant.

Afterwards, we rested for a while, talked a little and then started over again, taking more time, learning to enjoy each other, discovering what turned us on. If our first attempt had been good, then this one was incredible. I felt like a celibate priest who had finally flung off his vows of chastity and was making up for lost time. A couple of hours passed in blissful abandon and at the end of it we were left spent but happy, a couple of burned out fireworks.

'Told you,' murmured Roz, her face against my neck. 'We're like that.' She crossed her fingers and held them out to me and I did the same, putting the tips of my fingers against hers.

'Christ,' I said. 'The time we've wasted bickering with each other when we could have been doing this.'

She smiled.

'We're together now,' she said. 'That's all that matters.'

'Yes,' I whispered: but I thought about the masked ball tonight. What if something went wrong, what if Flynn made a mistake and let the killer get to me? How ironic to die just when I'd discovered how to live. 'Roz,' I said. 'If anything bad happens tonight . . .'

'Shh.' She pressed her fingers to my lips. 'Nothing bad is going to happen to you, darling. I'll look after you.'

'Yes, but . . .'

The mobile phone rang, interrupting my chain of thought. I sat up and looked about for it. It was in the pocket of my leather jacket, which was flung over the back of a chair.

'Don't answer it,' said Roz drowsily.

'I better had. It might be important.' I clambered out of bed, grabbed the phone and then ducked back under the covers.

'Hello. Danny Weston speaking.'

'Danny? Oh thank goodness you're there! It's Julia Moreno.'

'Julia?' I said; and felt Roz's naked body flinch beside me. 'Oh er . . . hi, how are you?'

'Not good. Danny, I am very frightened. Somebody has been following me.'

'Really?' I glanced at Roz and saw that she was lying there, looking daggers at me. 'Who?'

'I don't know who. A man. A bearded man. He was in the supermarket last night and then, when I looked out of my window later, he was standing across the street, watching the house.'

'Call the police,' I told her.

'I can't.'

'What do you mean, you can't? You must.'

'No, no, it's not possible. You have to help me, I don't know who else to turn to.'

'But Julia, what can I do? Call out the police and tell them what's happened.'

'You don't understand. I can't risk involving the police. You see I . . . I'm an illegal immigrant.'

This was a revelation to me. In one sweep it explained why Julia was so secretive, so careful about giving out information . . . and why I hadn't managed to find her on the electoral register.

'I have been living illegally in this country for years,' she told me. 'If the police found out about it, they would report me and I'd be deported back to Chile.'

'How come you never told me any of this before?'

'I was frightened. I didn't know if I could trust you.'

'Of course you can trust me . . .' Beside me, Roz gave a tut of irritation. She threw back the covers, got out of bed and started to put her clothes on. I motioned to her to stay where she was, while Julia continued.

'I am afraid. This man, he was staring at me in the supermarket. He wants something from me, I think . . .'

'Look, do you want me to come over?'

Roz glared at me, a look of pure hatred.

'How could you?' she protested.

'Roz, just a minute!'

'Danny?'

'No, sorry, Julia. I wasn't talking to you.'

'There is somebody with you?'

'Yes, just Roz. You know, my assistant?'

'Oh!' said Roz. 'So now I'm just your assistant again, am

I? That's funny, a minute ago you were saying you loved me.'

I put my hand over the ear piece.

'I do love you! But Julia's in some kind of trouble.'

'She'll be in trouble all right if I get my hands on her.'

'Roz, don't be ridiculous!' I removed my hand from the phone. 'Julia, what do you want me to do?'

'I don't know, I am confused. You . . . you are going to the ball tonight? At the Town Hall?'

'Yes . . .'

'I will be there. We can talk then.'

'But what about the man that's watching you?'

'I will be OK. A friend is coming to stay with me till tonight. He will escort me to the Town Hall. Look out for me at the ball, won't you?'

'Of course. But I don't know what costume you'll be wearing.'

There was a pause while she considered this.

'I'll make myself known to you. How will I recognise you?'

'I'll be wearing a skeleton outfit. But you realise, I'll be masked. The idea is you don't take off your mask until midnight.'

'Wear a red ribbon around your left arm. Can you do this?'

'Uh . . . yes, I suppose so . . .'

'Good. I have to go now. I'll see you tonight.'

'Yes, but Julia, I . . .' The line went dead. 'Julia?'

'Julia, Julia!' squawked Roz, doing a fair impersonation of a parrot. Then she gave me a look of pure contempt. 'You bastard!' she said.

I stared at her.

'Roz, don't be ridiculous. She only phoned me because she was worried. Somebody has been following her.'

'Hah! I shouldn't be at all surprised. One of the other fifty blokes she keeps on a string, no doubt.'

'Oh, come on,' I protested. 'What was I supposed to do? Hang up on her?'

'Why not? She's pissed you around enough, hasn't she? Running out on you the other night . . .'

'Just a minute.' I held out a hand to interrupt her. 'The only reason she ran out is because you drove her out. You came bursting in on us like . . . like some deranged maiden aunt. Of *course* she ran out.'

'Oh, and I suppose you'd rather I'd left you to it, wouldn't you? I suppose *I'm* just the bloody consolation prize.'

'Not at all! There you go again, putting yourself down. Look, what just happened between us was absolutely fantastic.'

'Oh yeah? Then how come you're galloping after that Moreno woman with your tongue hanging out?'

'I'm not! She was in trouble and she phoned me. What's so terrible about that? She said that she would be at the ball tonight and . . .'

Roz extended her arms in a theatrical manner.

'Oh well, that's *perfect*, isn't it? You can go to the ball with her and renew your relationship.' She prodded my left arm. 'You can show her your tattoo, I'm sure she'll be impressed!'

Now I was beginning to lose my own temper.

'Will you calm down and listen to me? I don't want to go to the ball with her. That's history as far as I'm concerned.'

'It certainly sounded like it.' She slipped into the screeching parrot voice again. '*Do you want me to come round, Julia? Shall I come now?*'

'You're being ridiculous. If you can't see that I was only being polite . . .'

'Oh, dry up! Polite! You think you've still got a chance with her and you'll do anything to try and make it up. Men!

454

You make me sick! I must have been out of my tiny mind climbing into bed with you. Well, that's it, I've had it, I'm out of here.'

'Roz, please! Where are you going?'

'Away from you.' She stomped towards the door and out of my room, grabbing her jacket as she went. I found myself scrambling out of bed and following her along the hallway into the kitchen, my hands over my privates in a pathetic attempt to maintain my dignity.

'You've got this all wrong,' I told her. 'If you'd just stop for a moment and consider . . .'

'Drop dead!' she snapped. She went out of the kitchen door, slamming it in my face. This was quickly followed by the sound of the front door closing as she left the apartment.

I stood there, stunned and quite a bit angry myself. What was the matter with that girl? Why did she have to fly off the handle at the slightest provocation? All right, it was awkward Julia phoning when she did, but surely Roz could see how it was?

I sighed and trudged back to my room. I stood there, gazing at the rumpled sheets of the bed, where only moments before I had been happier than I'd been in a long, long time. Oh well, I told myself, Roz would be back when she'd had a chance to cool down a bit. I bent over and picked up the skull mask from the floor, then turned to put it in the wardrobe with the skeleton costume.

And noticed the tie hanging from the rail, the tie that Roz had bought me for the opening of *Skin Flicks*. The silk tie with its printed images of Aztec gods. Remembering now how Roz had known all of their names; how evasive she had been when I asked her how she came to be such an expert . . .

*No, that's ridiculous*! I told myself. After all, I'd been
with her when Trevor Bird was murdered. How could she
possibly be involved? And there must be hundreds of
people who could give the names of ancient Mexican
dieties at the drop of a hat . . . mustn't there? But the
more I thought about it, the odder it seemed. Why choose
that particular tie? A coincidence? Or did it have some
deeper meaning?

I grabbed some clothes and threw them on. A few
moments later, I found myself sneaking into Roz's bedroom, looking around at the jumble of stuff she kept in
there. Suddenly it was hard not to see so many of her
possessions as downright suspicious. The large framed
cinema poster for *Psycho* that dominated one wall. The
squat, stone statue of some pagan Mother Goddess
crouched on the mantelpiece. A paper knife lying beside
her word processor, the handle carved in the image of a
snake's head.

*Anybody could have these things*! I told myself – but now I
was scanning the rows of books on her shelves and certain
titles seemed to leap out at me one after the other. *The
Encyclopedia of Serial Killers, The Secret Law of Magic,
Blood Sacrifice*. And even more startling, *Aztec Myths and
Legends*.

Now I couldn't stop myself. I started searching through
drawers, feeling like some sneak thief, telling myself that I
was being stupid and hoping against hope that I wouldn't find
anything I couldn't explain.

And that's when I found the flat wooden box tucked
away at the back of a drawer. I unlatched it and opened
the lid. Inside it, I found something that made me step
back with a gasp. It was a harmless thing and under
different circumstances, it would have elicited nothing

more than mild amusement. But now it made me feel very, very cold inside.

It was a professional stage make-up kit, containing amongst other things, a pot of skin darkening cream, a tube of theatrical glue and nestled into a small compartment, something even more sinister: a false beard and a moustache.

# Chapter Forty-One

I was still standing there staring at the make-up kit when the
phone rang in the kitchen, jolting me back to reality. I closed
up the box and pushed the drawer back into place, then
hurried through to answer the phone. I felt dazed and more
than a little confused as I picked up the handset.

'Hello?'

'Danny, It's Lawrence Flynn. I'm phoning from the car at
the front of your apartment.'

'Oh, hi. Look, I'm glad you called. I've just discovered
something really strange and . . .'

'Never mind that just now. Look, don't panic or anything
but a bearded man has just crossed the road to your place.
He's standing at the front door right now.'

The information kicked my anxiety levels into overdrive.

'What? Jesus! Who?'

'I don't know who he is. To tell you the truth, I didn't get a
clear look at his face.'

A wave of panic swamped me, jolting through my veins
like a zap of electricity. Then I jumped as the intercom
buzzed.

'Christ!' I said. 'He's ringing now! What should I do?'

'Stay calm. Find out who it is first. And what he wants.'

'Uh . . . right . . .' I went to the intercom and pressed in the mic button. 'Yes?' I gasped.

'Mr Weston? It's Philip Cassiday.' The metallic voice rasping from the speaker grill did not sound happy.

'Oh, uh . . . hi! What can I . . . what can I do for you?'

'I want to talk to you, right now.'

'Well I'm . . . kind of busy at the moment.'

'I don't care. You *will* spare me five minutes. I'm not going to leave until I've spoken to you.'

'Uh . . . yeah, hold on a minute, I . . . I've just got some prints in the developer. Give me a few minutes, OK?'

I released the button and talked into the phone.

'It's Philip Cassiday. You remember, the horror writer I told you about? He says he wants to talk to me.'

A brief pause.

'OK, you'd better let him in.'

'What? Are you crazy? Arrest him!'

'Danny, I can't arrest a man for simply calling at your house. We need a bit more than that. Listen, this is what you do. Buzz him inside but keep your finger on the button. I'll follow him in. Leave the kitchen door open. I'll come up quietly and listen in to the conversation. The moment he says or does anything suspicious, I'll step in.'

'No way! He could have me shish kebabbed by the time you get your act together.'

'Danny, trust me. I won't let anything happen to you.'

'That's easy for you to say!'

'Buzz him. I'm getting out of my car right now.'

'OK, OK, but for fuck's sake, don't hang around.' I put down the phone and pressed the intercom again.

'You can come up,' I said and jabbed my thumb on to the door release button. I kept it there and waited with a sense of mounting dread, for a knock on the kitchen door. It wasn't long in coming, but I hesitated, keeping my thumb in position, wanting to be sure that Flynn had got inside. Finally, when I was convinced that he must have had plenty of time, I walked across to the kitchen door and opened it.

Cassiday was standing there in his trademark black leather gear and I noticed with a deep sense of foreboding that he was wearing matching gloves. I forced a kind of manic smile but he scowled back at me, his dark eyes full of anger. I stepped back from the door and he stalked into the kitchen. To my dismay, he slammed the door shut behind him. He stood for a moment, gazing around at the room, as though suspecting an ambush.

'Alone?' he asked me.

'Er . . . yes,' I said; and felt like biting my tongue off. Why hadn't I told him there was somebody else working in the studio? *Idiot!* 'Look, I'm very busy at the moment,' I blustered. 'What do you want?'

He began to pace agitatedly around the room and I moved around to stand with my back to the door. I reached my hands behind me and surreptitiously turned the handle, pulled the door back off the latch. I glanced through the narrow gap I'd made but couldn't see anyone out there.

Cassiday whipped suddenly around to face me and I stepped involuntarily backwards. My heel hit the door, closing it again and I had to work hard to stop from giving a groan of despair.

'I am pissed off with you, Weston,' he growled.

'Oh?' I gave a nervous laugh, to try and cover the sound of me turning the door knob again, 'Why's that then?'

'A couple of things.' He started to pace again. 'First off, I had two police officers round my house this morning.'

'Oh, that's nice. Helping you with your research were they?'

He glared at me.

'On the contrary. They were asking me all kinds of questions. *Sticky* questions.'

'Oh.' This wasn't exactly a surprise. When I'd told Flynn about Cassiday's interest in the Sebastian Kennedy photographs, he'd announced his intention of checking the author out. Evidently, he hadn't wasted any time. 'I'm sorry, I don't quite—'

'Don't come the innocent with me! They were asking me about the recent murders. Gave me the bloody third degree. Did I know Sebastian Kennedy, or the other bloke that died?'

'And . . . and did you?'

'Did I bloody hell! Oh, of course, to some degree I should have expected it. Here's a bloke who writes nasty stories, naturally he's a suspect! At first I was patient with them, helpful even – but then I detected a pattern in their questioning.'

I managed to get the door open again. Then with a shrug, I moved aside, not wanting to get in Flynn's way.

'That's very perceptive,' I said. 'But as an author, you probably have a clear picture of the way they work.'

'What are you babbling about?' he sneered. 'And what's wrong with you? You look nervous.'

'Nervous, me? Good heavens, no! What would I have to be nervous about?'

'I'd say you have every reason to be nervous,' he said coldly. 'I'm not your usual kind of push-over. People get on the wrong side of me and they soon regret it.'

I was aware of a thick film of sweat on my forehead now and had to resist the urge to wipe it with my sleeve.

'I'm afraid I haven't got the faintest idea what you're on about,' I said.

'Oh, really? Don't give me that! These two policemen,

once they'd asked all the usual stuff – Where were you? Who saw you? What time was it? – they moved on to a slightly different tack. They started asking about those bloody photographs of yours. Why had I expressed such an interest in buying them, even when I knew they weren't officially for sale? Now as I recall, Mr Weston, I only mentioned that interest to two people: you and your so-called manager. So it's perfectly obvious to me that one of you must have given the police the tip-off.'

'Umm . . . well, I did mention it to them, yes. But it's not as if I made it up. You *were* interested. Quite persistent, actually.'

He gave a bitter and derisive laugh.

'You astonish me, do you know that? My interest was purely in the artistic content of those pictures. I'm not some kind of prurient weirdo who gets kicks from looking at dead bodies. I would have thought that as the person who decided to exhibit those works, you would appreciate that fact better than anyone.'

I stared at him.

'Well uh . . . I'm sorry if I misinterpreted your motives, Mr Cassiday. I've been under a lot of stress lately and I'm afraid I perceived your interest as uh . . . sinister. You have my apologies.'

He rounded on me, waving an index finger in my face. His cheeks had darkened and he looked as though he was within inches of losing his temper.

'Oh no, you don't get off that easily! The thing with the police I could possibly have forgiven; but then, this lunch-time, there's something else instigated by you. Something I cannot and will not forgive!'

I glanced nervously towards the kitchen door.

'Oh, er . . . what was that?' I muttered.

'Determined to play dumb, aren't we? And isn't that always the refuge of the scoundrel? Well you've gone too far this time, Mr Weston. I'm going to make you wish you were never born. People like you take too many liberties and it's time somebody like me fought back.'

I started edging away from him. I didn't like the way this was shaping up at all.

'Look, honest to God, I haven't the faintest idea what you're talking about!' I protested.

'Is that right? And you'll be telling me next you didn't have a clue what you were doing. You'll tell me that somebody went behind your back. Well, I don't happen to believe that, Mr Weston, not for one moment. The way I feel right now, I could quite happily kill you!'

Again I glanced towards the door, wondering just how long Flynn was going to hold back. It seemed to me that there was a pretty fine distinction between 'could kill' and 'will kill'.

'For Christ's sake calm down.' I pleaded. 'Shouting isn't going to solve anything.'

'I know, but it makes me feel a damned sight better! And I'll do more than shout, Mr Weston, let me assure you. Oh yes, I'll do a damn sight more than that.' With a quick movement, Cassiday reached into the inside pocket of his jacket – and I panicked. Before I could even think about it, I threw myself at him, slamming against his chest and knocking him backwards across the kitchen. He struck the wall with an impact that dislodged large chunks of plaster, then slid down, an astonished expression on his face; but his hand was still inside his jacket as he struggled back onto his knees.

'For fuck's sake, he's armed!' I yelled; and launched myself at him a second time, wrestling him to the ground and jamming his face down against the floorboards. At the same instant, Flynn burst into the room, nearly kicking the door off its hinges. Cassiday was struggling to get free and I twisted his left arm up behind his back, shoved my knee into his spine. I heard him make a muffled oath – then the barrel of Flynn's gun was against Cassiday's head and he stopped struggling, froze in a foetal position on the floor.

'Stay absolutely still,' Flynn told him, and I was amazed by the calm quality of his voice. 'Danny, where's this weapon you mentioned?'

'Inside pocket,' I said.

'What the fuck is this?' spluttered Cassiday, his face still pressed against the floor.

'Just do as I tell you,' Flynn told him. 'I want you to remove your arm slowly from your pocket and lay your weapon on the floor . . . slowly, I said!'

'You're making a big mistake,' Cassiday told him.

'The arm, if you please,' said Flynn. 'Let me assure you, if you give me the least provocation, I will shoot you.'

'For God's sake,' murmured Cassiday. 'You've got it all wrong. I was simply . . .'

'The arm,' said Flynn. 'I won't tell you again, Sir.'

Cassiday relaxed a little. Slowly, he brought the arm out of his pocket; and I saw that he was holding a rolled up copy of the *Evening Post* colour supplement. He set it down on the floor and moved his hand away. Flynn looked at me, his eyebrows raised.

'Danny, I've always thought that the *Post*'s editorial style was pretty deadly, but really . . .'

I stared at the magazine open-mouthed.

'I . . . I thought he was going for a knife,' I said helplessly. There was a long, embarrassing silence. Then:

'Page seven,' said Cassiday, quietly.

Flynn bent and picked up the magazine. He handed it to

464

me but kept the gun trained on Cassiday. He conducted a quick body search, patting the author's pockets with his free hand. He came up with nothing more unusual than a wallet and a bunch of keys, which he immediately handed back.

It was finally beginning to dawn on me that I'd made a major cock-up here. I unrolled the magazine and opened it to page seven. There was a large photograph of Cassiday, one of the pictures I had shot in Don Lynch's studio, what seemed like a hundred years ago. I saw that Barry Summerby had selected a particularly unfortunate picture. Cassiday was posed against the red gloss backdrop and he looked quite manic – his eyes bulging, his mouth open to show thick, harp strings of saliva, his hands outstretched and gesticulating, as though he was about to strangle the photographer. The revised headline only added insult to injury. SERIAL THRILLER, it read, in large blood-splashed letters.

'Ah,' I said.

Cassiday sat up slowly and dusted himself down. When he spoke, his voice was surprisingly controlled, but it was quite obvious that he was fuming inside.

'I came here quite simply to complain about the biased manner in which this . . . this so-called photographer has depicted me,' he said. 'He has deliberately selected a shot which makes me look like Manchester's answer to Norman Bates. I came here with every expectation of a spirited exchange of views. The last thing I expected was to be . . . pounced on by two maniacs . . . I've . . . I've never been treated like this in my entire life.'

Flynn winced. He slipped the gun back into its holster.

'Mr Cassiday,' he said. 'There would appear to have been an unfortunate misunderstanding here.'

'I'll say there has!' Cassiday looked from Flynn to me and back again. 'What the hell is this, a fucking police state?

Have you all gone completely round the twist?'

Flynn shook his head.

'In my defence, Sir, I can only say that I am in the middle of a surveillance operation. Mr Weston is thought to be in considerable danger of his life and . . .'

'Oh, he's in considerable danger all right. He's in danger of being sued for every penny he owns. And that goes for you, as well, Inspector . . .?'

'Flynn, Sir. Detective Inspector Lawrence Flynn. I will of course be available to answer any complaint you may wish to make.' He stepped back to give the author some room. 'Let me add that I quite understand your anger. I can only apologise and remind you that Mr Weston and I were acting under pressure.'

'This picture,' I said, holding out the magazine. 'I can assure you I didn't select it. It certainly wouldn't have been my choice. I . . . I think you're best to take the matter up with the editor, Barry Summerby.'

'Oh, I'll be taking it up all right,' Cassiday assured me. 'With my solicitor. You're quite clearly deranged, man. Do you hear me? Stark staring bonkers!' He snatched the magazine out of my hand and stalked towards the kitchen door. But he paused to fling back a final threat.

'You haven't heard the last of this, either of you! I'll see you in court.'

Then he went out, slamming the door behind him.

There was another silence, during which I prayed that the ground would open and swallow me. It was getting to be a familiar feeling.

'Well, said Flynn, after a lengthy pause. 'That didn't go quite as well as we might have hoped, did it?'

'I don't know what to say,' I muttered. 'He reached into his coat and I . . . I suppose I just kind of freaked.'

Flynn held up a hand.

'That's quite all right, Danny. Perfectly understandable under the circumstances. Though I must say, I do sense my future as a police officer growing more precarious by the moment.'

'Oh God, I'm really sorry,' I said.

He shrugged.

'Don't be. It's as I've already intimated. With every day that goes by I feel a little less committed to my chosen profession. If this incident speeds up my departure from the Force, I for one, won't be at all sorry.'

'You really mean that?'

'Yes, Danny, I do. There are other things I want to devote my life to now. More *enjoyable* things. I've had enough intrigue and bloodshed to last me a lifetime. All I want to do is wrap this case up and get on with my life.' He frowned, glanced at me. 'Now, what was it you said to me when I phoned? That you'd found something?'

'Huh? Oh, yeah . . . right. Well, I don't know if it's anything but it sure as hell seems odd.'

'Let's take a look, shall we?'

I led him through to Roz's room and opened the drawer. I showed him the make-up kit. He looked fairly startled by my discovery. When I explained about the tie and pointed out the odd books on her shelves, he seemed more than a little disturbed.

'That's something we haven't even considered,' he said. 'So far we've assumed that the killer is a man – but there's nothing to say that it couldn't be a woman. There's everything here to achieve the necessary transformation.'

'Except that it doesn't make sense,' I reminded him. 'I was with Roz when Trevor Bird was killed. We came back here and found him, remember?'

'Hmm.' He considered this. 'Well, the business with the tie could be mere coincidence . . . and I'd be willing to bet you'd find similar books on plenty of other people's shelves. As for the make-up kit . . .'

'Yes?'

'She's planning to go to the ball tonight, isn't she? It may be that she purchased it to help create her costume . . .'

'Yes, of course, that must be it,' I said. 'I knew Roz couldn't be involved.'

'Well, steady on! I was only theorising. I saw Miss Birchill leave earlier. She left in something of a hurry . . .'

'Oh yes, we er . . . we had an argument.'

'What about?'

'Oh it was just some silly row. Roz is kind of volatile, you know.'

'As I'm sure her father would testify. Any idea where she might have gone to?'

I shook my head.

'She didn't say.'

Flynn closed the make-up box and slid the drawer back into position. 'We'll simply have to wait and see what she does,' he said. 'If she comes back here, puts on her false beard and goes looking for you at the Town Hall, you'd better hope she wants nothing more sinister than the first dance.' He glanced at his watch. 'Now, I'd better have a look at your costume before I go.'

I led him out of Roz's room and down the hall to mine. I indicated the skeleton outfit hanging from the door of the wardrobe. He picked up the mask and examined it thoughtfully.

'Hmm. There's liable to be more than one skeleton in the closet at an event like this. We could do with some extra means of recognition.' He thought for a moment, then snapped his fingers. 'I know, take a camera with you and keep it hanging around your neck. That'll serve as an easy identifying device for my crew.'

'And for the killer?' I asked him suspiciously.

He shrugged.

'Possibly. But to be honest, even allowing for the unthinkable, that he manages to get past our face-check, I can't see that he'd be able to make a move until after midnight, when everybody unmasks. As you say, how could he be sure he had the right target? No, I think if there's any danger inside the building, it will come after midnight. But don't worry, I'll personally keep you in my sight the whole time.'

'What costume will you be wearing?' I asked him. He gave me an admonishing look.

'Danny, where's your sense of mystery? Naturally, I want to *surprise* you.'

We left my room and walked back to the kitchen. Flynn glanced at his watch.

'Actually, I've still got to organise my outfit for tonight, so I'd better make a move.' He opened the kitchen door. 'Now, I'd advise you to sit tight in here. The surveillance will continue as before. At ten o'clock, a couple of officers will call to drive you to the Town Hall. Naturally, we can't risk making our ploy obvious, so they'll pose as a couple of friends who've called for you. They'll be in costume and the same goes for the other officers who'll be deployed at the ball . . .'

'Christ, this sounds *confusing*,' I said. 'How the hell will everyone know who's who?'

'Well, we'll all be briefed beforehand, so we'll be able to familiarise ourselves with each other's costumes. And naturally, we'll all know what *you* are wearing . . .'

'Yes, but I won't know who the cops are!'

'That's probably just as well. Don't want you giving the game away by hanging around the "safe" people all night, do we?'

'OK,' I said. I glanced at my watch. 'And what am I supposed to do till ten o'clock?'

He seemed to think for a moment, then he grinned.

'You could always brush up on your dancing,' he said. 'I'd recommend *Abba's Greatest Hits*. Use a hair dryer as a microphone and make sure the mirror is positioned where you can see your feet. Oh, and Danny . . . don't forget to save the last dance for me, OK?'

He grinned, gave me a sly wink and went out of the room, closing the door behind him.

# Chapter Forty-Two

It was a long evening but despite Flynn's advice, I didn't practice my dancing. Instead, I sat in front of my battered old black and white television and pretended to watch it, listening all the while for the sound of footsteps on the stairs – but Roz didn't come back.

At about nine-thirty, I went to my room and got into my skeleton costume. I put on the skull mask, a bit of a tricky affair since I had to wear my spectacles underneath the damned thing. I spent some time adjusting it to the optimum position, to be sure of seeing out through the eye holes. I regarded my reflection in the wardrobe mirror. I looked an absolute fright, the tight-fitting one-piece emphasising the skinny, gangling quality of my arms and legs. Another problem with it was that there were no pockets in which to carry keys or wallet, so after some indecision, I strapped a black leather bum-bag around my waist.

Remembering Julia's request, I spent some time looking for a red ribbon but with no luck. In the end, I had to resort to an old red leather tie that I'd had hanging in the wardrobe since the day's when such items were considered a suitable fashion accessory. I knotted it around my left arm in a bow and studied the results doubtfully. At least it added a bit of colour to an otherwise funereal look. Then complying with

Flynn's instructions, I went into the studio and dug out a camera. I wasn't going to risk the Pentax on something like this, so I ended up with a light-weight Canon instamatic slung around my neck. The end result made me look like some macabre tourist on a day trip to Hell.

At ten o'clock sharp, the intercom buzzer rang and when I pressed the 'talk' button, a voice informed me that my two 'friends' were waiting to take me to the ball – so I went downstairs and opened the door to find that Count Dracula and the Phantom of the Opera were standing on the door-step.

'Bloody hell,' muttered Dracula, behind his mask. 'This poor bugger looks like he's dead already!'

I didn't oblige him with a laugh, but simply followed my two fiendish escorts to their car, a Mondeo in an appropriate shade of black. I was ushered into the passenger seat beside the Phantom, while the Count struggled into the back, hampered by his voluminous cape.

'Fuck this for a game of soldiers,' he muttered. 'Who's idea was it anyway?'

'Who do you think?' muttered the Phantom irritably. 'That bloody southern shirt-lifter. You know his sort, any excuse to dress up.'

'Watch your mouth!' I snapped; and was amazed that I'd said it. Amazed but pleased. So many times in the past I'd let remarks like that pass unchallenged, but I sure as hell wouldn't allow it to happen again.

We drove the short distance in a stony silence. It was a cold, clear October night and a round, white moon hung like a huge Halloween lantern in the cloudless sky. There was quite a bit of traffic on the roads, but as we approached the Library Theatre, a car pulled out of a handy parking space and we were able to drive straight into the vacant slot.

'Stroke of luck,' I observed.

'Luck's got nothing to do with it,' said the Count. 'You're working with the professionals now, son.' He pulled a miniature radio from under his cloak and talked into it briefly. 'This is Zebra One to Control. Am in position outside the Town Hall. We're taking him inside now. Over and out.' He tucked the radio under his cloak and looked at me over the back of the seat. 'OK, Mr Weston, we're going to see you safe inside. Once we're in we'll leave you to it – but there'll be other costumed officers in position at all times. The thing to do is just act natural.'

I almost laughed at that, wondering how a man dressed as a skeleton with a camera hanging from his neck and a red leather tie around his arm was supposed to 'act natural'.

We got out of the car. The Count glanced quickly around and led me through the narrow alleyway that led between Central Library and the side of the Town Hall. We approached the main entrance.

The building was lit up like some gigantic wedding cake, strategically placed spotlights seeming to emphasise its colossal proportions. I tilted back my head to take the lofty pinnacle of the clock tower and remembered being up there with Spike, not so very long ago, looking down from the balcony as the world spun sickeningly in front of my eyes.

We continued towards the arch of the main entrance, which was decorated with a huge, papier mâché skull, lit from within by an electric lantern. The eye sockets glowed a dark, blood red. There were throngs of costumed people on the stairs – witches and vampires and zombies and monsters of every shape and size. We joined the queue at the entrance and slowly progressed in through the doors to the foyer. The Count went first, then me, then the Phantom. At the first desk, I had to display my ticket. At a second desk, a couple of uniformed police officers were asking every new arrival to remove their masks and show their faces. This clearly wasn't popular with the party-goers, who hadn't expected to have to reveal their identities till midnight. A lot of people had evidently oiled themselves beforehand at their favourite hostelries and there was quite a bit of good-natured and not so good-natured banter going on. When it came to my turn, I dutifully pulled up my mask and displayed my features. If the uniformed men recognised me they gave no indication of it. I was ushered into the foyer.

I walked on, adjusting my mask back into position over my spectacles as I went. When I looked around again the Phantom and the Count were nowhere to be seen and I found myself wandering amidst the crowds of exotically costumed revellers. We made our way up the main staircase to the first floor and in through the open doors of the Great Hall, where the main party was in full swing.

The room was packed, hundreds of people attempting to dance to the uptempo strains of a *mariachi* band, who were set up on a rostrum stage at the top end of the room. The musicians wore white peasant outfits and huge sombreros and one beefy guy was playing a guitar that looked to be the size of a small cello. It didn't exactly strike me as ideal dance music but there were plenty of people giving it their best shot, desporting themselves wildly under the massive chandeliers. I moved off to one side and stood there beside one of the Ford Madox Brown murals, gazing around at the scene and wondering what I should do next.

It seemed to me in that instant that everybody I could see looked suspicious – why for instance was that Frankenstein's monster standing just off to my left, apparently looking straight at me? And why was a hideously disfigured witch leaning on her broomstick in a corner of the room, making a poor pretence of studying the murals? A creature with a face like a pile of melting gloop walked right up to me and stood there as though trying to puzzle me out, before turning away and marching off towards the exit doors.

*They could be cops*, I reminded myself; but then, I argued, couldn't one of them just as easily be the murderer? After all, that business of checking the faces wasn't exactly fool-proof, was it? The police were looking for the bearded man from the photographs . . . but it was a relatively easy matter to shave off a beard, dye the hair, even change the colour of the skin . . . and as Flynn had surmised before, maybe it had been a false beard in the first place. No, I didn't put too much faith in that first hurdle. If those cops didn't see a face that looked exactly like the photograph, they would happily usher the person through. So the killer could be here, for sure.

I suddenly felt the urgent need for a drink. I made my way out of the Great Hall and through to the crowded ante room that had been set up as a bar. It took me ages to get served with a half a lager and then I wondered how the hell I was going to drink it without removing my mask. Sensing my indecision, the barman pointed out a strategically placed container of straws. After some experimentation, I discovered that I could get the tip of a straw in through a gap in the skull-teeth and into my own mouth. I stood in a corner and sipped my beer.

I spent the next hour or so moving backwards and forwards between the two rooms, but I didn't want to drink too much, since it had occurred to me that in a costume like mine, taking a piss was going to prove a major undertaking. Furthermore, I didn't much care for the idea of somebody following me into the bog, whether it be undercover cop or psychopath. So I drew the line at three halves and sipped them slowly. I was just coming out of the bar for the third time when I noticed somebody walking towards me, somebody I couldn't fail to recognise. He was wearing a scuffed leather biker's jacket, torn blue jeans and a pair of mouldy trainers. As a token nod to the nature of tonight's event, he was also wearing a plastic Guy Fawkes mask of the kind that could be purchased in any newsagents for the princely sum of about sixty pence.

'Spike!' I said. 'How are you doing?'

He stopped in his tracks, the brightly painted mask looking straight at me and I sensed the bemused expression underneath.

'It's me,' I added. 'Danny.'

'Hey, Danny, way to go man! That's a cool costume, did you make it yourself?'

'No, I hired it. I er . . . like your costume too.'

'Yeah? How did you know it was me?'

'Just a lucky guess.'

'Where's Roz?'

I shrugged my shoulders.

'We had a bit of an argument,' I explained. 'I don't think she's coming.'

'Typical,' he said. 'It's about time you two stopped fighting and got together. That's what she wants, you know. A really good—'

'Uh . . . right.' I didn't want to get into that just now, it was far too complicated. 'Where are you off to?' I asked him.

'Where do you think, man? Up to the friggin' clock tower. Got to prepare for my J Arthur Rank routine, haven't I?'

I glanced at my watch and was astonished to see that it was eleven-thirty. Where had the time gone, for Christ's sake? It felt as though I had only just got here.

'Takes a while to set up, does it?'

He nodded, glanced quickly around and then reached inside his jacket. He pulled out a half bottle of tequila, then slipped it back into place.

'Gonna see in the New Year in style,' he said. 'I've even got salt and lemon.'

'The New Year?' I asked him. 'Spike, it's *Halloween*.'

'Yeah, well, same difference ennit? Listen, if you fancy a couple of slammers, meet me up there. You know the way, right?'

'Right. I might just take you up on that. See you later.'

I felt slightly cheered by the knowledge that I had at least one identifiable ally I could turn to. I watched him strolling off along the landing to the darker reaches around the circular staircase; then found myself wondering if he had some ulterior motive for inviting me up there.

'Oh, for God's sake, this is ridiculous!' I muttered. If I went on at this rate, everybody in Manchester would be a suspect. I walked back towards the Great Hall and stepped inside.

An hour ago, the *mariarchi* musicians had been replaced by a troupe of jugglers who flung burning clubs around the place. At one point they'd come perilously close to setting the stage on fire. They in turn had been superseded by a bunch of Mexican alternative comedians, who had probably been hilarious if you happened to speak fluent Spanish. Now, *El Lobo*, a gutsy Tex-Mex band who were the special guests for the evening, were up on stage giving it some stick. Their grinding R & B-based rock was proving to be a major hit with the audience and the dance-floor was now chock full of leaping, cavorting merry makers. Under different circumstances, I would probably have joined them but I didn't feel much like stepping into that frantic press of bodies at the moment. I was all too aware that midnight was approaching and that Flynn had suggested this might be the most dangerous time for me.

I was standing there watching the band when I suddenly felt a hand touch my thigh. I turned, startled, to see that a young woman had moved up beside me. She had on a beautiful flamenco dancer's dress in black satin and a mantilla in intricate black lace. The top half of her face was hidden by a silver lamé mask, but her gorgeous red-painted lips mouthed my name silently.

'Julia?' I whispered.

She nodded, then took my arm and led me towards the exit doors.

'Where are we going?' I asked her. 'I'm supposed to—'

She lifted a finger to her lips, silencing me and she swept me out through the doors and on to the landing. There were a lot of people hanging about here, sipping drinks and even attempting to smoke sly cigarettes through strategically placed holes in their masks. My companion glanced quickly this way and that, before leading me along the landing away from the others. I glanced nervously over my shoulder and didn't see anybody following us. I was beginning to get a bad feeling about this.

'Look, what's all the secrecy about?' I muttered. We were quite a distance away from the crowd now and moving into the dimly lit area close to the circular staircase. Julia paused in front of the opening, glanced quickly around, then stepped back into the cover of the spiral stairs and drew me in after her. I opened my mouth to speak but then her arms were around me and she pulled me to her, her beautiful lips slightly parted to kiss me.

*Roz would kill me if she saw this*, I thought, but what the hell, Julia was evidently glad to see me and she was a very attractive woman. So I lifted my own mask on to the top of my head and kissed her, pushing her up against one of the central columns, my mouth hard on hers, my tongue probing hers and for a moment, it was perfect, it was absolutely the best kiss ever . . . and then something struck me as odd.

For one thing, Julia *felt* different than I remembered, her flesh harder, more muscled. And for another, as I moved my head slightly to alter my position, I felt the rasp of closely shaven whiskers against my cheek. I opened my eyes wide and it took me a couple of seconds to react: but then I jolted back with a gasp of shock and almost tripped and fell down the stairs. I steadied myself, reached out a hand and whipped the mask off her face. It wasn't Julia at all, it was another woman who I'd never seen before and she was laughing delightedly at my horrified expression.

'Oh, Danny, I'm sorry. I simply couldn't resist it!'

It was the voice that gave it away, otherwise I could have stood there for a week and not worked it out.

'My God,' I whispered. 'Lawrence?'

'It's not Lawrence tonight, Danny. Tonight I'm Sonia, the beautiful belle of the ball! Play my cards right and I could walk off with the fancy dress prize!' He gave me a playful wink. 'I certainly had you fooled.'

I stared at him, open-mouthed.

'But you look . . . I mean you're . . . *beautiful*,' I whispered.

'I shouldn't say it, but I have to agree with you!' he admitted. 'I made a special effort tonight. Didn't I tell you I wanted my costume to be a surprise?'

I wiped my mouth on the back of my hand to remove the traces of lipstick.

'It was a surprise all right. How long have you . . . I mean, how long have you been dressing up like that?'

'In secret, for years. But it was Joey Sparks who showed

me that a man doesn't have to be covert about a thing like that. He can make a virtue of it. And tonight was my perfect opportunity! By God, you should have seen their faces when I turned up to the briefing dressed like this. I thought dear old Sergeant Potts was going to have a coronary!' I realised now why nobody else had followed us out of the Great Hall – the other cops had known that it was Flynn who was with me. I tried to picture him giving the briefing dressed as he was and I visualised something out of a Monty Python sketch.

'It could cause a lot of trouble for you,' I told him.

'Oh, I dare say they're already drawing up the papers to have me transferred to a police station in John O'Groats!'

I couldn't help laughing.

'And you really don't care?'

'Care? I tell you, Danny, I feel transported! I feel like I could fly. And it's all thanks to you.'

'To me? How do you make that out?'

'Well, if you hadn't tipped me off to the Joey Sparks connection, I would never have gone to his club – and I wouldn't have undergone my own personal road to Damascus.' He thought for a moment. 'Who's Julia, by the way?'

'Er . . . just a friend. You . . . you looked rather like her.'

'A very *close* friend if that kiss was anything to go by.' He put a hand on my shoulder. 'Seriously, Danny, it was just a bit of fun. You don't mind, do you?'

I shook my head.

'Tell you the truth, it was fun. You're a good kisser.'

He smiled with evident pleasure.

'My goodness, *you've* changed your tune! When I first met you, something like that would have had you climbing up the wallpaper.'

I considered this statement and saw that he was right.

'I guess I don't feel I have to defend my sexuality

any more,' I told him. 'What's that song Joey Sparks does? *I Am What I Am*. I think that sums it up, really. In the end, labels don't matter.'

'Good for you. But we mustn't lose sight of the fact that we're here to do a very serious job tonight. It's coming on towards midnight and I wanted to be sure you were ready.'

'I've been readier,' I admitted. 'But at least now I'll know who to run to if there's any trouble.'

'Good. And don't worry, I've come prepared.' He lifted the hem of his dress and showed me an automatic weapon, strapped to his stockinged thigh in a leather holster. 'Deadlier than the male,' he said; and let the dress fall back. 'Anyway, we'd better get back to the party. Oh, by the way, I thought you'd like to know that Miss Birchill is here.'

'Really?'

'Yes, apparently she called back at your apartment at about ten-thirty. She was in her room for half an hour and when she emerged, she was wearing the false beard you found.'

'My God . . . you're not saying . . .?'

'I'm not saying anything at this stage. But once you see her costume, I think you'll understand that . . . Danny, look out!'

Flynn suddenly threw an arm around my waist and pushed me sideways. Caught off balance, I sprawled on to the flight of steps leading up and turning on to my back, I saw the bizarre figure that had just stepped through the entrance on to the staircase. Enveloped in a floor-length black cape, the face was a white, round mask that I recognised only too well. The last time I had seen that mask it had been mounted in a glass case at the Manchester Museum.

It was the mask of the Aztec god, Xipe Totec.

Events seemed to go into a weird slow motion then; a

couple of frantic seconds stretching themselves out longer than I could possibly have imagined, so that I saw everything in vivid detail.

Flynn lifted the hem of his skirt with his left hand and reached for the gun with his right: but even as he stooped for the weapon, the masked figure's right arm was moving out from the folds of his cloak. It was a long, naked arm, richly illustrated with intricate and very familiar tattoos: and the hand at the end of that arm gripped a heavy stone club. The round head of the club hit Flynn once, hard, across his temples and I saw his body jerk as he was rocked backwards. The lace mantilla fell sideways on to his shoulder and he swayed forward again, trying to fight off the wave of unconsciousness that must have been rushing at him like an express train. His right hand brushed at the fallen hem of his skirt, the gun now hidden behind heavy folds of satin. Then his legs collapsed under him and he fell sideways on to the descending steps. He went sliding down the spiral, out of sight.

I lay there on the upper steps, mesmerised as the masked figure turned and tossed the club aside. The tattooed arm moved back under the cloak and re-emerged holding a stone dagger, a replica of the one that had cut Spinetti's arm wide open. Then the knife was lifting up above the figure's shoulder for the death stroke and I seemed to come suddenly out of a trance, the prospect of imminent death galvanising me into desperate action. I scrambled up and leapt to meet the descending blow, my fingers closing around the wrist of the tattooed arm.

'Kit!' I yelled. 'For God's sake, don't do this . . .'

And then the skin beneath my fingers tore in ragged strips and I became aware of the vile, putrescent smell that gusted into my nostrils. And somewhere in the back of my mind, I was reminded of Dr Hulce, telling me how the Aztec priests would wear the skin of their victims for twelve days . . .

I gagged involuntarily and almost released my grip, but the knowledge of my certain death made me determined. Instead, I twisted hard to one side, making the figure over-balance, making him fall headlong against one of the central pillars. The mask broke across the middle and fell aside in two pieces, and the figure kneeled there for a moment, one hand to his face, where a stream of blood was running from a cut in his forehead. I thought about leaping over him, out of the entrance and running back towards the Great Hall but it was already too late for that. Now the figure was rising again and in the shadowy stairwell, I saw that familiar bearded face glowering at me with eyes that burned hatred. He still held the knife in one hand and now he was clambering slowly up the steps towards me.

I had two options. I could fight, pitting my puny, unarmed body against the jagged razor edge of the Aztec knife: or I could make a run for it. Not much of a choice at all, really. Without a moment's hesitation, I turned and fled up the spiral staircase, with the cloaked figure of death hard on my heels.

# Chapter Forty-Three

I spiralled frantically upwards in the great echoing building, my heart thudding in my chest, my breath jolting out of me with every step. Behind me I was horribly aware of the clumping of my pursuer's boots on stone. It occurred to me that I was moving further and further away from my protectors but there was little I could do about that now.

I glimpsed a familiar sign above an exit to my right. Level 4. And without thinking, I ran into the long stretch of corridor beyond. Ahead of me, to my left, a familiar wooden door stood open and I realised it was the entrance to the clock tower.

Spike! He was up there now, getting ready to ring the thirteenth chime of the bell and though he wasn't much of an ally, he was all I had at this moment. Perhaps two of us would stand a better chance of fighting off the killer, who even now was racing along the corridor in pursuit.

I dived in through the low opening and pulled the heavy door shut behind me. I turned back, hoping to see a bolt I could slide into position, but there was nothing. Without the key there was no way of securing it, so I plunged onwards up the narrow staircase and behind me I heard a loud crash as the door was flung back again.

Stooped over and hampered by the poor light, I stumbled

upwards, turning around so hard on myself now that I began to feel a stomach-churning dizziness settle on me. Sweat oozed from every pore of my body, soaking through my tight-fitting costume and the camera that still hung around my neck, kept glancing off stone and bouncing up into my face.

I moved on for what seemed an eternity and then, on my left, I saw the dark entrance to the room that housed the clock mechanism. I was beginning to have doubts about Spike, remembering that he hadn't been much use when we'd tried to evict that drunk from my mother's house. Maybe there was another way of doing this.

I ducked in through the opening and stepped back into shadow, telling myself that once my pursuer had gone by, I could double back and head down in search of reinforcements. But as I hunched down into the cover of darkness I became suddenly aware of a greenish, luminous glow emanating from somewhere nearby. I held out my arms and looked at them stupidly. It was the first indication I'd had that the white-painted bones of my costume were designed to glow in the dark. I must have been shining like a beacon in the night. Before I even had time to think about what I might do next, the caped figure burst in through the doorway and hurled itself at me.

I was struck full in the chest and I reeled back against the banks of machinery. A huge cog wheel slammed me between the shoulder-blades and I cried out with the pain, just as a hand lashed down at me. There was a red hot stinging sensation across my ribs and the material of my costume tore open, blood spraying from torn flesh. Desperately, I fought back, lashing out with my fists. My knuckles connected with the dimly-seen face, bringing a grunt of surprise from my attacker. I threw out both my hands to claw at the face and my fingers locked into hair which seemed to come away in my hands. I sensed rather than saw the knife arm lifting again and I lunged forward, smashing my forehead into my attacker's face, putting every ounce of my strength into it. There was a gasp of pain and the caped figure reeled backwards, tripped and fell.

I leapt for the entrance and in a complete panic now, I stupidly started upwards again. By the time I'd realised my mistake, it was already too late: the cloaked figure was coming after me. So we twisted upwards through the gloom and this time, I wasn't going to stop till I had Spike with me to lend a hand. I was dimly aware of spasms of pain, lancing across my ribs and when I put down a hand to explore the spot, it came away wet and sticky with blood.

The realisation that I had been cut seemed to lend me wings. I lengthened my stride, going up the cramped steps three at a time, keeping my right shoulder pressed to the wall, so that the fabric of my suit began to shred against rough stone, the flesh of my shoulder burning as the skin grazed. I seemed to go on running for an eternity, my tortured lungs wheezing like an ancient pair of bellows; and I could hear the hoarse gasps of the killer, still some distance behind me but gaining all the time.

I went past the dark opening that was the bell-ringing chamber and knew that there was only a short distance to go. I prayed that Spike wasn't smashed on tequila when I got there. Without his help and wounded as I was, I surely didn't have a chance of survival.

At last, I saw the exit door up ahead of me and I scrambled out on to the balcony. It was eerily silent up there, almost serene, the round globe of the moon sailing in the empty sky. At the end of the balcony, I could see the open door that led into the bell chamber. There was a light on in there.

I sprinted along the balcony, aware now of the sheer drop to my left. I heard a clatter as my pursuer pushed out through the doorway. Now, if I only had time to warn Spike . . .

I burst into the bell chamber and saw that Spike was perched on a short ladder, the top of it propped against one of the wooden supports that held the great bell. He was in the act of drinking from his half bottle of tequila and he had a mound of salt and a slice of lemon in his free hand. Startled by my sudden entrance, he jerked around to look down at me. His face lit up in a smile of greeting and in that moment, he lost his balance. I saw his expression turn to one of dismay and he threw out his arms in a desperate attempt to correct himself. The tequila went one way, the salt the other. Then he fell sideways, striking his head on the wooden beam with a thud that was clearly audible to me down below. He dropped the short distance to the stone floor and lay absolutely still.

'Spike!' I yelled. 'You bloody idiot!' I ran to him, went down on my knees and shook him roughly but he was out cold. I was still kneeling there when the cloaked figure stepped into the tower and bolted the door behind it.

I got to my feet and backed off against the nearest wall. Glancing quickly around, I saw that a narrow walkway extended on all four sides of the chamber, though it was interrupted here and there by the diagonal wooden supports of Big Abel. If I could just keep some distance between me and the figure, then maybe . . .

The figure moved slowly towards me along the walkway and for the first time, I could see who it was. Only a few tufts of the false beard still adhered to the dark face that regarded me so coldly and the nose was bleeding from where my forehead had connected with it. There was a dark smudge under one cheek that would soon be a bruise. The short wig was gone too and the killer's long black hair fell down to her shoulders.

'Julia?' I whispered.

She smiled at my bewilderment and continued to walk towards me, the stone dagger held ready to strike. Recovering myself, I started to back away, one hand clutched to my ribs in an attempt to stem the flow of blood.

'I . . . I don't understand,' I said.

'You do not have to understand,' she told me. 'You only have to die.'

'No, wait . . . you can't . . . you must listen to me! You're making a mistake. I wasn't involved in any of this.'

She kept right on coming.

'You are a poor liar, Danny.'

'No, I swear to you—' I stumbled and almost tripped over a bell support, but managed to recover and step over it. 'Wait, please. The least you owe me is an explanation.'

She shook her head.

'All I owe you is a quick death. You will not suffer like the others. Zippy says I can be merciful, because your guilt is not as great.'

'Zippy. That's Xipe Totec, isn't it?'

She looked surprised by this.

'Well, well. Perhaps you are not as stupid as you look. Zippy is a pet name. I started calling him that when I was working on my thesis . . .'

'Your . . . thesis?' I remembered something else that Dr Hulce had told me. About a promising pupil of his who had been putting together a thesis about the ancient Aztecs. A quite extraordinary work, he'd said: but it had been abandoned. Intent as I was on other matters, I hadn't thought to enquire further.

'Look,' I said. 'I don't understand.' I had reached the

corner of the room and I angled back on myself, stepping over another wooden support, wincing with the pain this caused me. 'I know it has something to do with a video. The man that was killed . . . the one you've made yourself up to look like. Who was he?'

'Pablo, my brother. My *twin* brother. He wasn't able to avenge himself, so I became him. Zippy said that it was only right. If I performed this task, then Pablo would find rest in the spirit world.'

'But . . . you told me that your brother disappeared years ago. In Chile, during the junta. You told me he was a photo-journalist . . .'

'I told you a lot of things, Danny. It was easy to lie to you. I should have settled this the night of the exhibition. I had you there, half naked, the dagger was right there in my bag. But just as I was reaching for it the girl came in and ruined everything.'

I felt a chill run through me. Thinking back to how vulnerable I'd been . . . how trusting. Roz and I had rowed about it afterwards, I'd complained bitterly that she'd denied me the lay of a lifetime. In fact, she'd saved my life.

'Luck seems to be your strongest card, Danny. The next time I came for you, at your studio, some idiot got in my way and I had to kill him. A pity, because he'd done no wrong. Zippy made me pay a forfeit for that.' She paused for a moment and gave me a deranged grin that made the hairs on my scalp prickle. 'Would you like to see what that action cost me, Danny? Would you like to know the depths of my devotion to the Flayed Lord. Look!' She pulled back her cloak and tore open the rotting skin tunic she wore, revealing her naked breasts. Between them, a large square of skin had been neatly removed and the flesh was a raw, red nightmare, seeping pus. Then she indicated the camera around my neck.

'Why don't you photograph this, Danny? You like to take such pictures, don't you?'

I gave an involuntary groan and lifted a hand to my mouth. She started forward again and I shrank back, feeling my way along the wall, trying to anticipate where the next bell support would be. If I fell she'd be on me in an instant.

'How could you do that to yourself?' I asked her.

'I do whatever he tells me. He is a powerful protector but a stern one. He does not tolerate weakness.'

'Julia, you've got to listen to me! I know you were there when I found Kennedy's body. And I know I accidentally caught you on film . . . so . . . I can understand how you found your way to me at that reception. But the stuff about your brother. The guy who was missing?'

'Just a story I made up, Danny. I'm good at stories. Actually, I'm from Argentina. My parents were in the meat processing business. As children, Pablo and I often spent time at the slaughterhouse, watching the men at work. When I was a teenager, I worked on the killing floor, gutting and skinning the freshly slaughtered cattle. I didn't know it then but it has stood me in good stead for more recent work.' She laughed mirthlessly. 'Pablo and I came to this country only a few years ago, quite legally as it happens. Moreno isn't my real name, by the way, so it was little wonder you couldn't find me on your precious electoral register. The real name doesn't matter . . .'

She made a quick lunge forward and I jumped back. My heel connected with a support and I almost fell, had to throw up my hands to correct my balance. I stepped over the support and kept moving back as she came purposefully after me, still talking.

'My parents were killed in a plane crash several years ago. Pablo and I elected to sell our shares in the business and come to Britain to study. I was attending the University as a mature student, doing a degree in Ancient History. Pablo was an actor, a very talented actor . . . though he wasn't having much success. Oh, he had appeared in a few small stage productions and everybody thought that he had a big future. If he could only get a break. Then he met Kennedy and he seemed to change, almost overnight. Pablo was honoured by Kennedy's attention and, I suspect, very much in love with him. When Kennedy singled him out for a special project, Pablo was wildly excited. He told me this was the start of something incredible for him.' She shook her head. 'A week later, he disappeared.'

She stopped again and her eyes filled with tears. I crouched where I was, wondering if I could duck under the bell and make a run for the door, which was now diagonally opposite me. Maybe if I could distract her, keep her talking . . .

'So . . . you . . . you contacted the police?'

'Of course I did! But they were no help. To this day, they have found no trace of my brother, not one scrap of his flesh. I will never know what happened to him.' She lifted the edge of her cloak to mop at her eyes and I weighed up the distance I would have to run. I was aware that loss of blood was weakening me by the second. Meanwhile, Julia continued talking.

'I had what people politely refer to as a nervous breakdown. I abandoned my course, my friends, everything. I had to know what happened to Pablo, I had to *understand*. In my room, I had a small image of Zippy and I began to confide in him. My fears, my hopes, my dreams.' As she talked, her left hand fingered the small brooch that clasped her cape and I recognised it as one she had been wearing at our very first meeting. Little wonder the mask of Xipe Totec had seemed

491

so familiar to me. It was the same face in miniature.

'Then Zippy began to talk back to me.' She gave me a fierce look as though daring me to contradict. 'He advised me to look into the matter myself. I felt in my heart that Kennedy had been responsible for my brother's death – but when I'd spoken of my suspicions to the police, they'd all but laughed at me. After all, Kennedy was a respected citizen of the city and Pablo, just an out of work actor! So I took matters into my own hands. I waited for the right moment, when Kennedy was out of the country on business and I broke into his house. I spent several days searching the place from top to bottom. The video was well hidden but eventually, I found it.' Her face hardened. 'I could see that Pablo's death was genuine – and my first instinct was to go to the police with the evidence. But Zippy told me, "*No, Julia, don't do that! Take vengeance yourself in my name. Teach these pigs the meaning of* my *laws!*".'

She began to advance on me again and I moved backwards, turned the corner and edged along the next wall, realising that step by step, I was getting closer to the door . . .

'But the killings,' I gasped. 'Flaying the bodies like that . . . how could you possibly . . .?'

'It came back so easily, everything I learned back in the slaughterhouse. I had tried to civilise myself but now I realised that butchery was always my true skill – and Zippy told me of the ancient texts that listed the techniques I needed to know.' She laughed mirthlessly. 'Meanwhile, I practised. I practised on anything I could get my hands on. Cats, dogs, birds . . . sometimes I even practised on myself. You should see my stomach, Danny, that's a regular work of art. But don't worry, I will not do that to you. I will make it quick and clean. All I want is to feel your heart beating in my hand . . .'

I shook my head wildly.

'But why me?' I cried. 'I wasn't involved in your brother's death, I swear! I never even met him.'

'No . . . but you were willing to profit from the death of another man. You exhibited a flayed body for the entertainment of others.'

'That wasn't my idea,' I protested. 'Vincent wanted to do that, I just went along!'

'That is not what he told me,' she whispered. 'Shortly before he died. He claimed it was your idea. That you persuaded him to go along with it.'

'No, I swear it to you!'

'You think it matters to me now? It doesn't. Zippy has marked you for death, it is as simple as that. He decreed that what you did was wrong.'

'For God's sake, Julia, all right, I *know* it was wrong but . . . I don't deserve this. I would have thought you'd have been glad to see Kennedy displayed like that, after what he did to your brother.'

'I admit, it confused me for a while: there was a small part of me that relished seeing him like a pig in a butcher's shop: but Zippy was quite clear about your punishment. You have to pay for your sins, Danny. Just as they have paid, every one of them.'

'They'll catch you,' I warned her, knowing that I was babbling uselessly now, as I tried to delay the moment when I'd have to make my run for the door. 'This place is crawling with police, there are hundreds of them down there . . .'

She laughed at that, throwing back her head and cackling gleefully.

'Don't be ridiculous! They are down there and we are up

here. Don't put any faith in them, they can't help you. Look
how easily I got past their stupid check. I came here as a
woman. Then in a toilet cubicle, I put on my other face.
Pablo's face. I had all of his effects, you see. Amongst them
his make-up case. We were not identical twins, but there has
always been a strong resemblance, everyone remarked upon
it. It was the closest I could get to giving him the vengeance
he so richly deserved. You owe him, Danny. You owe him
your heart, you cannot deny him that. Now stop trying to put
off the inevitable. You are weak, losing blood. Nobody
knows we are here and nobody will hear you if you cry for
help. Come to me. Let us end this once and for all . . .'

I took my chance and tried to dash for the door, but she'd
seen it coming. She caught up with me easily, grabbed my
arm and pulled hard, whipping me around and flinging me
into the centre of the room. I tripped over a cable and fell
against one of the horizontal beams directly under the dome
of Big Abel. Then she came at me.

The bell mechanism gave a loud click as the metal lever
pulled back on the cable and in that instant, I realised what
was about to happen. I threw up my hands and clamped them
over my ears, as Julia lifted her arm to strike. Then the
wooden mallet swung back and hit the bell and the noise rose
like a great wave of sound, obliterating everything. Even
from behind the cover of my hands, the noise was awesome.
I saw Julia's eyes widen in shock and then the knife slipped
from her twitching fingers, as she opened her mouth to
scream, but I couldn't hear the scream over the ear-
shattering roar of the bell as the second peal followed on the
dying note of the first. Julia clapped her own hands over her
ears and that was when I lunged at her, ramming her in the
stomach with my head. She doubled over and went sprawling
to the floor.

I didn't hesitate but ran straight for the door. I took my hands away from my ears and struggled with the ancient rusty bolt as the third peal of the bell came at me like an aural explosion. I dragged back the bolt and clawed the door open, then started for the balcony. I was half through the doorway when there was an unexpected impact as Julia leapt on to my back, her hands clawing for my eyes, the red nails digging into the flesh of my face. I screamed, stumbled and staggered forward, hit the concrete balustrade ahead of me with an impact that drove all the breath from my body. I had a vivid impression of the lamplit streets, waiting for me one hundred and eighty feet below and I felt the stone lintel shift beneath my weight.

I roared in pain and terror and jabbed back hard with an elbow, catching Julia in the ribs and dislodging her. I turned to face her as another crash from the bell thundered out of the open doorway and Julia was up in an instant, her hands at my throat, pushing me backwards over the balustrade. I could see her mad, screaming face, the two trickles of blood pulsing from her ears and I struggled helplessly in her grip. I was weak now and the power in her hands was awesome. Below me, the ground seemed to swoop and swirl in a sick-making blur of light and shadow and my head was filled with the clamour of the bell. The soles of my shoes lifted off the surface of the balcony and Julia cackled with delight, tightened her grip.

And then I saw the devil; a devil in a bright red costume, bursting out of the doorway of the tower and coming along the balcony behind Julia in an eerie slow motion, red cloak flapping, dark bearded face scowling in concentration. In satin gloved hands, the devil held a wooden pitchfork. It was such a weird apparition for an instant I thought I'd lost my grip on sanity once and for all, just as certainly as I was losing my grip on the stone balustrade. The devil took his pitchfork in both hands and swung it back like a baseball bat. Then he struck Julia across the shoulders with such force that the pitchfork shattered and went whirling past me in tiny fragments. Julia released her grip and turned to face this unexpected adversary, giving me the opportunity to slide my feet down on to solid ground. The devil dropped into a defensive crouch, whirled suddenly around and threw out one foot in a savage kick, hitting Julia full in the face. She was thrown backwards against the balustrade. She performed an impressive back flip and then she tumbled into space.

Simultaneously, I was jerked backwards too. I whipped instinctively around as a band of steel seemed to tighten around my neck. The rough stone struck me in the chest and I felt myself being pulled forward by a prodigious force. Somebody (the devil?) grabbed my legs and hung on for dear life and I was held immobile, aware of the pressure around my neck increasing, threatening to cut my head off.

Looking down over the balcony I could see that Julia had grabbed the strap of the camera that was still trailing around my neck. She was clinging on for dear life and staring up at me defiantly through a mask of blood, intent on taking me with her. My legs began to slip through the devil's grasp and rough stone scraped my chest, tearing the fabric of my costume. I couldn't get my breath and the strap was pulled too tight for me to prise it from around my neck, it was cutting deep into my flesh. The camera itself hung inches away from Julia's face.

I saw one tiny chance and had to take it. I released my right hand from the stone lintel and reached down towards the camera. This caused my entire body to swing to the right and the devil was dragged sideways too but this was my only hope. By extending my arm the whole way, I thought I might just be able to do it. The twelfth peal of the bell blossomed on the night air and died away. Suddenly, everything seemed quite peaceful.

'You are coming with me, Danny,' said Julia.

I got my shaking index finger closer, closer to the camera. Then at last it was touching the shutter release.

'Watch the birdy,' I croaked, through gritted teeth – and Julia's eyes widened in shock, as I pressed the button.

The flash was only inches from her eyes. For an instant, her face was lit in a glare of electric light. Her hands opened and released their grip. Then she fell to earth, her cloak flapping around her like the wings of a great black bat. I watched her go, whirling and fluttering like a thing out of hell: but I turned away a second before the impact. I thought I heard the awful sound of her body shattering on the stone flags below, but maybe I only imagined it.

Now the devil was easing me back down on to the floor of the balcony, turning me around to face her. I slumped there, completely spent now and Roz kneeled beside me, enfolded me in her arms.

'Danny,' she whispered. 'Thank God I came looking for you. I thought maybe you'd be up here with Spike, but . . .'

I groaned. It seemed to me that every inch of my body had been torn apart and stuck back together, all wrong.

'Roz,' I gasped. 'I'm sorry. You were right . . . I couldn't see it, but you were right about everything . . .'

'Shhh, take it easy! You've got to rest.'

I indicated the great swathe of blood that soaked my costume.

'She cut me open, Roz. I don't know . . . I don't know if I'll make it . . .'

'Shut up, you pillock! Of course you'll make it! You have

to! We're like that, you and me, remember?' She crossed her fingers and held them out to me. With what seemed a monumental effort, I did the same and touched my fingers against hers. Then she leaned forward and kissed me. When she pulled away, I was laughing, even though it caused me agony to do it.

'What's so funny?' she asked me, indignantly.

'Nothing. It's just that I . . . I've never kissed a bearded woman before.'

She looked at me as though she suspected that I'd completely lost my marbles.

'Wait here,' she said. 'I'll go get some help.'

She hurried back towards the door of the tower and went down the stairs with a last flap of her red cape.

I lay there, feeling unconsciousness creeping rapidly up on me and I saw the battered camera still cradled in my lap. My last thought before I slipped into darkness was an odd one.

I wondered if there'd been any film in the camera.

# Epilogue

As it turned out, there was no film in the camera. In my haste
to go out, I'd forgotten to load it and on reflection, I was glad
about that. It absolved me from any responsibility. I would
like to think that if I had found a blurred shot of Julia's
blood-splashed, startled face, the only record of her last
moment on earth, I would have destroyed it. But still there's
a small part of me that wonders about that. After all, times
are hard for freelancers.

Looking at the dates, I see it's almost exactly a year ago
that I started writing this account. Getting it out of my
system has helped me enormously and I'm glad to say that I
don't get nearly as many bad dreams as I did when I first sat
down at Roz's word processor to begin my story. When I'd
concluded the chapter about what happened up in the bell
tower, I thought it was finished: so I gave it to Roz and asked
for her opinion. She read what I'd written, locking herself
away in her room and taking most of the day over it. Finally
she came back and told me she thought it was OK, but that
I'd left too many loose ends.

'You need to tie everything up,' she told me. 'It makes for
a more satisfying read.' She's started doing a creative writing
class recently, so I figured she probably knew what she was
talking about. So I told her I'd try.

★ ★ ★

I was a long time in hospital. I'd figured that Flynn might visit me but he didn't; so when I got out, I tried to get in contact with him. I phoned the police station and was told politely that Detective Inspector Lawrence Flynn had recovered quickly from the slight injury received at the Town Hall and had immediately resigned from the Force. No reasons were given, no forwarding address left, so they were unable to give me any information as to his whereabouts. There was no mention of him in any of the phone directories and he'd moved to the area too recently to figure on the electoral register. So that seemed to be that.

Not long afterwards, I booked myself some very expensive treatment at a laser surgery clinic and had the last reminder of Julia painlessly removed from my arm. A friend recently suggested that Roz had nagged me into this, but that simply wasn't the case. It was me who wanted it done and I wouldn't have been able to rest easy until it was.

After that I went through a long period of depression, rarely going out, not in the least interested in photography or art or anything else, come to that. Roz got me through it only with the greatest perseverence. There were many times when she must have been close to walking out and frankly, I wouldn't have blamed her if she had.

Three recent events seem of importance and I will mention them briefly. The first was about a month ago. It was very late at night and I was suffering from one of my periodic bouts of insomnia. For no better reason than to have something to occupy myself, I'd decided to empty out the trash from the kitchen. I went down to the street where the bins were located and was startled by a quick movement, in amongst them. My first feeling was one of panic, but it quickly turned to wonder as I caught sight of the culprit. It was an adult fox. It was standing in the shadows of the bins, looking straight at me, a beautiful, russet-coloured creature with white markings on its throat and chest. The light from the open doorway was reflected like two orbs of fire in its dark, intelligent eyes. It was only there for a moment and then it turned and loped silently off down the street.

I'd read somewhere that urban foxes were becoming more common all the time, so I suppose there was nothing remarkable about the encounter: but nevertheless, I was profoundly moved by it. I figured that if something so wild and elusive could survive amidst all the shit and debris of city life, then surely so could I. More significantly, I found myself wishing that I'd had a camera with me. It was the first time in a year that I had experienced such an impulse and it struck me as significant.

The second event was less spectacular. One morning, about a month ago, the postman delivered a fashion cata-logue called *Big and Bountiful*, which as the name suggests specialised in clothes for the 'fuller figured woman'. Nor-mally, it would have gone straight in the bin, but the cover model caught my eye. It was Mo, who had clearly taken my advice about joining an agency and against all expectations, had made good. That made me smile: I thought I had forgotten how to.

The third event happened only a week ago. It was a Friday, a cold, clear October evening and Roz and I were walking across town, to the Academy to attend the opening gig of Sepulchre's latest tour . . . oh yes, I should have mentioned earlier, Spike walked out of that clock tower with no more than a bump on his head and a dazed expression on his face. Shortly afterwards, the band signed with a prestig-ious management company and everything else seemed to fall into place for them. A well reviewed single, an album and a decent tour supporting a major rock band. Just lately there's a kind of buzz happening around Sepulchre and I can't seem to open a music magazine without seeing their ugly mugs scowling at me from the pages. Critics are claiming that they are spearheading a new wave of Northern Death-Metal.

So, anyway, there we were, Roz and I, walking across town. I was feeling good, more relaxed than I had done in a long time and I was even carrying my trusty Pentax over one shoulder, because I thought I might . . . I might take a few photographs of the band in action. What the hell, what did I have to lose? And you know, it might even be fun.

The streets were busy as people geared themselves up for the night with a few jars at their favourite watering holes, before moving on to the clubs. Roz and I were chatting and it was the usual topic of conversation for us, these days: should we make our relationship more official, or simply stay as we were, because things did seem to be working out pretty well for us at the moment.

And then, as we turned the corner onto Oxford Road, we noticed these three good-looking girls coming towards us. They were walking along, arm-in-arm, laughing and joking between themselves, looking like they were out for a night on the tiles and were determined to have a good time, come what may.

And as they drew near, I suddenly realised that the girl in the middle looked familiar. She had long dark hair and her lips were painted a deep shade of red. She was dressed very sexily in a black leather jacket, a lace bodysuit and a leather mini-skirt. Her long, shapely legs seemed to go on for ever. When she was only a few feet away, she glanced up and saw me and a warm smile of recognition came to her face. Impulsively, she detached her arm from that of the girl on her right and blew me a kiss. Stunned, I just kept walking.

Then we'd passed each other and I had to resist the impulse to glance back over my shoulder. I told myself there was no point in going after her. The person I used to know no longer existed. I would have been talking to a complete stranger.

Roz gave me a look then, a hard, suspicious look and I had to pull out all the stops to prevent myself from blushing.

'Who was that?' she wanted to know.

'Hmm? Oh,' I said, trying to sound cool. 'Just somebody I used to know.'

'An old flame?' she ventured.

'No, not exactly. Tell you the truth, it never got past the first kiss. She was a great dancer though.'

Roz seemed to accept the explanation: at least she didn't question me any further. She simply slipped her arm through mine and we walked on together through the gathering darkness of a late October evening.

## John Peyton Cooke

# TORSO

'AMONG THE BEST NOVELS EVER WRITTEN ABOUT A TRUE CRIME'
Colin Wilson

### A BREATHTAKING PSYCHO-CHILLER OF MURDER AND PERVERSION

There are a lot of people who might want to kill a punk like Eddie Andrassy. He could be the target of just about anybody – rival pimps, gangsters, narcotics suppliers or even a jealous spouse. Which still does not explain why his once-handsome body has been reduced to a headless and sickeningly mutilated stump.

Eddie is the first victim of the Cleveland Torso Slayer – at least as far as homicide detective Hank 'Lucky' Lambert can tell. However, he's certainly not the last. As the number of grotesquely dismembered corpses increases Hank, under mounting political and personal pressure, knows with horrible certainty that his luck has finally begun to run out . . .

'A powerful and atmospheric recreation of one of the most gruesome serial murders in American criminal history' Colin Wilson

'A slick, pungent reconstruction of the true case of the Cleveland Killer' *Time Out*

**FICTION / THRILLER 0 7472 4193 7**

*More Compelling Fiction from Headline Feature*

# SILENT WITNESS

## A FRIGHTENED CHILD HOLDS THE KEY TO A DOUBLE MURDER

## GALLATIN WARFIELD

For State attorney Gardner Lawson, violent crime comes too close to home when his eight-year-old son Granville stumbles in on an armed robbery and double murder at a local grocery store. The boy is found unconscious, suffering from concussion and with the imprint of a gun barrel on his forehead. Though the only one who can identify the killer, he wakes up with no memory of the incident.

As the police search continues for a coldblooded murderer it is increasingly clear that Granville's memory must be restored – though that might expose him to mental trauma. Lawson is faced with a terrible dilemma.

Meanwhile two suspects have emerged: a rich student at a nearby boarding-school and a local thug with a police record. One of these is a dangerous psychopath who is almost certain to strike again.

Under gentle therapy, Granville is beginning to recall bits and pieces of the horrifying occurrence . . . But will he remember enough in time, and is his own life now in danger?

**FICTION / THRILLER 0 7472 4065 5**

## *A selection of bestsellers from Headline*